FROM SPAIN TO THE UNTAMED PASSIONS OF A NEW LAND

DON DIEGO DE ESCOBAR.
Catarina's father. A proud nobleman banished
from Spain by the treachery of a jealous queen,
he was destined to carve a vast empire
out of the unlimited wilderness.

DOÑA INEZ.
Catarina's aunt. Beautiful and high-born,
she was ready for the wild adventure
of the harsh new world. Yet, though aloof
and independent, a secret desire filled
her nights and darkened her days.

CARLOS DE ESCOBAR.
Catarina's brother. Handsome and reckless,
he took to life on the frontier
with keen excitement. Then, he overstepped
the bounds of an Apache taboo.

A SAGA OF THE SOUTHWEST
★ VOLUME I ★

THE HAWK
AND
THE DOVE

Leigh Franklin James

BANTAM BOOKS · TORONTO · NEW YORK · LONDON

THE HAWK AND THE DOVE
A Bantam Book / published by arrangement with
Book Creations, Inc.
Bantam edition / June 1980

Produced by Lyle Kenyon Engel.

Drawings by Louis S. Glanzman.

ISBN 0–553–13452–3

Published simultaneously in the United States and Canada

Bantam Books are published by Bantam Books, Inc. Its trade-
mark, consisting of the words "Bantam Books" and the por-
trayal of a bantam, is Registered in U.S. Patent and Trademark
Office and in other countries. Marca Registrada. Bantam
Books, Inc., 666 Fifth Avenue, New York, New York 10019.

PRINTED IN THE UNITED STATES OF AMERICA

0 9 8 7 6 5 4 3 2 1

ACKNOWLEDGMENTS

My most appreciative thanks and gratitude for the heroic task of steering a first rough manuscript into a coherent and cogent book are due to Marla and Lyle Engel of Book Creations and to the ablest editors any author could hope to have, Leslie and Philip Rich.

I must also dutifully and gratefully acknowledge the informative aid given me by Lucille Lawler, of Ridgway, Illinois, whose great-grandfather was the first Catholic immigrant to Gallatin County, and whose authoritative book, *Gallatin County: Gateway to Illinois,* furnished definitive material on old Shawneetown, where John Cooper Baines spent his boyhood.

I am also indebted to Dave Richmond, former manager of the gun department at Abercrombie & Fitch in Chicago, for his invaluable documentation on the weapons and ammunition used in the period of *The Hawk and the Dove.*

THE HAWK
AND
THE DOVE

ONE

"Hush now, Lije," the lanky, towheaded boy whispered to the shaggy-coated Irish wolfhound standing patiently beside him as he cautiously flattened himself on the ground. He aimed his flintlock musket at a preening quail, momentarily perched on the branch of a cedar tree on the bank of the creek. "This'll make up for those ducks I missed." He made a rueful face. "Just the same, I'll bet Pa'll give me the dickens for wasting so much birdshot."

Holding his breath, he took careful aim and squeezed the trigger. But, with a shrill cry, the quail soared into the air. "Tarnation!" John Cooper Baines exclaimed angrily, "that does it for fair. We might as well head for home now. I'm out of ammunition and I bet I'll be hearing about it for quite a spell."

Disconsolately, he got to his feet and tied the free end of the rawhide thong, tethering the necks of the brace of mallard ducks he had shot earlier, around the barrel of his musket. Then, with a shrug and a mournful whistle of disappointment, he shouldered the musket and beckoned to his dog as he headed eastward on the three-mile walk back to his father's cabin in Shawneetown, on the bank of the Ohio River, on the southeastern tip of Illinois.

1

It was a warm, hazy September afternoon in the year 1807. Though two months away from his fifteenth birthday, John Cooper Baines, wiry, long-legged, and slim-waisted, lacked only an inch of being six feet tall. Suddenly, he turned to look back at the cedar tree, squinting as he cupped his hand above his keen blue eyes to shield them from the sun. "Bet if I'd had pa's Lancaster, I'd never have missed that quail," he muttered. "Or even Cousin Matthew's old squirrel gun. He always promised to lend it to me when I got older, but he and his Shawnee squaw left for Indiana land last spring. And Pa keeps saying this musket's good enough for me until I turn eighteen." John Cooper kicked at a small, jagged rock, sending it flying. Then his sun-bronzed, freckled face broke into a boyish grin. "Anyhow, these mallards are the fattest of the lot we saw, aren't they? And I'll save some bites for you, that's a promise, boy."

The dark gray-coated Irish wolfhound was five years old, stood three feet from shoulder to ground, and weighed one hundred and forty pounds. John Cooper's mother, a Dublin schoolteacher, had christened the puppy Elijah when she and her sawyer husband, Andrew Baines, had brought it, the only survivor of its dam's litter, along to America.

Andrew hadn't cared much for his British landlord or the British way of meddling in Irish politics. And when he received enthusiastic letters about America from his older cousin, Matthew, who had come to the obscure little settlement of Shawneetown back in 1799, he had decided, in 1802, to follow.

It had been a daring venture for Andrew to pull up stakes, cross the ocean with a wife and three children, and make the long trek from New York to Shawneetown, Illinois. Yet his gentle young wife, Ruth Cooper Baines, had never questioned the wisdom of that decision. And they had certainly prospered in these five years, what with the water-driven sawmill which Andrew Baines had built a hundred yards downriver from their big log cabin, and the trading with the friendly Shawnee Indians.

A little farther on, John Cooper noticed a patch of blackberry bushes, and his exultant whoop made Lije prick up his ears. The dog stiffened as if expecting the command to fetch fallen game. John Cooper chuckled goodnaturedly, then patted Lije's head. "No, not this time, Lije. Didn't I tell you I'm plumb out of buckshot? But maybe if I bring back some blackberries for Ma and Elsie, Pa won't take me to task so hard. You just wait now, while I fill my hat. But first I'm going to eat all I can hold!"

Laying down his musket and squatting before the bushes, John Cooper removed his wide-brimmed straw hat and set it down before him, to serve as a basket. Then he began to stuff himself with the biggest, juiciest berries. But when Lije nudged his master's shoulder with his muzzle, John Cooper gave him a sheepish grin. "You're right, Lije. I forgot all about taking some home, didn't I? Well, it won't take long, and anyhow, I've had plenty."

As if to make up for his momentary selfishness, he selected the biggest berries he could find. Soon the hat was filled to the brim. Then he straightened and scowled down at the hat. "Guess I wasn't thinking very good now, Lije. I can't very well carry the musket and the ducks in one hand and my hat in the other. Wait now—if you carry the musket, I'll have both hands free."

Grinning at his own ingenuity, John Cooper shortened the rawhide thong tied around the barrel of the musket, then held the gun out to Lije. Gently, with his left hand, he touched the huge dog's upper jaw. Lije obediently opened his mouth and clamped the musket barrel between his strong teeth. "Now we'll go back in style, won't we, boy? You're the smartest dog in the country, no two ways about it, Lije!"

Picking up the hat and balancing it between his hands, John Cooper retraced the path back home, Lije trotting beside him. Head erect, fierce brown eyes glowing with pride, the Irish wolfhound lifted the short-barreled musket as high as he could so that the ducks would clear the ground. From time to time, Lije glanced at his master, and John Cooper nodded and praised him. They were within a mile of home now, and the boy's high spirits had returned. "Not such a bad hunt after all, was it, Lije?" He glanced fondly at the wolfhound. "Next time we'll catch ourselves a deer, you'll see. Then Ma and Pa'll be real proud of me, and maybe Pa'll let me handle his Lancaster, just once. This old musket can't hit the side of a barn only fifty yards away, but Pa's Lancaster sure can."

He pondered a moment, then went on talking to his dog. " 'Course, that'll mean I'll have to do my chores and learn my lessons well enough so I can get a day off to hunt. But I'll earn our day together next week, you'll see, Lije." He shook his head in thought. "I'd be just as content to help Pa at the sawmill and float the logs downriver to his customers. Only he keeps saying that a boy's got to have book-learning if he expects to amount to anything. He says it's not the way it was back in Ireland, that if he'd had some decent schooling, he might have had a big fine house and been able to buy Ma pretty clothes and such. And he's always after me to wash my hands and face before supper and use my knife and fork like a proper gentleman. Gosh, I told Ma I didn't want to be a sissy, but she just laughed and kissed me and said it wasn't being a sissy to have good manners and something stored in my brain. Well, I guess she was right at that."

The well-trod path led past clumps of wild azaleas, brilliant dandelions, and, for long stretches, tall grass. Farther on there was a large grove of birch trees, many of them already stripped of their bark which the Shawnee used to build canoes and wigwams. Just past the birch trees was a shallow gully which John Cooper avoided nimbly. A bluebottle fly buzzed against his cheek and angrily darted away. He grimaced. The scent of the humid earth, the grass, and the flowers and shrubs filled his nostrils. He breathed deeply, content and proud as he glanced again at the wolfhound and saw that Lije still held the musket barrel firmly. Lije returned the glance with a soft little snort, his shaggy brows arching, and his tail scissored the air.

Now John Cooper could see a thin plume of smoke rising from the chimney of the cabin. He figured that his mother had started a fire for supper and anticipated her happiness when he presented her with two fine ducks for roasting. They'd go mighty fine with sweet yams. Hopefully she'd bake a pie tomorrow from the berries.

They had come now to a cornfield, some two hundred yards behind the cabin. There had been enough rain and heat this summer to produce a bountiful crop, and the tassled stalks rose as high as John Cooper's head. His father had already sent a dozen bushels to the village of Pesquetaba, chief of the Shawnee, and would doubtless send more before the season was over.

John Cooper knew that his father made whiskey from some of the corn, using the formula which his father had taught him back in Ireland. Sometimes, Andrew Baines sold jugs of whiskey to neighbors or visiting trappers. But when he first settled in Shawneetown, Andrew had told old Pesquetaba that this drink was only for the sick and the dying. And

Pesquetaba seemed to accept the white lie. Andrew had explained to his son that it was both dangerous and illegal to sell whiskey to Indians.

John Cooper was about to skirt the cornfield and head for the cabin when he suddenly froze. The sounds of shots and angry cries reached him. Lije pricked up his ears and growled softly. "Quiet, Lije!" John Cooper snapped in a hoarse whisper. He had gone very pale, and his eyes were fixed with disbelief on the scene beyond him.

There were at least ten of them, Shawnee braves, their heads shaved bare save for the scalplock, naked except for buckskin leggings, breechclouts, and moccasins. One of them lay sprawled near the door of the cabin. Even as John Cooper stared, a musket shot sounded from inside the cabin and another brave dropped his tomahawk, clutched his belly, and rolled over and over on the ground in his death agonies.

"Oh, sweet Jesus . . . oh, no . . . oh, God . . . they're after Ma and Pa and Elsie and Ginny!" the boy gasped. "I haven't even got any birdshot left in my musket. . . . Quick, Lije, into the corn, before they see us!" Still holding the berry-filled hat, he bolted into the thick cornstalks. The wolfhound followed, with another low growl which drew a warning "Shhh!" from the agonized boy.

Inching forward on his belly to the last rows of corn, John Cooper peered through the stalks while Lije obediently lay down beside him, still gripping the musket. Two of the braves had brought along a cedar log and were now battering the door of the cabin. One of them, from behind the high stump of an oak tree, was reloading an old long rifle. He took careful aim at the shuttered window of the cabin and fired. John Cooper could hear a faint cry from inside. He clenched his teeth, tears nearly blinding him. "What am I going to do? How can I help them in there? All I've got is my hunting knife. . . . They've got tomahawks and muskets and that old rifle. Oh please, dear sweet God, don't let them hurt Ma and Pa and the girls—I swear I won't ever lie again or shirk my chores and lessons if you'll just save 'em, Lord, please!"

Once again he heard the sharp bark of his father's rifle. One of the braves, who had been loping toward the back of the cabin, stopped in his tracks, then toppled like an ax-felled oak. But two more braves had joined their companions with the battering log. Drawing back and using all their strength, they crashed through the door with hideous whoops.

"Why, why?" John Cooper groaned as he turned to stare at

the wolfhound. "We never did the Shawnee any harm. They've been friends ever since we got here." The wolfhound stared back at him, his eyes angry and bright, still gripping the musket barrel between his jaws.

John Cooper stifled a cry of horror. Two of the braves had dragged his father out, and the Shawnee who had been crouching behind the stump flung down his rifle and ran forward, brandishing a tomahawk. As Andrew Baines struggled frantically, the tomahawk descended. John Cooper closed his eyes and bit his lips until they bled to control the shout of rage and horror which rose within him. The two braves who had been holding his father let the lifeless body fall and rushed into the cabin with the others.

Now John Cooper could hear screams and tearful pleas. He forced himself to look, trembling violently. One brave dragged out his gentle mother, her sweet, heart-shaped face contorted in agony at the sight of her murdered husband. "Oh, Andrew . . . why have you done this to him? Don't harm the girls . . . take me!"

Two braves ripped her homespun dress from her and then her underclothing. They flung her, naked, down on the ground. John Cooper buried his tear-drenched face in the earth and groaned aloud. He could hear his mother's sobs and groans as a young brave brutally and vigorously ravished her while two of his companions held her down on the blood-stained ground, near her husband's body.

By the time her fourth assailant had finished with her, she lay, moaning feebly, her face twisted to one side. The man who had had her last, the oldest of them, seized the musket she had used inside the cabin to defend her brood and, swinging it by the barrel, dashed out her brains with a triumphant bellow.

Now the others dragged out John Cooper's sisters—thirteen-year-old Elsie, and Virginia, three years older. Seeing her parents lying dead, Elsie broke away from her captors, flung herself to her knees, and hysterically begged them not to die and leave her. The Shawnee hooted at her childlike pathos, one of them twisting his fingers into her long, golden curls and dragging her out toward the stump, while two others followed. The other four amused themselves with Virginia, who fought them with her fingernails and desperate kicks . . . but all in vain.

John Cooper had retched. Now, his body still shaking, he watched the hideous aftermath of this inexplicable attack by these braves, many of whom he had known since his family's arrival in Shawneetown. Lije growled again, and the agonized boy put his hand to the dog's nose and shook his head. Then he watched until he could look no more. His sisters were violently ravished, and then they, too, were tomahawked.

The triumphant marauders rushed into the cabin. A few minutes later, three of them emerged carrying clay jugs of Andrew Baines's whiskey. Chanting and boasting, they passed the jugs among themselves until they were empty.

The sun had already set, and a gentle twilight bathed the cornfield and the cabin. John Cooper could hear the placid gurgling of the broad Ohio River as it flowed southward to meet the mighty Mississippi. Night birds began to twitter, but their sounds were drowned out by the Shawnee's boisterous, drunken bursts of laughter.

The boy waited helplessly for what seemed like an eternity. He was violently sick from what he had seen, torn asunder by his all-consuming grief and rage. Almost mechanically, he reached for his musket, and Lije obediently opened his mouth. John Cooper sobbed softly as he flung the useless weapon away, and the ducks with it. "Now quiet, we've got to wait until they go away, Lije," he muttered thickly.

The silver quarter of the moon had risen by the time the Shawnee began to stumble to their feet and move northwestward, back to their camp. Only two remained, a young warrior John Cooper knew, and the oldest brave, who had been last with Ruth Cooper Baines. They lay in a drunken stupor, the young Indian, Nisquah, clutching the barrel of Andrew Baines's Lancaster.

All was still now. The night birds called insistently to one another, and there was the sound of the water lapping. John Cooper could hear the croaking of a bullfrog as he got to his feet slowly, again putting his hand to Lije's muzzle to keep the dog quiet. He moved swiftly toward the cabin, trying not to look at the bodies of his murdered family. His eyes burned with tears and his throat was raw with unuttered shouts and curses. For a moment he stood staring down at the older brave, who was muttering in his drunken stupor. He saw the bloody tomahawk which had murdered his father, seized it, knelt down and, lifting it, smashed it with all his strength first against Nisquah's skull. Then he whirled swiftly and raised the tomahawk again to avenge his mother.

He left the tomahawk buried in the older brave's skull as he walked into the cabin. Lije uttered a low, angry whine as he saw the bodies of those whose protector and friend he had been since first Andrew Baines had carried him in a sling aboard the ship bound for America.

John Cooper came out with a spade and began to dig four graves. He sobbed while he worked. Gently, John Cooper lowered his father into the first grave and covered him. Tears were streaming down his face. "Oh God, if only I hadn't gone hunting today," he muttered when it was done.

Then, reverently, having brought out sheets from their bedding to cover the naked bodies of his mother and sisters, he lowered gentle Ruth Cooper to her final resting place. How kind, how good she had always been to him and how he had loved her. He remembered bolting down all those black-berries. "If you'd seen me, Ma, you'd have scolded me good and proper. You always taught me to eat slowly. . . . I'll not forget it, not ever." He broke down, covering his face with his hands, his wiry, young body shuddering violently.

He rose again and forced himself to bury Virginia. How often his big sister had teased him—she used to say that it was a shame he hadn't been born a hunting dog like Lije, so that he could spend all his time in the woods.

Again he got to his feet, drying his swollen eyes with the sleeve of his jacket. His mother had sewn it for him. There was something he had to do for little Elsie. He'd really brought back the blackberries for her—she loved them best. He remembered how she'd asked him to whittle toys and dolls for her. He hurried back to the cornfield. Stooping down, he retrieved the berry-filled hat and returned to the last grave, in which he had laid his younger sister. Kneeling down, he put the hat on her bosom and then, with an agonized sob, began to cover her.

The earth would be gentle with them, he knew—gentler than those damned Shawnee had been. But why had they killed his family? What he didn't, couldn't know was that they had turned renegade and defied Pesquetaba's order. They'd murdered old Henry Dolson, who lived about a mile down-river, and found two jugs of whiskey in his cabin. Putting two and two together because of Baines's big cornfield, they'd come back to demand whiskey from Andrew Baines and he'd refused them.

"What do we do now, Lije?" John Cooper turned to the wolfhound, his voice hollow and despondent. "There's noth-ing left for me here any more. Maybe we'll go west. I sure don't want to go to Indiana to see Cousin Matthew and his

Shawnee wife. . . . I don't want to think about Shawnee, ever again. Besides, he's got his life and his kids, and we'd just be in the way. So we'll go west. First, though, we've got to get some provisions. I'll take Pa's Lancaster and his powderhorn, lead and bullet mold, and all the balls he's got left. We might need all that if we run across hostiles on the trail."

He went into the cabin, his head bowed, his body slumped in despair. Lije followed hesitantly, silent and observing as John Cooper packed the supplies necessary for the journey.

Outside the cabin once again, John Cooper tugged Andrew Baines's Lancaster from Nisquah's stiffening hand. Then he headed toward the bank of the river, Lije at his heels.

"We'll get on Pa's log raft and float ourselves down the Ohio to a likely spot, then cross over and head out west," he thought aloud to himself.

Setting the heavy sack down on the raft, he shoved it toward the water's edge, remembering to take the long pole used for steering. Then, nimbly leaping aboard, he whistled to Lije, who leaped swiftly onto the raft and stood wagging his tail, looking up at his young master.

"You're all I've got left now, Lije. We'll see each other through this. God'll take care of us. Maybe someday I'll turn out to be the gentleman Ma always wanted me to be. Let's go now." John Cooper's voice had steadied. It was as if he were standing off to one side, hearing himself talk to the wolfhound. He felt drained, exhausted. He willed himself with all his waning strength to push from his mind what he had been forced to watch.

He heard the croak of a bullfrog as he shoved the raft out into the gently flowing waters of the Ohio. He did not look back at the cabin, receding in the distance, now dark, with only the silver of the moon in a cloudless sky to illuminate his forever abandoned boyhood home.

TWO

"If you will wait here, Don Diego, His Majesty will see you presently. He has matters of state requiring his immediate attention, you understand." The majordomo, resplendent in his red brocade coat and powdered wig, grasped his staff of office and gave the gray-haired nobleman a peremptory nod. Then, turning stiffly, he walked away, leaving Don Diego de Escobar alone in the great hall to await his private audience with His Most Catholic Majesty, Charles IV.

The night before, a royal courier had brought a summons to Don Diego's estate on the outskirts of Madrid, commanding him to present himself to the king this dreary September morning. The impersonal brevity of that summons had puzzled Don Diego. He, and his father before him, had served the Spanish crown with honor and dignity. Now as he stood gazing at the portrait of Philip II, painted by Juan Pantoja de la Cruz, he tried to compose his thoughts and prepare himself for this unexpected audience.

Don Diego de Escobar, forty-seven years old, was a man of medium height and stately bearing. His goatee and mustache were silver gray, and he disdained the formal wig. His head was leonine and his hair, though as gray as his goatee and mustache, was thick and full and showed no sign of thinning with his advancing age. He glanced back at the retreating figure of the majordomo and smiled wryly to himself. There, indeed, was a man who had need of a wig. Under it, the Count Pedro de Santorsalva was as bald as an egg.

He stared up again at the portrait, reflecting that the Escorial represented all the glory that was royal Spain. Built in a twenty-one-year period during the reign of Philip II, it included a massive palace, a monastery, and a church; and it housed the tombs of Spain's greatest monarchs. Everywhere one saw the decorations of great artists, and its library and collection of Spanish paintings were world-renowned. From this place, gloomy and dark with its centuries-old secrets, the man whom de la Cruz had so vividly immortalized with oils on canvas had brought Spain to its very zenith of colonization and prosperity.

Don Diego de Escobar could not turn his gaze from that portrait. He saw the heavy-lidded eyes, cold and merciless, the thin lips, the hand that clutched orb and scepter, and the other that was flung out contemptuously toward a map of the then-known world. He had, of course, seen other great portraits of this indomitable Philip—the ones by Titian, A. Coello, and the more familiar portrait by this same de la Cruz, which showed the king in full armor. Yet this was the one which always held his attention. The painter had captured the autocratic sovereignty which Philip II had so gloriously exemplified.

Don Diego sighed nostalgically. There had been a de Escobar, a young captain out of Seville, who had commanded a troop of arquebusiers during Philip's religious invasion of the Netherlands. Indeed, all of his descendants since then had served the king with joy and honor. The very father of the monarch whom he now awaited had bestowed the title of nobility on Carlos de Escobar, Don Diego's father. And he, Don Diego, had named his only son Carlos, after both monarchs, in gratitude for that honor.

At last he turned away from the imposing portrait to stare at the door of the antechamber in which he would be received when it pleased his royal master. The thought of his son, now sixteen, and of his lovely, willful daughter, Catarina, three years younger, brought sharply back to mind his deep concern over their mother's illness. Dolores de Escobar, his handsome, thirty-five-year-old wife, had been suffering from a strange fever for more than a month. Her spinster sister, two years older, Doña Inez de Castillana, had come to Madrid to nurse her and help care for the household and the children. When Don Diego had received the royal summons, he had said nothing of it to Dolores or Inez; there was no need to worry either of them. But he felt uneasy—he couldn't understand why he had been summoned so urgently.

Almost unconsciously, Don Diego de Escobar straightened his shoulders. He remembered with pride how the king had invited him, last February, to inspect the royal bodyguard at the Escorial. He had walked down the line of brilliantly caparisoned soldiers, their cabassets glittering under the rays of the cold morning sun, their boots immaculately polished, their muskets gripped tightly at salute. Charles IV had turned to him and said, "Don Diego, men like these truly inspire one to be a king, *¿no es verdad?*" Don Diego had smiled and inclined his head as he replied, "As they do me to be your most loyal subject, my king."

Yet now, remembering that moment, Don Diego was saddened by his own misgivings. If only Charles IV had shown the same forthrightness as his illustrious father. But instead, dominated by his queen, the dissolute Maria Louisa of Parma, and her lover Manuel de Godoy—whom he had made his chief minister in 1792—the fifty-nine-year-old monarch was weak and vacillating in this hour of Spain's greatest need.

Don Diego de Escobar had disliked Manuel de Godoy from the very first. Cunning and unscrupulous and even two-faced, he had first favored war on revolutionary France. Then, for some reason, he quickly changed and advocated peace instead. In Don Diego's opinion, if war had been declared, the threat of Napoleon would never have arisen. But Godoy had negotiated a peace in 1795 and, since then, seemed to side with the French on all issues, even those which would affect Spanish territory.

Gradually the colonies of Spain's glorious New World were being undermined by the king's own vacillation and his prime minister's treacherous loyalty to the French. To a *Madrileño* like Don Diego, it was a desperately trying situation, one which struck at his own devotion to his native land and his oath of allegiance to the monarch whom he now anxiously awaited.

Suddenly he heard the reedy voice of Count Pedro de Santorsalva, the majordomo. "His Majesty will see you now, Don Diego. Follow me, *por favor.*"

Don Diego de Escobar drew a deep breath and turned to

the majordomo. His thoughts had led him to a conclusion—he would be forthright with Charles IV. Of course, he would not dare slander the royal household by alluding to Godoy. That would serve only to remind the king of his own complacence in the face of cuckoldry. But he would urge Charles IV to strengthen the troops that guarded the peninsular boundaries. Despite the pact with France, he did not trust Napoleon. History had already shown the Corsican's greed and overwhelming ambition. If that mighty army moved against Spain—as it had against Austria, Russia, and Sweden—then Philip II's valor and all the glory of the Escorial would become mere legend.

Don Diego followed the count down a narrow corridor. He waited while the latter struck three times with his staff upon the floor and then almost reverently opened the door, bowing low as he announced, "Don Diego de Escobar, as you have bidden, *vuestro Majestad.*"

The count moved away and hurried back down the corridor as Don Diego entered the floridly decorated antechamber, carefully closing the door behind him. He went down on one knee, pressing a fervent kiss upon the limp, fat hand of Charles IV. As he rose to his feet, he declared, "I await your orders, my king."

Charles IV was portly. He wore a white wig and a jeweled sword hung at his side. His round face was mottled, his lips trembled, and he showed already the malady of dropsy which was to afflict him so sorely. He turned toward the velvet-curtained window, his back to Don Diego, and spoke in a querulous voice. "I fear the orders I have concerning you, Don Diego, will not be to your liking."

"In what way have I failed Your Majesty?" Don Diego stood stiffly, arms at his sides, head erect—but he was consumed by an uneasy premonition.

The king turned back to his writing desk, drew out the cherrywood chair before it, and sat down. Covering his mouth, he uttered a soft belch. He scowled, staring at the documents awaiting his signature. Then, again without looking at Don Diego, he went on, "My consort and my chief minister have asked that I punish you for treason, Don Diego."

"Treason? Your Majesty!" The gray-haired nobleman was aghast. "But surely you must know, my king, that my father and I have devoted our lives to the throne and that we are the most loyal Spaniards in your realm."

"That is what I argued, Don Diego." At last Charles IV deigned to look up at him. Don Diego perceived an almost pathetic expression in the king's watery eyes and twitching lips. "Indeed, had I not convinced them that you and your illustrious father had done much for the throne, I should be disconsolate at passing on to you their judgment."

"Judgment, my king?" Don Diego's voice quivered.

"Did you not say to the Count Jorge de Murciano that you believed it to be a fatal blunder of statesmanship to ally Spain with France?"

Don Diego de Escobar closed his eyes and shuddered. He remembered all too well that chance remark. Yet it had been taken out of context by Murciano, who, he knew, had long envied him his rank in court and the high esteem he had hitherto enjoyed. Yes, now it was all too terribly clear.

"But Your Majesty, that was not all I said. I do not know how it was that our casual conversation came to the ears of Queen Maria Louisa and Prime Minister Godoy, but I assure you that there was nothing traitorous in the implication. What I said—if I may be permitted to recall it to Your Majesty—was that Spain has always gained strength from its colonies in the New World, and that I feared only that preoccupation with French affairs would endanger our control of those colonies. Even if we are at peace with France, surely Your Majesty must realize that Napoleon would scrap a treaty in a minute if it suited his purpose. Even now he is devising a campaign that will tear us asunder and strip us as a world power, all the while pretending to maintain peace. Do you believe that statement to be traitorous, my king?"

Charles IV made an ineffectual gesture with one fat hand, as if brushing away the argument. Finally, he cleared his throat. "The unalterable fact, Don Diego, is that you have placed me in an untenable position. Her Royal Majesty Maria Louisa believes that a subject who does not concur with our statesmanship should not be attached to the royal court. Yes, I well know how you and your father have served Spain! Yet I must accede to the wishes of Godoy and Maria Louisa. You will be banished, your lands and your estate will be confiscated. . . ."

"Your Majesty!" Don Diego gasped, his face contorted with anguish.

Charles IV held up a placating hand and forced a wan smile to his trembling lips. "Hear me out, Don Diego. I know your worth to our nation. You are herewith appointed intendant in the province of Taos, in Nuevo Mexico."

Don Diego de Escobar uttered a choking groan. To be banished forever from his beloved Madrid—it was like a sentence of death. And to uproot his family, with his wife already grievously ill, and move to a desolate country in the New World appeared to be an irretrievable disaster.

But Charles IV had risen and approached Don Diego. He placed his hand on the latter's shoulder. "Come, my old friend, it is not so bad. Believe me, I argued earnestly against the wishes of Godoy and my queen. It was only by such argument that I prevailed in being able to grant you five thousand acres of good land and this position of intendant. It will bring you five thousand pesos in annual salary. I know you will find other benefits. I am quite certain of it, indeed." Again the king smiled wanly.

"I do not know what to say, my king. . . ."

The king patted Don Diego's shoulder. "Take heart from what I have been able to do for you. Do you not see that, in the broader sense, I agree with you that we must maintain our distant empire? I understand your wish to keep Spain great among the nations of the world. It is my wish, too—you know that. And it is my belief that you are best suited to this new station in life. You will be free of the intrigues of court. Ah yes . . ." Charles IV sighed and shook his head. "I know, far better than you, the wearisome pomp and formalities which surround me on every side."

Don Diego drew his sword and tendered it to his king, as a token of his resignation of all stature. But Charles IV shook his head and gently grasped the nobleman's wrist as he forced him to sheathe the blade. "No, you must not. You must, instead, look upon this new post as a reward for your valued labors. I, whom you call your king and to whom you have pledged your devotion, believe in and rely on you. You must think that always."

There were tears in Don Diego's eyes as he slowly knelt and kissed the king's hand. Once again, he swore allegiance, just as his father had done before him in the presence of Charles III.

"My majordomo has already received the documents you will give the governor of Cuba and, as well, a letter of introduction to our viceroy in Mexico. From there, you will be given a military escort to your new post in Taos."

This news, far from cheering Don Diego, only distressed him more. It would be an arduous journey for his sick wife and young children.

As if to emphasize the disaster even more, Charles IV spoke again, in a firmer, more decisive tone. "The galleon *Paloma* will carry you and your family on the journey, Don Diego. I should be grateful to you if you could arrange to depart no later than the end of this month. The *Paloma* is now being outfitted for the voyage."

"I hear and I obey, my king." Once again, Don Diego knelt and, bowing his head, kissed the hand of his royal master. Then, his face impassive, striving to control the emotions which welled up within him, he left the antechamber.

As he closed the door behind him, he stopped short and his eyes narrowed with a sudden, rising anger. There before him, chatting convivially with the majordomo, was the Count Jorge de Murciano. Don Diego's hand gripped the hilt of his sword, seized by the impulse to denounce the scheming rogue and to challenge him to a duel. Yet, mastering himself with the greatest effort, he straightened his shoulders and walked forward proudly.

"Oh, Don Diego de Escobar, what a happy and fortuitous meeting!" Count Jorge de Murciano approached the gray-haired nobleman and extended his hand in greeting.

"If you say so, Count de Murciano," Don Diego retorted. "If you will excuse me, my wife is ill and I must return home at once. To you, majordomo, my sincere thanks. And you, Count, I have the pleasure of wishing you a very good morning."

Without looking back, ignoring the soft, mocking laugh that he heard behind him, Don Diego de Escobar walked slowly out of the Escorial.

THREE

As the Ohio River carried the log raft downstream, John Cooper Baines directed it as best he could with the long pole to keep it on the western side of the river. Night had fallen, but the quarter moon was obscured by the catalpa, cedar, and oak trees lining both shores of the broadening river. The lonely, orphaned boy turned ever and again to the huge wolfhound for consolation. There were no friendly, familiar lights of cabins, nothing to remind him of human habitations or of people. Lije, accustoming himself to the movement of the raft, and seeing that his young master was safe enough, lay down.

"You see, Lije," John Cooper felt it necessary to explain, "we want to go west, but if we had crossed overland, the Shawnee might have spotted us. This way, we'll put distance between them and us. Pa told me something about this river and where it joins the Mississippi. Beaver trappers and hunters come up it and stop in Shawneetown. I remember listening to one fellow with a long, red beard. He came through last November and bought two jugs of Pa's whiskey."

The boy heard the sudden hooting of an owl and, far above his head, the flapping of wings as the owl sought another perch. John Cooper started at the first sound, then chuckled and shook his head. "Shucks, that was just an old owl, Lije. He won't hurt anybody. I remember Pa's saying that some Indians think an owl can tell the future. I sure wish it could tell me what's going to happen to us—it'd make it a lot easier for us both, don't you think?"

He reached down to pat the dog's head and then straightened, digging vigorously with the pole to keep the raft from veering toward the eastern bank. "Over that way's Kentucky, Lije, and we don't want to go there. In my geography lessons, Ma said that there's a lot more unexplored country out west. There's bound to be lots of good hunting and fishing and trapping in country where there aren't many people."

He fell silent a moment. Unconsciously, he had raised his voice in talking to Lije, as one might whistle in the dark out of a secret, gnawing fear of what lurked beyond that unknown darkness. More than that, he was still trying desperately to blot the indelible scenes from his mind.

Easing his hold on the pole, now that the raft seemed to be moving smoothly along the western bank of the Ohio, John Cooper tried to take stock. He knew they would have to live off the land once their supplies were gone. But he also knew they wouldn't starve; there'd be all sorts of fruit and berries, and deer and lots of fish wherever there was water . . . and rabbits and partridge and quail. They would survive.

He frowned as he glanced at the sack of provisions and ammunition. They'd been in such a hurry to get away he'd forgotten all about his father's greatcoat. It wouldn't be long before the snow and real cold weather came. "Maybe I can kill me a bear," he thought happily. "I think I could skin it all right—Pa taught me how to skin rabbits and squirrels, and even deer. He taught me lots of things that'll be mighty useful from now on, like how to scout and track, and read footprints and the signs on bark or bushes that tell you that Indians or outlaws aren't too far off. That's another reason we're not going to stay on this river once it joins up with the Mississippi. There are all sorts of river pirates, and from what Pa used to tell me, they're even worse than those Shawnee. . . ."

Suddenly he bit his lip, remembering. Once again anguish welled up in him. Then, carefully laying the pole aslant the edge of the raft, he turned to his dog. "Say, you didn't get any of those ducks I shot, and I promised you I'd share them with you. You must be starving, Lije. Here, try a little of this jerky. It's not too salty." Opening the sack, he burrowed in it to find the jerky, then took his hunting knife and cut off several pieces. He shared these evenly between the wolfhound and himself. Then, cupping his hands and dipping them into the water, he drank his fill. "There, that's a lot better. We can think straighter with some food in our bellies, can't we, Lije?"

The raft had reached a sluggish spot in the river and began to drift slowly eastward. John Cooper seized the pole and thrust it down vigorously, managing to reach the shallow bed of the river and correct the raft's direction. "That was a close one," he thought, hoping that by dawn they'd find a place for a landing and head west.

In the monotony of this all-encompassing darkness, John Cooper began to feel the physical exhaustion of the terrible, long day and the seemingly endless night. With a soft groan he hunkered down on the raft, placing the pole beside him and closing his eyes . . . only for a moment, he promised himself. His muscles ached, and he felt empty and weak. Lije nudged his thigh, and he came awake again instantly, fighting off the almost overpowering urge for dreamless sleep. "That's all right, Lije. I won't fall asleep—we might drift all the way down to the Gulf if I did, mightn't we? You and I'd be sort of out of place in a town like New Orleans. Guess all they speak down there is French. Leastways, Ma used to tell me that there were a lot of French settlers there . . . but she never got to teach me that. . . . I think she knew a few words. Well, I can talk English pretty good, and Algonquin . . . I picked that up from the Shawnee. . . ."

He winced and closed his eyes again. A swirl of tortured memory came back to him. Doggedly, he forced himself to stand and, retrieving the pole, jabbed it down to the left to make certain that the raft would continue its course along the western bank.

There was a broad turn to the southwest, and John Cooper called out, "It won't be long before we'll get back onto dry land, Lije boy! Then maybe we can catch a few winks of sleep. I figure we'll be where we ought to go by about dawn. It won't be much longer." He stared hard at the wolfhound, his eyes suddenly filling with tears. "I'm glad I've got you, Lije. You don't know how much . . . or maybe you do. You saw what happened back there—you won't ever forget them any more than I will." Once again he fell silent, staring out at the dark, moving water ahead as the log raft followed the bend in the Ohio and then began to move more swiftly.

He sighed, his hand stroking Lije's head as again he stared into the water beyond, wishing he could have seen Pesquetaba and told him what his braves did, so he'd punish the ones that got away. "He was a good man," the boy mused aloud. "Pa took me to their village the first year we came, and the two of them got along just fine. I don't think they're all like the ones who . . ." He did not finish, closing his eyes and bowing his head for a long moment. Then he remembered a Bible verse his mother had read to him: *Love thine enemies,* and *The wicked shall do penance for their sins against the oppressed.* "No, she wouldn't have wanted me to hate them just because of what a few of them did. . . . Oh, God, Ma and Pa and poor little Elsie and Ginny, I miss them so!"

He burst into uncontrollable sobs, covering his face with his hands. The wolfhound whined and tried to lick his face.

Recovering, John Cooper rubbed his eyes and gave a derisive snort as he rose to his feet. "That's all right, Lije. I'm all right now. You know, if we run into Indians or hunters when we get on land, they sure won't think much of a boy who cries like a baby! I'm a man now, and I've got to show everybody that's just what I am or I'll never get where I'm going."

He again thrust the long pole down to the left as dawn began to break over the river, dappling the dark trees with a reddish nimbus. The Ohio broadened suddenly as it joined the Mississippi, and as the raft neared a shallow inlet, he used his pole to beach it. Shouldering the heavy sack and gripping his father's Lancaster rifle in the other hand, he leaped off the raft and Lije followed.

Relieved of its double burden, the log raft, seized by a sudden swell in the current, edged away from the inlet and began to float down the river. John Cooper turned to stare at it, thinking, "Guess that settles it. Here's where we start from. Now let's find a shelter in these trees somewhere and rest up a bit before we head on west."

FOUR

Don Diego de Escobar walked slowly down the great stone steps of the Escorial to his carriage, his bearing still as stiff and proud as when he had ascended them for his audience with the king. He returned the salutes of the soldiers who stood on guard at the entrance and even nodded congenially to several minor officials. But his spirit was in chaos. It seemed that, at each step he descended, the oppressive weight of the king's sentence upon him grew to be a heavier yoke around his neck. Only rigid self-control allowed him to maintain the stately poise that he had always assumed at the royal court.

So little time had been given him to clear up his affairs and prepare his family for the long, taxing journey to Taos. Even for the healthiest, such a journey was sure to sap strength and energy. But Dolores was ill, and she had only a few short weeks to recover and to ready herself to accompany him and the children. It was almost unthinkable.

His elderly coachman, Manuel Arriaga, who had been engaged when just a stripling by Don Diego's father, hastened to open the door of the carriage for him. Don Diego nodded, smiled faintly, and then turned back for a last look at the Escorial, where he had spent so much of his life in faithful attendance upon his monarch. As he did so, Count Jorge de Murciano, just emerging, raised a hand to acknowledge the salute of the guards, his small thin lips curved in an ingratiating smile. Don Diego felt a flux of savage rage surge up in him. Instinctively, his right hand clutched at the hilt of his sword. Then, again mastering himself, he got into the carriage and snapped, "Drive me home, Manuel, without delay. I must see to my wife."

"¡Si, Don Diego!" Manuel Arriaga climbed back onto the driver's seat, took up the reins and called, "¡Adelante, caballos!"

Once again, Don Diego forced his thoughts away from the smirking count and drew his hand away from the hilt of his sword. He felt reassured that he had not yielded to the furious temptation of provoking a duel of vengeance. Not that the rogue did not deserve a Toledo blade through his black heart—but the repercussions could well condemn the don's innocent family to far worse punishment than even the king's decree of banishment. Even an honorable duel—for which there was, God Himself knew, more than ample justification—would surely be interpreted as a spiteful act of reprisal and mark him, Don Diego, as even more of a traitor.

As the carriage passed along the winding path that led from the Escorial through the magnificently tended gardens and lawns which bordered the palace, the gray-haired nobleman closed his eyes and forced himself to plan for the journey. First of all, it went without saying that Dolores would have to get well. Indeed, considering what little time had been granted to him to board the Paloma, it might even be necessary to petition the king to allow her to come later, after she had regained her health and strength. He would not endanger her life—she meant so much to him. She was still as beautiful and desirable as when he had met her, eighteen years ago. That had been a year after the death of Charles III, son of Philip V, who had been duke of Parma and Piacenza, and then king of Naples and Sicily, before succeeding his half-brother, Ferdinand VI, as king of Spain in the year 1759.

Once again, Don Diego cursed his folly in stating his opinion in the hearing of a man who was, at best, an opportunist and had profited so scurrilously from his own moment of unguarded confidence. But it was too late to make amends now. A single uttered reflection which, even used out of context, should certainly never have been construed as traitorous had served to shatter the settled tenor of his life and, worst of all, of his beloved family.

The two dappled geldings turned at last into the gateway of Don Diego's estate. There, industriously clipping a hedge to a pleasing symmetry, was his head gardener, Miguel Sandarbal. He smiled and waved. Here was a man who, despite humble birth, was far more honorable than the pretentious Count Jorge de Murciano—a true man of the Spanish people who had risen above his own personal misfortunes. Forty-two years old, Miguel Sandarbal's short black beard was flecked with only a little gray. Many years ago, he had inherited a highly reputed fencing school in Madrid from his father, who had given lessons to Don Diego himself when the latter had been a boy. Out of this, the two men had developed a lasting friendship. Miguel Sandarbal had always been a free spirit, impatient with the conventions and the hidebound traditions of the upper classes—and that had been his own undoing. His love for a convent-bred girl had led the girl's aunt to have him imprisoned on a trumped-up charge and sent to labor on a penal farm. There he had learned to care for animals and to ride. Now he was an expert.

After he had been released from prison, Miguel learned that his sweetheart had been quickly married off to an elderly nobleman, and he offered his services to Don Diego. The only post available had been as an assistant to the head gardener. Yet, through diligent work, Miguel Sandarbal had replaced him after the old man's death.

Don Diego drew himself back to the present with an effort. Perhaps this evening, after he had seen to his wife, he would visit Miguel and they would have a glass of wine together and talk about the old days.

The carriage stopped before the Moorish archway framing the patio of Don Diego's palatial house. His driver hastened down from his perch to open the door for his master. But as Don Diego dismounted, he uttered a gasp of alarm to see his sister-in-law, Doña Inez, hurrying toward him, her handsome face streaming with tears, wringing her hands.

"¿Que pasa, Doña Inez?" he asked anxiously.

"Thank God you have come, Don Diego!" her voice quavered with emotion and she dabbed at her eyes with a lace handkerchief. "Padre Benito is giving Dolores the last rites.

The *medico* told me that my poor sister will not last through the night. It was only a little hour after you had left for the Escorial, Don Diego. That was why I called Padre Benito. Oh my poor sister, and the children... and you, who loved her so..."

"Courage, courage, Doña Inez." Don Diego's voice was hoarse and trembling as he put a comforting arm around her shoulders. His face drawn and haggard, he looked up at the dreary, gray sky, then crossed himself. "Let it be Thy will, *mi Dios*. Only do not let her suffer, and do not let her know what has happened today, this evil, accursed day."

Doña Inez de Castillana blew her nose and bit her lips as she stepped back. Her tear-swollen, dark brown eyes searched his taut face. "What did you mean just then, Don Diego? What should Dolores not know?"

"The worst that could happen to us, Doña Inez. I have come from the Escorial and from a private audience with the king himself. It appears that the prime minister and the queen think me hostile to their cause—and so I am, if their cause embraces France and not our glorious land. I have been banished from Spain, yet with some small honor left me. I am to be—the king has so decreed—intendant in the province of Taos, in Nuevo Mexico."

Doña Inez de Castillana recoiled. A handsome woman, slightly taller than her younger sister, her dark brown hair coiffed in an imposing pompadour, she stared at him in confusion for a moment. "Nuevo Mexico?" she at last echoed. "But that is the very end of the world."

"It is still a part of Spain, my dear Doña Inez," Don Diego reminded her. Then, his face grave, he added softly, "I can not tell Dolores. To take her away from this beautiful house, where Carlos and Catarina were born... No, she must not know into what disgrace our name has fallen. And now I must see her. Pray God she can still recognize..."

"Yes, Don Diego. You will want to be alone with her. I shall pray," Doña Inez de Castillana agreed, again dabbing at her eyes with her handkerchief.

As he entered the house, Padre Benito came slowly down the stairs, his lips moving and his fingers touching his rosary.

"Padre... my wife..." Don Diego de Escobar began.

"She is with God, my son." The priest crossed himself. "It was a blessed death, there was no pain, and she confessed her sins before she drew her last breath."

"Sins!" Don Diego repeated the word bitterly, as he, too, crossed himself. "She was blameless insofar as any human being can be, Padre Benito. She thought only of the children and of me, and of all those around her. Never once did I hear her utter an unkind word, an impious thought. She was an angel."

"Then she will already be in heaven, my son. I too believe that her soul was blameless and that the good Lord will welcome her into His eternal keeping."

"So be it, Padre. I shall go to her now."

"Of course, my son. I shall wait for you if you need me."

Don Diego ascended the stairs and headed toward his wife's bedroom. Doña Inez, watching him, sighed and shook her head. Was this, then, the shabby reward of the royal court for all the devotion he had shown Charles IV? Ever since she had come to this house to be with her ailing sister, she had learned to hold her brother-in-law in high esteem, not only for his loyalty to king and country, but most of all for his kindness and gentleness with Dolores. As for Carlos and Catarina, she loved them as much as if they were her very own. And now Don Diego was being forced to leave decadent, enfeebled Spain for a new world.

That journey might be the restoration of both him and his children. Doña Inez had never cared for the pompous rituals and ceremonies of the Spanish court to which her brother-in-law had been obliged to adapt himself. True, the name of de Escobar was an honorable one, enhanced by the title of nobility granted by the king himself. Yet, she was quick-witted enough to perceive that it imposed a stultifying influence upon Don Diego's children. If they had continued to live in Spain, she would have had ever-growing concern about them—particularly Catarina, who was already vain and self-centered. Carlos was more malleable, more direct and honest, not unlike Miguel Sandarbal. The distinctions of class in the Old World had a rigid power when it came to influencing children; well, this might indeed be a blessing in disguise for quick-tempered, selfish Catarina.

Don Diego entered his wife's bedroom and sank down upon his knees beside the canopied bed on which Dolores de Escobar lay. Her face was serene, but the intense, warm brown eyes were closed. Her glossy black hair, of which she had always been so proud—and which Catarina had inherited—mantled her cheeks, caressed the bosom of her shift. Her hands were folded in prayer.

Don Diego bowed his head and wept softly. Then rising, he kissed his wife's hands. *"Querida,"* he murmured, "I am desolate without you. Yet our dear God has spared you the anguish of knowing that we can no longer be together here in Madrid, in our beloved home."

He put his hands over hers and now kissed her lips. Blinking his eyes to clear them of the tears, he said to her, "You have been all things to me, Dolores, my wife, my sweetheart and lover, my dearest friend, mother of Carlos and Catarina who are flesh of our flesh and will remind me always of you. Before God, I swear to you now that I shall keep your memory alive forever and that Carlos and Catarina will revere and love you as I always did and always shall to the end of my days."

No one had ever seen Don Diego weep. But now, straightening, he covered his face with trembling hands and gave vent to the agony of his loss. When he recovered, he kissed Dolores's forehead and walked slowly out of the room and down the stairs to the priest and to Doña Inez.

FIVE

The raft had brought John Cooper and Lije to a low bluff, the other side of which dipped into a thickly wooded glen, about eight miles north of Cairo, Illinois. Pine and spruce trees flourished just beyond a thicket of thorny brambles. The boy found a narrow opening in these and entered the forest. The smell of pine was redolent in the humid air, and he breathed deeply, turning a last time to look back at the river that had brought him to this new haven. Then he trudged on into the glen until he came to a grassy knoll, elevated a few feet from the moist earth. Remembering what his father had taught him, he explored the terrain for some fifty yards on three sides and then returned to the knoll.

As he stretched out, Lije lay down also, his head erect, his alert eyes scanning the surroundings. John Cooper reached out to pat him. "That's right, Lije, keep watch. But it's safe here, and you need sleep, too, after yesterday."

Before he slept, the boy checked the Lancaster to make sure that it was primed and loaded. It was indeed—his father had been unable to get off the last shot before the renegade Shawnee had dragged him out of the cabin to his death. Clutching the rifle in both hands, John Cooper closed his eyes with a weary sigh.

When he finally woke, it was midafternoon. The glen was silent, except for the buzzing of insects and the occasional twittering of river birds. The density of the trees dimmed the bright sun and made the forest cool. John Cooper sat up, at once alert, as Lije moved over to nuzzle his cheek and to utter a soft whine of greeting.

Laying down the rifle, John Cooper opened the sack and cut off more jerky for the two of them, as well as a large chunk of his mother's bread. This, too, he shared with the wolfhound. Then, to refresh himself, John Cooper walked back to the river bank and, kneeling down, bathed his face in the cool water and cupped his palms to drink. Lije followed him, his long tongue thirstily lapping up the water.

John Cooper had remembered to take along a chamois bag in which Andrew Baines had kept his compass and tinderbox. The boy had found this bag laid beside the powderhorn and the canister. Before starting the journey, John Cooper opened his sack and took the compass out to ascertain his bearings. Shouldering the sack and gripping the rifle barrel in his right hand, he strode off with brisk steps toward the northwest. Lije moved ahead of him, glancing back from time to time to make sure that he was not outdistancing his young master. By ten o'clock that night, the two had crossed into Missouri territory, near Cape Girardeau. Once again, John Cooper found a campsite inside a protective clump of spruce trees, on an elevated little hill. He shared his meager meal of jerky and bread with the wolfhound and then fell soundly asleep.

He wakened before dawn, refreshed and alert, bathed his face in a little stream from which he and Lije drank, then started off in the direction of Perryville. A little after noon, Lije's soft, warning growl alerted him to the approach of a dozen Indians on horseback. The boy quickly flattened himself on the ground behind a large boulder and bade Lije lie beside him. They might be friendly, but it was hard now to think of Indians as anything but enemies. They were strong, proud-looking men, and John Cooper sighed enviously as he watched them ride off. A horse like that would be a lot better than shank's mare, he thought, but then he realized it wouldn't be fair to make Lije keep up with a horse. They'd just have to make do. He decided to give the Indians plenty of time to head north, before they moved west.

By nightfall, he and Lije had put sixteen miles behind them and made camp on a low, wooded bluff overlooking a high-water creek. By now, John Cooper had regained all his wiry energy and contented himself with only four hours' sleep. It was still dark when he sprang to his feet and beckoned to the wolfhound.

One night during the first week of October, John Cooper and Lije made camp about fifteen miles southwest of Saint Louis, Missouri. Long before that, the small provisions of jerky, salted venison, and bread had been replaced by berries, apples, and rabbits that he caught in simple snares.

Each time he lit a fire, John Cooper was careful to survey the area to make sure that the glow would not be seen. Then, using his father's tinderbox, he would set sparks flying downward to ignite a small bed of punk, made of dried, decayed maplewood. After coaxing the tiny fire into flame by blowing upon it, John Cooper would add fine splinters of wood, dry leaves, grass, and twigs to enlarge the fire enough for cooking.

There was no problem in finding water. The land through which he was passing abounded in small streams, inlets from large rivers, and creeks. Apart from the Indian hunting party, he and the wolfhound had seen only an occasional trapper or hunter, and they had warily avoided any human contact up until now.

The weather was turning cooler, and John Cooper and Lije had several times taken refuge, during thunderstorms, in little caves atop bluffs. He had kept the skins of the rabbits he had snared, scraping them with both knife and a jagged piece of rock to cleanse the hides thoroughly. And he had found a salt lick in a shallow creek not far from Perryville. Before going to sleep, John Cooper would vigorously rub the coarse salt into the hides, stretching them out between four rocks on a flat surface. Though they were still odorous, they were tanned enough for his purpose. He managed to make a crude pair of mittens for himself and a kind of stocking for his feet.

By the second week of October, sudden early frosts had hit and John Cooper realized that he would need sturdier outer clothing for what promised to be an obdurate, long winter. He had reached a point not far from the little village of Marley, an area marked with stretches of rolling, verdant valley. There were clumps of fall wildflowers along the way and mound-like hills housing many abandoned caves. In one of these, John Cooper had found flint arrows and a badly rusted iron tomahawk.

A day later, just before twilight, the boy and the dog

stopped to make camp and prepare their evening meal. John Cooper laid his rifle aside as he began to build a fire to roast the quail he had shot that noon. He had always coveted "Long Girl," as his father had affectionately called the weapon. It had been made before the turn of the century and was an exceptional piece of workmanship—accurate at long range, with a clean bore, excellent rifling, and good sights. An experienced marksman could get off two shots a minute from it, which sometimes could mean the difference between life and death. In addition, the thick, metal plate fastened to one side of the hardwood butt allowed it to be used as a very effective club, should there be no time to reload.

Suddenly, John Cooper was roused from his thoughts by a curious, coughing roar. Springing to his feet, he could make out, through the dusk, the outlines of a lumbering brown bear. All he could think was, "There's my coat!" He seized the rifle and put an extra charge of powder into it for maximum carrying power. Then he dropped into the barrel the largest ball that would fit.

Hoping that the bear would not catch his scent, John Cooper ran swiftly along its trail. Lije bounded along beside him. "Go get him, but be careful, boy," John Cooper warned. With a joyous bark, Lije sprang forward and disappeared into a thicket of weeds which camouflaged a shallow gully. Above it rose a low hill, and, as the full moon emerged, John Cooper could see the bear plainly as it began to lope over the top of the hill, heading eastward. Lije barked again. The bear turned with a low growl, reared erect on its hind paws, and awaited the attack.

John Cooper knelt and took careful aim, allowing for the angle of trajectory. "I'd better make this shot count or Lije 'n me'll be in real trouble," he muttered to himself. Lije feinted toward the angry bear who made a swipe at him, then returned to its upright, menacing pose. Its deadly claws reached up in readiness to strike.

The report of the rifle almost deafened John Cooper. The bear staggered, uttered a ferocious howl of pain, and then fell backward and rolled over, thrashing in its death agonies. From a distance of sixty feet, the boy had put the ball into the bear's left eye.

"Careful, Lije, he may be playing 'possum'," John Cooper warned as the wolfhound, with a triumphant bark, approached the fallen bear. "Back to me, Lije!" He put his left thumb and forefinger to his lips and emitted a shrill whistle; the wolfhound gave the bear a last look, then turned and trotted obediently back to his young master.

"Good dog, good boy! Tell you what, I'm going to put another ball into him. Then we'll see if he's faking or not. I think I've got him, though." Moving behind a wide oak tree, he squatted down, reloaded, then moved forward to about twenty feet away from the bear. He aimed carefully at the great head and pulled the trigger. There was no movement, and John Cooper exultantly brandished the rifle as he cried out, "I did it! There's my coat, for sure!"

Remembering what his father had once warned him about bears, he waited, nonetheless, for another ten minutes until he was absolutely certain the bear was dead. Then he moved toward it, hunting knife in hand. It was a male, weighing about four hundred pounds, with a shaggy, thick coat. Squatting down, he began the arduous and gory task of skinning the animal.

Grimacing at the sight of the blood that poured from the careful slits he made in the skin, John Cooper forced himself to complete the task. It was well after midnight when he finished, and then followed another hour or two of scraping the skin with a sharp rock to remove the last fibers of flesh, gristle, and fat.

The wolfhound stood beside him, wagging his tail in approval. John Cooper appeared wirier and taller now than when he had started on his journey. His face was leaner, weatherbeaten, and bronzed. Except for his blond hair, bleached almost white by the sun, he could well have been mistaken for an Indian.

At last the job was done. John Cooper was bone weary. The bear meat was indeed a tasty treat—his mother had been able to serve it to the family only once or twice a year, and then they'd all had second helpings, he remembered. It was curious. Thinking about his parents and sisters didn't make him want to cry now the way it had those first few days. But he hadn't forgotten them—he never would. Remembering how the Shawnee believed that the spirits of the dead remained where they had been happy or, if banished, followed those with whom destiny had linked them, he was sure that they were all around him now. There had been times along this trail when he had caught himself bolting down his food and grinned sourly to remember how often his mother had scolded him about his table manners. And when, last week, he'd run into a wild boar because he'd failed to see some scraped bark on a tree and the crushed ferns along a path he was taking, he had shaken his head and said aloud, "Pa, that was downright stupid, that was. I'll watch it the next time."

With his hunting knife, he carved slices of bear meat and salted it in order to cure it. Then, at last, he and Lije made their beds on a pile of fallen leaves. He clutched the rifle to him as he closed his eyes and smiled happily. If Pa had seen him kill the bear—his very first—he'd know that his son was fending for himself pretty well. It was something to brag about.

SIX

It was an hour before dawn, and the waning moon was hidden behind a cloud. In the east, the first faint hint of the sun's round ball edged warily at the farthest and lowest point of the horizon. The sky was a somber gray, and a chilly October wind tugged at the branches of the giant elm tree at the base of which John Cooper lay sprawled in sleep. The bed of leaves that he had made for Lije was next to his, plainly showing the outline of the wolfhound's massive body. A few feet away, the hide of the bear was stretched out on an even expanse of ground, four heavy stones holding it flat. John Cooper, holding "Long Girl" in his right hand, lay with his left hand outstretched toward Lije's bed.

Just half an hour before, Lije had opened his eyes to see a fat rabbit scurrying inside the small forest on the edge of which he and his master had settled down to rest. With a last glance at John Cooper, the dog had bolted from his bed and taken off in hot pursuit. The rabbit was elusive and resourceful, doubling back, hiding in a thicket, then running at full speed toward the top of a little hill. It was seeking its hole near one of the little caves on the side of the hill, and it managed to outdistance Lije for a considerable time.

But at last it made the fatal error. Having found a small

opening, concealed by a large bramble bush at the side of the hill, it waited there, terrified, expecting Lije to rush past at full speed. Instead, the wolfhound crouched down, flattening himself, his eager eyes intent upon the bramble bush, uttering no sound, waiting.

After a few minutes, the terrified rabbit decided to go back toward the giant elm and then down toward the little valley. It emerged warily, its nose twitching, its ears waggling, but did not see the crouching wolfhound. When it made its frantic attempt at flight, Lije was ready and waiting and, with a low growl, sprang. The rabbit raced vainly toward the valley, only to be overtaken after some twenty feet. Lije's great jaws closed over its neck, and death was swift and merciful. Then, wagging his tail, proud of his accomplishment, Lije trotted slowly back.

Earlier that night, two men had seen John Cooper's small supper fire and later heard the two shots the boy had fired at the bear. They had exchanged wondering glances and fallen to speculating on the identity of the unsuspecting hunter. For both men were white renegades who occasionally traded with the Delaware Indians and supplemented that livelihood with robbing and often murdering unwary travelers.

Hank Schlosser was a burly, black-bearded man in his early forties. His beady eyes were set close together beside the bridge of a broad, bulbous nose. Squatting on his booted heels while he cut a piece of jerky with his clasp knife, he had started at the sound of the first shot and turned to his crony, Bart Maridew, a tall, gangling, red-haired and bearded man, ten years his junior. "Now who the hell d'you s'pose that could be? Sounds like a rifle shot to me, Bart."

"That's what I was thinking too, Hank. Hey now, you figger that fellow's all by hisself?"

"More'n likely. You know, I could use me a good long rifle. Meant to trade for one last trip, when we powwowed with Shantimo. But we didn't have enough to offer him, and besides, his rifle was a short one."

"I get your drift, Hank. You think we should have a look-see later on, when the fellow goes to sleep?"

"Sure." Hank Schlosser bared yellow, snaggly teeth in a vicious grin. "We got pistols 'n a musket between us, haven't we? And you've got that Spanish throwing dagger. If it's only one fellow, we won't have any trouble. Now, let's finish supper and rest a spell, then we'll go and see what's up."

"Sure, Hank." Bart Maridew's angular, freckled face twisted in a knowing leer. On his left cheek, near the bony jaw, was a livid, jagged scar, a memento of an encounter with a Saint Louis crib girl.

The sudden sound of the second shot had somewhat puzzled the two renegades. For a moment, they had thought that the unknown hunter might be defending himself against a band of roving Indians. But when a long silence had followed, Hank and Bart decided to wait until it was almost dawn and then rob and, if need be, kill the sleeping hunter.

Each had slept for an hour or two, while the other stood guard around their camp, until the first glimmering of the sun in the east. Then Hank and Bart crept toward the little hill and its bordering forest. The older man had primed and loaded his musket, while Bart carefully loaded his two pistols. Around his neck was a slim, perfectly balanced knife of Spanish steel, encased in a leather sheath.

Crouching to make themselves less visible in the faint, pre-dawn light, they approached John Cooper's camp in a wide circle from the north. They moved carefully, lest the snapping of a twig or branch or the crunching of the dry leaves betray their presence.

"Shucks, it's just a kid," Bart Maridew hissed as they stood staring down at the sleeping boy.

"Yep, but kids grow up to be men, and this one looks real strong and husky," Hank Schlosser whispered back. His beady eyes glinted with avarice at the sight of the long rifle clutched in John Cooper's right hand. "Now that's what I've been wanting all along, Bart."

"Look over there on the ground—it's a prime bearskin," Bart whispered back. "We can get seven or eight dollars for a hide like that. Say, the kid did a fair to middlin' job skinnin' it, too."

Hank Schlosser leveled his musket at John Cooper's chest. He kicked the boy's feet with the toe of his heavy boot. "Wake up there, sonny!"

John Cooper blinked as he fought his way out of the engulfing eaves of sleep. He stared blankly at the ugly, bearded face of the renegade and then at the muzzle of the musket pointed at him. "Who—what—" he stammered, instinctively lifting the rifle.

"No you don't, sonny, drop it," Hank Schlosser snarled, gesturing meaningfully with the musket.

There was a sickening feeling in the pit of John Cooper's

stomach as he remembered that he'd forgotten to reload "Long Girl" after putting that second ball into the bear's head. Obediently, he opened his hand and the Lancaster dropped to the ground.

"Now that's a mite better, sonny." Bart Maridew winked at his crony and grinned at the frightened boy. Both hands rested on the butts of his holstered pistols. "If you don't put up a fuss, we might jist let you live."

"That's as may be," Hank growled, glaring at his partner.

"Hell, Hank, if we take his rifle, the bearskin, 'n what food he's got, this cold spell'll kill him for sure. 'Sides, I ain't never yet killed a kid and he's no danger to us once we've got his gun. Now then, sonny, I'll just take that rifle along with me. Hank, see what provisions he's packin'. Then you can haul that bearskin along, too."

"Since when do you give orders to me, Bart Maridew?" the bearded renegade retorted. "Anyhow, the rifle's mine, I told ya how I tried to trade for one."

"We'll work it out once we get back to camp, Hank," Bart Maridew said as he stooped to retrieve the rifle, then straightened. "He's sure to have powder 'n balls 'n leather patches for loadin', so we'll jist take all the fixin's with us. He won't be needing 'em, anyhow."

"All right, fer once you've got your thinkin' cap on straight," Hank Schlosser agreed grudgingly.

As he turned to look at John Cooper's sack, which had been placed at the very base of the giant elm, Lije trotted out of the forest with the rabbit between his jaws. The dog stiffened, uttered a low growl, dropped the rabbit, and then leapt at the black-bearded renegade.

"Hey—what the hell—Bart, fer Crissake—it's a wolf—kill it!" Hank Schlosser bawled, petrified. But Lije's strong teeth had already closed around Schlosser's jugular vein and the wolfhound's momentum and weight hurled the renegade to the ground.

Hank Schlosser tried to grasp the dog's neck and draw those murderously sharp teeth away from his bleeding throat as he kicked and twisted. Bart Maridew, finally reacting to the suddenness of Lije's attack, drew one of his pistols, momentarily turning his back to John Cooper. The boy drew his hunting knife and sprang forward, crying out, "No, I won't let you kill Lije!" With all his strength, he drove the blade deep into Bart Maridew's back. Though the knife had been dulled by scraping the bear hide, its sharp point and John Cooper's determination to save the wolfhound inflicted a fatal wound.

Bart Maridew uttered a high-pitched yowl, stumbled back a step, and his trigger finger loosed the pistol ball to fly off harmlessly into the woods. With his left hand he reached back to grip the handle of the knife. "You—you li'l bastid—you've killed me—here I told Hank to let you go—aahh—"

His hand fell away from the knife as he lurched forward and lay still.

Trembling and panting, John Cooper groped for Hank Schlosser's fallen musket and lifted it, but there was no need. Lije, still growling ferociously, lay on top of the lifeless renegade, worrying the dead man as he shook his head this way and that, his sharp teeth still viciously imbedded in the man's throat.

"Let him go, Lije—oh my God—you saved my life, Lije." John Cooper gasped. "That's enough, I said! Do what I tell you, now!"

At last the wolfhound rose, his jaws bloody, looking up questioningly at his shaken young master, who was very pale.

"Oh my God, I never wanted to kill that man—but I had to—he'd have shot you, Lije. Why'd they want to kill me, anyway? I never saw them before, I never did them no harm—I mean, any harm—Ma would take me up on that for fair, wouldn't she now? They're both dead—oh I think—I think I'm going to be sick."

He turned away suddenly, his face ashen, then knelt down and retched violently. When the spasm was over, he rose and turned to face the wolfhound, whose ears had pricked up and whose keen eyes studied him solicitously. "It's over now, Lije. I guess I better bury them."

The wolfhound trotted over to his young master and nudged his leg with his bloody muzzle. John Cooper grimaced with revulsion, then knelt down to tear up a handful of grass and wipe away the blood. "All right, now. I'll bury them. You just stand and watch, in case they've got friends who'll come to see what's happened. I sure hope there aren't any more. I don't think I could go through this again. But how'm I going to bury them, Lije, when I haven't got a spade or shovel?"

He stood for a moment, his face twisted in tortured indecision.

Looking around dazedly, he decided at last to just drag

them into the woods and cover them up with leaves and grass. It was the best he could do. But he would say a prayer for their souls—anybody, no matter how low he was, deserved that much.

John Cooper flinched at the sight of the two dead men, but he steeled himself to bend and grasp the older man's booted ankles. Laboriously, he dragged the lifeless body into the copse. Then, swiftly, trying not to glance at the livid, distorted face of the black-bearded renegade, he covered Hank Schlosser with leaves and grass.

Slowly, he went back to the giant elm tree, leaning against it for a moment to steady himself. His eyes fell on the sheath tied around Bart Maridew's neck and, with boyish curiosity, he drew the bone-handled knife out of the sheath and examined it. Then he whistled with admiration. It was beautifully balanced, the blade finely honed, and the point murderously sharp. He walked a few feet away, faced the giant elm, and took the point of the knife between right thumb and forefinger. He balanced it in the air to get the feel and the heft of it and then flung it. He let out a shout of joy when he saw it sink into the tree, quivering like a living thing. "It's a dandy," he exulted aloud and resolved to keep it in place of his own. Remembering, he grimaced again, shook his head. He couldn't take his hunting knife back, not after what he did with it.

He went to the red-haired renegade's body and dragged that also into the copse, covering it as he had Hank Schlosser's body. Then, as a kind of afterthought, he picked up the latter's musket. It was a little one. It wouldn't be hard to find ammunition for and it would be better for birds and rabbits than "Long Girl." He chuckled wanly. "We'd best make tracks away from here, Lije. I sure wish we could have stayed longer to let that bearskin cure, but there's no help for it now. I'll just bundle it up as best I can."

Dawn was breaking, but the sky was even drearier than before. John Cooper had folded the bearskin carefully and wedged it partly into the heavy sack. Shouldering this with his left hand, and holding the barrels of the musket and his father's long rifle in his right, he uttered a long sigh and moved westward. Lije docilely trotted beside him, now and again glancing up at the stricken face of his silent young master.

SEVEN

It had rained on Monday, the day of the funeral of Dolores de Escobar. Don Diego, Doña Inez, and Carlos and Catarina had been driven in their carriage to the little cemetery two miles south of Don Diego's estate. There they had witnessed the interment beside the grave of Don Diego's father.

The rain had served to hide Don Diego's tears, and Doña Inez had tried valiantly to conceal her own while consoling her weeping young niece. It appeared that Catarina, of the entire household, was the most bereaved; she had wept inconsolably all through the weekend. And during the ceremony at the gravesite over which old Padre Benito had presided, she had clung to her aunt, burying her tear-stained, swollen face against Doña Inez's bosom.

Charles IV had sent his majordomo as emissary to tender his personal condolences to the de Escobar family. And, as a kind of final irony, there had been a neatly uniformed captain of the royal guard, Hernando Salvacez, who attended the funeral as the representative of Carlos Leonardo Luis Manuel de Godoy y Boegas. The young captain, a man in his early thirties, had maintained himself with a stiff military bearing throughout. At the conclusion of the ceremony, he had approached Don Diego. "If I may have a word with Your

Excellency," he had murmured, glancing nervously about, as if afraid of being overheard.

Don Diego had inclined his head and walked a few paces away from the grave, gesturing to Doña Inez to keep Carlos and Catarina with her. "I am at your service, Captain."

"My illustrious master has instucted me to offer his personal sympathies to you in your great loss, Don Diego."

"It is kind of him." Don Diego curtly inclined his head, his eyes quizzically appraising the suave face of the captain.

"He bids me tell you that you will not be disturbed during your preparations for the voyage, Don Diego. He respects your grief and wishes you to have ample time to recover from it while you prepare for your journey to Nuevo Mexico. And he asks me to tell you that he wishes you well in your new capacity."

"Again, it is kind of him. Will you tell him that my loyalty to the throne has never wavered and will, if anything, be stronger once I am in this new world. I see now how vital it is to do all that is possible to maintain the strength of Spain in all her remaining colonies," Don Diego said. He had permitted himself a faintly ironic smile while he seethed inwardly with a righteous anger over this new injustice. Manuel de Godoy was mocking him, reminding him that his Spanish estates were forfeit but that, out of consideration for his dead wife, there would be no formal confiscation until he had boarded the *Paloma.* It was, in a sense, the kind of courtesy an executioner would extend to a condemned man. He added tonelessly, "My family and I intend to sail from Cadiz when the *Paloma* is ready, Captain."

"I shall convey your message. I thank you for accepting my presence here, Don Diego. I did not have the pleasure of knowing your wife, but I have been told that she was a woman of great beauty and kindness."

Don Diego turned abruptly to one side lest the officer see the tears that had suddenly sprung to his eyes. He cleared his throat and, without turning back to the captain, replied, "I think Padre Benito spoke the most appropriate words of all. And now, I must not keep you from your duties."

Godoy's captain saluted, turned on his heel, and then strode off to his horse. Don Diego watched him go and then turned back to his family. An apologetic cough announced the presence of the Conde Pedro de Santorsalva. The frail little man, almost hidden in his great cape, stared at him. "I hesitate to intrude upon you again, Don Diego."

"You are the emissary of my king, to whom I have pledged my life and honor. Speak as you will, Conde," Don Diego retorted.

"As you know, Don Diego, His Most Catholic Majesty has entrusted into my keeping the documents which confirm you as intendant and also those which you are to convey to the governor of Cuba and the viceroy in Mexico. These will be delivered to you at the port of Cadiz on the last day of this month. Also, His Most Catholic Majesty has graciously decided to bestow upon you in advance your first year's salary as intendant, in the sum of five thousand *pesos*."

"I am deeply grateful for His Majesty's kindness, Conde."

The man looked around again and then concluded, "You understand, I am sure, the first minister's decree as to the confiscation of your estates in Madrid and Sitges. However, His Majesty bade me remind you that such monies or jewels which you have in your possession need not be left behind. He understands that you will want to defray the expenses of your journey and, doubtless, to acquire servants and necessities in your new post."

That, indeed, was a royal indulgence. Don Diego was more grateful for it than he dared tell the majordomo. He had lavished fine jewels on Dolores and, carefully concealed in a leather sack, hidden behind a camouflaged wall panel in his study, were some eight thousand *pesos*. At least he would not be destitute. Most of all, that sum together with his advance salary as intendant would enable him to provide all possible comforts for Carlos and Catarina. He had no illusions about what comforts might be available on shipboard. The cabins would be narrow and cheerless. Already he could foresee how peevish Catarina would be about exchanging the luxury of the life she had known up until now for a narrow space on a tossing ship.

He extended his hand to the majordomo. "You will catch your death of cold if you stay here much longer, Conde. It was good of you to come, and it was most gracious of my king. Tell him I shall always be his most loyal subject. And may God go with you."

"And with you and yours also, Don Diego." The majordomo hesitated a moment, coughed apologetically, then nodded and went back to the carriage that awaited him. The rain had nearly stopped, but there was a chill wind and the sky was mournful, like Don Diego's distraught thoughts. He gestured to Doña Inez to bring Carlos and Catarina to their waiting carriage and, as his son approached him, forced a smile to his quivering lips. *"Mi hijo,* now we must be thinking of what lies ahead of us."

"We go to the New World, do we not, Father?" Carlos demanded.

"Yes, my son. We shall talk about that over supper tonight. Be kind to your sister, Carlos. She is young, so lost without her mother. You must set a good example and be as much the man of the family now as I am. And I shall need your strength and you, too, my son."

Don Diego was even more conscious of his loss that evening at the dinner table. Until her illness, Dolores de Escobar had brought with her a warmth and light, wherever she went. Even at the most formal of the dinners which Don Diego had been obliged to give, he had been cheered by his wife's graciousness and charm as a hostess. She had the knack of setting visitors at ease and eliciting interesting conversation from even the most dull-witted guest. There had been no pretense to her, only a sincere devotion and love.

He glanced now at the empty chair where she had sat. Once again, he experienced a sudden swell of anger. He noticed that Doña Inez was staring at him, leaning forward with an intent expression on her handsome face, as if she wished to say something. He waited until Pablo Solera, their elderly butler, had filled the goblets with wine and gone out of the ornate dining room before he nodded to her. "You wish to say something to me, Doña Inez?"

"I have wanted to say it to you ever since last Friday, my brother-in-law. I cannot bear to think that Catarina and Carlos are to make that difficult, long journey with you and no one to look after all of you. Will you not consider letting me accompany you, as duenna to Catarina, at least? It will be very difficult for a young girl to adapt herself to so much that will be new and strange."

At this, Catarina, who had been chatting with her brother, stiffened and haughtily tossed her head. "I am quite old enough to take care of myself, Tía Inez!"

"That is not exactly true, Catarina," Don Diego gently reproved her. "You are thirteen, certainly not yet betrothed, and your education is far from complete. Indeed, Doña Inez, you have solved a problem that has been troubling me. But I could not ask you to leave Madrid. You forget, my dear sister-in-law, that it is I and the rest of my family who have been banished from Madrid, not you."

"What have I to keep me in Madrid, Don Diego, expecially when my niece and nephew and my esteemed brother-in-law are to leave it forever?" Doña Inez countered. Yet there was something wistful in the way her eyes held Don Diego's searching gaze, and her hands, hidden from sight, twisted nervously in her lap.

"There is so much to be done and so little time," Don Diego mused. "I must confess I know very little about the new province to which I am being sent. Of course, since my work at court was involved with the ministry of revenue, I was aware that the crown received taxes from Nuevo Mexico and that we imposed royal duties on articles of trade in that region. Yet, to the best of my recollection, it is not a colony that has brought gold and silver into the coffers of Spain, although perhaps that was what the *conquistadores* hoped for when they brought it under Spanish rule. I must learn as much as I can about it—after all, it will be my new home now, as it will be for Catarina and Carlos. Think again, Doña Inez, before you forsake the culture and beauty of Madrid."

"No, Don Diego, I have very little to give up when all is said and done." His sister-in-law shook her head, glancing with a smile at Carlos and Catarina. "You know very well that my parents are dead and that Dolores and I had no other relatives. A capable steward runs the little farm that they left me and would be happy to purchase it. He wishes to marry a pretty peasant girl from the village in which I was born, and to own such a farm would give him status in her parents' eyes. I shall arrange at once to sell the farm to him, and the money will enable me to pay my way and to make a new start of my own in Nuevo Mexico."

"If that is how you feel, Doña Inez, I am deeply grateful. And I know that Carlos and Catarina will look upon you as a foster mother in view of—" He could not finish, reached for his goblet of wine, drained it, and set it down with a clatter to hide his emotion. "What I must next do, Doña Inez, is to see to the matter of servants and workers for the new land which my king has granted to me. I think I shall speak with Miguel Sandarbal. I hope that he will agree to accompany us. He is a strong, honest man who has worked land and knows animals, and he could be of great service to us in our new home."

"Yes, Father." Carlos eagerly spoke up, having overheard

this last. "He can teach me how to hunt and ride, and to use the sword and the musket. And he is a good friend, Father."

"Pooh!" Catarina sniffed. "You forget yourself, Carlos. You are the son of a nobleman, and yet you speak of being friends with a common gardener."

Don Diego turned to his daughter and frowned. "He is much more than that, Catarina. He happens to be my friend. I said, too, that he was honest and trustworthy, and these virtues one does not always find, even among the nobility—and well should I know from my own experience."

"It is all very well for you to talk, Father, but I do not want to leave this beautiful house. Tía Inez has told me where we are going, how there are Indians and wild animals. . . . It will be dreadful, I know it will. And there will not be any balls and no handsome young men to ask me to dance with them—"

Doña Inez lifted her eyes toward heaven and, with an apologetic look at her brother-in-law, retorted tartly, "Well, my opinionated niece, would you prefer to spend your days in a convent? There, I promise you, you would see no young men whatsoever, and you would have only the nuns' hymns to dance to. Would you prefer that?"

"You are cruel, Tía Inez!" Catarina burst into tears and covered her face with her hands.

Carlos regarded his sister with a half-amused, half-irritated look, and then eyed his father. "I have no objection at all to going, Father," he volunteered. "It will be exciting. And there is certain to be hunting and a chance to ride my horse as much as I like—is that not so?"

"To be sure, my son. Only, we shall not be able to take the horses with us. We shall be traveling on a ship of the line—there will be just enough room for us. It carries cargo for the king, and we must not take up more space on the ship than is our due."

"Of course, Father. Besides, I am sure Miguel can find good horses for us to ride in Nuevo Mexico. Maybe they will be even faster and sturdier than the ones in our stable," Carlos readily agreed.

Don Diego smiled. His son's enthusiasm lightened his sorrow. It was a good sign, indeed. As for Catarina, one expected a girl of her age to be emotional. Once they had settled in their new home, once he began his new duties as intendant, there would be enough to occupy them all to relieve them of the sadness which he felt at this moment. He looked around at the sumptuous furnishings of this beautifully appointed room. All of these things were forfeit to the crown. Not that Charles IV would hold him to an itemized accounting of the antiques and heirlooms here, but since he was destined to begin life all over again in a new country across the ocean, the wisest course would be to abandon everything and begin anew. He rose with a courtly bow to his sister-in-law. "If you will excuse me, then, Doña Inez, I wish you a pleasant good night. And, Catarina, try to look on the brighter side of things. There is no profit in regretting what cannot be changed. After all, it is far worse for me, your father—at my age, I certainly had not planned on beginning my life over again. You are only just starting yours, and you are going to be a very beautiful young woman." He chuckled paternally. "I don't doubt your ability to attract very eligible and handsome suitors in Nuevo Mexico."

About five years before, in recognition of Miguel Sandarbal's faithful service, Don Diego had ordered that a little cottage be constructed for his head gardener, behind the spacious estate. It was to this cottage that he now walked, deep in thought, scarcely conscious of the intermittent gusts of wind which tugged at his cape. Somehow, in the bitter loneliness that had surged up within him tonight because of Dolores's absence at the table, he needed the comforting reassurance of a man like Miguel. Here was a man who had gone to prison unjustly, simply because he had been ambitious enough to want to marry a girl whose lineage decreed that she could not properly wed a commoner. Yet, instead of breaking his spirit, that punishment had been turned into a kind of valuable education. On the penal farm, Miguel had learned how to deal with cows, goats, and horses, and the rugged life had strengthened his body as it had sharpened his wits. There could be no more valuable companion to take with him to Nuevo Mexico, Don Diego was certain.

He could see the lamplight through the small shuttered window of the cottage and quickened his step toward the door, on which he knocked loudly. The head gardener opened the door hesitantly, then uttered a gasp of surprise and stepped back, respectfully inclining his head when he recognized his master. "Don Diego, you could have sent for me—I am ashamed to welcome you—I was just having a little supper—"

"Come now, this is no time to stand on ceremony." The gray-haired nobleman made a peremptory gesture with his hand. "If you have some wine left, I should be grateful for it. It is a cold, dismal night. Will it ever stop raining, I wonder?"

"If it rains in the provinces, Don Diego, it will be good for the crops," Miguel Sandarbal remarked as he drew back to allow his master to enter. Then, closing the door, he hurried back to him, uneasy and yet solicitous. On the little table was a half-filled jug of red wine, as well as the remnants of a stew and a loaf of black bread.

"A man who lives alone, Don Diego, is not always so neat as he might be," Miguel Sandarbal apologized.

"I did not come here to discuss your domestic arrangements, *hombre*. Go ahead, sit down and finish your supper. I shall just draw up this stool and share the wine with you, if you don't object."

"Of course not, Don Diego. I regret I have little more to offer you. . . ."

"I've already dined, but I came here to talk to you, Miguel. To talk to you as one man to another, not as your employer."

"How can I serve you?"

Don Diego picked up the wine jug and, holding it in both hands, set it to his lips and drank. It was strong, bitter wine, yet it sufficed for his mood. "I am going to take you into my confidence, Miguel. My children and I must leave Madrid by the end of this month—it is by order of the king."

Miguel Sandarbal eyed his master with wonder, but he was discreet enough to say nothing. That, too, pleased Don Diego. Decidedly, here was a man he could trust.

"The king," he went on, "has in his wisdom decided to appoint me intendant to the province of Taos, in Nuevo Mexico. I am desolate at the thought of leaving Madrid, but I am a loyal subject of His Majesty and I obey his order. Now then, Catarina and Carlos will accompany me, and Doña Inez has been kind enough to offer to go with the children as their duenna. It is helpful, you understand, in view of—"

He could not finish and resorted to the wine jug again.

"*Sí, comprendo*," Miguel softly ventured.

"Yes. Well, then, the king has given me five thousand acres of land in Taos. The position of intendant has to do with the financial affairs of the province, and in this I have been trained here at court. But for my own subsistence as well as my sanity, Miguel, it would be wise to put that land to some fruitful use. Perhaps cattle or sheep, I do not know yet."

"I have heard, Don Diego," Miguel Sandarbal suggested with some hesitation, "that sheep are profitable. Their wool and their meat are always in need. I myself, some years ago—when I was on the farm of which you know—worked with them. One needs patience, that is all."

"And you have that, Miguel, I'm certain. So, if it does not grieve you too much to leave Madrid, I would be pleased if you would agree to continue in my service. I shall make you foreman of my *hacienda* in Taos."

"It is too much honor for me, Don Diego," Miguel protested. "I am only a gardener—"

"You are the only one I can turn to, the only one I can trust. If you accept, Miguel, you will be responsible for engaging servants and workers for the *hacienda*. Of course, it will have to be done in Mexico. The *Paloma* will take us first to Cuba and then to Vera Cruz, whence we shall travel to Mexico City to see the viceroy. While we are there, you will be able to make all the arrangements—that is, if you are willing."

"I want to work for no one else, Don Diego. I am devoted to you, you know that. You gave me back my life after what happened—"

"And in a way, Miguel, you will help give me back mine. I shall not forget your devotion to my family and me, be sure of that." Once again, Don Diego took the wine jug and drank from it, then sighed. "I do not suppose that any of our servants would be willing to leave the comforts of Madrid, to go to this barren, new country. I am sure old Pablo would not, nor would the cook. . . ."

"There is this to consider, Don Diego. In Mexico, we are certain to find people willing to work for much lower wages than we should have to pay in Madrid."

Don Diego chuckled. "You are a practical man, Miguel. Yes, I see I have made no mistake. Bless you for agreeing to come with us." He rose and offered his hand. "I am proud to call you my friend, Miguel Sandarbal."

The gardener swallowed hard, struggling against his own emotion, then gripped Don Diego's hand. "I ask nothing better than to serve you well in all things," he said hoarsely.

EIGHT

Fearful that the two renegades he had been forced to kill might have friends nearby, John Cooper continued to travel northwest until early afternoon. He was careful to remain hidden as much as possible, skirting the edges of small copses of trees, already stripped of leaves as the early winter approached. Often, he would crouch low and move along the sides of small hills which bordered the terrain to the east. He had to pause several times—the heavy bearskin and the sack, together with the rifle and musket, proved a taxing load. By mid-afternoon, he came upon a large cave at the top of a jagged hill, bordered by sturdy cedar trees that provided a kind of camouflage for the cave. Exhausted by the arduous trek, and reacting to the violence of his encounter with Schlosser and Maridew, John Cooper flung himself down on the ground and pulled the bearskin over him. Its smell and unwieldiness scarcely bothered him; in a few moments, he was fast asleep. Lije lay down beside him, close to the mouth of the cave, from which he could keep watch. There was no one in sight, not the slightest sign of any habitation, not even an Indian village. Then, just before twilight, the wind subsided and the air seemed actually mild after the bitter morning and early afternoon.

When John Cooper woke, he found Lije standing before him, whining impatiently. Between his jaws, the wolfhound held a rabbit. John Cooper first gasped, then burst into almost hysterical laughter. Now he remembered. Lije had brought back another rabbit just as those two men were trying to rob him, maybe kill him. In their flight away from that terrible scene, he'd completely forgotten about Lije's hard-earned prize. When he was able to control himself, he reached out and took the furry little animal from between Lije's jaws, then hugged the wolfhound. "Good boy, good dog! I forgot last time, didn't I? Well, just for that, we're going to have a very late breakfast and you're going to get most of this rabbit, Lije!"

John Cooper noticed that it was pitch-dark outside. He had slept until well past midnight. He crawled to the mouth of the cave and peered out, to see that the moon was fringed by thick, rapidly moving clouds—a sure sign of a coming storm. Most likely snow, from what he remembered back in Shawneetown. The air was frosty again, a further indication of what was to follow.

Crawling back to the sack, he opened it and took out his father's tinderbox. Having found a pile of dry leaves and some twigs at the mouth of the cave, he began to make a fire.

The light showed him that the cave was deep and wide. It would make an excellent refuge in the event of a storm or blizzard. Then there was the bearskin. He would have to make it into some sort of coat—folding it and sticking it into the sack made it too heavy and unwieldy a load for him to carry. And, judging from the air wafted in from the mouth of the cave, it was high time he went about making the coat.

He found that he could stand nearly erect in the cave, and, after his long sleep, he felt strong and alert again. He'd have to think about where to go next. So far as he could tell, he was still in Missouri territory. A little farther north and then west, and he'd be in the land of the Osage and the Ayuhwa Sioux. He remembered now that his father had told him about the Ayuhwa. The name was taken from the Dakota Sioux term which meant "sleepy people," and they were friendly. His father's cousin's wife, he remembered now, had come from the Ayuhwa tribe. After a battle in which the Osage had defeated the Ayuhwa, she had fled with her mother to the east and taken refuge in one of the Shawnee villages. The girl had been brought up by the Shawnee and then married his father's cousin. Perhaps he should head for that territory—he would think about it after he'd made his winter coat But first he would cook the rabbit for himself and Lije.

The fire was blazing merrily, and just outside the cave he found a few broken branches which he added to it. Next, he skinned the rabbit and cut it with his new knife. Then, breaking off a green branch he had found outside the cave and skewering the rabbit with it, he set it onto the fire, while Lije gravely contemplated his master's handiwork, turning now and again to nudge his cheek or shoulder.

Suddenly he recalled the terrible, shattering violence, and he began to shudder uncontrollably. He turned his face away from the solicitous wolfhound who whined and nudged him again, as if to draw him out of this black mood.

"I never thought I'd have to kill anybody—not ever," he whispered into the darkness. "And now—besides those Shawnee—well, God forgive me, I couldn't help doing that, I think He knows I couldn't. . . . But now there's those other two—even if you did go for that fellow's throat, I was responsible for his dying. If I were ever caught and what I did to those two men were discovered, I might go to jail—maybe they'd even hang me. I'm just praying they didn't have any friends who'll come looking for them and then try to track us down."

But by this time the savory smell of the cooked rabbit began to dispel the boy's somber mood. Taking the improvised skewer, John Cooper made his way to the mouth of the cave and held it out into the cold night air for a few moments, then returned. He carefully sliced strips of meat from the bones and fed them to Lije, who gobbled them down and barked once to indicate his pleasure at this feast.

John Cooper continued to feed Lije until all of his share was gone, put the bones off to one side, and then picked up his share and ate ravenously. Although John Cooper knew that he should move on, he decided to use the rest of the night to fix his coat. It would be easier to wear the bearskin instead of hauling it around.

By dawn, he had finished the coat. He put it on and found that he had allowed for a kind of overlapping hood which he could pull over his head. The coat fitted surprisingly well. It was heavy, and he already felt warm in it. To test it, he moved outside and Lije followed him.

The night was still, except for the occasional call of a bird and, from the distance, the baying of a wolf. John Cooper shivered at that sound and then turned back to Lije and patted him.

Twenty minutes later, having extinguished the fire, John Cooper Baines and the wolfhound left the cave and moved westward, still following the line of hills to keep out of sight.

NINE

The ship of the line, *Paloma,* lay at anchor in the port of Cadiz on the last day of September. Its crew, neatly uniformed for the long voyage, was busy readying the vessel for its departure with the tide, late in the afternoon. Under the intent eye of the boatswain, and even more under the scowling scrutiny of a resplendently uniformed first lieutenant, the cargo had been stored in the hold, supplies taken aboard, and masts and sails inspected for the last time before sailing. The townspeople, gathering to watch the departure of the ship, buzzed with excitement and made way with shouts of acclaim for the carriage which was bringing Don Diego de Escobar and his family to begin the journey across the Atlantic which ultimately would take them to Taos.

There were men and women in that crowd who remembered the former glories of the Spanish navy and who, in their muttered exchanges to one another, could surely have been adjudged far more guilty of treason than Don Diego de Escobar. They could remember a time when the galleons of mighty Spain had coursed the seven seas and brought back gold, silver, and jewels. They also remembered how the trim fighting ships, which had supplanted the cumbersome and unmaneuverable galleons, had been copied by the English.

And they could see, too, the pompous figure of a French captain of marines haranguing the harbor master and demanding to see the captain of the *Paloma*, as was his every right. To be sure, if a Spanish ship of the line was putting forth from Cadiz, Napoleon must be certain that it was not being sent against his invincible forces which threatened to overwhelm all Europe. The papers indeed were in order, the cargo already inspected, and the identity of the passengers and the destination known in advance. Yet nothing must be left to chance. If a single Spanish ship, sailed by devoted Spanish patriots who detested the French, should leave Cadiz, it might ruin the peace upon which the prime minister had staked not only his honor but his very life.

The oldsters in that crowd remembered also how the *Paloma*, a three-decked, four-masted ship, had once been the flagship of Admiral Pierre de Villeneuve. Two years ago, he had taken French and Spanish ships of the line to face Viscount Horatio Nelson off Cape Trafalgar. There, although the English naval hero had been killed in action, Villeneuve had lost twenty ships and the power of Napoleon on the seas had been drastically reduced to a mere token force.

In those days, the *Paloma* had boasted seventy-two guns. Now it had exactly half that number, to make more room for cargo as well as passengers. Every bulkhead had been taken down in the after part of the ship to make spacious though low-ceilinged cabins. There were carronades on each side which suggested the former fighting power of the *Paloma*, and there were wind scoops at the scuttles to deflect the trade winds into the cabins. These, thanks to the double shade of awning and deck, would keep the cabins pleasantly cool until the *Paloma* turned into the Gulf of Mexico.

In the days of Spain's naval glory there had been galley slaves—but in the stormy Atlantic, oars were not practical. So what had once been the long tiers of rowers' benches had been replaced by a broader hold for cargo. If the *Paloma* were becalmed in the Atlantic, the captain and his crew would be left to whistle for a wind and lie helplessly becalmed until the great sails filled. Although Don Diego had been told that the voyage to Cuba should take no more than two months, it was quite possible that it might take three. The journey to Vera Cruz might take another three, and then they would face the long, overland trek to Mexico City and the viceroy. Beyond that lay the arduous journey by land from the viceroy's capital to distant Taos—it might be a full year before Don Diego, his children, Doña Inez, and Miguel Sandarbal would see their new home.

Nonetheless, as the coachman hurried to open the door and help his passengers descend, Don Diego put on a brave face for the crowd. He handed down Doña Inez as if she were herself a countess; and Miguel did the same for Catarina, who looked around her, a pout on her lovely face, a frown on her high-arching forehead. The crowd was distasteful to her, and the hubbub even more so. Carlos jumped down and slapped his thigh. "There is nothing like sea air, is that not so, Father? *Por Dios,* we could not have picked a better day for sailing!"

"Es verdad, mi hijo." Don Diego was heartened by his handsome son's buoyant outlook. Throughout the long journey by carriage from Madrid to Cadiz, Catarina had been almost tearfully peevish, and even Carlos's attempt to cheer his sister had little effect. Doña Inez had asserted herself with an occasional admonishment, but had at last given up and prayed silently for a divine inspiration that would mend her young niece's manners.

"I should like to go aboard and look over the ship, Father. Would it be all right?" Carlos pursued.

"I think we had best ask the captain, son. You can see that his men haven't finished loading—there are water casks being hauled up to the deck by slings, there at the end of the deck, do you see?"

"Yes, Father. How is it that they have not already loaded the casks?"

"Now that I can tell you," Don Diego chuckled with a pardonable show of paternal pride. "That water will have to suffice us until we reach Cuba, Carlos. If we should be becalmed during the voyage, the water, no matter how well preserved in those sturdy casks, will go stagnant. So the captain waits until the very last moment to take on fresh water so that it will stay fresh as long as possible."

"Yes, I see that, Father. You know a great deal about the sea."

"Not really, Carlos. In my position at court, I had to go over the accounts of the navy. . . ." Don Diego cut himself short, not wishing to recall bitter memories. He, as much as anyone in the crowd, was all too aware of Spain's fall from naval glory. "But there is the captain now, and I see His Majesty's courier beckoning to me. He will have the documents which certify me in my post as intendant. Follow me if you like, and then we can ask the captain if he would mind your going aboard for a moment." He turned to Catarina and Doña Inez. "It would be best for you both to remain near the carriage until the captain allows us to board."

"I should like to go to my cabin now and get away from all these noisy people, Father," Catarina complained.

"Please, child, it will be only a few more minutes," Doña Inez said. There was a tone of exasperation in her voice that she could not quite hide.

Beside the gangplank a short, thick-bearded, uniformed man stood chatting with Jaime Rodriguez, whom Don Diego recognized as he approached as the courier of Charles IV. Miguel followed a short distance behind. Don Diego saluted both the captain and the courier, and to the former declared, "My family and I are at your disposal, captain. My son, Carlos here, asks if he might go aboard your fine ship to inspect her before we take our places in whatever quarters you see fit to provide for us. It is the first time he has been at sea, you understand."

"But of course," the captain of the *Paloma* assented. "Take care, young man, my first mate will show you about once you've gone up the gangplank." Turning and cupping his hands to his mouth, he called, "Gonsalvez, show this young gentleman how the *Paloma* is rigged!"

"*¡Sí, mi capitán!*" a swarthy, heavy-set Andalusian called back. Carlos, with an excited laugh, hurried up the gangplank.

Miguel approached Don Diego. "*Con permiso,* I will accompany Carlos aboard," he said. "I, too, am anxious to become acquainted with the vessel."

"Of course, Miguel," Don Diego replied. "And I'd appreciate your keeping an eye on my son for me." With a wry smile, Miguel followed Carlos on board the ship.

"I am Captain Ferdinand Otero, at your service, Don Diego," the bearded officer introduced himself. "You will find two comfortable cabins, one for yourself and your son, the other for your daughter and Doña Inez de Castillana. It will be my pleasure, as well as that of my officers, to make your journey to Vera Cruz as pleasant as possible."

"I thank you for your courtesy, Captain Otero. We have brought with us as little baggage as possible, and we shall try not to discommode you and your crew during the voyage." He bowed to the captain, then turned to the courier. "A pleasure to see you again, Señor Rodriguez."

"My pleasure also, Don Diego. These documents include letters of introduction to the governor of Cuba and the viceroy in Mexico City, as well as your appointment as intendant to Taos. And this is a draft upon the Banco de Mexico in the amount of five thousand *pesos,* as His Majesty agreed. In addition, you will find in this packet confidential letters from His Majesty to both the governor and the viceroy."

"Convey to His Majesty my warmest thanks and my assurance that I shall place these documents in the proper hands. It is a trust I eagerly accept as a proof of my loyalty to the throne."

The courier bowed, then turned to salute Catarina and Doña Inez. He was a personable young man in his early thirties, wearing a brilliant white uniform with a silver sword buckled to his side. Catarina at once forced a dazzling smile to her pouting lips and dropped him a curtsy. Doña Inez eyed her niece and muttered something inaudible under her breath.

As Don Diego turned back to the captain of the *Paloma,* the French captain of marines came forward. Tall and lean, with a cadaverous face, he wore on his uniformed chest Napoleon's own Order of the Eagle for heroism in battle. He sneered superciliously as he confronted the two men. "If I may be permitted to see your papers, gentlemen. Yours, Captain Otero, which designate the sailing orders of your king. And you, sir, to identify yourself as a passenger aboard this vessel."

Some of the onlookers moved slightly forward after the courier left. Seeing the uniform of the hated French, an elderly woman called out, "*¡Abájo Godoy y Carlos, viva Ferdinand!*"

The marine captain turned with an angry scowl on his face. "Where is your civil guard, captain? That woman speaks treason against your prime minister and your king—she calls for the king's son, Ferdinand, to sit upon your throne. My imperial master will not be happy to hear that the man who negotiated the wise peace between our two countries is so reviled in public!"

"As to that, Señor," Captain Otero countered, "I am a sea captain, not a *político.* I simply follow orders, as you must yourself."

"*Ventre Saint Gris,* Captain Otero, I can draw my own conclusions. Now let me have your papers, and yours as well, monsieur!"

The French captain examined Captain Otero's sailing orders at some length, scowling all the while; and then he rather rudely took from Don Diego's hand the sheet on which Charles IV had inscribed the appointment as intendant. This he glanced at summarily and then handed back to Don Diego without a word. Turning to the captain of the *Paloma*, he declared, "All seems to be in order. Permission granted to sail. I have already inspected your cargo. It is well that there are no weapons aboard, or the emperor would consider that such cargo would endanger the peace treaty which has unified our great countries. I bid you a pleasant voyage."

"*Vaya con Dios, Señor.*" Captain Otero returned the French marine captain's salute.

As the French officer left the dock, Captain Otero sighed. "This is what we are reduced to these days, Don Diego. I said I am not a politician, and that is true. Yet all the same, as a midshipman I sailed on men-of-war and fought such dogs as that one, and I am sad at what I observe today."

"I share that sadness, Captain Otero. But I shall say no more on the matter. I fear I have said too much already. And now, whenever you wish us to board, we await your command. I know enough about ships to understand that you alone are the law on the high seas," Don Diego said with a faint smile.

"Yes, that is true, Don Diego. But you will not find me a tyrant. And my first duty is a happy one—to invite you and your family to dine with me, my first lieutenant, and my other officers this evening. As soon as we are safely out to sea, we shall serve you an excellent dinner. I have aboard a most capable cook, and we have taken on many delicacies. With luck and a fair wind, you will not starve before you reach Cuba."

He turned, after a polite gesture to Don Diego, to call up to his first mate, "Stand ready to cast off!" And then, with a genial smile and an inclination of his head in recognition of Don Diego's noble rank, he added, "If you will do me the honor of escorting your daughter and your sister-in-law aboard, Don Diego, we shall begin our voyage."

TEN

The gnawing fear that the two renegades might have friends who would pursue him and Lije made John Cooper set a determined pace for the rest of the night, heading westward and using the protective covering of trees, hills, and bushes wherever possible. By dawn, the boy, totally exhausted, found shelter in a grassy knoll, framed by towering oak trees; after telling Lije to stand guard, he slept till well past midday.

The weather had grown noticeably colder, and John Cooper figured that the winds from the north and the northwest foretold an early winter. The winters had been rugged enough in Shawneetown, but the cabin had been well built, and the roaring log fire kept it snug. What he missed most these lonely nights was the easygoing companionship which he had known, which he had taken for granted without ever having been aware of it, of his father and mother and his teasing but always loving sisters. True, Lije had become a staunch, indispensable companion: there were times when it seemed to John Cooper that he and the wolfhound could communicate almost as well as two men. Yet, of course, it wasn't the same, could never be the same again.

By November, he reached the outskirts of the little settlement of Hannibal. His luck had held very well thus far. He had encountered neither Indians nor white men during his journey, with the exception of Schlosser and Maridew. Careful to double back on his tracks now and again and to make Lije follow him so that no possible pursuer could readily track him, he kept as close as he could to clumps of forests and bushes, to hills and caves, to low ravines and the banks of creeks.

One night John Cooper and Lije came in sight of a towering hill which stood apart from the succession of little, mound-like hills. It was topped by a clump of gnarled oak and cedar trees. It would give a good view of the valley, and he could see a cave near the summit. But it might also be a bear's den, so John Cooper pointed to it and, patting Lije, urged, "Go see if anything's there, boy!"

The wolfhound bounded forward, loping along with long strides, his tail extended stiffly, his ears back. John Cooper followed, checking to make certain that his rifle was loaded. He had opened his sack and put the musket inside, then shouldered the sack again, gripping it with his left hand as he held his rifle in the other, ready for immediate action. The wind had begun to howl along the valley, and he was grateful for the warmth of the cumbersome coat.

As he ascended the hill, he could see Lije warily sniffing and peering into the cave. Then the dog turned back to him, wagging his tail as if to signify that all was well. With a chuckle of approbation, John Cooper hurried up to the summit.

Soon he had a fire going and then began to clean the trout he had caught that afternoon. Using strong, long green branches, the boy speared the trout and stuck them in the ground, angling the fish in toward the fire. He had found a small piece of bark at the mouth of the cave and used this as a serving dish on which he piled Lije's portion of the fish.

As he waited for his own fish to cook, he decided to explore the rest of the cave. Fashioning a torch from a branch, he cautiously approached the black hole at the back of the cave. As the cave narrowed, he was forced to crawl on his hands and knees. Suddenly in the torchlight, just before he stumbled into it, he saw a skeleton—bones with only shreds of clothing left and boots. He shuddered at the sight of a feathered arrow imbedded in the breastbone of the skeleton. "Some poor trapper or hunter holed up here a long time ago," he explained to himself and to the wolfhound, who had followed him and was whining uneasily. "Some Indian shot him and he must have crawled back in here to die. Gives me the shivers. What's this?" Overcoming his revulsion, he reached down and held his torch toward something that glinted on the dry earth beside the skeleton. It was a knife, in a buckskin sheath. Gingerly he reached for the boned haft of the knife, turning it over and over, inspecting it intently. It was a good blade, and once it was sharpened, John knew, it would be invaluable.

Later as he ate his trout with the knife, he rationalized, "I don't figure that poor fellow will care much if I use his knife now. Wonder who he was, whether he had a family, whether they're still looking for him and missing him—best not to think about things like that."

John Cooper reassured himself that at least they were safe. They hadn't seen any Indians for a long while. Soon he had stretched out on the ground in the cave, with Lije lying down beside him at the very mouth, on guard as usual. He flung out one arm to stroke the dog until, at last, sleep claimed him.

John Cooper woke to hear a howling wind and to see the almost blinding brilliance of snow just outside the mouth of the cave. Several inches had fallen during the night, and he blinked his eyes and stared out along the valley. A soft, white mantle covered the entire area, only the dark outlines of trees standing starkly to break that ghostly pattern.

"It's a blizzard, Lije!" he exclaimed. "It'll be hard to find food in weather like this. I've still got part of that rabbit salted down in my sack, so we'll have that for breakfast. It won't be much, though. You and I had best go foraging before the snow gets too deep."

He commended himself on having thought to bring into the cave an armful of broken branches and a few fallen trees last night, to replenish the fire. Now he started up the fire, while the wolfhound watched approvingly.

What was left of the rabbit provided a somewhat meager meal, but it contented them both. In good spirits, John Cooper moved out of the cave and stood blinking his eyes and cupping a hand over them to shield them from the intense, white glare. He scooped up snow and ate it to quench his thirst. Lije watched him and did the same. The sun was hidden behind clouds, and the wind still howled and blew snow against his face.

Suddenly Lije stiffened, and John Cooper uttered a delighted gasp. "It's a buck, a big, fat one, too! Wouldn't it be lucky if I could bag him, Lije!" he whispered. "We'd have enough food for a week. Not a sound out of you now, boy, and let's hope he doesn't catch sight of us. He's about three hundred feet away. Well, Pa's rifle ought to manage that. I'm going to try it."

John Cooper knelt down, adjusted the butt of the rifle against his shoulder, and peered through the sight. Under his breath he was praying that the buck wouldn't stir, and luck was with him. He squeezed the trigger, felt the heavy recoil of the butt, and winced. Then he let out a cry of joy as he saw the buck stagger, seem to run forward a few feet, and then fall onto its side in the snow, kicking convulsively.

Lije bounded ahead, turning back now and again to make sure that his young master was following him, as John Cooper carefully made his way down the side of the hill. When he reached the buck, it still continued to thrash, lifting its head, its black eyes glazed. John Cooper groaned as he reached for the dagger in the sheath round his neck and swiftly and mercifully slit its throat. Shaken, he vowed to become a better shot, to learn to kill the first time and not let an animal suffer.

From its antlers, John Cooper surmised that the buck was about three years old, and it was heavier than he had thought. Perplexed a moment, he finally decided, "I'll trust you with Pa's rifle, Lije. Here, hold it tight, don't you dare lose it. That's going to keep us alive and give us plenty of food all through this winter. Now you just follow me back to the cave like a good boy, you hear me?"

Obediently, the wolfhound gripped the barrel of the rifle between his strong jaws, watching as his young master bent down and, taking hold of the deer's front legs with both hands, began slowly to drag the carcass up the hill to the cave. It took almost a half hour, and John Cooper had to rest several times. The wind, which had momentarily subsided, now began to blow again, this time with blinding drifts of snow. As he looked around him, the utter desolation and eerie barrenness of the land was set before him. Nothing moved except the tall trees, swaying to the buffets of the wind, and the bushes and brambles whose coating of snow was shaken off by savage gusts.

At last he reached the cave and knelt down, inhaling deeply to regain his breath. His muscles ached, but the knowledge that he had braved the elements to find food for himself and Lije exhilarated him.

He took the knife he had found in the dead man's sheath

and began to skin the buck and then to cut sizable portions of the haunch and side. Remembering how his mother often praised the liver as a rare delicacy when his father had bagged a deer, he decided on sharing that with Lije for their supper. He still had a supply of salt, and he proceeded to salt down some thin slices of meat he had cut and store them in the sack to sustain them when they traveled again. Yes, they could manage for at least a week on all of the meat that was here. He could hang the carcass of the buck near the entrance of the cave and the wintery blasts of cold would keep it fresh. And the skin would make warm leggings for him later on.

As he worked, he could hear the howling of the wind increase and feel the frosty air at the mouth of the cave.

When he had cut away all the edible meat, he debated for a moment on how to dispose of the remains. To fling it outside the cave might draw unwelcome scavengers, perhaps wolves —though so far he hadn't seen any of those and he hoped he wouldn't. If they traveled in packs, they could be lots deadlier than Indians, and they were just as patient when it came to tracking you down or lying in wait for you. Pa had told him that much. No, he wouldn't leave the carcass outside, but he'd bury it at the back of the cave.

John Cooper used his hands to scoop out the dry earth, and that was tiring, too. By the time he had scooped out a hole big enough for the carcass, he was so tired he could hardly think of supper. But seeing Lije stare at him reminded him of his chores, and with a weary little chuckle, he set to work making a fire and cooking the liver.

Night fell again, the wind seemed to gather greater fury than before, and the swirling snow began to block the mouth of the cave. The firewood supply would do for another day or two, John Cooper estimated. Maybe tomorrow, if it let up any, he'd go out and get some more. Some of these old trees, especially on the top of the hill, were very dry and perhaps he could break off branches. He didn't have an ax or a saw, but he'd just have to do the best he could. That was all anyone could do.

ELEVEN

Brisk winds sped the *Paloma* out of Cadiz the first week of her journey across the Atlantic. With all sails unfurled, the four-master seemed to glide across the blue waters, dipping to the swell of the ocean, rising and surging forward under bright skies. But the rolling and pitching of a ship of the line was as new to young Catarina as to Doña Inez, and both were seasick during that first week. Catarina's aunt, however, was able to maintain more composure and cope with her niece's pouting and sometimes hysterical complaints. Nor did the young girl enjoy the close quarters of her cabin after the spacious luxury of her own bedroom and bath chamber. Indeed, had this week of seasickness continued, Doña Inez would have been sorely tempted to assume the role of the girl's mother and administer a few slaps where they would do Catarina the most good.

Valiantly, however, she contented herself with sharp rebukes. "You know, my girl, you prattle so much of being a grownup young lady, what do you think your brother and your father would say if they could see and hear you now? And these fine officers and sturdy seamen on this ship, if they could watch you sulking and giving in to your tantrums, do you think they'd believe you to be the daughter of a grandee of Spain? Remember your position, Catarina."

"Oh, *Dios*, it is all very well for you to talk, Tía Inez," Catarina gasped, her face pale and drawn and damp with sweat, "but I did not dream it would be so awful! I am seasick, I cannot eat a thing. I can hardly drink a glass of wine, and this cabin is so dreadfully cramped—oh, why could they not have given us better quarters?"

"Because, you thoughtless minx, we are occupying the cabins which would usually be used by the captain and his first lieutenant, that is why. On a ship of this kind, Catarina, one works and sails, one does not lie abed in luxury. That is a lesson you must learn now that you are on your way to your new home."

"*Válgame Dios*," the girl groaned as the ship seemed to turn from side to side and then move forward to the surging of the waves, "I almost wish you had sent me to that convent you threatened me with, Tía Inez! Oh, I'm going to be sick again, I cannot help it—"

"You must learn to get your sea legs, Catarina, and as soon as you can, go out on deck. The weather is still fine and sunny. And walk about a bit, show everyone that you are not a child," her aunt counseled.

On the eighth day, the winds died down, and the *Paloma* moved slowly, with only the sounds of the timbers creaking as she drifted westward. Catarina at last was able to go out on the quarterdeck with her aunt and walk around. When the officers tipped their hats to her, she began to forget her seasickness, so delighted to find that she was once again the center of attention. Doña Inez eyed her with a faintly indulgent smile, understanding her niece all too well. Privately, she told herself, the best thing that could have happened to Catarina—to all of them, in fact—was this sudden severance with the past and this renaissance in a strange new world, where there would be no hoary rules of conduct nor decadent traditions to follow. With that, since she could not very well talk of so intimate a matter with her niece, came the comforting thought that now, alone with Don Diego, she would be able in due time to show him the depth of her affection for him. By mothering Catarina and by encouraging good-natured, energetic Carlos to take his position as a man to be reckoned with, she would become closer to their father—perhaps even to the point where he would realize that she was indispensable to him—at least, that was the lovely spinster's secret dream.

During that first week, to be sure, there was no question of either Doña Inez or her niece dining in the officers' mess room. A seaman had been dispatched to bring meals on a tray to the two indisposed members of Don Diego's family. Although there were such delicacies as roast chicken, fruit tart, and rich coffee from Cuba, neither was able to take much nourishment. On the other hand, Don Diego and Carlos seemed to have been born with sea legs, for after the initial day of accustoming themselves to the pitching and tossing of the ship, they ate well and took their exercise as if all their lives had been spent at sea.

Miguel Sandarbal had also adapted from the very first. The captain of the *Paloma* had not expected that Don Diego's party would have more than four members and had frowned with annoyance to discover that Miguel was to make the voyage. But the gardener had urged, "Let me stay with the rest of the crew, and I shall earn my passage by giving them a hand. I am a quick learner, and I know how to work with ropes and such." Vastly relieved, Captain Otero had agreed, and from the very first day at sea had observed that Miguel Sandarbal did not only his share, but more than any other seaman. He performed cheerfully the chores assigned to him by the boatswain and readily lent himself to the discipline of the ship.

During the several days of calm which followed the brisk winds of the first week at sea, young Carlos became restless. For one who had been accustomed to riding a spirited gelding back in Madrid, the long days of relative inactivity on board ship were a burden. Also, Carlos began to observe how his young sister preened herself when she was out on deck. And from the admiring glances of the officers, he knew that they, too, noticed her. Watching several of the midshipmen climb to the tops of the towering masts, Carlos turned to his father and eagerly demanded, "Do you think the captain would allow me to climb the way they are doing, Father? It would be good exercise. There is not much chance of it in that little cabin of ours or even pacing this deck."

"It is much too dangerous, Carlos," Don Diego protested. "Those men are practiced, they have been doing this for years. Just one slip and you would fall to your death."

"Not I, Father. I am strong, and I can balance myself very well—you know that the first week at sea didn't bother me in the least. For that matter, you yourself are as fit as I am."

His son's flattering appraisal drew a quick smile of pleasure from Don Diego. "You had best ask the captain's permission first, Carlos, and be careful. Do not forget you are my only heir. My career is at an end, I can see that now. So it is for you, my son, to carry on the traditions of the de Escobars."

"I shall not fail and your career isn't over, Father," Carlos exclaimed as he hurried over to Captain Otero. Don Diego shook his head and sighed. During the past ten days, he had been closer to his son than ever before, it seemed; sharing the small cabin had brought about not only physical proximity but also a greater communication of ideas and thoughts. He had told Carlos the entire story of the episode at the Escorial, and his son had shown a bright, keen anger for the treacherous Count de Murciano. But more than that, Don Diego had been amazed at the hope and ambition which Carlos expressed for the life which awaited them both in Nuevo Mexico.

He frowned as he watched his son and the captain, feeling a momentary anxiety over this proposed boyish escapade. Yet he knew that it would be wrong to deny Carlos his request. The boy had courage and an assurance which belied his youth, and to impose his own fears on his son might thwart his bright, eager spirit.

So he watched, his face tense, his nails digging into his palms, as he tried to maintain a nonchalant attitude. The slim youth began the difficult climb up the futtock shrouds, which, thrusting outward from the mainmast, made it necessary to climb several feet while hanging back downward with fingers and toes locked into the ratlines. Finally, with a sigh of relief, he saw Carlos ascend the main shrouds and lay out along the main topsail yard. It was a good hundred-foot drop below, yet Carlos seemed to manage it with little hesitation, and when he had reached the yardarm, he waved jubilantly to his father. Don Diego nodded affirmatively, but his heart was pounding and there were beads of sweat on his temples.

Carlos descended nimbly, transferring his grip to the brace and sliding down it to the deck. He did this with such aplomb and balance that some of the seamen, who had turned to watch his display of bravado, cheered. Flushed with pride and exertion, Carlos made his way back to his father. "You see, Father? There was not any danger. Of course, I would not want to try it during a gale."

"I should think not, may the saints protect us all," Don Diego exclaimed. Then, his admiration overcoming the misgivings he had suffered during Carlos's perilous ascent, he hugged the youth to him and declared, "¡Muy hombre, mi *hijo!* But you know, my son, although it is a good thing not to show fear, a little respect for danger is to be encouraged. It is a wise man who can understand what there is to fear and how best to circumvent it."

"I think I understand, Father. But there really was not any danger, you see. I had hold of the ropes all the time, and the foot-rope was there when I reached the yard. Even if I had slipped, I could have grabbed it, and I should only have been a few feet away from the yardarm."

"Well then," Don Diego concluded with another sigh of relief, "you did anticipate what there was to fear and planned how best to overcome it. That is good, my son. You have distinguished yourself. But you need not do this every day of the voyage."

"Well, if there is no other way to get exercise, and if there is no storm, and of course if Captain Otero does not mind, this is as good a way as any of exercising," Carlos chuckled. Don Diego's eyes were suspiciously moist as he gripped his son's hand and, in a gruff voice, remarked, "Well, in any case, it is time for our *almuerzo*. I have no doubt you have worked up an appetite for it, my son."

After the lull of the second week, bitter northeastern winds buffeted the *Paloma*, driving her several degrees off course. Carlos and his father kept to their cabin. The relentless creaking of the ship's timbers and the constant pitching and tossing of the vessel tested their composure. Even Don Diego was made queasy from the week-long storm, but wanly managed to set a good example for his son. Catarina, seasick once again, taxed Doña Inez's patience almost beyond its saintly limits with her incessant complaints and hysterical tirades. On the seventh day, when the gale at last began to subside, the young girl, shaking and sobbing, dressed herself and declared, "I am going to ask Father to turn back—I hate this ship. I am going to die aboard it if I stay on much longer! I don't want to go to Nuevo Mexico, I want to go back home, Tía Inez!"

"Catarina, you know that is impossible. Stop talking like a child," her aunt replied. "I am suffering nearly as much as you, but you do not hear me complaining."

"Oh well, that is because it doesn't matter to you what happens. You have not got a husband or children or anything to hold you—"

Doña Inez compressed her lips and glared at the fuming

young beauty. "I am quite aware that I have no husband, my girl," she responded tartly, "but I came along because I happen to be devoted to you and Carlos. Yes, and to your father as well. Of course I could have stayed in Madrid—I was not the one who was exiled, you know. But I could see in advance what that poor man would have to deal with if he came on this journey with no one to put up with your tantrums, Catarina. Now lie down on your bed and make the best of things. Say a prayer for good weather again—that is what all the sailors do, but they work and they keep their minds off the storm because they know they have to sail this ship. And we have been very comfortable, thanks to them."

"Oh yes, comfortable," Catarina groaned. She stamped her foot and then sat down on the edge of the narrow bunk. "I am sick, I cannot eat, and my complexion is dreadful, I know it is."

"No one expects you to be beautiful at such a time. Besides, you are far too young to think of such things. I saw how you paraded yourself on deck last week and let the officers ogle you, girl," Doña Inez broke in. "Now it is true that I am only your aunt, but I am also your duenna—your father himself has given me that authority. And I promise you, Catarina, if you continue acting in this way, I shall give you a good, hard slap."

"You—you would not, Tía Inez!" Catarina stared incredulously at her aunt who, though very pale, faced her and concealed as best she could her own discomfort.

"Try me," her aunt retorted. "Don't let me hear any more about running to your father and having the captain turn the ship back to Spain. First of all, your father would not be allowed to return to Spain, and by orders of the king he has a post in Nuevo Mexico. As an honorable man and a royal subject, it is his duty to obey such an order. And it is your duty, as his daughter, to accept that life. Look at your brother, he is making the best of things and even enjoying himself."

"Oh yes, that is all very well for you to say, Tía Inez," Catarina burst out, "but he is a boy and boys are always stronger! I cannot help being seasick and I hate it, and I hate Father for making me suffer like this—oh—oh—you—you— slapped me, Tía Inez!"

Just as Catarina had uttered those last words, Doña Inez had dealt her a resounding slap across her pale, white cheek. Catarina stared up at her aunt, then burst into tears and covered her face with her hands, her shoulders shaking with her sobs.

Doña Inez sat down beside her and put an arm around the girl's shoulders. "You must never say such a thing about your father again, little one," she murmured. "What do you imagine he would think if he heard you speak of him as you did just now? You would shatter his life. Do you not understand that it is torture enough for him to leave Madrid and take this long journey to a place he has never seen before? And yet he is ready to do it, for your sake as much as for Carlos's. You must try to be courageous, *muchachita*, and pray to the good God for the strength your brother and your father have. Now, will you forgive me for slapping you?"

Catarina nodded. Turning to her aunt, she flung her arms around her and kissed her.

That same afternoon, Carlos stood beside Miguel Sandarbal. The slim youth's face was bright with enthusiasm as the brisk wind ruffled his hair, and he turned to the former gardener and exclaimed, "It is exciting, this journey, Miguel! And how different it is from all the frills and folderol of court. You know, *hombre*, maybe Catarina and Father are not happy over this change in our lives, so far away from Madrid—but I am, that is for certain."

"And why, young master?" Miguel eyed him sharply.

Carlos de Escobar shrugged, his eyes fixing the unruly sea, his smile deepening. "It is because I think I can be my own man in this new world we are going to, Miguel. I did not much care for growing up and taking my place in the king's court as Father and Grandfather did. I would rather see new sights, meet new people, learn from them how to live my own life."

The following week, fair winds guided the *Paloma* back onto her course for the port of Havana. Despite the chilliness of the moderate gusts that filled the lofty sails, Catarina and her aunt took their morning and afternoon walks on the quarterdeck. This time, abashed by that unexpected slap, the impetuous young girl did not openly seek out admiring glances but kept her eyes demurely fixed either on the horizon or the deck before her, much to Doña Inez's approval. As they had during the second week, when the vessel had been becalmed, the two of them took their meals at the officers' mess. It was apparent to Doña Inez that Catarina was doing her best to adapt herself to her circumstances and doing so with better grace than she had displayed at the outset. It was encouraging. Indeed, it made her long all the more for the bond she desired between Don Diego and herself. Perhaps there was hope, she thought. If he could see how Catarina, under her guidance, was growing into a proper young lady, Don Diego would be sure to recognize the value of her influence—an influence which, she sincerely felt, was exactly that which her dead sister would have shown to this tempestuous girl.

TWELVE

When he wakened on the morning after he had killed the deer, John Cooper found the mouth of the cave nearly blocked by packed snow which the furious wind had driven throughout the long, dark night. With his mittened hands—he had made some crude mittens out of rabbit skins—he managed to push away the snow and emerge. The wind still raged, though not so strongly as it had during the night, but the landscape was almost unrecognizable. Even the tops of the trees on the summit of the hill were bowed down by clinging snow, and as the wind stirred, the snow dropped with a soft thud to the ground. It was desolate. So far as the eye could see, nothing stirred. There was no sign of even a rabbit or a deer. The sky was sullen, the sun hidden behind gray clouds.

John Cooper knew they would have to wait out the storm. It would be useless, even dangerous, to travel through the snow. But he would have to collect more firewood if he and Lije were to survive.

The footing was treacherous, and the ground uneven beneath the thick drifts. Several times he slipped back, but at last he reached the crest of the hill and began to tug at the branches nearest to him. They fell with a dry crack, yielding readily to his grip. Soon he had collected a heavy armful, and trudged back to the cave where he stored it, then went back for more.

In an hour's time, he was satisfied that he had enough. The branches, some quite thick, could be easily broken to keep the fire going.

Alone in this cave with Lije, John Cooper was doing a lot more thinking than ever before. He knew he had to figure out exactly where he wanted to go after the blizzard let up. Until now, he'd been heading northwest, but pretty soon he ought to start going due west. Sooner or later, he was bound to run into some Indian tribes, and he hoped they'd be friendly. He'd picked up a little of the language of the Shawnee—he knew the words for "friend" and "peace," and some of the signs that the Indians used instead of talking. Unless he got so far west that he met up with tribes he'd never heard of, most of the Indians around these parts ought to recognize the signs, even if they didn't know the words. He would just have to take things as they came, and get along as best he could.

He had kept a crude record of the days spent on the trail since boarding the log raft with Lije. On a piece of leather, he had scored each day with a prick of a knife. It wouldn't be long before his fifteenth birthday. He wondered what sort of birthday it would be, where he'd be by then. If he headed toward the northwest from here and then changed his direction to due west, he should reach the Wisconsin territory soon. His father had told him about friendly Indian tribes in that neck of the woods. They did a lot of trading with trappers and hunters. There were beavers, and prime pelts to be had there, which could buy a good deal of trade goods. And if you were honest and gave them a fair shake, the Indians didn't drive too hard a bargain.

He would continue on his way with dogged determination because something inside him said he had to. He didn't know where he'd wind up or what it would be like when he got there. All he knew was, he had to keep going. He and Lije had to find a home, a place where they could be free and start all over again and maybe, years into the future, he would be part of a family again. But he wasn't fifteen yet, and a boy didn't start thinking about girls until he was seventeen or eighteen.

Besides, he wouldn't know how to act around a girl. With Virginia and Elsie, there'd been teasing and fun and sharing things, but they'd been his sisters, after all. Well, there was no sense thinking about that now. But maybe, someday, it would be nice to have someone care for him. . . .

John Cooper made an exasperated noise in his throat, wanting to drive out thoughts like this, and Lije looked at him and whined a little and put his head on his shoulder. John Cooper, seated on the floor of the cave while he looked over at the deerskin and wondered how long it would be before he could start making the leggings from it, turned to hug the wolfhound and then heaved a deep sigh.

Several days passed, but the storm still showed no sign of abating. John Cooper and Lije remained in the cave except for an occasional short walk for exercise. Snow continued to fall, and every few hours the boy had to brush away the drifts from the mouth of the cave, not only to see outside but to allow the smoke to drift out.

On the eighth day, the sky cleared and the wind became milder. John Cooper had made his leggings and wrapped them round his calves and thighs. He had also made some more bullets, melting part of the lead bar and pouring it into the mold. With the old hunting knife, he trimmed the rough edges down and removed the mold marks so that the balls would carry true to their maximum distance when fired.

It was slow going for the next week, traveling through the heavy snow. John Cooper was content to cover four or five miles a day.

On the ninth of December, his fifteenth birthday, John Cooper camped not far from the little village of Kirksville, atop a low hill from which he could see the few cabins which comprised that little settlement. At nightfall, he looked yearningly at the feeble lights of oil lamps flickering in the windows of those cabins. He sat, hugging Lije. It was so different from his last birthday. Ma had baked a special cake for him. Tonight, all he'd had for supper had been half of a squirrel. For the first time since he'd set out on this journey, he felt lonely. But it didn't do any good to dwell on such thoughts. First thing he knew, he'd get to feeling sorry for himself, and then he'd really be in trouble.

By the tenth of January, 1808, John Cooper and Lije had come to the Raccoon River, about twenty-five miles south of Des Moines. Several heavy snowstorms had slowed them down.

That morning, after a frugal breakfast, John Cooper and

Lije had headed due west. The air was clear and bitingly cold, but there wasn't too much wind to slow them down. "We'll follow the river for a spell, Lije," he told the wolfhound. "It's probably frozen over for a good ways, so we won't be able to get any fish. But we'll make out. . . . Winter isn't going to last forever."

Taking a deep breath and readjusting the heavy sack over his left shoulder, John Cooper trudged on, following the bank of the river which wound slightly to the northwest after a long, narrow, straight stretch. By late afternoon, he neared a small woods and halted for a rest, beckoning the wolfhound to him. "There might just be some game in those woods, Lije. We'll be quiet now and go slowly, so we don't scare it." He looked around and shook his head. "I haven't seen a cabin or even a village for a long time—not even an Indian, for that matter. I think I'll just make sure the rifle's loaded and ready for action, in case you flush out something for our supper, Lije."

Setting down the sack, he squatted and inspected the priming. He was really hoping for deer. A fat deer would provide enough meat for at least a week, maybe ten days if he eked it out. And the skin was useful, too. No doubt about it, it was going to be a very long winter, and the farther west he got, the harder it might be.

Just then, he thought he saw a movement at the edge of the woods and cocked his rifle. Sure enough, it was a deer, and it was coming toward him, running swiftly on the thickly packed snow. He could see its frosty breath as it seemed to quicken its gait. Then, just as he was about to shoot, he saw a tall Indian running swiftly in pursuit of the same deer. He had an arrow already notched at his bowstring. Suddenly, the Indian slipped along the edge of the bank and lost his balance. The deer turned sharply toward the north, and John Cooper pulled the trigger. It seemed to lunge forward and then fell heavily on its side, kicked, and lay still. Lije barked joyously, but John Cooper shook his head.

He laid his rifle down on the sack and ran toward the river. The ice had broken through, and the Indian was up to his waist in the cold water, his fingers scrabbling at the icy bank, trying to lift himself out. His round face was tilted back; his strong white teeth clenched in a grimace of agony as he tried to draw up his right leg.

When he saw John Cooper approach, he put his left hand to his buckskin belt, trying to draw a hunting knife from its sheath. John Cooper extended his hands, palms out in the sign of peace; he shook his head and came slowly forward. "Friend, I help you," he called, remembering the words he had learned from the Shawnee.

The young brave, a hawk feather thrust through his black scalp lock, did not seem to understand the words. He tried to tug his knife out as John Cooper approached. Lije followed warily, the hairs at the back of his neck bristling as he thrust forth his muzzle with a low, menacing growl. "No, no, Lije, it's all right, he won't hurt me. Quiet, boy!"

Carefully kneeling down on the edge of the bank, John Cooper held out both hands to the young brave. The latter, his face still contorted in pain, stared at him a moment, then dropped the knife back into the sheath and extended both his hands.

Grasping them, John Cooper pulled with all his strength, crawling backward, panting with exertion. Slowly, the brave emerged from the water, and crawled groaning onto the snowy bank.

As the Indian pulled his body out of the water, John Cooper saw that one foot was caught in a large metal beaver trap.

The young brave had rolled over onto his back, and tried to sit up and reach his hands out toward the cruel metal jaws. There was a long chain attached to the trap. John Cooper carefully crawled to the water's edge, reached down, seized the chain with both hands, and tugged with all his strength. At last the trap stake came out of the river's shallow bottom.

The brave's right foot had come down upon the pan of the trap, snapping the jaws shut upon his ankle. He stared at John Cooper, and, gritting his teeth, nodded in approval. "I just have to push down the springs and get you loose from it," John Cooper said. Pressing his palms down on the springs and exerting all his strength, he saw the jaws begin to open and nodded to the brave, who at once drew out his foot with a gasp. John Cooper picked up the trap and was about to fling it into the water when the brave shook his head and held out a restraining hand, saying something in a guttural tongue which he could not understand. "All right, I'll put it in my sack. Your ankle's pretty bad. Let's see if it's broken."

Carefully, John Cooper grasped the young Indian's ankle, pressing here and there. Stoically, he endured it without a sound. "I don't think it's broken, but I'll bet you've got a bad sprain there, and there's a big bruise. I'll try to find a branch you can use as a crutch."

He rose to his feet, gazing down at the young Indian, who looked no more than eighteen. He wore a buckskin jacket, leggings, and moccasins. His forehead was high, as were his cheekbones, and he had a thickly bridged nose and a sturdy chin. His teeth had begun to chatter, and John Cooper observed aloud, "Sure, you're cold after taking that swim in the river, I shouldn't wonder. I wish I could speak your language—"

"Kandaka speak some English, white-eyes," the young brave suddenly announced.

"My gosh—you do, don't you!" John Cooper was both startled and delighted. Then he turned to Lije and added softly, "Say, maybe we're in luck, maybe we'll get a good supper tonight after all." Then, to the brave, "Are your people far from here, Kandaka?"

"Not far. Village of Ayuhwa there—" He gestured toward the west, "when sun sets."

"That'd be about an hour's walk—if you can walk, Kandaka. My name's John Cooper Baines. I'll get you that crutch now. And say, that deer I shot, that belongs to you—you flushed it out, after all. Maybe, if you can walk, we can carry it back to your village."

He turned and strode toward the woods, peering around for a sturdy branch. There was one just above his head, and he grasped it with both hands and pulled it down until he heard it crack. He pulled it again and it broke off. Then, setting the twiggy end under his right foot, he pulled it up toward him and broke it off until he had improvised a crutch.

"Try and see how good you can walk with it," the boy urged. Kandaka nodded and grunted, adjusted the sturdy branch under his right armpit, gripping it tightly with his right hand, and took a tentative step or two forward. He winced with pain but managed to go forward a few more steps before he stopped to turn back and nod to his young rescuer.

"Well, it'll take longer than sunset, I'm thinking, but you'd best get back to your village and get out of those wet clothes before you catch a real chill." John Cooper stared over at the fallen deer. "I'll have to drag this, I guess."

"No. When we get to village, my father, Mikanota, send

braves for deer. You will be welcome, you with the long stick that thunders and kills. Come, we go now."

"Sure, Kandaka. If that crutch doesn't work so good, you can put your arm around my shoulder and lean on me," John Cooper offered. He put the rifle back into the sack, shouldered it, then beckoned to Lije, who turned back for a last look at the fallen deer, then obediently trotted along as the young Sioux and his master began the slow walk back to Kandaka's village.

The moon was out before they neared the village of the Ayuhwa Sioux. John Cooper perceived rows of large circular houses flatly covered with earth, with a smoke-hole at the top. Each house had a covered, projecting entrance, and a low wooden stockade encircled the village. Women were already busying themselves around the cooking fires, and at the sight of the hobbling young brave with his tree-branch crutch, the strange young white-eyes, and the wolfhound, they began to cry out. Several braves emerged from the nearest houses. They had pleasant features and round faces, and wore no war paint. Kandaka began to talk, but John Cooper could not understand a word. He saw Kandaka turn to look at him and make gestures with his hands, and the other braves smiled as they turned toward him.

"My father comes," Kandaka proudly announced. The other braves respectfully made way as a tall, gray-haired Sioux in full headdress, beaded buckskin jacket, and buffalo robe approached, his face grave and his eyes narrowed with concern.

"It is Mikanota, the chief. I will tell him what you have done. Already, I said to my friends how you killed deer with long stick that thunders and spits fire. They go now to bring it back for feast," Kandaka explained.

Then, turning to his father, inclining his head, and touching his chest in a gesture of respect for Mikanota's rank, he swiftly explained what had happened. Mikanota turned to John Cooper, nodded, took hold of the boy's shoulders and, in a deep voice, spoke words which John Cooper again could not understand.

Translating, Kandaka explained, "He says you are good friend to Ayuhwa, you saved my life, and you are great hunter. I told my father of long stick which makes the sound of thunder and spits fire. He asks that you stay with us. We will talk tonight after feast. My father says, will you show

him how long stick kills deer and buffalo. He says you are
welcome here as hunter, we will share food and give you
lodge, because you are good friend."

John Cooper frowned for a moment; he hadn't really
thought about settling down yet, but with the bad winter
coming on, it might be wise to take shelter from it. These
Indians were friendly. Besides, he was just beginning to
realize how tired he was, after the last few months. Yes, he
could try it for a spell, see how it worked out. He could
always move on when the spring came, if he didn't like the
life. Maybe they could tell him about the other Indians, even
about some of the settlers who lived farther west. He could
learn a good deal, and it would all come in very handy.

He turned to Kandaka. "Tell your father I'd like to stay for
a spell, and I'll be glad to show him how 'Long Girl'
works."

" 'Long Girl'?" Kandaka repeated, confused.

"That is what I call the stick that thunders and spits fire,
Kandaka. Do you see the coat I am wearing? I killed a bear
with 'Long Girl' to get the skin to make it."

"That is good!" Kandaka nodded vigorously. "We hunt a
bear, an old bear who has killed some of our braves. But we
have not caught him yet. Perhaps you help us kill him. Now
come, I take you to my father's house." He looked down at
his discolored ankle. "The women will rub my leg with strong
medicine, I will be well again soon. Come, my friend John
Cooper Baines."

John Cooper was touched to hear the young Sioux so
faithfully pronounce his name. Well, certainly he could use a
friend now. And, although he wouldn't admit it to anybody,
he was just as glad to call a halt to the trek west. He'd rest up
and get some good food into him and Lije and wait for better
weather before they went on to find wherever was really
meant to be their new home.

THIRTEEN

Majestically moving past the grim fortress of Morro Castle, the *Paloma,* all her sails billowing in the soft tropical wind, headed into the great bay of Havana on the late afternoon of December 13, 1807. It had been a long and trying voyage, with periods of storm and calm alternating, as if by nature's caprice, to delay the long-awaited landing.

Captain Otero had given orders to have the *Paloma* steered toward the trade winds because the initial storm and the periods of calm forced the great ship off its original course. Also, finding his food supplies dwindling, he had put into the Canaries for provisions. Moreover, the mainsail mast had been badly damaged during a two-day squall, necessitating a further delay. The first step of the de Escobars' journey had thus proved a far more arduous ordeal than Don Diego himself had anticipated.

But now these hardships could be momentarily forgotten under the blue Cuban skies and the warmth of the sun, which seemed loath to set as it bathed the Spanish ship in a brilliant light. The sun's rays glistened, too, on the ominous cannons of the Cabañas which menacingly guarded the seaward approach to the harbor. In dazzling contrast, they also fell on the white traceries of the villas and the purple bouganvillea

79

and scarlet frangipani which rose along the edges of this magnificent island.

The water was glassy-smooth, its colors varying from a moody indigo to clear sapphire and pale green. And the sight of flowery gardens fringed by palm trees made this island seem a paradise after the rigors of the long journey aboard the *Paloma*.

Don Diego de Escobar stood at the railing beside his son, with Catarina and Doña Inez close by, and sighed in satisfaction as he said to Carlos, "This will be a welcome break in our long travel, *mi hijo*. Do you see the trees and the flowers? They remind me of my own beautiful Andalusia. What a pity it couldn't be here that the king sent me to live!"

"It is very beautiful, Father," Carlos agreed. "All the same, I do not think there would be the chance to hunt and ride here that we shall find in Nuevo Mexico."

"It is true, an island can be confining. But when you are a man, you will find more important things to do than hunt and ride. I hope, when we dine with His Excellency tonight, you will not embarrass him by disparaging his island. Do not forget, my son, he is by far my superior."

"Have no fear, Father. I only hope that while I am here, I shall have a chance to exercise. Captain Otero says they often go hunting for wild boar in the mountains. That would be great sport!"

"It is also dangerous sport, Carlos. And I hardly think His Excellency has planned such a hunting party in our honor," his father responded dryly. Then he turned to Catarina with a kindly smile. "You look very lovely, my daughter. The warm air has brought the color back to your cheeks. We shall be well entertained here, and you will have a chance to wear your prettiest gown."

Catarina brightened. "Oh yes, Father! I am so longing to walk on land again I can't think of anything else—it is really very beautiful. And just think, I shall have a room of my own for a change instead of that dreadfully narrow cabin."

"Well," her aunt said indulgently, "these last few weeks, you have really tried to make the best of things. You deserve your comfort. And I do not mind admitting that I, too, shall enjoy an honest to goodness bed, in a room that does not sway up and down. Oh, look, Don Diego! There is a boat coming toward us—is that the one that will take us to meet the governor?"

"That is right, Doña Inez," Don Diego said, smiling.

"Miguel will bring our trunks on the return journey so that we may dress presentably for the dinner tonight."

"Oh, that is wonderful; I shall wear my pretty blue silk gown—may I, Father?" Catarina asked, in excitement.

"But of course, my dear one. We shall all try to look our best this evening, for we represent His Majesty. But Captain Otero is beckoning to us—we'd had best go down to the boat and take our places."

The longboat, with three black oarsmen and two Spanish soldiers had drawn up alongside the *Paloma*. Its gunwales were painted with the red and yellow of the flag of Imperial Spain. Miguel Sandarbal approached Don Diego. "As soon as the longboat comes back, Don Diego, I shall have two men help me with the trunks. We shall have them at the governor's mansion in time, have no fear."

"Good man!" The gray-haired Spaniard gripped Miguel's arm. "Captain Otero is very pleased with you. Indeed, just a little while ago, he tried to talk me out of your services. You have handled yourself so ably aboard his ship that he would be willing to give you the papers of a second mate."

"I am grateful to the captain, Don Diego. But I shall not leave you. You will need me to pick good workers in Mexico for your new estate and to get your ranch in order."

The two men regarded each other in silence. Then Don Diego coughed, nodded, and turned to take his place in the longboat.

At the wharf, two carriages drawn by paired black geldings awaited the de Escobar family, with military coachmen dressed in white tunics, black Napoleonic hats with reddish orange plumes, gray skin-tight breeches, and knee-length boots. There was also a military escort of four smartly uniformed Spanish dragoons astride white horses, and Catarina was greatly impressed. Her dark eyes widened and she blushed self-consciously as the under-lieutenant of dragoons smartly saluted her father and then bowed low to her. After she and her aunt had been helped into the second carriage, she turned to Doña Inez and giggled, "Oh, it is just like Spain, Tía Inez! So handsome, so gallant—I have almost forgotten what a tiresome voyage it was!"

"That is because you are a forward minx, young lady. Now sit back and enjoy the sights. Havana is indeed, as I have heard, a beautiful city—see, Catarina, the yards of the houses form squares in their centers, and look at the wide flights of steps leading to the second story. See the balcony corridor onto which all of the rooms open? That is because of the climate. And look at all the flowers and the wonderful palm trees—it is like a great tropical garden. So you see, my dear one, this voyage is in a way like going to school. You are learning ever so much more than you would if you were back in a dry, dusty room poring over your books."

Catarina tossed her head. "Well, it started nicely anyway. That handsome officer seemed very impressed with me."

"You are a little too young to have your head turned by a man's attentions, Catarina. It does no harm so long as you realize that he is only being polite. That is good breeding."

"I know." Catarina sighed. "I only hope when we finally get to Nuevo Mexico, there will be some nice young man who will ask father for my hand in marriage."

"And that, you impudent baggage, is still quite a few years away. May the saints preserve us, thinking of marriage and you not yet fourteen!" Doña Inez lifted her eyes heavenward, but she was unable to hide an amused smile.

The governor's mansion was a magnificent structure, set on a small, rolling slope which overlooked the great bay. The rooms were spacious, with lofty ceilings, and the floors were made of squares of thick slate, marble, and brown jasper. One rarely found carpets or even wooden floors in Havana because of the intense heat. The governor's secretary, Estaban Reduro, a tall and very personable man in his early forties, welcomed the de Escobars and escorted them to their rooms. To her great joy, Catarina was given a room all to herself, with a shuttered window that looked out onto the magnificent patio. Doña Inez had the room next to hers. Don Diego and Carlos shared one of the largest rooms on the second floor. "The house servants have been assigned so that your orders to them will be as punctiliously carried out as those of the governor-general himself," Reduro remarked. "He craves your indulgence, for he has just finished his *siesta* and is dressing now for the dinner at which you will be the guests of honor."

It was nearly eight that evening before the de Escobars were ushered into the magnificent dining room where—at the head of a huge rectangular table set with the finest linens, silverware, and goblets—the tall stately Marqués de Someruelos, Salvador de Muro, governor-general of Cuba since 1799, rose to welcome them to Havana. His face was grave, made even more austere by his neatly pointed beard and the elegance of his military uniform. Don Diego was seated at his right, with Carlos beside his father, while Doña Inez was at his left with Catarina at her side. The other guests at the table were merchants, officers, and plantation owners, and the servants silently and swiftly began to serve what for the de Escobars was the most luxurious meal they had tasted since they had left Cadiz.

"Tomorrow evening, if you are sufficiently rested from the long voyage," the governor-general declared toward the conclusion of the festive dinner, "we shall hold a ball. It is my hope that both of the charming ladies of your household, Don Diego, will inspire and honor us with their presence."

Don Diego smiled and inclined his head. "Your Excellency is very gracious. I am sure that Doña Inez and my daughter Catarina will accept your most hospitable invitation."

"Oh yes, Father—" Catarina exclaimed, then clapped a hand over her mouth and blushed furiously while some of the guests smiled tolerantly. Don Diego contemplated his daughter and reflected that, despite her tender years, she was at the threshold of becoming a very beautiful young woman. Then his gaze fell upon Doña Inez. She was more striking than he had ever before noticed. She wore a simple gown of white, with puffed, short sleeves which left her graceful arms bare. There were delicate green leaves on a tiny trellis of gold embroidering the hem at her ankles, and in front of the narrow waistline was an intricate bow. Around her neck there was a ruching which, like the bow, was of an intense emerald green. She wore soft, white, satin slippers, tied with crisscrossed ribbons which made her ankles look even more trim. He had not noticed before how youthful she was and how very presentable. But now, even as he thought this, the governor-general raised his glass of brandy and rose. "A toast, good friends, to our visitors from Spain. It has long been known that Spanish women are the most beautiful and intelligent in all the world. Now, tonight, we may see with our own eyes how true this is!"

Doña Inez could not help blushing. She had noticed Don Diego eyeing her. It was almost as if he were seeing her for the first time—and indeed he was.

True to his word, the governor-general held a formal ball in honor of his distinguished visitors from Spain. The musicians were freed men of color who, to Don Diego's unconcealed delight, played with great feeling music which he knew well. Carlos, dashingly handsome in his black satin breeches and waistcoat, found himself dancing with a gawky fifteen-year-old girl. Don Diego chuckled, watching his son execute the intricate maneuvers with a grace and suppleness that reminded him of his own youth. Then the memory of how he had danced with his beloved Dolores made him turn away, his eyes misty with unbidden tears.

Catarina was squired by the diffident, punctiliously proper fourteen-year-old son of the under-lieutenant of dragoons who had escorted them to the mansion, and the boy's flowery compliments enchanted her. So much so, indeed, that she gave him two dances, much to the disapproval of Doña Inez. As for Doña Inez herself, she had worn her most elegant gown of fine brown silk. She was spoken for by Estaban Reduro, who led her out onto the floor, bowed low to her, and then joined her in the stately measures of a saraband.

In his turn, Don Diego danced with the buxom, somewhat garrulous wife of the governor-general, but he could not help observing how radiant Doña Inez was. He heard her soft laughter respond to one of Reduro's witty comments, and he frowned. "Is something the matter, Don Diego?" his partner asked.

"Oh no, Señora, it is only that I was concerned about my dancing. You see, I have not done much of it recently."

"But you have no reason to apologize, Don Diego! You are so distinguished, and you dance beautifully, truly!" his hostess gushed.

When the saraband ended, Don Diego courteously offered to bring his hostess a cup of punch and observed, as a liveried servant ladled it into a silver cup, that Doña Inez was already being approached by a handsome captain of the governor-general's personal guard. His frown deepened. Then he rebuked himself. After all, there was no reason that she shouldn't enjoy herself. It was selfish of him to deny her pleasure—and, after all, she was unmarried.

At the conclusion of the ball, after Doña Inez, Catarina, and Carlos had thanked their host and hostess and retired to their rooms, Don Diego found himself alone with Salvador de Muro. "I have read the documents which you brought me from His Majesty, Don Diego," the governor-general declared. "If you will come into my study, I should like to hear some of your impressions of the court. I may tell you that I shall dispatch, by the next ship bound for Cadiz, a letter of thanks to His Majesty for the cargo and, above all, the personal gifts which he was kind enough to send to me as his representative in this Spanish colony."

"I am at your service, Excellency." Don Diego bowed.

The governor-general closed the door and gestured toward a comfortable chair facing his desk, behind which he seated himself. "Now then, Don Diego, I am deeply concerned not only with the events in Spain, but in all of Europe. Napoleon's strength seems to grow daily, and that bodes ill for our beloved country. I speak to you in all confidence—and what will be said between us this night will not go beyond the walls of this room."

Don Diego stirred restlessly in his chair. "Again, I am at your service," he repeated.

"What concerns me most—and this is what I wish to discuss with you privately, of course—is that I fear the age and infirmity of His Majesty. Equally, I am alarmed by the power which his prime minister has diverted from the throne, especially in the alliance with France."

"Your Excellency touches on a subject that is painful to me. You know, from the letter I brought you, that I have been named intendant of the province of Taos, in Nuevo Mexico. That assignment, if I may trust Your Excellency's pledge of confidence, was brought about by the prime minister himself. I had said to an acquaintance in the court that I regretted Spain's gradual loss of so many of its colonies, its loss of control, and of course my feeling was that the pact with the French was lessening Spain's power in the world."

"But that is quite accurate, Don Diego. I myself believe this."

"It heartens me to hear you speak so, Your Excellency. Yet all the same, it was the kindness of His Majesty which persuaded the prime minister to allow me, as a kind of favorable banishment, to become intendant, so that my presence at court would not continue to embarrass him. I do not think it wise to say more than that."

The Marqués de Someruelos rose and extended his hand. "I thank you for your honesty, Don Diego. I do not think you would have been made intendant of Taos if His Majesty did not have a high regard for you. Now that you have been so long delayed in reaching us—and with the holiday of our blessed Savior nearly upon us—I entreat you, your children, and Doña Inez to remain with us until after the first of the year. I have asked Captain Otero to postpone his sailing until then. It is quite likely that we shall have some cargo to send on to Vera Cruz, for I wish to send my own gifts to the viceroy and his family—we are old friends, you know."

"It is most kind of you." Don Diego uttered a deprecating little laugh. "My daughter and Doña Inez had a difficult time of it aboard the *Paloma*, with the storms and squalls which beset us. I know they will welcome your lavish hospitality, and it will strengthen them for the long journey still ahead of us. Again, I thank Your Excellency for all your kindness to my family and me, and I wish you a pleasant good night."

FOURTEEN

Four young braves brought back the deer which John Cooper had shot, and the women hurried to skin it and cut the meat, which would be used for the feast to welcome this young *wasichu* who had saved the life of the son of their chief.

Kandaka, his ankle already poulticed with bark in which cooked herbs had been placed, sat at his father's right hand, with John Cooper at Mikanota's left. In this largest of the earth-covered houses, five of the tribal elders had joined the chief and his son to welcome Kandaka's new friend, as well as Petimaka, the wizened old shaman of the Ayuhwa village. In addition to deer meat, the feast consisted of dry buffalo meat, a kind of corn pudding, squash, and a strong, hot tea brewed with wild sassafras.

The meal was served by two attractive Ayuhwa girls dressed in beaded buckskin. Kandaka, who acted as John Cooper's translator, gestured toward them and said, "These are the daughters of Petimaka. Their mother died many years ago. Letalto is a year younger than I, and Yumiquya, which means *pretty round face,* is three years younger." John Cooper flushed and nodded to the two attractive Indian girls. Letalto was slim. Her black hair was formed into a single, thick braid which fell nearly to her waist, and her features

87

were sensitive and dignified. Yumiquya was far less reserved; she could not suppress a soft giggle of amusement, which drew an angry glare from her father.

"My mother died during the hard winter of last year, as did my sister," Kandaka explained in a whisper. "My father has not yet taken another squaw to his lodge. Perhaps he will in the summer, for we have another small village to the west where we plant the corn and cut wood for the campfires. There's a squaw there, Sentigata, who looks with soft eyes upon my father, and I think one day she will be his squaw."

Petimaka had been eyeing John Cooper and now leaned toward Mikanota and spoke in the Sioux tongue, upon which the Ayuhwa chief turned to his son and interrogated him. Kandaka nodded and spoke to Petimaka, then said to John Cooper, "Petimaka sees that you wear a coat made from the skin of the fierce black bear. I have told him that you killed it with the stick that thunders and spits fire."

Petimaka contemplated John Cooper with keen interest, then engaged Mikanota in excited conversation.

"The shaman says that perhaps the Great Spirit has sent you here to hunt down the great black bear which has already killed one of our braves and two squaws."

"Tell him that I will be glad to hunt the killer bear, Kandaka. My wolfhound, Lije, will help me. But I don't know what your people think about my dog—will they treat him as my friend, for that's what he is?"

"I have seen that already, John Cooper. Some of the Sioux eat roasted dog, but we will not harm your friend. We are a peaceful people. We plant crops and we hunt the deer and the buffalo, and sometimes we trade beaver skins and the things our women make out of bark and buckskin to the *wasichu* who come to our village with trade goods. Some of our people are from the tribe of the Missouri, who were defeated in battle by the Osage, and they came to us to live in peace."

"I'd like to learn your language, Kandaka. Will you teach me?"

"It is good that you say this. I will tell my father and Petimaka that you wish to be our good friend." With this, the young brave turned to his father and began to talk quickly, both Petimaka and Mikanota listening and grunting with approval.

"My father and the shaman say I am to teach you. They say also there is a small lodge at the end of the village which will be yours now. Latiwaka, who died trying to slay the great black bear, and who was my good friend, lived there. But his spirit will rejoice when you, so strong a hunter and yet so young, take his place among us. Come!"

Before he left the chief's lodge, John Cooper respectfully inclined his head and extended his hands with the palms upward toward both Mikanota and Petimaka. Both men gravely returned his salute, and the old shaman muttered something to Mikanota, who nodded vigorously and then grinned. The shaman's two daughters moved away from the door of the lodge, and John Cooper smiled and said, "Thank you for the food." Although they did not understand his words, Letalto inclined her head slightly to indicate that she understood what he wished to say. But Yumiquya turned away and hid her face in her hands with a smothered giggle. This again drew a rebuke from her father, who spoke sharply to her. Somewhat embarrassed, John Cooper emerged to find Kandaka waiting for him. But as they were about to walk toward the far end of the village, the boy suddenly heard an angry growl. He had momentarily forgotten about Lije, but two mongrel dogs which had skulked around the campfires earlier that night had decided to investigate the intruder and had trotted toward the wolfhound, their fangs bared as they prepared to attack.

"They challenge your dog," Kandaka muttered. "Let us see how he answers them."

"I don't want him to hurt your dogs, Kandaka, but he'll fight—careful, Lije!" John Cooper cautioned his dog, seeing that one of the mongrels had sidled behind the massive wolfhound while its companion stood, snarling, a few feet away, facing Lije to distract his attention.

Suddenly the dog behind Lije sprang at the wolfhound, its teeth sinking into Lije's flank. With a yelp of pain, Lije turned on his attacker and seized him by the throat with his great jaws. At that same moment, the other mongrel—a yellowish, gaunt hound with a long muzzle and short tail—sprang from Lije's side, its teeth seeking his throat.

John Cooper clenched his fists and took a step forward, but Kandaka put a hand on his shoulder. "No, let them fight. They are like our braves, they challenge the enemy to see who is the stronger. Let them fight!"

Surprised though he had been by this twofold attack, Lije parried it adroitly. With an angry growl, he shook off his first attacker, a lean brindle cur which was bleeding from tooth marks in its neck, then reared on his hind legs and with his strong front paws shook off the other mongrel whose teeth, thanks to Lije's thick shaggy fur, had not quite reached his throat. As the dog rolled onto its side, Lije sprang upon it and seized its throat between his teeth, shaking his great head while the dog thrashed and yowled in agony. The other dog, returning to the attack, harassed his flank, but Lije stubbornly ignored the scoring pain of the mongrel's teeth. The dog beneath him writhed, then stiffened in death, its jugular slashed.

Swiftly whirling, Lije sank his teeth into his second attacker's side, drawing another yowl of pain. The yellowish, gaunt survivor, now seeing itself without aid, turned tail and fled, bleeding from its wounds.

"Stop, Lije, that's enough! Come, boy!" John Cooper cried out as he clapped his hands. Lije had begun to give chase, but at his young master's command, stopped and looked back, growling softly, and then docilely trotted back to John Cooper. The boy reached down to stroke Lije's head, frowning at the sight of blood on the wolfhound's flank. With his other hand he felt Lije's throat to determine whether the mongrel's savage attack had drawn blood. "You did fine, Lije, just fine. He didn't get your throat, thank God for that. I guess you taught those mangy curs who's boss around here—now that they know you're a real fighter, they won't bother you."

Kandaka shook his head in admiration. "I have never seen a dog so large or so fierce. Those two of ours kill many dogs from other villages and stray dogs that come in packs, starving for food in winter. That other one will know better now. He will not attack your dog again."

"That's good. I didn't mean for Lije to kill that other dog of yours, Kandaka."

"It could not be helped. If he were a brave, he would have acted the same way. But now you are tired and want sleep. I will take you to your lodge."

"Lije will stay there with me. He won't bother anyone around here, he'll obey me."

"This I have already seen. And he will hunt with you, and there will be much game for our campfires, John Cooper."

The lodge was small but comfortable, and one of the old women had already started a small fire to take away the chill of the night air. Before crawling beneath the blankets, John Cooper washed away the blood from Lije's wounded flank. It was not a deep wound, and the wolfhound licked his young master's face as John Cooper attended to it. Then, seeing the boy stretch out under the blankets, he lay down beside him, resting his head on John Cooper's chest. He gave a soft, little whine, and the boy stroked his head and murmured sleepily, "We're going to be just fine here. Thanks, Lije. I didn't want you to hurt their dogs, but they started it. I guess by now everybody'll know we can rely on each other and get along peacefully unless someone stirs up trouble."

FIFTEEN

There could have been no more gracious host than El Marqués de Someruelos. Having learned that young Carlos de Escobar was an avid horseman, he presented the delighted youth with a spirited brown gelding which would be reserved for Carlos alone during his sojourn in Havana. And when Carlos, thanking the governor-general, blurted out that he wished Miguel Sandarbal might accompany him, the official gave orders that Miguel was to have his pick of the horses in the stable and assigned a young under-lieutenant to act as guide for the two. Carlos at once took a liking to Antonio Romero, who was only four years older than he. Romero, despite his rank, was a most personable and enthusiastic companion.

Nor did the governor-general neglect Catarina and her aunt. His buxom wife, Doña Anna, took them under her wing and often drove with them into the city, in her own carriage. There she took them to the finest shops, and Catarina and Doña Inez were enchanted at the sight of the elegant gowns, slippers, and other fashionable fripperies displayed. On such shopping expeditions, it was almost as if they were back in Madrid. Warm-hearted Doña Anna made Catarina a present of an exquisite bracelet of sea shells held together with intricate, handworked silver chain links. It was so delicate and fragile that Catarina was almost afraid to slip it onto her slim wrist. She kissed and hugged the governor-general's wife, and Doña Inez sent their hostess a look of intense gratitude. This gift, perhaps like nothing else which had happened since the de Escobars' departure from Cadiz, served to pierce the young girl's defensive armor.

But an even more enchanting gift awaited Catarina. On Christmas Eve, after a lavish dinner, the governor-general rose and clapped his hands. A servant hastened in with a large, round object concealed by a voluminous silken shawl. "On this happy occasion," the Marqués declared, "it is my hope that our distinguished guests have enjoyed their stay on our beautiful island. So that they will long remember the pleasure their presence has afforded us, my wife and I present to them these gifts, which we hope will serve to keep those memories bright for a long time to come of the friendship which we have enjoyed with our honored guests." He gestured and the servant removed the shawl, then handed it to Catarina. But the girl ignored it completely and let it drop to the floor as she clapped her hands in amazement and stared, wide-eyed, at the silver cage that held a majestic white cockatoo. It perched on a bar and tilted its head prettily at her. "Oh, it is—it is so lovely, oh thank you, Your Excellency, for the wonderful present—what is his name?"

"Pepito, Señorita Catarina," the Marqués replied. "And for your beautiful aunt, my wife has selected a gift which I hope will not only please her, but remind her of her gracious beauty which has won all our hearts."

Doña Inez blushed and looked down at her napkin, aware that Don Diego, seated across the table from her, was eyeing her with a benign smile. Another servant entered and stood beside her, offering a magnificent ivory case in which lay two tortoise-shell combs, a silver-backed hairbrush, and a little hand mirror framed in silver. "Your Excellency, it is magnificent—I shall never forget such a gift, nor how kind you and your lovely wife have been to my niece and myself," she exclaimed, her voice quivering with emotion.

"Nor shall we forget you, Doña Inez." The Marqués gave her a courtly bow as he stood at the head of the table. "Now, Don Diego, for you I have the finest spyglass to be found in all of Cuba, so that you may survey your estate in Taos from a distance and find it fair to look upon." The first servant approached Don Diego with a leather case that contained the finest telescope the nobleman had ever seen. It bore the imprint of a famous Madrid marine shop which he at once recognized. "I shall treasure this touching memento of our acquaintance and friendship, Your Excellency," he acknowledged, clearing his throat and blinking his eyes. "The respect and affection I have for you and your gracious wife will hearten my family and me when we are in distant Taos."

"And to your son, with your permission, Don Diego, since my young under-lieutenant, Antonio Romero, has told me of his expertise as a horseman and his knowledge of the weapons of a gentleman, I wish to present this Toledo rapier. May he draw it always in honor, to right a wrong and to defend all of you against the enemies of His Majesty, our beloved Carlos IV! Your son has endeared himself to all of us, Don Diego, by his unfailing courtesy and gentlemanly qualities which, nevertheless, do not conceal his strong young heart and good nature!"

"You do us too much honor, Your Excellency," Don Diego protested, but again his eyes were misty and he had to clear his throat.

Carlos pushed back his chair and rose to accept the magnificent rapier with basket guard and tooled leather belt which the second servant now tendered to him. He took the weapon, turning it over and over, examining it, and overcome with joy, could only stammer his thanks. Then, turning to Don Diego, he exclaimed, "Look, Father, it is such a wonderful blade, so flexible and so well balanced! I shall have Miguel show me how to use it."

"Yes, my son. Let us pray God, however, that it will prove to be a symbol of your honor and manliness, and that you will not have to face danger with it," Don Diego responded.

Don Diego and his family bid farewell to the Marqués and his genial wife, boarded the *Paloma* on the second day of January in the new year of 1808, and with fair, warm winds, docked at Vera Cruz ten days later. Doña Inez and Catarina had a room to themselves in the best inn of that port, while Don Diego and Carlos shared another room, across the corridor. Captain Otero and his crew busied themselves unloading the cargo bound for Mexico City, including the king's gifts to the viceroy, His Excellency José de Iturrigaray, who had been appointed five years earlier and who, apart from the prime minister, was perhaps the most important man in Spain's waning empire.

Catarina's spirits had been greatly restored by the comparative placidity of the voyage from Havana to Vera Cruz and, still more so, by her treasured cockatoo. Doña Inez found herself answering her niece's countless questions. Was Pepito getting sufficient exercise? Wasn't his snowy plumage thinning just a little? Whenever time weighed heavily on her hands, Catarina would open the cage and hold out her hand to the cockatoo, which dexterously perched on her slim wrist and sometimes climbed to her shoulder, often to the girl's delight, playfully pecking at her hair.

Doña Inez was greatly encouraged by Catarina's change in attitude, as symbolized by her affection for Pepito. She could well understand the girl's need for love and companionship. After all, she had mourned her mother sincerely, had been suddenly uprooted from a luxurious home, and forced to embark upon a long sea voyage. And the prospect lay before them of an arduous overland journey. Doña Inez blessed the governor-general's wife for her thoughtfulness in giving Catarina Pepito. Decidedly, if there were to be any problems in her role, they could come only from Catarina. Carlos would adapt and do so readily, without any regrets. Catarina, because of her youth and her mercurial temperament, would find the process more difficult. But with her help, Doña Inez vowed, Catarina would turn at last into a beautiful, compassionate, and warm young woman. And when that came about, perhaps Don Diego would notice his sister-in-law's dedication and at last realize that it had been inspired by her own love and admiration for him.

On the following morning, the pompous little magistrate of Vera Cruz, Jaime Montrero, officially called upon Don Diego, read the king's order of appointment, and assured Don Diego that by the next morning he would have carriages and an escort ready to convey them to Mexico City. Shortly before noon, Don Diego and his family entered the spacious carriage, while the gifts for the viceroy and provisions for the journey were loaded into a second carriage. A military escort of twenty Spanish soldiers would see them safely on this journey of some two hundred and fifty miles.

Doña Inez, seated opposite Don Diego, observed that her brother-in-law seemed unusually pensive. Indeed, Don Diego had been seized by a sense of melancholy, caused by the knowledge that he was being taken even farther from his beloved Madrid. With this came the renewed sense of loss at the death of his beautiful young wife.

It was Carlos who, seated beside his father and stunned by the remarkable beauty of the countryside, finally lifted Don Diego's somber mood. Miguel Sandarbal rode alongside the carriage with the de Escobars; an extra horse tethered by the reins to his saddlehorn trotted next to him. On the second day of their journey, Carlos appealed to his father, "Please, may I not ride with Miguel? I need to stretch my legs and I want to feel more a part of this beautiful country."

"Well, if you wish," Don Diego replied. "It is true that it is a long journey, and I can understand that you do not want to be penned up in a carriage with your old father."

"Now, Father, that is not true," Carlos answered. "You are not old—it is only that Miguel tells such wonderful stories about duels and the breaking in of balky horses and the adventures he has had."

"Well then, my son, amuse yourself if it pleases you. Tell the coachman to stop the carriage so that you may mount that extra horse Miguel brought along—I should not be surprised if the rogue planned it just for this reason!"

Joyously, as soon as the carriage halted, Carlos got down and nimbly mounted the brown gelding, self-consciously adjusting his rapier at his side. "Ah, that is much better, Miguel! Just smell the air, it is marvelous!"

"Sí, Señor Carlos," Miguel responded with a smile. "But you must not let your father think that you prefer my humble company to his. Why not suggest to him that he ride beside me a few times on the way to Mexico City. You know, the good Lord has given him health and strength, and he is as much a man in his prime as I am, maybe even more. Well then, do not forget what I tell you."

Carlos and Miguel rode up to the head of the escort, exchanging a pleasant greeting with the captain. "I see your soldiers have lances, sabres, and muskets, Captain," Carlos declared. "Is there any danger on this route?"

"The highway to Mexico City which we take will skirt the most dangerous regions, but it is true that on occasions there are attacks from hostile Indians or bandits. Have no fear, however—my men and I have chosen the safest way, even though it may take one or two days more."

"Well," Carlos boasted, "if there is any danger, I shall pitch in and help." He patted the basket guard of his rapier with a confident smile, which drew a chuckle from Miguel.

Inside the carriage, Don Diego sighed and remarked, "Doña Inez, he is my only son, he will be my heir to the land in Taos and whatever wealth I may amass during my intendancy. It is important that he learn to be a nobleman, to carry on the traditions of the de Escobars."

"I understand what you say, my brother-in-law. But from what I see of this new world, I think the boy's education will surely require less ceremony and more practical common sense. He has vitality and all his life ahead of him, Don Diego. Forgive me for saying so, but you rely too much on memories of the past. For your son, and for Catarina too, it will be an exciting new life precisely because it will have no traditions. They will have to adapt themselves to the demands it will force upon them. And, in my humble opinion, my dear brother-in-law, that is the proper way to bring up children in this new world which is to be our new home."

SIXTEEN

Kandaka's ankle healed quickly. Within three days he was able to throw away the tree-branch crutch and walk with hardly a limp. Most of that time, much to John Cooper's gratification, the young Ayuhwa brave spent with the tow-headed boy, teaching him the language of the Sioux. John Cooper realized that there were many tribes of Sioux to the west and the north, and that while each tribe's dialect might differ, there were bound to be basic terms and words which would stand him in good stead if he should decide to pursue his journey.

When John Cooper asked Kandaka how the latter had learned to speak English, the young brave explained, "A *wasichu* squaw and her man from Saint Louis had left in a wagon for the west. They were attacked by warriors of the Missouri tribe, and the man killed. She was taken captive and, a year later, one of our warriors exchanged four horses for her with the Missouri brave whose squaw she had become. So she came to this village. My father, Mikanota, and this warrior, Beniqua, were good friends. I was then this high"—with his hand, he indicated the height of a boy of perhaps ten—"and I had never seen a *wasichu* to that time.

After Beniqua had taught her how to speak with our tongue, and because I was kind to her, she taught me hers."

"Does she still live with your tribe, Kandaka?"

Kandaka shook his head. "No, John Cooper. She could not give Beniqua a child—though I am certain that she longed for one—and he put her aside and took another squaw who was cruel to her. One day, she ran from the village and flung herself into the river. I mourned her, for she was kind and gentle and she made me understand that the *wasichu* and the Sioux can live in peace when they understand one another."

"Yes, I believe that too, Kandaka. That's why I want to learn to speak your language—so that your people will understand me and know that I am their friend."

"But you, John Cooper, you yourself are a *wasichu* and yet you come from your home to stay with us. How is this?"

John Cooper's expression became grim, and he hesitated. Yet he knew there was no point in dissembling. Briefly, he told Kandaka how his family had died and how he had come west with Lije, seeking not only refuge, but also a place where he could live and make a new start. Kandaka nodded sympathetically. "You have great courage, John Cooper. I knew that when you pulled me from the river. And yet, you have told me that the Shawnee killed your people—do you not, then, hate the Indian as many other *wasichus* would have done?"

"No, Kandaka. I knew the chief of the Shawnee, and he was always fair to my mother and father. And there were other braves I knew who were friendly. The ones who killed my family were not like the others—I've thought about that a lot since I started out, and I'm pretty sure their chief would have stopped them if he knew what they planned to do."

Kandaka stared at him, an intent look on his young face, then gripped his shoulder and nodded. "Your heart is good, and you speak with a straight tongue, John Cooper. You have learned much already for one so young. I think, too, that he who comes without hate to us and to all the other tribes in this vast land can be a friend, even if he is a *wasichu*. My father and Petimaka saw this in you that night when I told them your words and your deeds. Now we will help each other so that you will soon be able to speak for yourself to the elders and to the young warriors of our tribe."

Within two weeks, John Cooper had acquired a rudimentary vocabulary of Ayuhwa words and phrases, enough to make himself understood throughout the village. His first act was to go to Mikanota's lodge and thank him for the way in which he had been received. The chief's grave face wrinkled with a smile of pleasure at the young *wasichu*'s halting but sincere words of thanks. He replied fluently, and John Cooper was able to understand enough of the words to realize that Mikanota was eager to see how 'Long Girl' could bring fresh meat for the campfires. Kandaka, who stood beside his young friend, turned to John Cooper and murmured, "He says he would like to see you make the thunder with 'Long Girl' and show the keenness of your eye as a hunter."

John Cooper pondered a moment, then remembered something he had heard his father say years ago: *If you show an Indian a fine trick, it will impress him and he will have respect for your magic.* He turned to Kandaka and whispered back, "There is nothing to hunt in this village, but if you will take one of those cooking pots and throw it high into the air, I will shoot at it and hit it. Then your father can see that I know how to use 'Long Girl,' and you will tell him that I promise to bring back my share of meat for the cooking fires of this village."

"That is a good thing, my father will be pleased." Kandaka turned and spoke to his father again, and Mikanota nodded and grinned agreement.

Hurrying back to his lodge, John Cooper picked up the Lancaster, primed and loaded it, and tamped it down skillfully with the ramrod. Returning to the chief's lodge and standing in the wide clearing between it and the other mound-shaped houses, he watched as Kandaka returned with a large, earthen pot which the young brave gripped in both hands. Mikanota stood at the door of his lodge, his arms folded across his chest, his face impassive. Petimaka had also come out of his lodge, his two comely daughters on either side of him. Yumiquya was whispering to Letalto, who gave her sister a warning look and put her fingers to her lips. John Cooper adjusted the butt of the rifle to his shoulder, squinted along the sight, and nodded to Kandaka. "Throw it whenever you're ready, and throw it as high as you can or it won't be much of a shot."

"Now!" the young brave exclaimed as he flung the pot high into the air. John Cooper lifted his rifle to allow for the trajectory, and, squinting through the sight, pulled the trigger. Several of the other braves had come out of their lodges, and one of them uttered an approving whoop as he saw a shard fly away from the pot. Kandaka hurried to retrieve it and brought it back to his father to show him. There was a large hole in the side.

"This *wasichu* will bring us much meat, even that of the buffalo," Mikanota exclaimed. He held out his hands and John Cooper, understanding his desire, handed the Lancaster to him. Mikanota turned it over and over, examining it with great interest, peering down the barrel, regarding the sight and the trigger before handing the weapon back to the tow-headed youth. Then he called to Petimaka, "It was a lucky day for us when this young *wasichu* came toward the River of the Racoon to save my son and to come in friendship as a mighty hunter to our village."

John Cooper could hear the grunts of approval from the other braves who had watched his feat. Then he spoke haltingly to Mikanota in Sioux. "Mikanota, your son is my friend and my teacher. I wish to give him a gift to thank him for this in the eyes of the Great Spirit."

Then, turning to Kandaka, he whispered, "I want to get something from my sack, and it's for you, Kandaka."

John Cooper hurried back to his small lodge, again delved into the sack, and came back with the musket he had taken from the black-bearded renegade. Handing this to Kandaka, he said, "This is for you. It will bring down small game like rabbits and ducks so you will have meat when you go hunting, Kandaka."

The young brave's face glowed with pleasure as he took the musket from John Cooper's hands. "This is a fine thing," he exclaimed. "I have seen the *wasichu* traders hunt with these. My friend Latiwaka, who was killed by the great black bear we shall hunt when he comes out of his winter hiding, once owned just such a musket. He showed me how to put little bits of iron into it."

"Yes, buckshot," John Cooper interposed.

"You will kill the bear, I know it. Come, we shall go back to your lodge, and I will teach you more of the words of the Ayuhwa." Kandaka grinned. "If you learn our tongue as well as you begin to learn our ways, John Cooper, it may be you will soon win a squaw and become one of us. Did you not see how Yumiquya looked upon you when she saw you put a hole in the cooking pot?"

John Cooper turned crimson with embarrassment. "Gosh, Kandaka," he blurted, "you'd better not give her ideas. I'm a mite young to think about squaws. And I haven't even started paying your father back for taking me in and feeding Lije and me and giving me a place to sleep."

"But you are strong and young, and our braves take squaws once they have counted a great success in the hunt, or sometimes in battle," Kandaka teased him. "But I will say nothing more about Yumiquya, because there is much time for both of you. Now, I will tell you the word for a trap that we set, sometimes for the rabbit and sometimes for the deer. It is *wikmunke*. Since few of us have weapons such as your 'Long Girl' or the musket you have given me, we set traps where the rabbit or the deer run. Sometimes they are very good. Sometimes the rabbit and the deer are more clever than we are, and this makes us work harder to show who has more cunning."

"*Wikmunke*," John Cooper obediently repeated. Then he gulped and thought to himself, *Let's hope that Yumiquya doesn't try to set a* wikmunke *for me. My gosh, I don't even know how to act around girls yet—how could I be thinking of a squaw? I just hope Kandaka doesn't keep pestering me about things like that!*

SEVENTEEN

The journey to Mexico City, the capital of New Spain, took two weeks and was without any incident. To be sure, there were discomforts, since many of the roads were little more than dried-up riverbeds with great rocks in the middle, and occasionally the carriages halted while some of the soldiers dismounted to clear a path. Perhaps the worst part was the ascending road climbing into the Chiquihuite Mountains to reach the little valley town of Córdoba.

From there, they proceeded to Orizaba, a little town situated in a narrow valley, shadowed by the volcano which gave it its name and surrounded by orange groves and banana and coffee plantations. Then the carriages began to ascend formidable Cumbres. The travelers were halted half a day by a torrential rainstorm. Even Carlos, for all of his love of the outdoors and enthusiasm for riding the gelding, was reluctantly compelled to take refuge in the carriage until the storm subsided and the journey could be continued.

But the next day all discomfort was forgotten under the brilliant blue sky and a radiant sun which glittered on the tiled domes of the city of Puebla. Since it was Sunday, the church bells pealed as if in welcome to the carriages in which the de Escobars rode as they entered the city. From Puebla, they rode to Cholula, once the mightiest of all Aztec cities but now only a small town. Don Diego and his son both remarked on the colorfully garbed Indians and were saddened to see how many of them lived in squalor, in tiny adobe huts.

Finally, the carriages reached the pinewoods of Río Frío. Below them, over seven thousand feet above the sea, there stretched the great, luxuriously fertile valley of Mexico, studded with its white-walled towns with baroque spires, patterned at its interstices by gleaming lakes, and surrounded by snow-capped volcanoes.

Here, in this capital city, one could see the remnants of Spain's ancient glory. The carriages crossed the tree-shaded Alameda, traveled along the commercial thoroughfare of Plateros, and finally arrived at the *zócalo*, that great central square in front of the cathedral, flanked on one side by the Palacio Nacional.

Carlos mounted the steps to the entrance of the Palacio beside his father. As an officer bowed to them and opened the great door to the Palacio, Don Diego straightened with pride. Doña Inez, following behind with Catarina at her side, watched him closely and sighed to herself. There was no doubt of it, her brother-in-law was still under the spell of the court of Madrid, and she knew how deeply his pride would keep him harnessed to it. And yet, Nuevo Mexico was far away, distant even from this capital of New Spain. Her hope grew that the spell could at last be broken by the practicality which this new life would force upon him. Besides, he was still mourning Dolores. It would be importunate of her to break in upon that grief by any affirmation of her own growing desires. She, too, had an obligation to fulfill—caring for Carlos and Catarina. As she crossed the threshold of the imperial palace of Mexico City, she breathed a prayer that God would condone her secret yearning for Don Diego.

Miguel Sandarbal took leave of his master at the palace. He would stay at an inn on the outskirts of the capital and there begin to recruit workers for the estate in Taos. "It is best, Don Diego," he had explained, "that I find men with families, for they are the most likely to be loyal and industrious. I can find the rest of the workers we shall need in Nuevo Laredo, where I can purchase also the flock of sheep."

"Besides my salary as intendant, Miguel," Don Diego had responded, "I have brought enough gold with me to be able to offer decent wages to men of good heart and vigor, so do not stint. I trust your judgment about a man's character as much as I would trust my own. I estimate we shall be here a week before we start on the final lap of this long journey, so you will have time to make your choice."

The viceroy's aide, a fussy little man with huge spectacles, received the de Escobars and at once had servants escort Doña Inez and Catarina to their rooms. Then, ostentatiously, he led Don Diego to the lavish furnished office of José de Iturrigaray, who had just emerged from a cabinet meeting.

The viceroy, a tall, bearded man with melancholy features and an elegant Castilian accent, came forward to greet the gray-haired nobleman. Don Diego opened the confidential packet he had brought with him and handed him the letter from Charles IV, adding that gifts the king had sent to the viceroy were being unloaded from the carriage which had conveyed them from Vera Cruz.

"All seems to be in order, Don Diego," the viceroy declared after he had perused the king's document of appointment. "But you must be tired after your long journey. Perhaps we might postpone matters of state until tomorrow."

"With your permission, Your Excellency," Don Diego intervened, "I am eager to know how I may best serve the throne. I know very little about Nuevo Mexico nor what function I shall be expected to perform as intendant there."

"I admire your directness, Don Diego. Well, then, since I am free at the moment, I shall be happy to acquaint you with the duties of your new post. Perhaps you are aware that the Ordinance of Intendants for New Spain was implemented in 1786, for the purpose of curbing corruption, halting laxity in obeying royal and viceregal orders, and promoting greater administrative efficiency." The viceroy permitted himself a humorless smile. "This order had the purpose of improving fiscal administration and augmenting the revenues to the crown, and with it were swept away the governors, the *alcaldes*, and other civil officers who helped themselves to the royal treasury and diverted considerable sums which should have gone to the king."

"I understand, Your Excellency."

"We have in effect a dozen governor-intendants to manage the newly created districts of New Spain. Just as you have been, the others were selected by the king, and their powers extend to the departments of justice, general administration, finance, and war. Your duties will be to collect revenues, to handle civil administration and cases of justice, and all economic matters. As such, you become my own assistant and are directly subordinate to me."

"I promise you every loyalty, as I did to the king, himself, Your Excellency," Don Diego responded.

"Of that I have no doubt." José de Iturrigaray rose from his desk and moved toward the window, gazing out at the magnificent cathedral. "It was long the hope of the kings of Spain that Nuevo Mexico would pour vast sums of gold and silver into the royal coffers. Regrettably, this has not yet occurred. It is a dry and dusty land in parts, verdant in others, with many mountain ranges. It is populated by perhaps as many *Indios* as Spaniards, but where you go you will find the *Indios* of the *pueblos,* who are peaceful and who work under administrative direction, as well as under that of the good priests.

"You will send reports by courier once a month directly to me, Don Diego. As soon as you have spent a few months becoming accustomed to your new office, I shall expect your collected revenues to be sent by trustworthy and well armed guards to the palace."

"That is understood, Your Excellency."

"*Bueno.* You and your family will do me the honor of being my guests until you have recovered your strength and spirits—I know what an arduous journey you must have had."

"God has blessed all of us with good health, Your Excellency, and me with a tireless desire to serve the king. I would not abuse your hospitality, and I have told my foreman that perhaps we might leave within a week."

"Your forthrightness does you credit, Don Diego. I understand why His Majesty chose you for this post. Well, we shall not quibble about a few days more or less. I shall need some time to arrange carriages and a suitable military escort—it is a journey of some sixteen hundred miles to Taos, you know. Also, there are areas in New Spain where the Indians are hostile, and it is best to be prepared for attack, particularly by *bandidos,* who are the scourge of our country where they believe themselves safe from the patrols of our royal troops."

"I am grateful to Your Excellency."

"The news I have received from Madrid in the past few years has been disquieting—though much of it I have pieced together for myself, reading between the lines, as you might say."

"Your Excellency?" Don Diego politely murmured, eyeing the viceroy warily.

"I myself, before I came here, Don Diego, enjoyed the culture and ceremony of our beautiful Madrid—just as you did. I confess to you that I am not fond of the French, and I find myself somewhat embarrassed that the great Spain of Ferdinand and Isabella and of Philip II has been seriously weakened by the alliance with the French. You have come recently from Madrid; how does the populace regard this?"

Don Diego de Escobar squirmed uneasily in his chair, searching for a diplomatic answer. "The pride of a Spaniard is legendary, Your Excellency. I daresay even the commoners feel as you do—and as I do myself."

"Well, then, we understand each other. Tomorrow night, you will be my guests at a banquet and a ball. Heaven knows that the duties of state at times require diversion, and I for one am in need of it. I welcome you officially to your duties, Don Diego, and I am glad to have you here as my guest." He extended his hand, and Don Diego shook it gravely.

Don Diego and his family were entertained as lavishly as they had been in Havana. There were many officials at the huge banquet tables, and the presentations seemed endless. The food was magnificent, accompanied by the finest wines. The luxury, indeed, reminded Don Diego of the brilliant court of Madrid.

Observing that Doña Inez looked particularly attractive in a yellow silk gown which she had not previously worn, Don Diego approached her at the ball which followed and asked to be her partner during a *paso doble*. Color flushed her cheeks and it was with an effort that she restrained herself from accepting too eagerly as she rose and allowed him to take her arm and lead her out onto the floor. Yet, as she danced with him, she noticed the faraway look in his eyes that told her he was comparing this palace with the Escorial. He was still preoccupied with thoughts of his banishment and the life he was leaving behind.

At the end of the dance, he bowed to her courteously and complimented her, then turned to dance with Catarina, who had just been released from the arms of the fat, nearly bald minister of the interior. Doña Inez stared after him. "It is said that time will heal all wounds," she told herself philosophically. "Well, with the will of God, I shall be on hand to help that assuagement. Tonight he held me in his arms for the first time—but he did not really see me. Oh, perhaps he noticed my fine new gown, saw that I did not dance too clumsily, and that I am not yet too old to be of interest to a man. But I must be patient and bide my time. I can only pray that one day he will seek me out because of his own need, as much as I yearn now to seek him out because of mine."

EIGHTEEN

By the middle of February, John Cooper had completely adapted to the easygoing life of the Ayuhwa village. His friendship with Kandaka had deepened, for the latter spent at least an hour or two each day teaching the youth the language of his people. Gradually, as John Cooper became more fluent in the Sioux tongue, he was able to speak with other braves, who plied him with eager questions about his rifle and Lije. He felt a sense of belonging, however temporary, which comforted him more than he realized. Moreover, he observed that this Indian tribe maintained strong, lasting, family and tribal ties. An old man or an old woman would not be cast aside if there were no relatives to provide food and shelter. This solidarity helped to ease the deep, abiding hurt which he had carried with him ever since leaving Shawneetown.

Kandaka had told John Cooper the buffalo had been plentiful last fall and so, even through this bitter prolonged winter, there was meat enough for everyone. Dried meat and tallow were kept in parfleches, a kind of envelope of sturdy rawhide which kept out air and water and preserved the contents. Chokecherries and berries, picked in the fall and dried for winter use, were stored in bags made of skin from buffalo calves. The Ayuhwa considered pemmican a particular delicacy: thin slices of buffalo meat, dried, cooked, and pounded fine, then mixed with melted fat and either berries or cherries.

Much to John Cooper's delight there was plenty of hunting that winter. He was eager to show how Lije could retrieve fallen game. Many nomadic tribes neither fished nor trapped but subsisted almost entirely on the buffalo. The Ayuhwa, however, ate fish, deer, rabbit, and squirrel meat, enjoying them almost as much as the buffalo. Toward the end of February, John Cooper, Kandaka, and Lije set out into the woods some distance from the village. It was like old times for the dog. His keen, brown eyes scanned the landscape, as he sniffed in search of the scent of quarry. A rabbit suddenly broke out of a copse of elm trees, and Kandaka leveled his musket and fired. The rabbit seemed to leap into the air, turned over, and then fell dead. "It is indeed a fine musket you have given me, John Cooper, and it has given me good luck the first time I have used it!" Kandaka exclaimed.

"Let Lije bring the rabbit to you, Kandaka. I want to show you how he hunts with me," John Cooper urged. When his friend nodded assent, John Cooper called, "Fetch, Lije," and pointed to the dead rabbit. The wolfhound loped forward, picked the dead rabbit up by the neck, and trotted back to his young master, proudly wagging his tail. "Good dog!"

He took the rabbit from Lije's jaws and handed it to Kandaka. The wolfhound let out a soft growl and stared quizzically at John Cooper, who shook his head. "It's all right, Lije. Kandaka is my friend. He shot the rabbit."

Almost dejectedly, Lije turned away with a soft, little whine. John Cooper burst into laughter, knelt down, and hugged the wolfhound, who licked his face.

"It is almost magic," Kandaka declared. "Now I understand how you and your dog could come so far to our village and still have food to keep you strong. Before you gave me this fine musket, I would try my skill with the bow and arrow against the rabbit, and sometimes I would set traps for him. Shall I show you how I made a trap?"

"I'd like to see it, Kandaka. I've made a few—Pa taught me—" John Cooper's voice faltered a moment, then resumed. "But I'm sure you know a lot more about setting traps than I do."

"I have set traps here in these woods before and caught many rabbits." Kandaka could not help boasting as he led the way. "You know, of course, that to set such a trap, you must find a rabbit run. It is a place where the rabbit goes back and forth for his food when there is no danger for him. Here is one of my old traps. Of course, there is still snow on the ground which covers the tall grass. It will be better soon for hunting in this place, I know it well."

He showed John Cooper a small sapling, from which dangled the noose of a rotten vine. "You see? The sapling holds the noose in the air as high as the rabbit's head. When he runs into the noose, it bends back and pulls him up into the air. I make the noose strong enough so that it will strangle him quickly and he will not suffer. Sometimes, though, if the sapling bends too much, and the noose is lowered, it will catch the rabbit by the foot."

"My traps are made sort of like that, Kandaka. Only Pa told me to use hairs from the tail of a horse to make my noose."

"Yes, I do this also. And I——"

John Cooper had suddenly spied an antlered buck about a hundred feet away in the woods. It had not caught their scent, and it was turned sideways to them. He plucked at Kandaka's arm and put his finger to his lips, then swiftly loaded the Lancaster. Kandaka followed his gesture, took a deep breath, and grinned, then squatted down to watch.

John Cooper tucked the butt of the Lancaster against his shoulder, squinted down the sight, his finger slowly moving to the trigger, then fired. The buck collapsed in its tracks, and Kandaka let out a whoop of admiration. "Now I know you will kill the bear, and you will kill many buffalo for us! You have truly counted coup today, John Cooper!"

"I'll let Lije carry your rabbit to the village, and the two of us can haul the buck back," John Cooper proposed.

"Yes, that will be very good. And do you know, my friend, that when Yumiquya sees you and when she hears that you have killed the buck with 'Long Girl,' her eyes will be soft and tender for you."

"Now don't talk like that, Kandaka!" John Cooper blurted out, angry with himself for turning red again at his friend's teasing allusion to the giggling teenaged Indian girl.

"I do not speak so to anger you, John Cooper, only to tell you of our customs," Kandaka protested with a straight face. "My father says that soon I must think of taking a squaw into my lodge, for at eighteen summers I am old enough for this. My poor friend Latiwaka, whom the great black bear killed last spring, was only three summers older than I am now, and he had wed the squaw Degala five summers before, when he was almost two summers younger than I am now. So you see, it is not too early for you to think of having a squaw to cook for you and mend your clothes and share your blanket, John Cooper."

"I'd just as soon not, if you don't mind, Kandaka. Now let's get this buck back to camp," John Cooper declared in exasperation.

"Now I see that I have indeed made you angry. We will speak no more of squaws. This buck is heavy, it will have much meat. And I see how your great dog holds my rabbit, so gently between his strong jaws. I am glad that he sees that I am your friend, for I should not like to have him as my enemy. You have told me how he killed one of those *wasichus* who tried to rob you of the bearskin and 'Long Girl.'"

"Of course we're friends, Kandaka, and Lije won't ever be your enemy. But I meant to ask you, where did you get the buckshot for the musket?"

"I told you that Degala must surely have kept what Latiwaka had, and I went to our other village two moons ago. It is not far on horseback, though it is nearly half a day's journey on foot. She gave me the little round pieces of metal which I put into this musket and said that she hoped they would bring me good luck."

"And they did, as you saw."

"That is true. I told her about you and 'Long Girl,' and how you have promised to help us hunt the killer bear when he comes out of his hiding place in the spring."

"She must be pretty young. Why doesn't she take another man, Kandaka?" John Cooper asked.

"The parents of Latiwaka came to us many summers ago. They were from the Missouri tribe and fled to us for refuge as many others did, from the Osage. They believe that if a brave is killed by an animal, his squaw may not take another man until that animal is slain. Otherwise, it will be bad medicine. And I think, too," Kandaka's face grew solemn, "she has always been sad that she could not give him a papoose. Sometimes it is said that such a squaw is barren, and if that is so, even if she should take another man, she would not be his favorite wife if he could find one who would give him a papoose."

John Cooper frowned, trying to piece together the Ayuhwa logic. Then he asked, "But if she has no man, who brings meat for the lodge where she lives with Latiwaka's mother and father?"

"Latiwaka's father still hunts, even though he is as old as Petimaka, who they say has seen fifty-two summers come and go. He can still kill rabbits and sometimes even a deer. Then, too, Latiwaka's mother plants corn and is given her share for the three of them."

"I see. And Degala's mother and father?"

Kandaka's face grew even more solemn and he looked away as he replied, "Now that is even more bad medicine. Two summers ago, Degala's mother was picking berries when the killer bear came upon her. And the father of Degala was bitten by a snake and died of its poison a week after he saw his daughter wed to Latiwaka. That is also why few of our braves think of taking Degala into their lodges. They fear that the bad luck of the evil spirits still clings to her and they, too, may be slain in such a manner."

John Cooper shook his head. "That's terrible, Kandaka. But she's not to blame."

"I think that, too. But Petimaka says that until the bear has been slain, she may not go to another brave's lodge. As to the snake, another warrior killed it with a stick after it had bitten her father, so it is only the evil spirit of the bear which must be lifted from her."

"I understand, Kandaka. Just the same, it's a shame that poor girl had such bad luck. Well, it isn't much farther back to the village—I'm glad of that, this buck is really a fat one."

"Since you've got no squaw for yourself, John Cooper, one of the old ones of the village will skin and cook the meat for you if you wish," Kandaka ventured.

John Cooper glowered at him, again feeling his face redden. "I'm not going to keep it for myself, if you don't mind."

Now it was Kandaka's turn to eye his friend, questioningly.

"You'll see," John Cooper answered the unspoken question. "I might just ask for a piece for Lije, as a sort of reward for fetching your rabbit."

"All the meat is yours; it is your right to say what will be done with it, my friend." They had reached the outskirts of the village, and the old women cackled with glee and called out encouragement to both John Cooper and Kandaka as the two carried the deer between them, both trying not to show the exertion demanded of their sturdy, young muscles by such dead weight.

"Where shall we take this buck of yours, John Cooper?" Kandaka asked.

"To your father's lodge, Kandaka. It is my gift to him to say thanks for his kindness."

"This is a very good thing." Kandaka's face glowed. "Already you begin to think more like an Ayuhwa than a *wasichu*. Our shaman has already said to my father that you have come among us with kindness and respect as if you were one of us. We know the traders who visit our villages, and they are good men, but they often take more than they give. With you, it is different, John Cooper."

Once again the youth was embarrassed, this time by his friend's words of praise. Mikanota had emerged from the lodge and stood gravely in the doorway watching the two boys carry the heavy buck toward him.

In the Ayuhwa tongue, John Cooper declared, "This buck, which I have killed with my thunderstick, is my gift to you, Mikanota. I gave my word that I would bring meat for your cooking fires. And I will do more, again I give you my word."

The tall chief smiled, put his hands on John Cooper's shoulders, and said gravely, "I give you thanks for this fine gift. And I ask that you share it with me tonight in my lodge."

John Cooper grinned boyishly. "I'd like that a lot, Mikanota. If it's all right with you, I'd like just a piece saved for my dog."

"The dog deserves that and more, Father," Kandaka broke in. "Do you not see how he carried the rabbit I shot with this musket all the way from the woods?"

"It is so," Mikanota chuckled as he observed Lije standing attentively beside John Cooper, still gripping the rabbit in his jaws. "He shall surely have his share."

By the first week of April, an early spring had banished the snows and dreariness of winter, and the warm sun had made the once barren trees bring forth new leaves. The verdant grass added vivid beauty to the plains and forests, and Kandaka proposed to John Cooper that they visit the other Ayuhwa village.

Kandaka chose a brown mare and roan gelding from the crude wooden pen which served as corral for about twenty horses. He rode bareback, using rawhide reins and a bit made of bone, and nimbly mounted his mare. John Cooper had never ridden bareback, and he hesitated, until he saw Kandaka smile teasingly down at him. Then, gritting his teeth, he swung himself astride the gelding, adjusted the reins, kicked his heels against the gelding's belly, and prayed for the best. But the gelding was docile enough and readily followed Kandaka, who led them in a westward direction.

The other village was smaller and, as Kandaka explained, had only fifty inhabitants. At one end was a large round granary made of earth, logs, and bark, in which the corn was stored, and in a similar edifice, firewood was kept. As they neared the village, John Cooper could see the Ayuhwa squaws out in the fields planting corn.

"I will see if Degala has any more buckshot, though I think she gave me all that Latiwaka had when I was here before," Kandaka suggested. Dismounting in front of a small, earth-covered lodge, he greeted a white-haired, stooped old woman who stood sunning herself at the entrance. "*Hau,* mother of Latiwaka, it is a good day for corn."

"Yes, a good day, Kandaka. My man, Maniwoka, has taken his bow and gone hunting," the old woman proudly declared.

"Perhaps I will see him when he returns. And Degala?"

The old woman grimaced, made an abrupt gesture, "She brings firewood, the lazy one. Her curse is still upon her."

"I have come to ask if she has more of those round, little bullets for the musket. My *wasichu* friend here is named John Cooper, and he speaks our tongue very well—I myself have taught him."

The old squaw regarded John Cooper and grunted, eyeing him warily.

"I am glad to know you, mother of Latiwaka, who was my friend's good friend," John Cooper said in Sioux.

"You do speak well for a *wasichu,*" the old woman admitted grudgingly. "Wait, Degala comes now. You will ask her. I know nothing of such things. I know only that my son is dead and that his slayer, the evil bear, still lives. And it was the same one that slew this lazy one's mother. Truly is she accursed."

John Cooper turned and saw a young woman coming toward them, her arms laden with cut pieces of firewood. Her jacket, leggings, and moccasins were made of buckskin, and her forehead was smeared with black ashes. Her round, sweet face was shadowed with a look of dejection and utter weariness. With downcast eyes and slightly bowed head, she approached the lodge. The old woman, with a cackling little laugh, seized a willow switch which stood propped up against the wall of the lodge beside her and, lifting it, cut the young woman across the hips. "Lazy one," she shrilled, "you take all morning to bring a single load of wood. I do not know why Maniwoka lets you live with us and gives you meat and salt. But you will work harder or you will not eat—I, Tisingua, tell you this!"

"I ask pardon, Mother," the young woman responded in a humble, husky voice. Wincing under the vicious cut of the switch, she went into the lodge and laid down the firewood, then emerged, crossing her arms over her full, round breasts and bowing her head, in the attitude of a slave.

"Kandaka will speak with you, lazy one. I have no wish to hear what he has to say to you. When he is done, you will bring me food for the noonday meal. If it is well prepared, I may let you eat of it yourself. And do not take too much time talking, there is work to be done in the lodge!" The old woman made a threatening gesture with the switch. Then, with a cackling laugh, she went back into the lodge.

John Cooper stared incredulously at the young Ayuhwa widow. She was no more than twenty-four and of medium height. Her soft, black eyes were misty with tears as she looked up at Kandaka. Her lips quivered, and the wings of her nostrils dilated sensuously. The perfection of her features— soft, copper-toned skin, high-set, angular cheekbones, a high-arching forehead—made her the loveliest Indian girl John Cooper had ever seen. But what struck him most was the torment and anguish in her eyes, and the almost hangdog attitude with which she stood before his friend. He stared, feeling himself a helpless intruder upon her grief, and glanced questioningly at Kandaka.

"This is my friend John Cooper, Degala. You know, I told you that he had given me a musket as a gift of friendship. That was why I came before to ask you for the little round bullets that Latiwaka used to put in his musket when he went hunting. Do you have any left?"

"I think there are still some in a buckskin pouch, Kandaka. I will give them to you."

"I thank you, Degala. My friend has a long gun, and it kills from afar. He has told me that we shall go hunting the evil bear."

At this, Degala turned to stare almost piteously at John Cooper, who felt an inexplicable lump in his throat at the wistful melancholy of that look. "This is so?" she faltered.

John Cooper replied in Sioux, "I have promised the chief, Mikanota, that I will go with Kandaka to kill the bear, Degala. Yes, it is so. And I promise you this, I will do my best to kill it."

The young widow caught her breath and put a hand to her smudged forehead, and John Cooper saw great tears form in her eyes. "I will pray to the Great Spirit that it will happen, *wasichu*," she said in a soft, husky voice. "I will pray that the Great Spirit will keep you and Kandaka safe from the killer bear."

"If the bear dies, Degala, the curse will be lifted from you," Kandaka said gently.

"I know," she murmured, again lowering her eyes. "But now I will give you the pouch and then I must do my work." She hurried back into the lodge and returned with a buckskin pouch which she handed to Kandaka. Then, without a word, she looked at John Cooper, bit her lips, turned, and swiftly went back into the lodge.

NINETEEN

On February 12, 1808, Don Diego de Escobar, his two children, and his sister-in-law began the last lap of their journey to Taos. The day before, the viceroy had summoned Don Diego to his private chamber to discuss with him the final details of the journey itself, and what Don Diego might expect when he reached Taos.

"In a sense, Don Diego," José de Iturrigaray said as he gestured to the gray-haired nobleman to take a seat, "your visit here enables me to inform myself more explicitly on the conditions of New Spain. You will have a strong military escort, well-armed and under the command of an able, young officer. Although he is only a lieutenant, I intend to promote him to captain as soon as he returns with his report. I shall not conceal from you, Don Diego, that there is some unrest in several of the provinces of Mexico, particularly as regards the levying of taxes. You and I understand that, because of Spain's dependence upon the French, greater revenues are needed so that Napoleon can effect a peace which will protect the borders of Spain itself."

"That is true, Your Excellency. But Napoleon is ruthlessly ambitious. I fear that one day he may seek to override the Spanish boundaries themselves."

"God grant your premonition be false, Don Diego!" the viceroy exclaimed. "But now, to immediate matters which concern you and your family. Your predecessor, Juan de Morena, was an old man who was ailing almost from the day he became intendant at Taos. Six months ago, he went back to Spain to die. A widower, and perhaps too impractical for the post he held, he contented himself with a small house which I am told is now dilapidated and surely no fitting home for you and your family. His duties for the last year of his intendancy were assumed by the *alcalde* of Taos, Don Sancho de Pladero. He is a capable, gracious man and will be of inestimable help to you in locating yourself suitably and acquainting you with the matters of revenue, government, and trade in the province."

"I shall be grateful for his assistance, Your Excellency. It will be all so new to me."

"Yes, but because of that newness, you may be able to give us a fresh approach to a local government that will strengthen the community, keep the *Indios* peaceful, and establish more profitable trading—do not forget that I rely on you to increase our revenues."

"I shall devote every energy to that pursuit, Your Excellency."

The viceroy smiled and nodded and then rose to open a cut-glass decanter filled with amber-tinted wine. He filled two silver goblets and held out one to Don Diego, who took it as he rose and touched it to the viceroy's goblet, saying, "To your health, Your Excellency, and with it my pledge of constant devotion to my duties in Taos!"

"*Salud, mi compadre.*" José de Iturrigaray replied. "And to His Majesty, and the greater glory of our beloved Spain!"

"*¡Viva el rey y España!*" Don Diego toasted.

The viceroy put down his goblet and extended his hand to the gray-haired nobleman. "You have told me that you plan to raise sheep on your land, Don Diego. Well, Don Sancho de Pladero is one of the principal ranchers of Taos, and there, too, he can be of help to you. In addition, he is a *Madrileño*. He left Madrid twenty years ago to come to Taos with his wife, Doña Elena. I think you will be good neighbors and friends, and that will help you work together harmoniously for the good of the realm."

Don Diego de Escobar brightened. "Indeed, Your Excellency, it will be almost like being back home to have a *Madrileño* as friend and neighbor. We shall have much to talk about, the two of us—after our day's work is done, to be sure."

"I have no doubt of that," the viceroy chuckled. "You plan to buy your flock in Nuevo Laredo, I understand. Doubtless your foreman will find good workers there as well."

"That is true, Your Excellency. However, he has already engaged four young men from this city who grew up on farms and who are familiar with sheep and cattle. I have thought, also, that it would be a wise precaution to arm them, and my foreman as well, so that in the event of any attack, we should have sufficient strength to beat it off."

"A very good idea, Don Diego. I shall send thirty men with you, soldiers who have been under fire before and know how to handle themselves. Lieutenant Cortez, who will head the escort, will take a route that should be relatively safe. Tomorrow, when you leave the palace, I shall not miss the opportunity of bidding a most reluctant farewell to your handsome son and beautiful daughter, as well as to you and the very charming Doña Inez."

"Your Excellency has been most kind to my family and me, and I am personally grateful to you for the comforts we have received. I look forward to sending you my first report —one that you will read with pleasure."

"That is my hope, too, Don Diego. Until tomorrow, then."

True to his word, the viceroy, in full military uniform, escorted Don Diego and his family out of the palace the next day and led them to the large, sturdy carriage drawn by four horses which would convey them to Taos. Their trunks and provisions for the journey were loaded into a second, equally large carriage. In front of the carriages, the troop of thirty smartly-uniformed soldiers armed with muskets and sabres was drawn up in review. Some carried lances as well, to which were tied cloth pennons displaying the colors of the flag of New Spain and the sign of the crown in the center. A slim black-haired lieutenant, Maximiliano Cortez, twenty-eight years of age, dismounted and saluted the viceroy, then bowed to the de Escobars. "At your service, Your Excellency, Don Diego and Señor Carlos, Doña Inez and Señorita Catarina," he declared, then bowed again to the two women. Catarina, who was carrying the silver cage which held Pepito, favored him with a dazzling smile. Decidedly, she thought to herself, he was very handsome. Doña Inez glanced quickly at her niece and uttered a faint, knowing sigh. It would do no harm for her impetuous young charge to have a distraction like this in view of the hard journey ahead. So long, of course, as Catarina forgot neither her station nor her immaturity.

"Well, Don Diego, I wish you and your family Godspeed and a safe journey." The viceroy turned to the gray-haired nobleman. "Lieutenant Cortez will take you first to Santa Fe, where you will meet the governor of Nuevo Mexico, His Excellency Reál Alencaster. I have written a letter to him, and I entrust it to you, Don Diego. It will introduce you and indicate that I have acquainted you with your duties and that, while you will send the revenues from Taos to him for ultimate dispatch back to Mexico City, your written reports of the situation in Taos will come directly to me. Out of courtesy, to be sure, you should send at least a brief summary of such reports to the governor."

"I shall carry out your wishes to the letter, Your Excellency."

"¡Bueno! And you, young man, I see in you your father's image—you would make an excellent officer one day, if your ambitions extend in that direction." The viceroy had turned to Carlos and given him his hand. Now, with a gracious bow, he approached Catarina, took her free hand, and brought it to his lips. "Our palace will be drearier now that you and your beautiful aunt are leaving it," he commented gallantly and then took Doña Inez's hand and kissed it as well. As he did so, the handsome spinster glanced quickly at Don Diego, and then blushed when she observed that he was watching the ceremony of leavetaking. She wondered whether, in the coming weeks of hardship and proximity, he would begin to appraise her in a different fashion.

Behind the carriages, Miguel Sandarbal and four sturdy Mexicans stood beside their horses, the men awaiting Miguel's orders. He had engaged them and purchased horses for the journey as well as weapons—two Belgian flintlock widebore muskets, sabres for them and for himself, and a dozen long-barreled fowling pieces, with a plentiful supply of ammunition. As Don Diego approached him now, Miguel quickly explained to his master, "I shall get the rest of the men we shall need in Nuevo Laredo, along with the sheep, Don Diego. These four men know how to use weapons, and that will be of great help to us on this long journey. They are not married, but they are eager to try their fortunes with us in Taos; and I have told them that if they work well, they will be rewarded for their labors. Also, that they will find pretty *señoritas* in Taos, so that they will soon be family men."

Don Diego chuckled and clapped Miguel on the back. "And I hope for their sake that is true, Miguel! You know, we shall need a good cook and a housekeeper, among other things, so I count on you to find them in Nuevo Laredo. Let me meet these men now and make them welcome."

"*Ciertamente,* Don Diego." Miguel Sandarbal turned to the first man, who was stocky and wore a heavy mustache. "This is Pedro Garcia, who grew up on his father's farm not far from here."

"I thank you for coming with us, Pedro." Don Diego extended his hand and the delighted peon, after a moment's hesitation, warmly shook it.

"And this is Felipe Gonzalez, Don Diego. He has worked with burros and sheep, too."

"An honor, *Patrón.*" Felipe Gonzalez grinned from ear to ear as Don Diego shook hands with him. He was tall, lean of face and form, not quite thirty.

"And this, Don Diego, is José Corrado. He is as handy with tools as with horses, and this is his brother, Jorge. They are eager to work for you, Don Diego."

"And I am eager to have them. *Hombres,* we shall get along, I am sure." Don Diego extended his hand to each of the brothers. José was twenty-seven, plump and good-natured; his brother, Jorge, was a year older, thin and somewhat taller, more reticent in nature.

"Well then, we are about to begin," Don Diego concluded. "I see you have brought along two extra horses, Miguel."

"Yes, Don Diego. One is for you, when you choose, and the other is for your son. Oh, and there is something else. I think it would be wise for you and Carlos, as well as the ladies, to arm yourselves with these fowling pieces. I pray that Señorita Catarina and Doña Inez will never have to use them—but perhaps, since you know weapons well, Don Diego, you could teach them. Or at least they could learn how to load the weapons, and then, if we should be attacked—may our Savior protect us from that!—you or your son would be able to shoot again more quickly than you could if you reloaded your own weapons."

"Yes, that is a good idea. These are fine pieces. I should think they come from France or Belgium."

"That is what I think, too, Don Diego. Here are four of them, and ammunition and powder in the pouch. Well then, I shall have our men mount up, and we shall follow behind you. In that way we shall be able to watch, in case someone comes up behind us and plans an ambush."

Don Diego smiled and patted Miguel's shoulder. "I am very pleased with you, Miguel. Now we shall start without delay." He went back to the steps of the palace and tendered his arm to Catarina, who hugged him and smiled up at him as he helped her into the carriage. Carefully, she put Pepito's cage on her lap, put her forefinger in through the bars, and cooed, "Pretty Pepito, say my name. Go on, I have told you what it is."

Don Diego offered his arm to Doña Inez and helped her into the carriage to sit beside her niece. She put an arm around Catarina's shoulders and murmured, "Has it spoken yet, *querida?*"

"No, but I think it will. I have been talking to it several times a day for the last week, Tía Inez."

"Yes, I know, you minx. But you have been trying to teach Pepito something else beside your name. I did not quite catch the word—what is it, Catarina?"

Catarina made a sulky *moue*. "Well," she whispered, "if you will not tell anyone, it is, *quiero*."

"I see," Doña Inez had to suppress a smile. "That is to say, *I love you, Catarina*. Well, so long as it is just a cockatoo— remember, you are still a little too young to think of such things."

Don Diego and Carlos had taken their places in the carriage, facing Catarina and Doña Inez, and Carlos grinned at his sister. Just then, the cockatoo, preening itself on the bar, called out, *"Quiero, Ca-ta-rina."*

"¡Por todos los santos!" Carlos exclaimed. "You have found an admirer at last!"

"Do not tease her, Carlos," Doña Inez put in. "It is good that she has a pet to cheer her."

TWENTY

"Come, John Cooper, today we hunt the buffalo!" Kandaka exclaimed as he strode through the opening of his white friend's small lodge and peered inside. It was a week after the two boys had visited the other Ayuhwa village, and the weather had continued unseasonably warm.

John Cooper, trailed by Lije, came out of the lodge, yawning and stretching. He sniffed at the warm spring air and grinned. "It's a great day for hunting, Kandaka. How far is this herd of buffalo you're going after?"

"Many miles past the village where you met Degala," was Kandaka's reply. He patted Lije's head and added, "This time not even this great dog can bring back the game as he did the rabbit. And it would be too far for him to run with us—we go on horseback, you, I, and six other braves. There will be much meat. This time, we shall try to kill only the young bulls or the heifers. Then, when the leaves begin to fall, we pick the fat cows out of the herd for the most meat."

"It sounds like fun. But if you say so, I'll make Lije stay here." John Cooper squatted down, cupped the wolfhound's head between his hands, and crooned to Lije, "Good dog, good boy, stay here." Then, with his left hand, he gestured toward the lodge. Lije whined softly, wagged his tail, then trotted docilely into the lodge and lay down just inside the entrance. He rested his head on his front paws, staring intently at his young master. The mournful look and the drooping shoulders spoke more than words of Lije's disappointment at being left behind, and John Cooper reached in to pat him a last time before he turned back to Kandaka. "Am I going to ride that same roan gelding?"

"No, John Cooper. In our corral, we have buffalo horses. They are well trained; your roan has never been on a buffalo hunt, and it might be dangerous for you. When you shoot, or when we strike our arrows or lances into the great shaggy ones, they sometimes turn. They would trample you if your horse did not move away quickly from their horns and hooves. Come!"

John Cooper had brought his Lancaster, along with a large, rawhide pouch which Kandaka had given him some weeks before, in which he stored his gunpowder, his father's cylindrical measuring cup, spare flints, and a plentiful supply of lead balls. At the same time that Kandaka had presented him with the pouch, the young brave had brought to John Cooper a jacket and leggings made of beaded buckskin, the work of an old squaw in the village. In addition, the squaw had made a pair of moccasins. John Cooper, as he strode to the center of the village with Kandaka, would have resembled a young Indian brave except for his shock of blond hair and his bright blue eyes. He moved quickly, his body wiry and lithe, his sun-bronzed freckled face alert and taut with excitement. The other six braves waited beside the corral, all of them stripped to breechclouts and moccasins. Three of them were older braves, and John Cooper guessed them to be in their early thirties. One was armed with a lance, while the other two carried the old, wide-bore muskets of which Kandaka had spoken. Two others were about Kandaka's age and armed with bows and arrows, as was the brave John Cooper had already met.

"You know Migawa already," Kandaka turned to John Cooper as he nodded toward the stocky brave, who smiled and lifted his hand in recognition. "The one who carries the lance is Ekanebe, and those with the muskets are brothers, Tisoulata and Winimato. These two, who have seen one more summer than I, are Depoinke and Semokime. They are all as eager as I to see you kill the buffalo with 'Long Girl.'"

"If we're going so far from that other village, Kandaka, how will we bring back the buffalo we've killed?" John Cooper asked.

"That is women's work. These six braves have squaws. They and some of the old women who have no men will come after us when we have finished the hunt. They will come with pack horses. But do not worry about women's work, John Cooper. I have told my friends you will kill more of the great shaggy ones than any of us because you have 'Long Girl.' Now let us go."

Opening the gate of the corral, Kandaka brought out a small, hardy, black mustang, on whose back was placed a piece of buffalo robe secured by a wide banded cinch of self-tanned leather. The horse was guided by a thin rawhide thong, looped over his lower jaw. Kandaka gestured to John Cooper. "This one is for you. He is swift, and he is not afraid of the sound of the musket—both Tisoulata and Winimato have ridden him and brought down many of the great shaggy ones. He is so good that when he hears the twang of the bowstring or sees the spear drawn out of the buffalo, he moves out of danger."

John Cooper mounted the mustang. "The band is loose so you can put your knees under it during the run and control 'Long Girl,' " Kandaka explained. "And you tuck the ends of that thong under your belt so you will have both hands for the rifle." John Cooper nodded, adjusted the buckskin sling that held his rifle over his shoulder, and took firm hold of the thin rein in one hand. With the other, he leaned forward to stroke the horse's neck and muttered in Sioux, "We will be friends, we will ride together this day."

Kandaka and the other braves mounted their mustangs, and then the group rode out of the village, heading west. Several miles beyond the village where John Cooper had met Degala, they came to a broad valley, flanked by clumps of cedar and birch trees. Kandaka held up his hand to halt them, and leaning forward, pointed southward. "There, a large herd, many of the great shaggy ones, enough for all of us. We will attack them from both sides. You, John Cooper, you, Depoinke and Semokime, will ride with me to the left. You others will go at them from the right. Now!"

Kicking his moccasined heels against his mustang's belly, Kandaka led the charge from the eastward direction, John Cooper riding beside him and the two young braves with bows and arrows alongside. Migawa and Ekanebe with his lance, and Tisoulata and Winimato with their muskets, rode at a gallop toward the west. "We will circle upon them, John Cooper," Kandaka called. "Then they will see the others coming from the other side, and there will be confusion in the herd. If we are lucky, they may move about but not run, and they will be easy for us to pick off!"

As the four of them rode toward the east and then prepared to charge against the grazing herd, Kandaka turned in his saddle, cupping a hand over his eyes and squinting toward the distant clumps of trees. "The women have already come with their pack horses; they will be waiting for us to make much work for them, John Cooper!" he exclaimed, baring his strong teeth in an exuberant grin. Then, tucking his knees beneath the cinch of the saddle, and swiftly tucking the ends of his rawhide bridle under his breechclout belt, he drew the bow from behind his back, reached with his other hand into the quiver of arrows slung over his left shoulder, and fitted the feathered shaft to the bowstring. John Cooper was caught up in the exhilaration of the hunt. As his mustang neared the edge of the herd, he pulled his rifle out of the sling, having already primed and loaded it, and took careful aim at a young bull that stood near the old, shaggy leader. His fingers squeezed the trigger, and the young bull staggered, then began to run. Suddenly it tumbled onto its right side and lay kicking.

"Did I not say you would bring us luck today, John Cooper?" Kandaka cried as, bringing his mustang closer to the southern edge of the herd, he chose a plump heifer and, drawing the bow back to its maximum, loosed the arrow. It struck just behind the last rib and about a third of the way down from the backbone to the belly, piercing the hide and a thin muscle layer to penetrate the intestinal cavity. The heifer uttered a bellow of pain and veered toward Kandaka's mustang, which had already swerved away from its anticipated charge. From the other side of the valley, there came the sounds of musket shots. John Cooper rode off a short distance to reload the Lancaster. As he did so, he saw Depoinke and Semokime circling on their mustangs, drawing their bows, and speeding their arrows toward two young bulls. Depoinke's arrow was too hastily aimed. It hit one of the bulls but deflected off a rib, inflicting only a minor wound. The enraged buffalo lowered its horns and charged the young Ayuhwa, but he had already jerked at the rawhide bridle and sent his mustang galloping out of danger. Semokime's arrow was better placed. It pierced the young bull's liver, and the wounded buffalo stumbled on about a hundred yards before suddenly collapsing. John Cooper turned his mustang toward the herd, which was now milling in confusion, aimed at a heifer, and squeezed the trigger. His shot went through the eye to the brain, and the heifer dropped in its tracks.

The sounds of muskets resounded from the other side of the herd, and John Cooper, pausing to reload the Lancaster again, watched Ekanebe ride up to a young bull, lean forward, and, with both hands gripping the haft of his lance, thrust downward into the bull's left side. Then he dragged out the lance and thrust again before swerving his mustang away from the fatally wounded buffalo.

By now, the herd, which numbered about two hundred fifty, had panicked. The animals began to run in several directions. Kandaka called to John Cooper, "The calves are too young to run well and will tire quickly. They will drop on the grass to hide. With the squaws and the old women have come boys who are too young for a big hunt like ours—they will practice their hunting skills on the calves. We will feast, we will feast, my friend."

John Cooper had by now gotten the knack of riding the well-trained mustang, who seemed to sense that he had a novice astride him. With his knees tucked under the cinch and the bridle firmly pressed under his belt, the boy found that he had ample time to prime and load the rifle and, as the hunt progressed, to choose his targets more carefully. His next two shots, however, only wounded a young bull and a young heifer. They stood stubbornly, with braced feet and lowered heads, bellowing their agony. Ekanebe had already slain six buffalo with his lance, though he narrowly avoided being knocked off his mustang by a wounded young bull which charged viciously and nearly gored the mustang. Moving away, Ekanebe wheeled his horse back against the bull's left flank and, lifting his lance as high as he could, thrust down with all his might. The bull staggered, lifted its head, then crumpled to the ground, kicked, and lay still.

Near John Cooper, Depoinke and Semokime were busy. Between them they killed five of the beasts within ten minutes. The two braves with muskets had accounted for a dozen buffalo by now and had drawn to one side, panting and sweating, to rest a moment and then to reload. Migawa was notching another arrow in his bowstring when a young heifer turned and charged his mustang. The mustang stumbled in a prairie-dog hole and went down; but Migawa nimbly leaped astride the heifer and, seizing the hunting knife from its sheath at his side, circled his left arm round its neck and thrust the blade repeatedly into its throat until at last the heifer went down on its knees and toppled over. Springing away from the dead heifer, Migawa put his fingers to his mouth and uttered a shrill whistle, but the mustang could only squeal in pain and shake its head as it tried to respond —it had broken its leg.

Migawa hurried to the thrown horse and swiftly ended its suffering with his knife. Then he ran a safe distance to the perimeter of the buffalo herd.

"Let the rest go, we have enough. There are all those calves for the boys to hunt down—the meat is good, tender, young," Kandaka called. "Migawa, you will ride behind me back to the village!"

Then the young brave turned to John Cooper with a grin. "It was good sport this day! Do not worry about those two which still stand—they will soon die or else the boys will come upon them with lances. Now, leave the work to the boys and the squaws. We ride back to tell my father that you have more than kept your pledge to him of meat for the fires!"

John Cooper turned his mustang back toward the smaller village. Cantering up beside Kandaka, he hesitated for a moment, then said, "Kandaka, I know I told you that the buffalo I killed are for the village, because I promised your father I'd earn my keep. But would it be all right if I gave one buffalo to your friend Latiwaka's mother and father? Maybe then—well, I mean, Degala might not be treated so badly if someone gave them meat."

"Now I see which way the wind blows for you, John Cooper!" Kandaka halted his mustang and smiled at his white friend. "You wish Degala to come share your blanket in your lodge, is that not so? But I have already told you she may take no man till the evil bear is slain. That is the tribal law of Latiwaka's parents."

John Cooper's face turned nearly as red as the sunset. "I wish you'd stop talking about me taking a squaw all the time, Kandaka. That wasn't what I meant at all. I just meant, if I give her a whole buffalo, that might make them a little less angry at her, and maybe they wouldn't take the switch to her so often. That's all I meant. Now what's wrong with that?"

Kandaka's teasing expression gave way to one of gentle

compassion. "Your heart is good, John Cooper. No, there is nothing wrong with what you want to do. I will tell Jiscanse, the old woman who came from Degala's village, to bring the meat and the hide of one of your buffalo to the mother and father of my dead friend. And I say to you once again, John Cooper, that I am proud to be your friend!"

TWENTY-ONE

Soon after leaving the outskirts of Mexico City, Lieutenant Cortez turned his horse back from the head of the troop and rode up to the carriage in which Don Diego and his family traveled, to make sure all was well with them. Once again, he enchanted Catarina by doffing his plumed hat to her and making a courtly bow from the saddle. But the young girl's pleasure at such male gallantry was short-lived indeed when she heard the handsome lieutenant converse with her father.

"We are quite comfortable, Lieutenant Cortez. What road do we take to reach Taos?" her father had asked.

"Excellency, it will be *El Camino Real* for a good way along the inland route toward Durango. We shall try to avoid the mountains whenever we can, as well as some of the provincial villages which are known to be hostile."

"My foreman and his men will go on to Nuevo Laredo, as you know, Lieutenant Cortez," Don Diego explained. "I count on you to tell them the fastest route and at what point they should take it from our own journey."

"Of course. When we reach Mapimi, in the province of Durango, they may head northeast to Nuevo Laredo—a journey of perhaps three hundred miles. They will make better time than we, *Excelencia*. On good horses, they should travel twenty-five miles a day, whereas, because of the size of this expedition and the obvious necessity to stop over at night in villages where comforts can be procured for the ladies, we shall probably average no more than fifteen to eighteen miles a day."

"I see." Don Diego frowned as he did some fast calculation. "Since Taos is about sixteen hundred miles away, Lieutenant Cortez, it will take us at least three months to reach our destination, is that not so?"

"That would be a reasonable estimate, *Excelencia*."

Catarina, who had been eavesdropping, could no longer contain herself. "Oh no, Father!" she burst out. "Surely you do not expect Tía Inez and me to stay cooped up here in this awful carriage for three whole months? I shall never be able to stand it, I know I shall not!"

"Believe me, Señorita," the handsome officer assured her, "my men and I will do everything in our power to ease the discomforts of this journey for you. There simply is no other way to get to Taos. One could break the journey by remaining a night or two in some little town, it is true, and naturally we shall discuss the route with your father."

"All the same," Caterina exclaimed, angry tears shining in her dark eyes, "I do not like it one bit! To have to be shut up in here, jolted about all the time, along dusty roads and dirty little towns with all those *Indios* and *peóns*—that is no way to treat the daughter of a nobleman!"

"Please, Catarina!" Doña Inez gripped the girl's elbow and whispered fiercely, "Can you not see you are making Lieutenant Cortez uncomfortable? It is not his fault—and he told your father that he and his men would do everything they could to make us comfortable. I am willing to endure this, and you must, too. If you are truly the daughter of a nobleman, Catarina, you should act like one!" Then she leaned toward the window. "For myself, Lieutenant Cortez," she said graciously, "I am already grateful to you for your thoughtfulness concerning all of us. We shall try to make this journey a pleasant one for all concerned."

"I have not the slightest doubt of that, Doña Inez." The officer gave her a dazzling smile which only served to make sulky Catarina jealous. Then he turned to Don Diego. "The road will be good for at least a hundred miles," he declared. "We shall make good time this first day. Perhaps it would be well, *Excelencia*, to break up the monotony of the journey by staying in a town for the first night, and then again on the third or fourth. I am at your orders, as always."

"*Gracias,* Lieutenant Cortez. I could not ask for a more solicitous escort, and we are in your hands," Don Diego told him.

Carlos had listened silently to all this. He rolled his eyes upward to denote irritation over his younger sister's tantrum. As for himself, he knew what the remedy for boredom would be. He would simply ride one of those extra horses Miguel had brought along. And there was an extra one for his father, too, so he couldn't be accused of wanting to escape Don Diego's company.

Don Diego caught Doña Inez's eye and found himself smiling. He had tried to ignore his daughter's willful outburst, and he was grateful for the way his sister-in-law had handled the embarrassing scene. But he told himself that, after all, Catarina was the one who had suffered the most in all this upheaval. It was far too much, he thought, to expect a girl of thirteen to put up calmly with a long ocean voyage, then a journey by land to Mexico City, and now yet another journey that would take at least three months.

At sundown, Lieutenant Cortez wisely broke the journey at a rambling, white house, about twenty miles from Mexico City. It belonged to a wealthy merchant whom he knew to be a loyal supporter of the viceroy. The man had come from Spain a decade ago, and when he and his white-haired wife came out to offer a night's hospitality to the de Escobars, Don Diego's spirits lifted. They rose even more during dinner, as he listened to his host's anecdotes about the days of his youth in Seville.

Catarina had exclaimed with delight when she saw the huge patio decorated with towering palm trees from which hung bird cages containing parrots, macaws, hummingbirds, and scarlet tanagers. She hurried back to the carriage to bring out Pepito, holding his cage up so that the cockatoo might observe his distant cousins.

The white-haired hostess, Doña Serafina Macaragay, observed Catarina' interest in the patio and the birds, and she mentioned that she had a servant who might be able to make a bell to hang around Pepito's neck. Catarina greeted the idea with great enthusiasm and momentarily forgot her irritation over the intolerably long carriage ride to Taos. Don Diego and Doña Inez exchanged knowing smiles as they observed her, at dinner, plying Doña Serafina with excited questions about the birds in the patio.

Carlos's interests had been piqued by a magnificent stable, which he had noticed at the back of the house. He asked hesitantly if he might visit it. Alvarado Macaragay was only too happy to grant his request. After dinner, he insisted on taking a lantern and escorting Carlos through the various stalls. Señora Macaragay had taken Catarina to one of the little cottages where old Antonio, a former silversmith, lived with his ailing wife. So Don Diego and Doña Inez found themselves alone at the table.

"The first day goes well, does it not, Doña Inez?" Don Diego smiled at his sister-in-law.

"Very well, and I hope it is a good omen. If only we can find enough to occupy Catarina, these three months will slip by before she becomes too unhappy—at least that is what I am hoping for."

"As I am. I must compliment you on how well you have handled her, Doña Inez."

"It has been my pleasure. Now, since we have a long day ahead of us, I shall say good night to you and excuse myself." As she was about to rise, Don Diego hurried around the table to draw out her chair for her. "*Gracias*, Don Diego. And may you sleep well and have pleasant dreams," she thanked him.

He bowed low to her and watched her leave the room. He sighed. Pleasant dreams, she had wished him. If truth be known, he would give a great deal to be back at the Escorial, to be back again in their lovely house, and most of all, to be reunited with his beloved Dolores.

He could not know that on this very day there had been a palace revolution at the Escorial, and that the tall, supercilious, twenty-four-year-old son of Charles IV had deposed his father and proclaimed himself *El Rey* Ferdinand VII.

Eight days later, Lieutenant Cortez and his troop entered the old Spanish city of Querétaro. There, the de Escobars were entertained for the night in the house of a Dominican cleric, in whose chapel Don Diego and his family knelt to pray and to receive a blessing for the rest of their journey. Five days later, they passed through the town of Guanajuato and headed on toward San Felipe. Here, a violent thunderstorm turned part of the road into a quagmire and compelled them to break their journey for three days. They were given hospitality by a wealthy farmer. It was here that Catarina celebrated her fourteenth birthday. Her aunt gave her a beautiful silver crucifix on a gold chain as a present, and at dinner their host, who had learned of Catarina's birthday, presented her with a beautifully crafted doll which represented an Aztec chief. Catarina exclaimed with wonder over the workmanship and thanked the man effusively. Don Diego completed the evening by putting onto his daughter's finger a tourmaline ring which had belonged to her mother.

The next stage of their journey took them to San Luis Potosí, at the foot of the eastern range of the Sierra Madres. Over a hundred miles of winding mountain road consumed twelve days before they arrived at Zacatecas. By now, Carlos had taken one of Miguel's extra horses to ride along, urging his father to emulate him. But the tediousness of the journey thus far had caused Don Diego to return to one of his earlier nostalgic moods. So, when Carlos rode back alongside the carriage to converse with his father, Don Diego, who had seen him talking with the men Miguel had hired in Mexico City, irritably declared, "You must not forget, Carlos, that you are the son of a nobleman. It is not seemly to descend beneath your station and act like an ordinary *compañero* to those men whom Miguel has hired as our servants."

Doña Inez sighed and shook her head. She, too, had chafed at the seemingly interminable journey. It was all she could do to cope with Catarina's fretfulness as the mountain ride continued. Exasperated, she commented, "It is good for his health to ride, Don Diego, and as for talking to honest workers, I do not see that he lowers himself. If anything, it shows a fine character that he can be compassionate and understand what is in the hearts of the common people. And since Miguel was thoughtful enough to bring along another horse, it would not do you any harm, either, to ride every now and then. You are a fine figure of a man—but, may the saints be my witness, by the way you talk you seem to want to grow old before your time."

Hardly had she finished these last words when she turned red and put her hand over her mouth, aware that she had been treading on dangerous ground. But Don Diego did not suspect her real motive. His mind was occupied with plans for the future. Though startled by her outburst, he stroked his beard and replied, "Well, it is possible you are right, Doña

Inez. I do not suppose a little exercise would do me any harm. But do not think that I hold my son and myself so far above these *peóns* that we must not converse with them—it is only that Carlos is still so young and not yet aware of his heritage."

"When you say heritage, Don Diego, you mean Madrid," Doña Inez countered. "You told me how the viceroy himself was concerned over Napoleon's ambitions, and I could not help but think that until Napoleon is finally ousted from all of Europe, Spain can never be what it was. Is it not more sensible and practical, then, for us to concentrate on what is in store for us instead of on the past which, even if it is restored, surely will have drastically changed?"

Don Diego looked at her as if for the first time. He did not expect such forthrightness and logic from a woman. Dolores had been interested in the arts, culture, costumes, and traditions. She had loved music and dancing and enjoyed the happy life of a wife and mother who loved her husband and her children dearly. Never had Dolores ventured to express political opinions.

Doña Inez flushed and lowered her eyes. "Forgive me, my brother-in-law," she stammered, suddenly ill at ease. "I did not mean to sound like a shrew and I have no right to tell you what to do."

"You need not apologize, Doña Inez. Perhaps you are right. I shall follow your advice and ride beside my son."

"He needs and admires you, Don Diego," Doña Inez said softly. Then, lest she say more that was in her heart, she turned to Catarina and began to amuse her niece by poking her forefinger through the bars of the cage so that Pepito might nibble at it.

In the next three days, they covered seventy-five miles to the little town of Nieves. Here, they had their first glimpse of the almost interminable desert through which they would travel to Durango and Chihauhau and then, finally, across the river which separated Mexico from Nuevo Mexico. After a night's stay in Nieves they resumed their journey. Five days more took them to the outskirts of Matamoros. Late that afternoon, Catarina insisted that she be allowed to walk about a bit and stretch her legs, so Lieutenant Cortez brought the troop to a halt. He rode up to the carriage, dismounted, opened the door, and helped her down as if she were royalty. His courtliness elicited from her an enchanting smile. Then, carrying Pepito in his cage, she walked toward a large clump of manzanilla, set the cage down on the ground, and disappeared. Carlos, who had been chatting with Miguel, dismounted and walked over toward the cage. He chuckled as the white cockatoo hopped from its perch onto the bars of the cage, clinging to them and cocking its head as it peered inquisitively at him. "Catarina *quiero*," he teased it, and laughed aloud as the cockatoo repeated the one phrase it knew.

Just then there was a scream. "*Ayudame*, Carlos, come quickly—I am afraid—"

Carlos straightened, drew his rapier, and ran behind the clump of manzanilla bushes. His sister stood trembling, pointing a finger at a large lizard nearly two feet long, its skin studded with orange and black beadlike tubercles. It stood about two feet away, its tongue flicked out and its beady eyes fixed unwaveringly upon her.

"Do not move, do not make a sound, Catarina," Carlos whispered. He moved to the right, circled behind the lizard, and suddenly thrust the rapier down, transfixing it. Then he lifted it and flung it far beyond, into a bed of small cacti. "There, little Catarina, do not be afraid any more. It was only a lizard and it was probably more afraid of you than you are of it. Come now, I shall take you back to the carriage."

She had burst into tears and flung herself against him, holding tightly to him as she sobbed out her fright and desolation. "Oh, it is just that everything is so terrible out here, all this lonely country and the desert and the long journey through the mountains—I am so tired of riding and being jostled back and forth—when shall I ever have a room to myself again—oh, Carlos, you do not know how awful it feels to be so alone!"

"Come now, little sister, do not let all those handsome soldiers see you crying. Why, your beauty gives them courage to protect us all. Come now, dry your eyes. We shall have dinner tonight in Matamoros, and you will be able to rest the night in a fine bed—Lieutenant Cortez told me so."

"*G—gracias, mi hermano*," Catarina sniffled as he led her back to the carriage. "Oh—*Dios*—I forgot poor little Pepito—"

"No, little sister." Carlos smiled indulgently. "I remembered to bring back the cage. There you are. Now forget all about the lizard."

"I—I shall. *Gracias,* Carlos," Catarina faltered as she sank back into her seat. Doña Inez turned to her and put a consoling arm around her shoulders.

As Carlos was about to remount his horse, Don Diego exclaimed, "So you have blooded the rapier the Marqués gave you. A good omen, *mi hijo.* I hope you will not have to draw it again until we reach Taos, and then only in practice!"

TWENTY-TWO

It rained during the last week of April and then turned unseasonably warm and sunny once again. Mikanota and Petimaka had gone to the smaller Ayuhwa village to celebrate the ritual of the planting of corn. The old shaman had welcomed the rain during this ceremonial week as a good omen, signifying that the Great Spirit was pleased with his people and that the harvest would be bountiful. The braves of the tribe would dance—their bodies painted with the cabalistic signs of the sun, the rain, and the ripe corn—and the women would prepare a great feast. Then, Kandaka explained to John Cooper, he who was not yet wed among the pledged braves would show his wish to court an unwed maiden by casting an arrow before her as he concluded the dance. If she accepted him, she would kneel, take the haft of the arrow in both hands, and dig it into the soil at her feet. If she rejected him, she would break the arrow or fling it over her shoulder behind her.

"I think my father will cast the arrow before Sentigata this time." Kandaka winked knowingly at his young friend. "I am his only son, and he wishes others so that the leadership of our tribe will pass on to those who are blood of his blood. He has been a long time grieving for my mother. Sentigata's man died last year—she is a kind woman, and she will give my father sons, as he wishes."

"And you, Kandaka, you always tell me to think of taking a squaw—haven't you chosen one for yourself yet?" John Cooper couldn't help asking somewhat maliciously.

"It is not yet time. The son of a chief cannot act like any other brave, John Cooper. First, the maiden must be willing —that is understood. But more than that, he must choose the one who is respected most by all the village because her own father and mother are worthy and have brought great honor to our tribe. And for such a maiden, the son of the chief must give many horses, trading goods, or guns to show what great price he puts upon the maiden he has chosen. I have not yet earned the price by my deeds, I have not yet counted enough coups to be worthy of her, John Cooper. Now, do you wish to go with me to hear Petimaka's prayers, to see the dancing, and enjoy the feast?" Then teasingly, as if to repay John Cooper for his intimate question, Kandaka added, "If you wish to dance before the maidens, I shall lend you an arrow that you may cast at the feet of her who most pleases you."

"I don't know anything about dancing. Besides, I'd sort of be an outsider—I know this must be an awfully important thing for you and your people, Kandaka. I think Lije and I will just go hunting. Say, maybe Lije can even flush that bear who killed your friend Latiwaka."

Kandaka's face grew solemn and he nodded slowly. "I read your thoughts, John Cooper. Since I told you of the curse upon Degala, it has troubled you. And the buffalo meat was given to the mother and father of Latiwaka, as you desired, and they have said they are grateful to you. But the great shaggy one is hard to find. He has been wounded by some of our braves and he is cunning. It will not be easy, and he may not have yet come out of his hiding place. Or he may have chosen another, farther from here, so that we shall not seek him and try to kill him."

"How will I know him if I see him, Kandaka?"

"He is taller than a full-grown man when he stands upon his hind legs and paws at the air and growls—that is when he is angry, when he sees a brave come upon him with bow or lance. He is black and his coat is thick, and his jaws are large and terrible. But you will know him best because a piece of his left ear is gone. I told you that he had killed one of our braves—so it was, and there were three dogs from our village who ran at the bear to bite and worry him while Mistantoma notched his bowstring with his sharpest arrow. One of the dogs leaped at the great shaggy one's head and bit off part of that ear before the bear killed him with a single blow of its great paw; and then it fell upon Mistantoma and killed him, too."

"I think I can recognize him from that, Kandaka. Besides, even if I don't come across the bear, I can kill a deer or two. I meant to ask you, Petimaka doesn't have a squaw, does he? Who gives him meat, if he doesn't kill it himself?"

"The squaw of Petimaka died of the river fever as did my own mother, John Cooper. He went into the forests and prayed to the Great Spirit, and when he came back, after nearly a moon, it was as if the Great Spirit had touched him. My father asked him to bless the planting of the corn, and that autumn the harvest was greater than we had known for many years. So it was that he became shaman, but he would never take another squaw. An old woman who had lost her man and her own children helped bring up Letalto and Yumiquya. Since he is shaman, my father sees to it that a share of the game which our hunters bring to the village goes to him."

"I understand, Kandaka. If I kill a deer, I'll make sure that Petimaka gets most of it. I owe him that for the kind things he said about me. It was what he said, and your father too, that made me welcome here to live with you."

"Yes, but now everyone in both our villages knows that the *wasichu* who shares our lodges is a good friend to all the Ayuhwa. Your heart is good, your tongue is straight, and you are brave. These things we respect—and I think that all through the land the tribes who hunt and farm, and even those who make war, respect them even in a stranger, John Cooper." Kandaka gripped his friend's shoulder and smiled at him. Then, swiftly changing his grave mood, he said, "Then you will not mind if I cast my arrow at Yumiquya's feet?"

"Now that's enough of that, Kandaka!" John Cooper stooped to pick up a handful of dirt and pretended to throw it at his Ayuhwa friend. With a merry laugh, Kandaka hurried out to the corral for his horse, and John Cooper came out of the lodge to watch him mount and ride away to join his father, the shaman, and the other braves. He stretched and yawned and looked up at the sky. "It's going to be a fine day, Lije. I'll just load up 'Long Girl,' and then you and I will go foraging for ourselves and see what we can find. All right with you, boy?"

Lije answered with a soft bark and a vehement wag of his long tail. John Cooper grinned and patted the wolfhound's head. Then he went back to get his rifle, primed it, and loaded it with an extra charge of powder.

The air was pleasantly warm, and John Cooper felt the old excitement come upon him. It was the same feeling he had always had in Shawneetown when he had been given a free afternoon. He left the village with Lije at his heels and headed north toward the gradually rising slopes dotted with cedar, elm, oak, and birch. "Now, if I was a bear, Lije," he reasoned aloud, "I'd hole up for the winter in one of those caves, the way we did during that blizzard—remember, boy? You didn't get too much to eat during that spell, I recollect." John Cooper spied a steep hill in the distance that looked as though it might conceal a cave. He and Lije headed for it.

The rising slope was half a mile away, and as he neared it, John Cooper watched the ground for tracks. Here and there, where the soil was softer and moister, he could see the footprints of rabbits.

The sun grew brighter, the air warmer, and John Cooper sniffed it with relish, his keen blue eyes narrowing as they studied the broad expanse of the ascending slope. Far up at the top and to the west, there seemed to be a small, partially concealed opening. Perhaps that was the cave he sought, he told himself. Turning to the wolfhound, he put his hand on the broad, shaggy neck and murmured, "Now don't you go ahead of me, Lije, and don't make any noises. I don't want the bear to come charging out of that cave before I'm ready to shoot him, hear me?"

Despite trees which grew along the rise of the slope, he could still see the cave as he ascended. His eyes constantly searched the ground for signs. The cave's mouth was narrow and dark but, in his estimation, it was wide enough for a bear. About two hundred feet from the entrance he squatted down and inspected the Lancaster to make sure that it was ready to fire. Then, almost automatically, he reached for the pouch at his side which contained the powder and balls to make sure it was handy. This done, he straightened and, crouching low, moved cautiously up the steepest part of the slope toward the cave.

His heart beat faster, and he reached down for a large

rock, transferring the rifle to his left hand, and flung it with all his might into the dark mouth of the cave. There was no sound. Nevertheless, he moved well to the left so that he would be out of the bear's line of vision if, indeed, it was skulking inside. He didn't think he was good enough yet with the rifle to meet a charging bear head-on and bring him down with one shot. "Quiet now, Lije," he murmured as he patted the wolfhound's head again. His eyes narrowed as he saw the unmistakable footprints of the bear, leading upward over the slope and away from the cave. Quickly he scrambled to the top of the rise and looked down into a small valley studded with a profusion of trees and bushes. Then he caught his breath. About six hundred feet away, the great black bear was moving past a clump of elderberry bushes and heading northward.

John Cooper began to run down the slope with Lije loping alongside him, glancing up now and again at his young master, his brown eyes intent and eager as he reached the level of the little valley. There was the bear again, lumbering methodically in a northward direction, apparently not yet having caught sight or scent of them.

John Cooper quickened his pace until he was about two hundred feet away from the bear. The size of the beast made him hold his breath. Yes, it was bigger than the one he'd shot near his camp that winter night. And black bears could climb trees, so if he didn't kill it, he'd just have to say a prayer because climbing a tree wouldn't do much good. He realized that he would have to make his first shot count, at least wounding the beast badly if he couldn't kill him. Once again he inspected his rifle and made sure that it was ready to fire.

Lije had seen the bear, too. He uttered a low whine, his ears flattened, and his eyes narrowed. "Shhh, Lije, not a peep out of you, boy," John Cooper muttered. At that moment, a fat jackrabbit ran out of the bushes just ahead of the bear, paused, saw the terrifying carnivore in its path, and bolted off to the west. The bear halted, slowly turned its head. John Cooper shivered as he knelt down and adjusted the butt of the Lancaster to his shoulder. It was even higher than Lije at the shoulder, and almost six feet long, with coarse, heavy fur and an almost rudimentary tail. Its limbs were short and massive, and John Cooper could only guess how cruel those claws would be.

The bear uttered an angry growl and reared up on its hind legs. Its jaws opened to reveal the terrible, sharp teeth of the true carnivore. John Cooper held his breath, squinted through the sight, and reached for the trigger.

Just as he was about to fire, Lije could no longer contain himself. With an angry bark, he sprang forward.

"No, for God's sake, Lije, come back, come back, you fool!" John Cooper cried out. He moved his eye away from the gun's sight to look after the wolfhound, and at the same moment his finger squeezed the trigger.

The bear uttered a yowl of pain and dropped to all fours. Frantically, John Cooper reached for the pouch to reload the rifle, calling out again, "Lije, come back here, do you hear me? Come back this minute!"

But even as he scrambled to reload the rifle, knowing with a sinking heart that, fast as he might be, he couldn't have it ready in time if the bear should charge, the wounded black bear began to lumber away toward the northwest. It disappeared into a clump of cedar trees and was gone.

Lije came back, wagging his tail; and John Cooper, kneeling on the ground, bowed his head and shuddered. He shook his head slowly. "I thought you were a goner then, Lije, I thought we were both goners. Don't you ever go running after a bear again! If I'd lost you—I don't even want to think about it—but we hit him, I can see that stain of blood on the ground over there. Let's go see what happened."

Fighting the nausea that surged in him, John Cooper finished reloading the rifle and then shakily got to his feet. He moved carefully, but when he stared off in the direction which the wounded bear had taken, he saw no sign of it. Then he came to where the bear had confronted him and stopped dead in his tracks. The ball had shot away the toe pads and claws of a paw—they were lying on the ground a few feet off to one side of where the bear had risen to challenge its hunter.

"Doggone it, Lije, if you hadn't run off like a fool just then, I might have killed him," he said disgustedly, shaking his head. "Now there's no telling where he's going to hole up. One thing's certain—he won't come back around these parts, least of all to that cave. That means Degala is going to have to go on working her fingers to the bone and taking sass from Latiwaka's folks. I wish I could have killed the bear, Lije, so that old curse upon her would be lifted, I sure do."

He stared somberly down at the ground, then shrugged and stooped to retrieve the bloody vestige of the bear's paw.

"Well, leastways, Lije, now there'll be no mistake picking that bear out the next time I see him. He'll have part of an ear and part of a paw missing, and the next time I'll get him for sure. Now let's head back to camp."

TWENTY-THREE

Much to Catarina's relief, Lieutenant Cortez decided to remain two days and two nights in Matamoros. Since he and the *alcalde* were friends, he was able to procure gracious hospitality for the de Escobars at the latter's sumptuous villa. To Catarina's great joy, she had not only a fine wide bed in which to sleep, but also a room all to herself. It even boasted a silver-framed mirror set above a magnificent teakwood dresser. Perching Pepito's cage on top of the dresser, she pirouetted before the mirror, gaily urging the cockatoo to see how pretty they both were and exhorting it to say once again, "*Quiero,* Ca-ta-ri-na," of which she never tired.

The *alcalde*, Jaime Consuelgo, was a widower in his midfifties, with two rather homely but goodhearted daughters in their early twenties. At dinner, both of them effusively complimented Catarina on her pretty gown, as well as her handsome aunt, without the least hypocrisy or affectation.

Lieutenant Cortez sat at Catarina's left, and further charmed her by plying her with his own compliments. Most of all, he commended her on her courage in facing the lizard—which he knew to be poisonous, though of course he did not even hint at this. To accompany the meal, there was wine from the Canary Islands, an old Jerez sherry from Lisbon, and potent French brandy.

After dinner, the men retired to Jaime Consuelgo's game room where, to Don Diego's delight, there was a billiard table imported from Portugal. The gray-haired nobleman had often played this game with his father, and after the first several games—in which he showed himself to be completely out of practice—he began to demonstrate a dexterity which won the *alcalde*'s admiration. Lieutenant Cortez was almost as much an expert as the *alcalde* himself. Even Carlos was persuaded to try some practice runs.

The men had brought their brandy and cigars—Carlos politely refusing both—into the game room. Lieutenant Cortez turned to his host while Don Diego was essaying a difficult shot and murmured, "Can you give me any news of the *Indios* in the province ahead, Señor Consuelgo? We go on to Torreón and then into Durango by way of Mapimi, and on into Chihuahua until we reach the border of Nuevo Mexico."

The plump, genial, little man frowned and glanced at Don Diego who, his back to his host, was pondering the strategy necessary for a long run. Then he said in a low voice, "My *peóns* tell me that they have heard of a renegade band of Toboso Indians. They are said to have murdered a *hacendado* and his family, burned the house, and stolen some guns from it."

"That is not good news, Señor Consuelgo. You have seen the two charming ladies who are traveling with us, and I wish to convey them safely to Taos."

"Understandably, Lieutenant. But the *peóns* tell me that there are perhaps at most thirty of these *Indios,* and your troop of fine soldiers is certainly well armed. Even though they succeeded in stealing a few old guns and *pistolas,* they would not have the skill to use them with much effect before your men could annihilate them. At most they have knives, lances, bows, and arrows. Just outside Torreón, as you must know because you have taken this road several times as far as Chihuahua, there are small rolling hills and much cacti, giant species behind which men can hide. Have your men be on guard and go through that region as quickly as you can. Some fifteen miles beyond is the town of Gómez Palacio, and I know that there are some soldiers there. So once you reach Gómez Palacio without danger, you need have no fear."

"I thank you for your information, Señor Consuelgo."

"But," the fat, little man went on, again glancing at Don Diego, "it would be well for you to obtain more ammunition and weapons when you cross into the province of Chihuahua. Those *Indios diablos*—the Apache—often raid the towns there. Many of them have guns which they obtained in the *Estados Unidos* from *gringo* traders—may their souls be accursed for helping those demons ravage our poor people!" He put a finger to his lips as Don Diego, having missed a difficult shot, swore under his breath and turned to face the two men with a resigned shrug.

"What a pity, Don Diego! Never mind, tomorrow evening you will beat me, I am sure. It takes constant practice—I can see that you have considerable skill," the little *alcalde* consoled him as he went back to the table for his own turn.

After the conclusion of the game, Lieutenant Cortez excused himself and went out to the *peóns'* quarters to find Miguel Sandarbal and his four workers. "When we leave here day after tomorrow, Señor," he told Miguel, "it would be well for you and your men to be on the alert against an attack from a band of renegade *Indios*. Señor Consuelgo has just advised me that he has heard of their presence near Torreón. Since you and your men ride at the rear of our party, you may be the ones most exposed to the danger of such an attack."

"I thank you for your warning, Lieutenant Cortez," Miguel Sandarbal responded. "I have shown both Doña Inez and Señorita Catarina how to load the fowling pieces, and there are six of them in the back of the carriage, hidden under a bolster. They are all loaded and ready to use. For myself, I have a Belgian gun and a sabre in my belt as you see, and my four men have sabres and fowling pieces. Don Diego has another gun and it is loaded, too. Have you any idea of the strength of the Indian force, Lieutenant Cortez?"

"I am told that it numbers about thirty. According to Señor Consuelgo, we should be in most danger between Torreón and Gómez Palacio, but once there safely, we can be supplemented by *soldados*. No, the *Indios* would not be strong or bold enough to attack that town."

"I shall tell my men to be on their guard, be sure of that, Lieutenant Cortez. And again, *muchas gracias*."

"*De nada*, Señor Sandarbal. I bid you and your men *buenas noches*."

The next afternoon, wanting a little diversion before continuing their journey, Doña Inez and her niece went to visit some of the picturesque shops of Matamoros. In one of them, a white-haired Mexican woman was selling lace and—as Catarina and her aunt waited their turn to examine the exquisite doilies, mantillas and centerpieces and to ask the prices—they observed that the old shopkeeper was engaged in a dispute with one of the soldiers of her escort. The man was a corporal in his early thirties, with the florid moustache and insolent bearing one might have expected of an officer.

"I will give you *dos pesos*, that is all this wretched work is worth," he rudely declared as he tugged a shawl out of the old woman's hands and fished in the pocket of his trousers for the coins.

"*Perdoneme*, Señor *capitán*," the shopkeeper sought to propitiate him by entitling him as one of high rank, "but it took many hours to make and the material is dear these days. I do not think five *pesos* is too much—"

"But I do, *mujer!*" the corporal sneered as he tossed the coins onto the table and, turning his back on the disconcerted old woman, prepared to leave the shop.

Catarina had overheard this dialogue and recognized the corporal as a man who used his spurs and whip on his horse far too often for her liking. Impulsively, she stepped forward and barred his path. "*Soldado*," she said icily, "you will give the *señora* five *pesos* as she asks, or you'll give back the mantilla and apologize to her for your rudeness. Besides, you had better do that anyway. My father would not like to hear that a soldier of our escort behaves badly to humble folk— and also how badly you treat your gelding. I myself mean to have a word about that with Lieutenant Cortez."

Doña Inez was listening with an appreciative smile. Catarina had suddenly taken on a new stature in her eyes—her niece could indeed think of someone else besides herself.

The corporal flushed hotly, muttered a half-audible apology, then plunged his hand into his pocket and reluctantly placed three more silver pesos before the old woman. "*Gracias*, Señora. I am sorry," he mumbled. Then, to Catarina, with a covert, angry look, "I did not mean to offend you, Señorita. A good day to you and to your esteemed aunt."

With this, he marched out of the shop, and the old woman began to thank Catarina effusively. "There is no need, Seño-ra," the young girl responded. "But your work is so lovely, I could not bear to think of that soldier insulting you. Now, might my aunt and I see some other mantillas? I think I should like one—and you, Tía Inez, I want to buy you one as a present for looking after me so well since we left Madrid."

"My dear child!" Doña Inez was more deeply moved than she cared to show. "But it is only my duty. I pledged that I would care for you after your mother died, Catarina. But I will tell you one thing—in heaven right now, she is very proud of her daughter, and so am I!"

On the forty-seventh day of their journey, Don Diego and his family bade a reluctant farewell to the little *alcalde* of Matamoros and resumed the arduous route to Taos. By late afternoon, they reached Torreón, some twenty miles distant. After spending the night in an unkempt little inn with small and sparsely furnished rooms and food that was almost unpalatable, they continued on their way to Gómez Palacio. There they would be the guests of a recently retired captain who had seen personal service in the viceroy's *palacio*.

About two and a half hours after leaving Torreón, there was a giant clap of thunder and a sudden, but brief, downpour. Lieutenant Cortez had anticipated the bad weather, and his soldiers wore their ponchos to keep their muskets and *pistolas* dry. The air had been humid just before the downpour, and Don Diego had opened one of the windows of the carriage. When the drenching rain abated, Lieutenant Cortez gave the order to proceed, only, a few minutes later, to call an exasperated halt.

Don Diego peered out of the window and called, "*¿Que pasa?*"

"My apologies, Don Diego." The officer bent down from his horse. "One of the wheels of the carriage behind you has come off. But, with luck, it should not take more than an hour to put it back in place. Fortunately, nothing seems to be broken."

"Well, then, there is no real harm done," Don Diego replied.

Six soldiers dismounted and hurried back to the carriage behind the de Escobars to replace the wheel while Miguel, wanting to be helpful, dismounted and told the Corrado brothers to lend the soldiers a hand. It was a heavy wheel and it took the combined efforts of all nine men to put it back into place.

Pedro Garcia and Felipe Gonzalez had reined in their horses and were chatting with each other as they waited for the wheel to be restored. Suddenly Pedro's mouth opened, his eyes bulged, and he slumped forward against the neck of his horse, an arrow between his shoulder blades.

"*¡Guarda! ¡Mi compadre es muerto!*" Felipe cried, tugging on the reins of his horse until the animal, pained by the sharp bit, reared and pawed the air with its front hooves.

Even as he called out, two brown-skinned Toboso Indians wearing dirty red headbands, breechclouts, and sandals, their hair plaited into two long braids framing bony angular faces, rushed from behind a giant cactus. Brandishing their lances, they fell upon the soldiers who were just lifting the wheel of the second carriage back into place. Miguel was first to see them and, cupping a hand to his mouth, bawled out, "*¡Los Indios! ¡Cuidado!*" He drew a fowling piece from his belt, leveled it at the first Indian and pulled the trigger. The renegade staggered back, dropped his lance, and sprawled like a rag doll flung onto the ground. But the second Indian was able to fling his lance into the back of one of the soldiers before José Corrado drew his own fowling piece and shot him through the heart.

From the other side of the road, to the west, there was the sound of a musket shot; the barrel had been poked through a dense thicket of mesquite by a grinning brave, and a soldier standing near Lieutenant Cortez uttered a gurgling cry, put his hand to the spurting blood of the wound in his throat, and toppled backward. Cortez wheeled, drawing a *pistola* from his sash-belt, leveled it at the thicket, and fired; there was a choking cry, and the renegade dropped the musket he had been trying to reload, rolled over onto his back, and lay still. Beside him were two others. One was armed with a lance, the other with a bow and a quiver of arrows slung around his left shoulder. Backing away from the thicket and crouching low, he seized one of the arrows, notched it, and, running out into the open, launched it at the carriage in which the de Escobars rode. The arrow sped through the window which Don Diego had opened and imbedded itself in the wood paneling on the other side, near Catarina's head.

"They are attacking from both sides, Carlos!" Don Diego shouted hoarsely, glancing at his daughter. "Doña Inez, pass me several of those fowling pieces, behind that bolster beside you, and you and Catarina crouch down as far as you can to be out of danger!"

"Oh, we shall all die, I knew we should never have come to this horrible country! *Mi padre,* I want to go back home, please, I cannot stand this any more! It is too awful—those terrible savages—they are going to kill us, I just know they . . ." Catarina had begun to shriek hysterically. She flung herself forward toward her father just as he was trying to aim the wide-bore musket at the mesquite thicket in which he had glimpsed a warrior with a lance.

Doña Inez, forgetting that she might expose herself to danger, moved forward swiftly, seized her niece by the shoulders, and dragged her back beside her. Then, in exasperation, she delivered a fierce slap to Catarina's cheek. "Stop it, you little fool! Now get down there on the floor, you will be safe there! If you start screaming like that again, I shall slap you even harder, I promise you that!"

"T–Tía Inez—you—all right, all right, please do not hit me again!" Catarina babbled, staring incredulously at her aunt's flushed, angry face. She promptly lay down on the floor of the carriage, while the handsome spinster turned to the bolster, delved behind it, and began to hand the fowling pieces to Carlos and Don Diego. At that moment, the Indian with the lance rushed out of the thicket and headed directly toward the de Escobar carriage, his teeth bared in a vicious grimace. He ran at top speed, intent only on killing one of the hated Spaniards before he himself should be slain. Doña Inez gasped, steadied the butt of a long-barreled fowling piece in her right hand, aimed it and pulled the trigger, then closed her eyes. The renegade stumbled, slumped down right in front of the carriage door, and then rolled over onto his belly, his eyes staring in death.

Don Diego lowered his musket and stared open-mouthed at his sister-in-law. He was unable to speak for a moment. Then he gasped, "¡Incredible, maravilloso! I cannot believe what I have just seen—" Then, suddenly realizing the danger which his sister-in-law had so unthinkingly braved, he paled and called out, "Por favor, Doña Inez, get down with Catarina, I beg of you. This is men's work! Carlos, watch that side of the carriage—there should be more of them, they are attacking from both sides!"

Lieutenant Cortez barked hoarse orders, and his men swiftly deployed themselves, a number of them crawling under each carriage with muskets at the ready. Lieutenant Cortez reloaded his pistola and knelt beside his horse, watching for the Toboso warriors to emerge from their hiding places behind the huge cacti which grew like a kind of spreading, malignant garden in this stretch of desert land. The twang of a bowstring sounded now, and another soldier who was scurrying toward one of the carriages yowled with pain as the arrow thudded into his right shoulder. Miguel

Sandarbal had already reloaded his fowling piece and, seeing the Indian who had moved out from behind a cactus to wound the soldier, took quick and careful aim and pulled the trigger. The almost naked Toboso flung his arms up in the air, then pitched forward and lay motionless.

The soldiers under Don Diego's carriage leveled their muskets and rifles toward the east, and those under the second carriage trained their weapons toward the mesquite and cacti on the west. A Toboso bowman rose from behind a mesquite thicket and drew back the bowstring, the muscles of his wiry brown arm strained against the sweating skin. His arrow sped at Jorge Corrado, grazing his right leg. Don Diego squinted along the musket sight and pulled the trigger. The bowman staggered backward, dropped his bow, then clapped both hands to his bleeding belly. He knelt down slowly, bowing his forehead to the earth, and died.

The soldiers' horses had begun to whinny and snort with terror, rearing and pawing the air. Three of them broke away and raced along the road to Gómez Palacio. Another Toboso arrow caught Felipe Gonzalez in his side; immediately one of the soldiers under the second carriage pulled the trigger of his musket and turned the Toboso's face into a bloody, unrecognizable mass.

Suddenly, a dozen Indians burst from behind a huge thicket of mesquite to the northwest. Brandishing lances and stone tomahawks, they headed toward the de Escobars' carriage. Don Diego seized one of the fowling pieces, aimed it, and pulled the trigger. The foremost Toboso dropped in his tracks. The others came suicidally on, their faces twisted in grimaces of murderous hate. One of them flung his tomahawk, and the sharp edge sank into the door of Don Diego's carriage. The soldiers opened fire, and four of the charging renegades fell dead or mortally wounded. One of the others, the tallest and lithest of the dozen, raced on with a frenzied burst of speed, his lance gripped in both hands. Carlos grabbed one of the fowling pieces that lay on the rear seat of the carriage and quickly fired at the renegade, but the weapon was jammed. With a howl of rage, the Toboso thrust the lance at Diego's young son. Carlos flung himself back to escape the deadly point, then drew his rapier and, with a single lunge, transfixed the renegade in the chest. The dying Toboso's eyes widened, glaring insanely at Carlos. Then, as the latter wrenched out the bloody blade, the Indian fell backward and lay still upon the sandy ground.

Miguel and the two Corrado brothers knelt down and fired fowling pieces and muskets at the other attackers, and the soldiers under Don Diego's carriage fired a deafening volley. The renegades were cut down before they could reach the carriage.

"*Teniénte, Teniénte,* the rest are running away to the hills!" one of the soldiers under the carriage called.

It was true. Only a handful of the band of renegades had survived the effective and courageous defense of the soldiers and the de Escobars themselves. Crawling out from under the carriages, the ten soldiers knelt down and fired at the fleeing Tobósos, but they were, by now, almost out of range. One of them stumbled, then began to hobble, and two of his companions steadied him and helped him ascend the rising slope until, at last, they disappeared behind the cacti.

"Don Diego, I pray God that none of you was hurt," Lieutenant Cortez panted as he straightened, his face damp with sweat.

"By the grace of the good Lord, we have come through without a scratch," Don Diego's voice was hoarse and trembling. Then, setting aside the musket, he reached down to lift his sobbing daughter and to take her onto his knee as if she were still a little child. "Do not cry, *muchachita,* it is all over now. Just forget it—it is like a bad dream. And none of us is hurt, eternal thanks to God and all the saints!"

As he comforted her, making soft shushing sounds till her sobs finally began to diminish, he stared at Doña Inez. She had sunk against the upholstered backrest of her seat, very pale, her eyes closed and a trembling hand pressed against her forehead.

"You are as brave, my sister-in-law," he said softly, "as any man I have ever known. I, Don Diego de Escobar, salute you as a *compadre* on the battlefield."

Then, leaning toward the window, he said to Lieutenant Cortez, "if you have a little *aguardiente*—perhaps some of your men carry leather flasks on their marches—I think Doña Inez would appreciate it."

TWENTY-FOUR

Lieutenant Cortez detailed four soldiers to bury their dead companions as well as young Pedro Garcia, who had been the first to fall to the Toboso attack. Don Diego, standing with Carlos beside the graves, crossed himself and murmured a prayer, then turned to Miguel. "When you stop in Chihuahua to buy the flock and recruit more workers for us, Miguel, please see to it that two hundred pesos are sent to Pedro's family."

"It will be done, Don Diego, I give you my word."

The Spanish nobleman turned to his son. "You were *muy macho, mi hijo*. I am very proud of you—but sorrowful that it was necessary to take human life. Those poor *Indios* had no reason to hate us. Perhaps there is a lesson here. When we reach Taos, you and I shall strive to treat the Indians of the pueblo as befits men of good will. In that way, we shall both cleanse our hearts of any prejudice or hatred we may have learned when we were very young."

"*Si, mi padre*. Miguel has told me that those who attacked us were renegades from their tribe, and that the Toboso are mainly at peace with white men. I would not condemn all of them because of the act of a few."

"You talk like a man, Carlos. It heartens me greatly. Now,

be very gentle with your little sister. Try to drive away her terror of this attack by being the affectionate brother. And above all, do not tease her too much."

"I shall not, *mi padre.*"

"*¡Bueno!* Now, since the wheel has been repaired, let us go on to Gómez Palacio."

From Gómez Palacio to the city of Chihuahua was a journey of over three hundred miles. It was on April 22, 1808, that Lieutenant Cortez and his troop reached it. By then, on the other side of the world, the ambitious Corsican had invaded Spain, Charles IV had abdicated in favor of his son Ferdinand, and both father and son were summoned by Napoleon and compelled to renounce the throne. Ferdinand was imprisoned, and Napoleon's brother Joseph installed as king of Spain.

At Chihuahua, the de Escobars stayed for four days and four nights at the home of the cordial *alcalde,* Hernando Villapuesta, before resuming their journey to Taos. Miguel Sandarbal stayed behind, with Felipe Gonzalez and the Corrado brothers. Miguel had already met a wealthy sheep owner who was on the verge of retirement and more than willing to dispose of most of his flock, if the price could be agreed upon.

Shrewd in the ways of the world, the former gardener indicated his interest in the flock and declared that he would settle the transaction within the next several days. This done, he and his three workers went to a local *posada* which he had been told sheepherders and *peóns* frequented. There he met Teofilo Rosas, a short, plump, and jovial man in his early thirties. Over several glasses of strong *pulque,* the two men became cordial acquaintances, and Teofilo Rosas soon impressed Miguel as a man who knew all there was to know about sheep. He had worked with them from his boyhood, and he knew their breeding habits and their worth.

"*Si,* Miguel," he declared, "it is true that Señor Corbazon has a fine flock. But he is charging you too much. At the price he is asking, you ought to be allowed to select the ewes and rams you favor. Do not take the entire flock, *amigo.* You will do well with about five hundred. They will multiply quickly once you give them plenty of land to graze on."

"Don Diego will have five thousand acres in Taos, Teofilo."

"That is certainly enough for five hundred good sheep, and you should triple your flock in two years' time if they stay healthy. Besides, I know this man, Miguel. Let me go with you tomorrow, and between the two of us, we will get you the best ones at a fair price."

Early the next afternoon, Miguel Sandarbal and his new friend Teofilo Rosas paid a visit to the *hacienda* of Emiliano Corbazon, a tall, stooped man in his early sixties, who cordially welcomed his former *peón* and Miguel. He insisted that they enjoy a cigar and some *aguardiente* before getting down to the business of looking at his flock.

"I look forward to spending what few years I have left in Almería, where I was born. How beautiful it is, on the great Mediterranean, with sun, blue sky, and water, instead of this dusty desert of Chihuahua where I have spent so many years." He chuckled nostalgically and raised his glass. Miguel and Teofilo emulated him, politely wishing him long, happy years. *"Gracias, amigos.* Now, let us go see the flock. My sheep are hardy, Señor Sandarbal, and they will easily stand the long drive to Taos. Now, come!"

At the back of the *hacienda*, several of the old manservants had brought up saddled horses. Emiliano Corbazon invited Miguel and Teofilo to ride with him to the broad stretch of land where his flock grazed. "I have in all a thousand sheep—perhaps a few more than that, since my rams are vigorous and my ewes responsive—that is their nature." He gave them a ribald wink.

"I had thought, Señor Corbazon, of buying about five hundred," Miguel tactfully interposed.

"Well, I suppose I cannot expect you to take the entire flock—although I would prefer it. Well, come along, you may see for yourself what I have. Naturally, a ram brings more *pesos* than a ewe."

"Naturally," Miguel agreed with a smile, while Teofilo Rosas favored his new friend with a broad wink.

"There, you see them. Of course, we have already had our spring shearing." The old man gestured toward the flock in the distance. "But they will have their wool back again by the time you drive them into Taos, at least enough to protect them from the colder weather that is sure to come with winter." He eyed Miguel shrewdly and demanded, "Of the five hundred that you wish to buy, how many will be rams and how many ewes?"

On this point, Miguel had already solicited Teofilo's opinion, so he was well prepared. "One ram for every fifteen ewes, Señor Corbazon."

"*Caramba,* you know something about sheep, it would appear!" the old man cackled gleefully. "Now, if you had shown me that you knew nothing, I might have been a rogue and tried to sell you as many rams as ewes. Then, I fear, you would have problems with your flock, is that not so, Teofilo?"

"*Ciertamente,* Señor Corbazon," the Mexican replied.

For the next several hours, Miguel and Teofilo inspected the placid animals, and the ingenious Teofilo marked with a piece of charcoal those sheep which he advised Miguel to select. This was not accomplished without a good many genial but guileful attempts on the old man's part to urge Miguel to choose this one over that one. But Teofilo came to Miguel's aid at such times, saying "No, no, Señor Corbazon, you know yourself this old ram has no *cojones* left. Now, this one beside him, that is a different matter. Any ewe he mounts will be sure to have a lamb in five months."

"You rascal, perhaps I was wrong in giving you your freedom so soon. Now you are trying to spoil my sale to Señor Sandarbal," his former master wryly rebuked him. Then he shrugged philosophically. "Well, what does it matter, after all, Señores? I am only sorry, Teofilo, that I cannot persuade your friend to take the whole flock so that I can leave for my beloved Almería all the sooner. Well now, you have marked your five hundred well enough, Señor Sandarbal. Now to the price. I should say six silver pesos for each ram and four for each ewe."

Miguel had brought along a sturdy leather pouch which had been given to him by Don Diego filled with silver pesos from the bank of Mexico City. He glanced at Teofilo, who surreptitiously shook his head and held up first four fingers and then two. Miguel took his cue, pursing his lips and frowning. "That is more than I was prepared to pay, Señor Corbazon. I had thought of four pesos for each ram and two for each ewe."

"Oh, had you now?" The old man glared at Teofilo Rosas, who rolled his eyes and adopted an innocent expression as he remained silent. "I see the scoundrel has been telling you how anxious I am to get back to Almería. Well then, for a quick sale, and since the sun is getting too hot to sit here on our horses talking business, I shall agree to it. But, since I have given you the privilege of choosing the very finest animals of my flock, the least you can do is to add another fifty pesos."

Miguel Sandarbal nodded. In his opinion, even with that

added premium, he was paying a fair price for an excellent flock. "Agreed, Señor Corbazon."

"¡Bueno! Now, you may be able to recruit some good workers from the people who have spent so many years here with me, and you will find others, I am sure, here in Chihuahua. Besides, I am certain Teofilo will help you there, just as he has swindled away the best of my sheep."

"Oh, Señor Patrón," Teofilo protested, "after your kindness to me, I swear by all the saints I would never try to swindle you!"

"Get along with you, you rogue, you rascal, you unmitigated scoundrel! I know your tricks. But then, you served me well, and there is no reason why you should not make a good bargain for yourself. Let us go back to my house and seal our bargain. You will stay for supper, Señor Sandarbal?"

"You are most kind, Señor Corbazon. It will be my pleasure."

The very next morning, Miguel and Teofilo Rosas returned to the *hacienda* and, after paying their respects to Emiliano Corbazon, went out into the fields to talk with his *peóns*. Teofilo had agreed to work for Don Diego de Escobar at the wages of twenty pesos a month, and as they rode out to the fields, he remarked, "Now, since it was I who aided you in obtaining the very best rams and ewes of my former *patrón's* flock, and since also I am the first you have engaged to go to Taos with you, Miguel, I think it only right that I should have the highest wages. Besides, I know these good men and their families. They would be eager to leave Chihuahua. So I think that if you offer the six best of the lot—and of course I will tell you who these are—fifteen pesos a month, it would be quite enough."

Miguel could not help laughing at this suggestion. "Very well, Teofilo," he replied, "it is true I owe you something for your inestimable help."

"I thank you, Miguel. And do not worry, I will not boast of it. Now, let us get off our horses and go talk with Juan Ortiz—that tall one with the huge mustache. He shears sheep even better than I do, and that is the highest praise I can give any man in Chihuahua."

Juan Ortiz brightened at the prospect of employment in Taos and readily agreed to accompany Miguel Sandarbal. He was nearly forty, direct of manner and practical as well. After he had shaken hands with Miguel, he took off his sombrero, twisted it about in his hands for a moment, and then suggested, "Señor Sandarbal, your *patrón* will need a cook in the *hacienda*, is that not so?"

"Why, yes, it is," Miguel nodded.

"My wife, Margarita, can make even *frijoles* and *tacos* taste like food for the angels, Señor Sandarbal. And what she does with *carne asada* is a little miracle." Juan Ortiz rolled his eyes and smacked his lips.

"If that is true, I will engage her as cook for my *patrón* and his family. But she will be on trial, and she will have to please them. They come from Madrid, and they are used to fine meals," Miguel warned.

"Margarita could please the viceroy himself, Señor Sandarbal," Juan stoutly declared. "I count myself as the most fortunate of men that such a woman is my *esposa*. We have two *niños*, but then you did not say that we could bring our families, Señor Sandarbal?"

"Oh that is understood, *amigo*," Miguel chuckled.

Again they shook hands, and then Miguel and Teofilo rode on until the latter pointed out another likely recruit.

"That is Esteban Morales, Miguel," Teofilo murmured as the two men dismounted. "He is always full of jokes, always happy, works hard, and hopes to make enough money to marry his *novia*, Concepción Alfindar. He has a way with sheep, that one, and he is brave too."

"Then he is a valuable man to have with us," Miguel agreed.

It did not take Esteban Morales long to agree to terms, particularly when Miguel hinted that the wages of fifteen silver pesos a month should surely impress Concepción.

By noontime, Miguel, relying not only on Teofilo's opinion but also his own instinct, had engaged four more *peóns* and their families to follow him and the sheep to Taos. These were Porfirio Locada, Manuel Miraflores, Sebastiano Cardenas, and Benito Romigar—the first three being sheepherders and the last not only an accomplished horseman but also an excellent carpenter. Porfirio and Manuel were in their late thirties, both married and each with two little daughters; Sebastiano, thirty-one, had a four-year-old son; and Benito, an affable, wiry, little man of forty-six, had two boys and two girls. This family solidarity impressed Miguel, for it was his desire to hire those who would be loyal and likely to link their own futures with that of Don Diego.

When he and Teofilo returned from the fields, Miguel

informed Emiliano Corbazon of his choice and received the old man's approval. He cordially invited them to keep him company at supper, and Miguel and Teofilo gratefully accepted. When they finally left the *hacienda* late that evening, Miguel turned to Teofilo and expressed a thought that concerned him greatly. "I ask myself, Teofilo, what protection these men and their families, and you and I shall have, driving five hundred sheep from here to Taos—a journey of almost six hundred miles."

"Ah, Miguel, here again I can help you," Teofilo retorted with a broad grin. "Two years ago, Señor Corbazon entrusted me with helping drive three hundred sheep into Ciudad Juárez, and thence to Las Cruces, which is in Nuevo Mexico. There were eight other *peóns* who went with me, and we were armed. But we had no trouble from the *Indios*. Besides, didn't you tell me yourself you planned to hire more men here in Chihuahua? I know a few who have fought the *Indios* and lived to tell about it. Also, there is an old gunsmith here in Chihuahua, and with your silver *pesos* you can buy some very good guns and *pistolas* and plenty of ammunition to protect you."

"That is good advice, Teofilo. Tomorrow evening, you and I shall go back to that *posada* where we met, and you will point these men out to me, if they are there. And, in the afternoon, we shall visit this gunsmith you speak of. I shall buy some horses, also, for the two of us—and our workers, will they need them?"

"Perhaps those you will meet at the *posada*. But these men you have seen in the fields today, they all own burros and they have carts. It's a pity we can not get the sheep to move as fast as horses."

Miguel chuckled. "In my opinion, if we travel ten miles a day, we shall be doing well."

"That is about right, Miguel—maybe even eight miles. So we shall arrive in Taos by early July."

"That is what I am thinking, too. Well then, I shall go back to my men from Mexico City, and you to your little hut, and we shall meet again tomorrow. *¡Buenas noches,* Teofilo!"

"And to you, also, Miguel."

On the last day of May, 1808, Don Diego and his family, with their military escort, entered the town of Santa Fe. This thriving capital of Nuevo Mexico, which boasted nearly five thousand citizens of Spanish blood, seemed drab at first sight, with its squat, whitewashed buildings. The universal building material was adobe, sun-dried earth laid up in walls three feet thick and roofed over with still more adobe, supported by horizontal timber poles. The palace of the governor, Joaquin del Real Alencaster, and the church were the largest and most imposing buildings of all and the only ones with glazed windows. Yet even these were only a single story.

In the central section of Santa Fe was the plaza, row upon row of single-story adobe buildings compactly set together. This arrangement originated out of sheer necessity as a protection against the marauding Apache and Comanche bands who had, in the early days of Nuevo Mexico, massacred many isolated homesteaders. In 1772, Governor Pedro Fermín de Mendinueta had urged his colonists to imitate the peaceful pueblo Indians and form communities in plazas so that a few men could defend themselves against many.

Beyond the plaza, Santa Fe seemed much more haphazardly constructed. There were no clearly defined streets or regular pattern of houses. Carlos mentioned this to his father, and Don Diego smiled and replied, "The viceroy explained to me that we Spaniards cherish our privacy and prefer ample space between our neighbors. It makes for more gracious living— you will see in due course when we arrive at our own new home."

Although he was visibly weary from the long journey, Don Diego could at last look upon the brighter side of things. The journey from Chihuahua to Santa Fe had been without incident. Just before they crossed the Rio Grande they had seen a band of Apache, but the presence of the well-armed and well-disciplined troops evidently frightened them off. The roads were quite passable, although the elevation of Santa Fe was seven thousand feet.

The viceroy had told Don Diego that there was only about a foot of rainfall a year in Santa Fe. The rivers were fed by melting snow from the mountains, and the colonists had learned how to tap these watercourses to irrigate their crops. They used techniques learned centuries before from Spain's Moorish conquerers.

During their trip from Chihuahua to Santa Fe, Don Diego had noticed that the hillsides were covered with grama grass, a short pale growth, very different from the verdant, green grass of Spain's countryside or in the tropical jungles between Vera Cruz and Mexico City. Again, the viceroy, singularly well informed for a military man, had told him that this grass was rich in nutrients for sheep and cattle, even when burned dry by winter sun and wind. Sheep, however, were far better suited than cattle to this mountainous terrain, and there was another virtue in having sheep rather than cattle: even if Indian raiders occasionally stole a few head or sometimes even slaughtered a flock to harass the Spaniards, the animals could not be stolen in large numbers because it was difficult to round them up and drive them away.

Before he had left Chihuahua, Don Diego had closeted himself with Miguel Sandarbal. He found that Miguel had adapted to his new situation with dedication and enthusiasm and had already learned that wool was traded and sold almost exclusively to Mexico. The only trails from Santa Fe ran south, back into that country. Supply trains of ox-drawn, two-wheeled *carretas* took two months to carry merchandise such as sugar, coffee, hardware, and textiles up from Chihuahua. Other trains, bringing military equipment and ammunition from Mexico City, took five months to complete the eighteen-hundred-mile journey. There was hardly any communication with either the Texans or the Californians.

The following January, the annual fair would be held in Chihuahua. It would provide Don Diego with a splendid opportunity to make himself known as an astute sheep rancher. Every January, the Spaniards of Nuevo Mexico renewed ties with their countrymen at that fair—bargaining, gambling, celebrating, and trading. Wagon trains of coffee and chocolate from South America were sent to Chihuahua from Mexico City along with silk hats and gloves from China, jewelry from the Philippines, and stationery, utensils, arms, and ammunition from Europe.

Pondering all of this information during the last stage of his journey across the Mexican border, Don Diego began to perceive the latent opportunities of this new life. He realized that, in order to bring these opportunities to fruition, he would have to make use of his own ingenuity, as well as the loyalty and industry of his workers. Gradually he felt his ties to his Spanish heritage loosening. By now, his connection with Madrid and with the throne seemed almost non-existent.

Doña Inez had observed him critically from time to time, without his being aware of it, during the last week of their trip to Santa Fe. She, perhaps better than anyone else, understood the conflict that was stirring within him. She knew he felt abandoned, set down in a strange, primitive, and even savage new world without any past to bind him. On the other hand, the rugged vigor which the countryside itself seemed to demand of those inhabitants brave enough to survive its perils and hardships presented him with an intriguing challenge. It was, indeed, as if he would begin life anew; and it would be, she realized, a life of continual adaptation. It was Doña Inez's private opinion that nothing could be more sanguine for all of them. She hoped that, in these new surroundings, she would be able to make him see that she could and would be more than aunt to his children, and more than sister-in-law to him.

Don Diego and his family remained two days in Santa Fe, as guests of Governor Real Alencaster, to whom Don Diego presented the viceroy's letter. He was officially welcomed by the governor as the new intendant of Taos. His interview with the governor sobered Don Diego and reinforced his awareness of a vast disparity between this isolated colony and the royal court of Madrid. Apart from the Franciscan friars, Nuevo Mexico had no professional class. There were the very poor, and the very rich, and between these two social strata existed a mere handful of metal craftsmen, leatherworkers, carpenters, and artisans. Their tools were crude and improvised, and they had little opportunity for trade and commerce which would have improved their skills. There were no lawyers, and in criminal matters the *alcalde* functioned as both judge and jury. Infrequently, a doctor would visit Taos or Santa Fe and sometimes stay as long as a year before moving on; but no trained physicians anywhere in New Mexico had set up practice on a permanent basis. There were no public schools and very few private teachers. As Governor Real Alencaster pointed out, a *rico* who wished his heir to be educated might send him to Mexico City or to Madrid, or turn the boy over to the Franciscans for instructions. Girls, even the daughters of the wealthy, were educated only in the household arts.

As for the poor, they subsisted almost entirely on the produce of their irrigated gardens and the milk and flesh of sheep and goats. They lived in adobe homes, known as *jacales,* and the dimensions of those crude houses were determined by the length of roof poles that a man could cut from the scrubby trees nearby. Of course, a *rico* could dwell in more spacious surroundings. He could afford to send woodcutters to fetch longer poles from timber in the mountains.

When Don Diego sought information on the area around

Taos, the bluff, hearty governor smiled sadly. "You will find perhaps two thousand Spaniards in Taos, Don Diego. In many ways, it is even more primitive than Santa Fe. You will arrive there in good time for the annual August fair, which will be celebrating its thirtieth anniversary. In the early days, the Comanche, Ute, and Navaho came into Taos with pieces of chamois, many buffalo skins, and, from the plunder which they obtained elsewhere, horses, muskets, munitions, knives, and meat. The Spaniards at Pecos came to Taos with blankets, beads, and other trade goods, as well as what surplus they could spare from their farms and pastures. That, indeed, is how Taos was settled and how it grew. Yet today, it prospers, and we do not have too much to fear from the Indians. Those of the pueblo who have settled among us and who have become Christianized have turned to simple crafts and produce articles for commerce among us. Some of them have even created works of art for our churches."

When he took his leave of Governor Real Alencaster on the morning of the third day, Don Diego de Escobar reflected somberly on the future. To have come from the brilliance and luxury of Madrid to a dusty town inhabited by peaceful Indians and impoverished *peóns* was punishment indeed. For one self-pitying moment, he wondered if he should not have taken his personal fortune and gone to Portugal, or even Italy, where there was still some vestige of culture and society. Now he was to become no more than a backwoods collector of royal taxes.

And what of Carlos and Catarina? His gifted son, so full of vibrant life, so much the man already and so fearless a horseman—Carlos had ridden most of the way on horseback from Chihuahua to Santa Fe!—was the last of the de Escobars. Into what high-born family could Carlos expect to marry? And how could Catarina, whose impressionable mind had been grounded in the rich Spanish culture of Madrid, find an *esposo* worthy of her?

Having said his farewells, Don Diego de Escobar handed Doña Inez into the carriage and took his place beside her with a heavy heart. Carlos had already swung into the saddle of his mount and had ridden up to Lieutenant Cortez, his handsome face aglow with anticipation of the end of their seemingly endless journey. If only he had Carlos's energy and enthusiasm, Don Diego thought. But that was because the boy was young, and did not realize yet all the hidden overtones of this abrupt change of fortune.

He sighed deeply, took out a silver snuff box, and resorted to it while Doña Inez eyed him solicitiously. For her, the journey had been both wearisome and exhilarating. She rejoiced inwardly that she, a spinster, had come so far and seen so much that was new and strange and wondrous, albeit terrifying at times. Because she could believe in the future and hope for it, she did not count her life finished. On the contrary, she was poignantly eager for it to begin

TWENTY-FIVE

Three days after leaving Santa Fe, Lieutenant Cortez and his men escorted Don Diego's carriage into the town of Taos. It was a bright, sunny afternoon and the Sangre de Cristo mountains were visible to the east. To the west was the majestic northern tributary of the mighty Rio Grande. Don Diego's heart sank. Taos, by comparison, was even shabbier and smaller than Santa Fe. Doña Inez turned to watch him and saw again his disappointment in the dullness of his eyes and the severe tightening of his lips.

The military escort had been halted on the outskirts of the town, and Lieutenant Cortez rode back to the carriage to tell Don Diego that their journey was at last at an end. "That is the *casa* which your predecessor, Juan de Morena, occupied, Don Diego. The viceroy ordered me to convey you to the house of the *alcalde,* Don Sancho de Pladero, knowing that you could not be expected to take up residence in such shabby quarters."

Don Diego peered out through the window of the carriage and disconsolately shook his head. What he saw was a large adobe house, wide and deep, but already crumbling into ruins. A vision of his luxurious estate in Madrid swept back into his mind with an almost overpowering sense of loss. "It is hardly a good omen, Lieutenant Cortez," he observed with a shrug. "Well, it seems that I have no choice but to throw myself upon the hospitality of the *alcalde*."

"You need not disturb yourself, Don Diego," Lieutenant Cortez answered courteously. "I personally know him to be a man of great warmth and understanding. Under his regime as *alcalde* there has been no trouble with the *Indios*, and he administers the town's affairs with justice and compassion. It is only a few minutes from here to his estate, and you will be warmly welcome, I assure you."

"That is heartening news indeed, Lieutenant," Don Diego replied slowly. "Yet, all the same, it places me in the position of a beggar seeking alms."

"Why, not at all, Don Diego," Doña Inez interposed. "After all, you are his superior by appointment of the king himself. Do not forget, he is a *Madrileño* like yourself, and you will have much in common with him."

"I suppose that is true," Don Diego mused. Then, with a wry face, he added, "All the same, beggars can hardly be choosers. Yet I confess that at this moment I am selfish enough to long for some little comfort after our prolonged journey."

"It will only be a few minutes, Don Diego," Lieutenant Cortez assured him. Then, doffing his plumed hat and bowing from his saddle to both Doña Inez and Catarina, he rode back to the head of the troop and gave the order to proceed.

As they rode through the dusty town, Don Diego could observe the same compact pueblo in the square formation that he had seen in Santa Fe; and then, further off, the familiar, distantly spaced houses of those more fortunate. On the other side of the town, they came to a huge, one-story *casa* made of adobe and strongly reinforced with timbers. It was in the shape of a kind of divided rectangle, in the center of which was a flowery patio flanked by a narrow enclosed passageway which united both long halves of the rectangle. Beyond this imposing dwelling and to the north stood the huts of workers and sheepherders, and beyond these, a broad stretch of grazing land for the sheep.

The driver of the coach clambered down from his perch and opened the door to help Don Diego and his family descend. Doña Inez was first to step down, looking around her with eager interest and a smile on her handsome face. "Why, it is like a palace, even compared with the *haciendas* we have stopped at since we left Mexico City, Don Diego," she announced. Catarina was next, carefully holding her silver cage and peering at Pepito. Carlos himself handed his father down. Lieutenant Cortez, having dismounted, bowed low to the de Escobars and then strode to the door of the *casa* of Don Sancho de Pladero, reached for the handpull of a silver bell mounted on the door, and yanked it vigorously.

After a moment, the door was opened by a white-haired, deferential Mexican servant dressed in red waistcoat and black *pantalones* who, recognizing the officer, beamed and exclaimed, "¡*Bienvenido, Teniente* Cortez!"

"¿*Cómo está*, Augustín?" Lieutenant Cortez cordially replied. "Is your *patrón* at home? If he is, would you be kind enough to tell him that the new intendant of Taos, Don Diego de Escobar, awaits his pleasure?"

"At once, *Teniente!* He is just finishing his *siesta*. I shall go tell him." The old man bobbed his head and hurried back into the house. A few moments later, a genial, rather corpulent man of fifty with sparse gray hair and an elaborate mustache emerged. The old servant followed him. "Ah, it is you, *Teniente* Cortez, welcome to Taos!" he exclaimed cordially. Then, seeing Don Diego, he advanced toward the carriage, a gracious smile on his plump face, and extended his hand. "¡*Bienvenido a Taos, Excelencia!* The viceroy wrote to me months ago, telling me to expect Juan de Morena's successor, and, just yesterday, I received a courier from *el gobernador* at Santa Fe who informed me of your appointment. I am your servant!"

"Not that at all, Don Sancho!" Don Diego clasped the *alcalde*'s hand and shook it warmly. "Say rather that I have the honor of being associated with you. His Excellency, General José de Iturrigaray, has already told me of your inestimable services to the crown. I look forward to the privilege of working with you on the administration of this province."

"You are most kind, Don Diego. But you and your family must be exhausted after your long journey from Mexico City. Augustín! See to it that rooms are prepared for my guests."

"At once, *Patrón*," the white-haired servant replied.

"My house is yours, Don Diego. Please do me the honor of entering it. Ah, this must be your son—what a fine, strong, young man, and how well he carries himself with that rapier at his side!"

Don Diego's somber features relaxed into a warm smile. This compliment to his son was a ready anodyne to the fretful misgivings that had returned to harass his mind upon their entry into Taos. "Yes, Don Sancho, this is *mi hijo,* Carlos. I may say that when we were attacked by *Indios* near Torreón, he valiantly defended us."

Carlos flushed with embarrassment and stepped forward to shake the *alcalde*'s hand. "I am honored to meet you, Don Sancho."

"This is my daughter, Catarina." Don Diego turned to the black-haired girl with a smile of paternal pride, and gestured to her to come forward.

"She is very beautiful, Don Diego," Don Sancho de Pladero exclaimed. To Catarina's delight, he took her hand and kissed it as if it were that of a princess.

"And this is my sister-in-law, Doña Inez de Castillana." Don Diego stepped back toward Doña Inez and offered her his arm, which she took with a quick smile of pleasure as she advanced toward the beaming *alcalde*.

"You honor my poor house, Doña Inez. I bid you welcome to Taos." Don Sancho bowed to the handsome, brown-haired spinster and kissed her hand even more effusively. Lowering her eyes, Doña Inez could not suppress a quick, self-conscious blush.

"I'm told you are a *Madrileño* like myself, Don Diego," Don Sancho remarked as he escorted the Spanish nobleman into the spacious living room. "We shall have much to talk about."

The elderly servant had returned and now approached his master to announce, "Doña Elena wishes me to tell you that the rooms are ready for your guests, *Patrón*."

"Thank you, Augustín. My steward will show you and your family to your rooms, Don Diego. I shall have my servants take your baggage from the carriage. You will want to take a *siesta*, and my wife, I am sure, has already given instructions to our cook for dinner to be served tonight after you have rested sufficiently from your journey. Doña Elena and I both look forward to hearing your news of Madrid over the dinner table."

"You are most kind, and I am deeply grateful for your hospitality, Don Sancho," Don Diego replied. "I had hoped to move into my predecessor's house, but the viceroy advised me that it was in a deplorable state—which I saw for myself as we entered Taos. It distresses me. . . ."

"Please, Don Diego," Don Sancho interrupted, "I am only distressed that Taos can offer you no proper shelter. As I have already said, my house is yours. I insist that you and your family remain as our honored guests until such time as a proper dwelling can be constructed."

"That is most gracious of you, but I have no wish to impose upon your hospitality and to disarrange your household, Don Sancho."

"Be sure that we have rooms enough to accommodate you, and it is I who regret the inconvenience to which the new intendant of Taos must necessarily be subjected. As you know, we have had our shearing this spring, and my *trabajadores* have little to occupy them at the moment. It would be my pleasure to lend them to you to help build your new house in Taos, Don Diego."

"I am overwhelmed at such generosity, Don Sancho," Don Diego almost stammered. "I have had my foreman engage workers and sheepherders in Chihuahua, and they should be here within a month, if God wills it, together with the flock of sheep he has purchased."

"Until then, I shall lend you my own men to begin the work, Don Diego. Ah, so you and I shall be friendly competitors in a sense, then. I pride myself upon my own extensive flock, and here again my workers will be only too happy to instruct yours in the proper caring of these docile animals, in the event they reqūre it. And now, I keep you from your *siesta*. Doña Elena and I look forward to meeting you all at dinner." With a gracious little bow, the *alcalde* took his leave of Don Diego and his family.

There could be no doubt that Don Sancho de Pladero had prospered during his twenty years as *alcalde* of Taos. Though his *hacienda* was constructed of the same unburnt adobe brick with which Don Diego was fast becoming all too familiar, its furnishings were opulent. There were well over twenty rooms, all opening onto the central patio. There was a small garden, also, beyond the walled-in connective passageway. The floors were puncheon, the interior walls were papered with calico, and the windows decorated with crimson worsted curtains. In Don Sancho's own study there was a massive table topped with white marble and a gilt-framed mirror, as well as a teakwood secretary. There was also an exquisite little chapel.

The beds in each of the guest rooms were assuredly the most comfortable Don Diego and his family had enjoyed since they had left Madrid. And there were fine Brussels carpets on the floors of these guests rooms, and commodious dressers. The dining room furnishings were equally elaborate —with a long table that could seat twenty if need be, the finest silverware and napkins, and a lace tablecloth. There were cut-glass goblets for wine, and plates of delft. As Don Diego seated himself for dinner, his eyes widened with wonder at such luxury. Don Sancho explained, "I promised my good wife, Doña Elena, when we left Madrid, that I should make certain she enjoyed the same advantages here as we had there. It is true these things you see took months and even years to bring by *carreta* from Mexico City, but the waiting only added to our enjoyment. Is that not true, *querida?*"

The woman to whom the plump *alcalde* addressed himself was tall. At forty-one, her black hair was graying slightly and was coiled in an imposing mass at the back of her head. She wore a black silk gown, and around her thin neck was the chain of a golden crucifix. Her face was prim and disapproving, with a nose that was almost bony, and a large but thin-lipped mouth. Her gray-green eyes became piercing as she spoke with slow emphasis, pausing between sentences to glance around at those who were listening, as if she wished to detect their reaction to her words. To Don Sancho's almost bubbling vivacity of speech, she offered a dampening and restraining austerity. Don Diego had the impression that she was shrewish, and, indeed, that all this ostentation and wealth had not yet compensated her for having had to leave Madrid.

Across the table from Catarina sat Tomás de Pladero, Don Sancho and Doña Elena's only child. At eighteen, he was an amiable young man, about five feet ten inches in height and stocky of build, with black hair and pleasant features. Catarina smiled at him and inclined her head like a young princess when she was introduced to him. "It is a pleasure to meet you, Señorita Catarina," he responded in a soft, low voice.

At this, his mother, from the other end of the table, spoke sharply. "Speak up so everyone may hear you, Tomás! You are almost a grown man now, not a boy." Then, as if to apologize for him, she addressed herself to Don Diego. "We do not often have such distinguished visitors here, Don Deigo, so you must forgive my son's shyness." At this, Don Sancho closed his eyes and compressed his lips for a moment, then cheerily broke in with, "*Querida*, would you not ring the bell so that our servants may serve *la comida?* Our guests must be hungry."

His wife sent him a swift, almost pitying glance and then

replied condescendingly, "But of course, *mi esposo*. I should be the very last to wish to have our guests complain about the hospitality of the de Pladeros." She reached for the silver handbell, lifted it, and rang it peremptorily. At once, servants entered the room carrying platters of roasted mutton and potatoes, stewed rabbit cooked with herbs, and an imposing roast of beef. The old steward carefully filled the goblets with Madeira from a superbly wrought decanter and supervised his subordinates' service of his master's family and their guests throughout the dinner.

When it was over, Don Sancho invited Don Diego to take brandy with him in his study, while Doña Elena invited Doña Inez, Catarina, and Carlos to tour the huge *hacienda*. Tomás went back to his room to read. Once inside the study, Don Sancho poured a generous portion of fine French brandy and tendered it to his guest. "Would you care for a *cigarrillo*, Don Diego?" he inquired.

"A *cigarrillo*?" Don Diego echoed.

"Oh yes, this is our universal, petty vice. Everyone smokes here in Nuevo Mexico, yes, even the *niños*. But, of course, so long as Mexico is loyal to the Spanish crown, the sale of tobacco is the king's monopoly. Therefore, we do not try to raise the tobacco weed privately for fear it will be confiscated. And if the viceroy showed you any of the revenue reports collected from the provinces, you must have observed that the tariff on the tobacco weed is extraordinarily high."

"Yes, I observed that."

Don Sancho had opened an inlaid box, and begun to roll tobacco in a piece of cornhusk. With an almost fatuous smile, he explained, "This is the way a *vaquero* does it, Don Diego. He can roll and light the *cigarrillo* with one hand while he rides at full gallop. Try the brandy, it is really superb. Now then, I hope you are somewhat rested from your tiresome journey."

"Thanks to the comforts you and your charming wife have so graciously extended my family and me, indeed I am, Don Sancho."

The portly *alcalde* held up a hand. "First of all, it is my duty, but most of all, it is my pleasure. You will embarrass me if you continue to thank me for it, Don Diego. Tomorrow I shall talk with José Ramirez, my *capataz*, and tell him to send a dozen of my *trabajadores* to begin the construction on your hacienda. They will start by tearing down that old ruin of poor Morena's, and they will be able to recover some of the timber used in building it. I assume that you have been granted land here in Taos?"

"Yes, Don Sancho. His Majesty was kind enough to bestow five thousand acres upon me."

"That is some fifteen hundred more than I was allocated, which is only fitting and proper since you are my superior. Let me suggest to you a site for your new home, Don Diego—about three miles to the north, where there will be plenty of grazing land for your sheep. There is level ground there for quite a stretch, sufficient for the house and also the cottages of your workers. And that way, your sheep and mine will be separated by about a mile, so there should be no difficulty in keeping them apart at shearing time."

Don Diego sipped his brandy. Then, frowning slightly, he pondered aloud, "There will be the matter of furnishings for this new house of mine, once it is built, Don Sancho."

"But that is not difficult at all, Don Diego! After all, are we not both *Madrileños?* I have more than enough beds, tables, and chairs to lend you until you have your own brought from Mexico City. Besides, there is the January fair at Chihuahua, and most of us go there to see what new comforts we can add to our homes to please our *esposas* and ourselves." Don Sancho sent smoke lofting from his nostrils, then crushed out the stub of the *cigarrillo* in a little copper bowl and finished his brandy. "Well, there is no need to talk of official matters on your first evening here, Don Diego. Perhaps tomorrow afternoon, you and I can have a little chat. It is as you say, we shall need each other's help."

"We shall get along very well, I am convinced of it, Don Sancho." Don Diego smiled as he lifted his brandy glass to his host.

Don Sancho chuckled again and glanced at the closed door of his study, as if fearful that someone might enter at any moment. Then, leaning forward, he said in a confidential tone, "You must not think that Doña Elena was unhappy to have you and your family here this evening. She is really very warmhearted, but in the last week or two she has had a difficult time with some of the servants. She had to discharge a few lazy girls and it has tried her patience."

"Of course. Domestic affairs are bothersome indeed," Don Diego courteously replied. "And you must convey to her our most appreciative thanks for a magnificent dinner. My family and I have not been so feasted since we left Madrid."

"Ah yes, Madrid . . ." the *alcalde* murmured dreamily, a

faraway look in his eyes. Taking up the decanter of brandy, he approached to replenish Don Diego's glass, and then his own. "Tell me how you left it. How is the Escorial? And who is the most famous matador in Spain these days, Don Diego?"

Doña Inez, who had been given a room next to Catarina's in the southern wing of the *hacienda*, knocked at her niece's door. She observed on entering that Catarina had already removed her dress and was standing before the mirrored dresser in her camisole, drawers, and hose, tilting her head this way and that and fluffing up her long black hair.

"Oh, Tía Inez, you do not know how wonderful it is to have my own room again!" Catarina exclaimed as she turned to her aunt with a radiant smile. "And just look at that big, comfortable bed—I think I shall sleep all day long tomorrow. And a nice maid brought in a bowl of water so I could wash before going to bed."

"Don Sancho de Pladero is truly a generous host, Catarina. Be sure you thank his good wife for all these comforts. They must not think us ungrateful, you know."

"Oh, of course, of course," Catarina replied impatiently, turning back to the mirror and studying herself.

"Well," her aunt remarked, "you seem to be taking special pains with yourself this evening, Catarina. I wonder if that very pleasant young man who sat opposite you could have anything to do with it?"

"That Tomás, you mean?" Catarina flashed, turning to regard her aunt with a saucy look. "Pooh! He is afraid of his own shadow, if you want to know what I think. And of his mother, too. She is a real Tartar, is she not, Tía Inez?"

"Now, Catarina, that is no way to talk about Doña Elena. She is your hostess, and if she seemed stern at the table, it was probably because she had to go to a great deal of trouble to prepare that wonderful dinner for us and to arrange for our rooms on such short notice—after all, they could not have known exactly when we would arrive."

"You are a fine one to talk, Tía Inez!" Catarina made a sulky moue into the mirror. "You like pretty things as much as I do, and you know it. And I do wish you would stop talking to me as if you were my mother—you are not, you know."

Doña Inez bit her lips and flushed hotly. Catarina's shaft had struck perilously near the mark, but in no way did she wish to have the impulsive young girl guess this. In as steady a voice as she could manage under the circumstances, she replied, "I am sorry if you felt that way, Catarina. Of course, I know how much you miss your mother—I miss her, too. She was my sister, after all. Well, say your prayers, and sweet dreams to you, my dearest niece."

TWENTY-SIX

During the next two weeks, Don Diego de Escobar entered upon his official duties as outlined by the viceroy. Don Sancho de Pladero was eager and cooperative in helping his superior become oriented to his new post.

Twenty-two years earlier, the reforming zeal of the Spanish Bourbons had implemented the Ordinance of Intendants for New Spain. The act was designed to improve fiscal administration and augment the flow of revenues to the royal coffers. New Spain had been divided into twelve intendancies, plus the separate department of the Californias which was administered by the commandant general.

Don Diego thus became an assistant of the viceroy and was directly subordinate to him. Yet, as the viceroy himself had pointed out during one of their conferences, the new intendant of Taos would deal in fiscal matters with Bartoloméo Navarro Calezon, the intendant general. Don Diego would be responsible for the collection of revenues, civil administration, and cases of justice, as well as all economic matters. He was to cooperate with Governor Real Alencaster in maintaining the peace among the Indians. When there were serious crimes, the accused were to be conveyed to Santa Fe, where they would be imprisoned until their trial had been concluded. There, also, death sentences for capital crimes would be carried out by the military.

For the protection of Taos itself, Governor Real Alencaster had disposed twenty troops commanded by the company's second lieutenant. The duties of these men, since there was currently peace in Taos, comprised guarding the horse herd, participating in weekly patrols under a corporal commandant, and acting as couriers to carry important news whenever it arose, as well as bringing, every month, copies of the reports to Santa Fe.

Don Sancho de Pladero held the title of *alcalde mayor* and received no salary. He was allowed to collect certain small fees and judicial fines, but the office was mainly one of prestige. Whenever he acted in his official capacity as an arm of the law, he carried a black cane with a silver tip. His duties included the notarization of official documents and wills and the handling of land grants.

Finding his guest extremely sympathetic and congenial, Don Sancho had taken him into his confidence and explained why he had left Madrid to serve in an honorary and unremunerative post here in Taos. He had inherited great wealth from his father, who had been a minister in the cabinet of Charles III. He had fallen in love with Elena de Mendoza, the only child of a widower of as great wealth as Don Sancho's own father. One of his friends had been in love with her also, and, having been rejected, maliciously began to spread the rumor that Don Sancho's only interest in Elena was her dowry. Don Sancho had confronted the man and demanded that he apologize publicly. When the latter refused, Don Sancho had felt compelled to challenge him to a duel. "I meant to wound him, nothing more, Don Diego," he explained, "but he turned at the last moment as he fired at me, and my bullet killed him. We had been friends for many years, and the knowledge that I had taken his life bore heavily upon me. I entreated His Majesty to let me serve him in New Spain, and thus it was that I came to Taos. My wife loved me and came willingly, and then our son was born. But now . . ." he shrugged hopelessly and fell silent. Thus, Don Diego came to understand the bitter austerity of Doña Elena de Pladero.

Meanwhile, under the supervision of José Ramirez, Don Sancho's workers began to demolish Juan de Morena's crumbling house to salvage the timber and start work on Don Diego's new home. While eagerly awaiting the completion of the house, he was invited by Don Sancho to sit in judgment upon a merchant who had contracted with one of the pueblo Indians to make a religious statue for his chapel. The Indian, a short, crippled man in his fifties, had been paid only half of what he had been promised, the merchant claiming that the statue was of poor artistic quality. Therefore, the Indian had petitioned Don Sancho to right the wrong on that contract.

The Indian had whittled the figure from the soft root of the cottonwood tree, then coated the carving with plaster, made from gypsum and animal glue. Finally, he had painted it with yellows and greens made from plants and roots, browns from iron ore, and blacks from charcoal. It was, in fact, a masterpiece of workmanship, and its creation had been arduous and time-consuming.

The merchant, one Luis Saltareno, was an arrogant man in his late forties who had come to Taos five years before. He was a bachelor with an Indian girl as his housekeeper, and the artist was none other than the girl's own father.

Don Diego listened attentively to the testimony given by both men, the Indian speaking in halting Spanish, and then asked to see the statue. It was a three-foot carving of Jesus dying on the cross. Don Diego crossed himself and then asked, "Señor Saltareno, on what grounds do you claim that this statue lacks artistry?"

"Excelencia, you can see for yourself," the merchant responded. "The face of the *Cristo* is ugly, *¿no es verdad?"*

Don Diego shook his head. "We are taught, Señor Saltareno, that God made man in His own image. This Indian conceived of Him with the features of an Indian—if you accept Holy Scripture, is it not logical that an *Indio* would see the blessed *Cristo* as like unto him and his own people?"

Then, before the surly merchant could object, he gently added, "If you will allow me, Señor Saltareno, I will buy this statue myself and pay the artist what I believe it to be worth."

"Take it then, *Excelencia!* I will not keep it in my chapel. It is a disgrace."

Don Diego beckoned the Indian to come before the table at which he and Don Sancho were seated. He handed the Indian ten silver *pesos* and said, "With your permission, I shall put it in the chapel of my new house as soon as it is built. And when the house is finished, I shall ask you to make others for me."

The Indian gasped, then nodded, and burst into voluble Spanish, much of which was unintelligible. His face radiant with happiness, he walked out of the little adobe building in the plaza where Don Sancho presided as *alcalde*. The merchant gave Don Diego a look of disgust and hatred and then left the room abruptly.

Don Sancho turned to Don Diego. "You have made an enemy, Don Diego. But what you have done for the Indians of this village will outweigh that by far. Castamaguey will tell his people that there is justice in Taos."

On July 22, 1808, Miguel Sandarbal, bronzed and weather-beaten from the scorching sun of his six-hundred-mile journey, rode into Taos with his flock of five hundred sheep and his crew of sixteen men, having engaged six more in Chihuahua. Luck had been with them, and apart from several days of drenching rain, Miguel and the workers had fared well during their seventy-five-day trek. Miguel had anticipated that both Catarina and Doña Inez would need maids to serve them, as befitted their station in life. Accordingly, of the six additional workers he interviewed in Chihuahua, he had chosen three in their late twenties whose wives were young and personable enough to be trained in the duties of ladies' maids. These were Luis Delgado and his wife, Gertrudes; Andrés Barceló and his wife, Luisita; and Salvador Costilla and his wife, Dolores. In addition, he had engaged Estevan Muñoz, Francisco Sierra, and Fernando Sanchez, all of whom were somewhat older. They were unmarried, the latter two being widowers.

Finally, out of his own savings, Miguel had purchased two horses which he intended to give to Catarina and Carlos: a spirited, young, brown mare and a magnificent, gray stallion.

Upon arriving in Taos, Miguel went directly to the house of Don Sancho de Pladero. He had met Lieutenant Cortez on the trail, and had been informed that his master and the three members of his family were being lodged there until such time as a proper house could be built for them. Don Diego embraced Miguel, was introduced to the workers and their families, and welcomed them cordially and with the greatest enthusiasm. He thanked them for their trust in him and promised that they would find him a just and kind employer.

Esteban Morales, upon having been engaged by Miguel, had rushed to see his *novia,* Concepción Alfindar, a slim, shy, black-haired girl of eighteen, and urged her to accompany him to Taos as his bride. They had been married hurriedly on the very day of their departure from Chihuahua by a kindly old priest, and Miguel had learned that Concepción was an expert seamstress and cook. She would be invaluable to the de Escobars.

Catarina was enchanted with the mare and promptly named her Marquita. Much to Miguel's discomfiture, she hugged and kissed him for his generosity. He had also purchased a side-saddle for her, and Don Diego indulgently permitted her to try Marquita out. "But only as far as that patch of mesquite, Catarina. Once we have our house and the corral and everything ready for us, you may ride Marquita whenever you like," he promised.

As for Carlos, he was ecstatic over the gray stallion, and, not bothering with the saddle, mounted it bareback, took the reins, and immediately put it through its paces. It was a yearling, and since Miguel had ridden it part of the way from Chihuahua, it was docile enough to follow its new young master's directions. When he dismounted, Carlos exclaimed happily, "I shall name him Valor, Miguel, because he has both courage and worth—what a beautiful horse he is, and what a good friend you are to bring him all the way from Chihuahua for me! I shall care for him day and night." Then, gripping Miguel's hand, he shook it vigorously.

Don Sancho de Pladero, Doña Elena, and Tomás accompanied Don Diego and his family to the August fair, to which the Comanche, Ute, and Navaho came to trade with the Spanish settlers. Don Diego purchased chamois, several buffalo skins, and hand-tooled belts and beautifully woven blankets. He presented Don Sancho with a splendid mustang, sold to him by a Comanche brave. And he made gifts of a necklace of beads and another of semi-precious stones to the delighted Doña Elena. For Tomás, there was a fine, bone-handled knife and a pair of leather riding boots.

While in Chihuahua, Miguel had bought six well-trained sheepdogs to guard the flock. Two of the workers were sent immediately with the dogs to let the sheep graze on the slope of the mountain range, while the others were put to work at once felling timber and constructing Don Diego's new house, as well as building temporary adobe huts for themselves and their families. The following year, the house was ready, as well as improved cottages for the workers, a large corral into which the sheep would be driven at shearing time, a stable, and a large shelter comprised of roof and walls only, in which the sheep could take refuge during the winter snows and blizzards. By March, the estate of the new *intendente* of Taos had been completed. And at that time the shattering news had at last reached Taos: first, that Ferdinand had succeeded his weak and aging father Charles IV to the Spanish throne; and then that the wily Napoleon had confronted both father and son, compelled them to renounce the throne, and set his own brother upon it.

José Ramirez, the *capataz* of the de Pladeros, had no love at all for his master's new neighbor and still less for Don Diego's workers. Inadvertently, Teofilo Rosas had bragged about his wages in José's hearing, and the disparity had angered the squat, thirty-five-year-old *capataz*. Moreover, he resented being ordered by Don Sancho to put his men to work building Don Diego's *hacienda*, although he would have readily forgotten his rancor if Don Diego had seen fit to reward him personally. But, since Don Sancho had indicated that he would be indignant if any recompense were offered to the men, Don Diego had pursued the matter no further. Thus, José felt himself abused by his own master and cheated by Don Diego.

José was short and coarse-featured, with beetling brows, a thick mustache, and squinting, suspicious eyes. His face reflected a perenially surly expression. His father had been a sheepherder in Durango, and, from boyhood through his teens, José had worked with him, learning all there was to know about sheep. When José was twenty-two, his father's *patrón*, an elderly widower, married a flirtatious, eighteen-year-old girl from Mexico City. Carmen soon discovered that her husband was not only impotent, but a miser into the bargain. Frequently, she saddled her horse and rode out to watch the sheepherders at their work. It was not long before she noticed young José Ramirez. Bored and spiteful, she met José one night, out in the fields, and became his mistress.

Inevitably, Carmen's trysts with José were discovered by her husband, who summoned José to him, denounced him in front of Carmen, and promised him a sound flogging, after which he and his father would be discharged without wages.

But before he could carry out his threats, José wrested away the quirt which the old man was holding, lashed him viciously across the face, and felled him with a blow of his fist. As the man fell, his head struck the wall, and, seeing him lying motionless on the floor, José believed that he had killed him. Without a word to Carmen, he went to the stable and stole the best horse. Without bothering to inform his father of the incident, he rode for the border. He made his way to Santa Fe, and then on to Taos, where he had heard that Don Sancho de Pladero was seeking a new *capataz*. Accordingly, José presented himself to Don Sancho, and the genial *alcalde* took him out to the fields to work with the flock and observe his skills. By the end of the week, José had been hired. The older workers grumbled over this choice, but José's brutal vigor soon ended their attempts at harassment.

Partly because of her disappointment in having had to accompany her husband from Madrid to Taos, Doña Elena had become somewhat of a tyrant with her maids. At times, when her mood was especially bitter and one of the girls had been clumsy or inattentive, she ordered José Ramirez to administer a whipping, which he did in a little shed not far from his own cottage. He lost no time in exploiting this new authority by bargaining with the unfortunate girls to submit to him in return for a milder chastisement than would otherwise be administered. Brutish and sadistic as he was, the girls had little choice.

The year before, Doña Elena's personal maid, Maria Concepción Bernado, had left her mistress's employment to marry. To replace the girl, Doña Elena engaged Consuela Viola, a voluptuous girl of nineteen. José Ramirez had observed her with lecherous anticipation, but she had been so diligent in her duties that Doña Elena had thus far no reason to complain of her.

A week before the completion of Don Diego's *hacienda* and the adjoining buildings, Don Sancho, Doña Elena, and Tomás rode off to Santa Fe to visit Governor Real Alencaster. Don Diego rode with them, for there had just been news that the viceroy had been deposed and that the archbishop of Mexico City had selected Pedro Garibay in his place. There would be, Don Sancho and Don Diego knew, a serious discussion on what was to be done with the revenues which had hitherto been sent from Mexico City on to Spain: now that Napoleon's brother wore the crown, both men staunchly believed that these monies should be held in safety until such time as a rightful monarch was returned to the throne of Spain.

José Ramirez, in a black mood, entered the *hacienda* and, as was his wont, exchanged ribald conversation with several of the maids who had visited his cottage at night. He did not see Consuela Viola, and so, out of a predatory and suspicious instinct, walked down the corridor to Doña Elena's bedroom. The door was partly open, and he quietly pushed it open a little more and looked in. Then his cruel, sensual mouth twisted in a vicious smile. Consuela had her back to him, and she was standing before Doña Elena's dresser, evidently searching through one of the drawers. His eyes glittered with lustful excitement. She wore a short, full, brightly colored skirt and a loose, low-cut blouse, with a *rebozo*. The skirt emphasized her ripely rounded hips and thighs, and he had already observed that she was endowed with a sumptuous pair of *tetas*.

"*Buenos días, Señorita*," he said in a low, insinuating voice.

"*Jesu Cristo*—you—you frightened me!" Consuela whirled, paling, a hand at her mouth.

"No doubt I did, Señorita Consuela. I wonder what you were doing in your mistress's dresser? Trying to steal something, I'll be bound."

"No, no, Señor Ramirez, I swear it," she protested.

"But if I were to tell Doña Elena that I found you going through her things, can you not imagine what she would do, little Consuela? She would have you whipped, that's what. I know that you are new here, but you have only to ask the other *domésticas* what happens when the mistress gets angry with a wicked girl. She sends her out to me, and I take her to the little shed near my cottage, *¿comprende?* There I tie her hands very tightly above her head to a peg in the wall, and then I take off her garments so that the quirt can stripe her soft skin."

"*Dios—por piedad*, Señor Ramirez, I beg of you, don't tell on me—truly, I—I wasn't going to steal anything—I wanted to look at Doña Elena's—" Consuela stammered, her ripe breasts rising and falling in agitation.

José's smile deepened, and, with a little snigger, he suggested, "Now then, I might be persuaded to forget what I have just seen, little Consuela, if you would come to my cottage tonight. You don't have a *novio*, I know that much. And you work very hard. But your mother and father are dead, and you are all alone in the world. You need a protector and friend. You will find me both, little one, if you are good to me. And I could tell the mistress what a fine, industrious worker you are, even when she is away, how you polish and dust the furniture. Perhaps then she would increase your wages—you see what a good friend I can be to a girl who is obliging?"

Consuela shuddered, but she could not lower her eyes before the glittering dark eyes that seemed to strip her naked. She understood only too well, for one of the maids had told her what it was like to be whipped by José Ramirez.

"I—I will do what you want, Señor Ramirez," she murmured in resignation.

TWENTY-SEVEN

It had been a good year for John Cooper, this past twelve months of outdoor life with the Ayuhwa. He had spent all of this summer and the fall hunting with Lije, often accompanied by Kandaka and sometimes with a group of other braves. Game had been plentiful, and he had improved his skill with his father's Lancaster. One July day he had shot a heavily antlered buck through the heart at a distance of five hundred feet. Kandaka had shown him how to set ingenious traps for rabbits and squirrels that greatly surpassed his own crude efforts. Kandaka had taught him how to speak without words, by using a kind of universal sign language which neighboring Indian tribes would readily understand. And by now, John Cooper spoke the Ayuhwa tongue as fluently as did Kandaka himself.

There had come with all of this a gradual sense of belonging, grateful awareness of being accepted. As this feeling deepened, the earlier, stark sense of loneliness and isolation had ebbed away. It was not that John Cooper had forgotten the violent death of his family; but rather, thanks to the new life he shared with Kandaka and the others, the agonizing memory of that dreadful September afternoon in Shawneetown had receded to the very background of his mind.

In late August, a party of six French trappers visited the Ayuhwa village. Chief Mikanota entertained them with a great feast. The French *voyageurs* were surprised to find a young white man living with the Indians, and questioned John Cooper with great curiosity. When they learned of the tragedy which had befallen him, they expressed sympathetic concern and the hope that he would find his new life satisfying. For the towheaded youth, it was a rewarding opportunity to communicate with his own people. As all of them spoke English, it was easy to explain to them the Ayuhwa customs and the simple, peaceful life of the villagers. Before the trappers left, John Cooper traded several deer and beaver skins in return for lead and powder for his long rifle; he would need plenty of ammunition for the great fall buffalo hunt. He bade farewell to them with a sense of loss, though their leader urged him to join their expedition.

In the fall, there was the buffalo dance, complete with rituals invoked by Petimaka and in which all the braves took part, in preparation for the great hunt. There were joinings of braves and maidens to perform in front of the shaman. John Cooper watched several of Kandaka's friends stand beside their chosen squaws and, when the ceremony was done, watched them go together into the lodge of the husband where the young girl would begin her new duties.

There had been many buffalo on the plains that fall, and now the Ayuhwa hunted down the fattest cows, which would provide the most meat for the winter ahead. A month before the hunt began, John Cooper took part in the ritualistic sun dance. The Indians chose a tall, slim tree with a fork near the top for the center pole of the ceremonial sun lodge, and this tree was felled by someone beloved of the tribe. Once the tree was down, each warrior attacked it like a fallen enemy, striking it with a weapon as the branches were broken off. Then the pole was carried to the lodge site, where a bundle of brush and a buffalo hide was bound to the fork before the pole was raised. The sun lodge was constructed with rafters reaching from the center pole to posts which marked the outer wall. Near the base of the pole, there was a cleared space decorated with buffalo skulls to serve as an altar.

Each hunter wore on his head a mask made by tanning the skin of an entire buffalo head from which the skull was removed and the horns and the hair retained. Kandaka had asked permission of Petimaka for John Cooper to take part in this ceremonial dance, and the old shaman readily agreed.

Before the ceremony began, Kandaka instructed John Cooper in the rhythms and steps of the dance, the purpose of which was to make the buffalo come in plentiful numbers and to let each hunter count many buffalo hides as his trophies.

"When you become tired, John Cooper," Kandaka explained, "you show it by bending forward and sinking your body toward the ground. Then one of the other braves will draw a bow upon you and hit you with a blunt arrow. You will fall like the buffalo, and those around you will seize you, drag you out of the ring by the heels, brandishing their knives about you. They will pretend to skin and cut you up, and then they will let you up. Your place will be taken at once by another, who dances into the ring with his mask on. We shall dance three days and three nights, for the shaman has said it will take this time to make the buffalo come."

Kandaka also taught John Cooper the songs and chants of the sun dance. As he learned, John Cooper realized that such rituals reflected communal purpose, faith, and devotion which could not be questioned and which linked men everywhere, whether they were white or red.

Then there was the sheer excitement and exhilaration of the buffalo hunt itself, which followed quickly after the three days and nights of incantation and dancing. The hunt evoked all the age-old pulsating drama of the eternal hunter and his dangerous quarry and became the climax to which all his senses and young vitality were channeled. Riding with Kandaka and some of the younger braves, John Cooper savored the companionship, forged out of communal action. He breathed in deeply the crisp, autumn air and felt himself uplifted into this panorama of life and death. He heard the shouted approval of his fellows who, though busy in their own pursuit of the buffalo, acclaimed his prowess as a hunter, as one of them.

When it was done, Kandaka rode up to him, his round face shining with excitement and joy, to tell him that never before could the young brave remember so many kills, so much meat to be stored for the long winter ahead. John Cooper had killed fifteen buffalo cows, and this time he asked Kandaka to give the meat of two of them to the parents of Latiwaka so that Degala's bondage might be eased. The women of the tribe followed the hunters, bringing the meat back on travois to the village.

The previous year, an amiable squaw had taught John

Cooper how to make pemmican by pounding the dry buffalo meat into a powder and mixing it with hot fat and dried berries, then pressing it into a loaf or small cakes. He and Lije had lived on pemmican many a time when a day's hunting had proved fruitless. This year again there would be a plentiful supply of meat for both of them.

That night, there was a great feast in the Ayuhwa village, and the chief, Mikanota, bade John Cooper sit at his right with Kandaka at his left to symbolize the honor paid this brave and skillful *wasichu*.

The next afternoon, as part of the celebration of the success of the buffalo hunt, they played the game of *tokon-hay*. Just outside the village, a playing ground had been formed by cutting down trees, uprooting the stumps, and leveling the soil. The field was a quadrangle about ninety yards wide and a hundred and fifty long, with two towering poles set six feet apart forming goals at either end. Each brave used a racket about two and a half feet long made of cedar wood and covered with deerskin. The ball was made out of a rag-filled buckskin bag, and the elders and the older warriors who did not take part in the sport gambled horses, bows, or knives on the outcome of the game.

John Cooper found himself on the team which opposed his friend Kandaka. Mikanota handed the ball to Petimaka, who lifted it and murmured a prayer, then flung it far into the air. The running and jostling, the felling of opponents in one's path, the constant action that swirled from side to side, caught John Cooper up in the exuberant vortex of healthy competition. And when the sun began to set, and his bruised, sweating body had reached what he believed to be the end of its endurance, the ball hurtled toward his racket; deftly catching it, he began to run toward the enemy goal, dodging and leaping away from braves who sought to stop him until, with a final burst of speed, he crossed the goal to win the game for his team amid exultant shouts from those who had successfully gambled on the outcome.

That night, after the game, Mikanota gripped him by the shoulders at the feast and said, "You are one of us, young *wasichu* with a straight tongue and a good heart. It is time you thought of taking a squaw into your lodge. It is not good for you to live alone, to have no one to care for you." When Letalto, the older daughter of the shaman, served them both with maize pudding, Mikanota watched her go back to her father and then turned again to John Cooper. "Now there would be a fitting mate for a mighty hunter. And I think her father would look with favor upon you." John Cooper turned red and bit his lip. Finally, he managed to speak in the Sioux tongue. "It is too great an honor, O Mikanota. And I am too young to think of a squaw."

Mikanota eyed him and then smiled knowingly. "Stay with us, young *wasichu*. You are almost one of us now. And I think that within not too many moons, you will cast the arrow before one of our maidens. I have taken Sentigata into my lodge and I am young again. So it is the way with all men, whether it be the young or the old."

The winter was not so long nor so cruel as the year before. By April of 1809 John Cooper was already into his second spring with the Ayuhwa. Four months past his sixteenth year, he had grown a full inch since he had left Shawneetown behind him forever. He was more wiry and sturdier, with increased stamina. He had patience, too, for the long trails which he and Kandaka often took. With the coming of spring, he thought again of the killer bear which still eluded him and which had not been seen since the day he had shot off part of its paw. One bright April day, he had accompanied Kandaka, Mikanota, and Petimaka to the ritual of blessing the planting of the new corn in the other village. There he had caught sight of Degala, her forehead still smudged with ashes and her braid streaked with them, carrying a heavy load of firewood back to the lodge of Latiwaka's old mother and father. Her face was more mournful than ever and her eyes were downcast. Kandaka eyed him intently, but John Cooper did not let his friend know what he was thinking. When they returned to their village that evening, John Cooper asked casually, "Have any of the braves seen the killer bear, Kandaka?"

"No, John Cooper. He has vanished. Perhaps your wounding him was a sign that there would be great danger for him, and he is cunning. Maybe he has gone far to the west or to the north, to seek another village where there is no one with a weapon like 'Long Girl.' "

"That could be true."

"If that is so, Degala will bear the curse for many moons yet. If the bear is never seen again, it is possible she will bear it to the end of her days."

"I know that, Kandaka."

"But to track the bear alone would be too dangerous, and foolish."

"That is so, also. A good hunter is not foolish, Kandaka."

"I am sure of that, John Cooper. Well, I must go back to my lodge. Sleep well."

John Cooper went into his own lodge, Lije following him. He stretched out upon his bed, pillowing his head in his arms, while Lije nuzzled and licked his face. He reached out to pat the wolfhound's head and then said softly, "Tomorrow morning, bright and early, Lije, you're coming with me and we'll see if we can't track down that bear. You're even stronger than you were last year, boy, and it's going to be a long hunt. I'll have to go on horseback, and you'll have to keep up with me, and be careful, too."

It was dawn when he woke, and, after he had eaten a piece of dried buffalo meat and washed it down with water, he went to the corral and let out the mustang he had ridden during the buffalo hunt. Lije trotted at his heels, his brown eyes keen with anticipation. John Cooper mounted the horse. He gripped his rifle in his right hand, the mustang's reins in his left. He had tied to his belt a long leather pouch with powder and ball. John Cooper quietly wheeled the mustang northward and trotted out of the sleeping Ayuhwa village.

He rode easily toward the gradually rising slopes where he had encountered the huge black bear the spring before, glancing back now and then to make sure that Lije was keeping pace. Once within range of the cave at the top of the slope, he turned the mustang west, staring intently down at the ground for tracks. There were no fresh paw marks, as he had suspected. He nodded to himself, frowned, looked around, and then decided to range westward.

Lije loped on ahead of John Cooper's mustang. As the sunlight grew brighter, John Cooper stared down at the ground, eyeing the bushes and the trees along the path he took for signs that would direct him. By noon, he had covered nearly ten miles to the north, without having stopped for food or water, and he dismounted and tethered the mustang to a sturdy elm tree. Above him sounded the gossipy chirping of birds, and as he looked up at the bright blue sky, a sparrowhawk wheeled overhead, hovered on a lofty branch of a giant oak, uttered its shrill cry, and then took flight again.

He had come to a long stretch of forest, but with many

spaces between the trees so that his view was hardly impaired. There was a little stream ahead and a low ravine well beyond it, curving to the northwest. Mounting up again, he urged the mustang toward the ravine and then uttered a stifled gasp of excitement. There, on the edge of the ravine's north bank, were the prints of a bear.

Calling Lije to halt, he got down again and squatted to stare at the prints. The feeling of excitement swirled in him and his heart began to beat faster. Unmistakably, these were the prints of the crippled black bear. There was only a partial outline of the animal's right paw, and the set of tracks moved toward the northwest and had been made only a few hours ago. Beyond the ravine, on the grassy knoll which surmounted it, the imprint of those paws in the grass showed the same characteristics; and their freshness told him that the bear had come this way about dawn, the same time that he had left the Ayuhwa village.

He pointed to the marks in the flattened grass and Lije sniffed, as if identifying the spoor of the quarry. Then, mounting his mustang again, he headed it along the trail which the bear had left. As he rode, he inspected the rifle to make certain it was loaded with an extra charge of powder, and that the pouch was within ready reach at his left side. As he quickened the gait of the mustang, the knife which he wore around his neck danced in the air, forward and back, against his sturdy, young chest, and its hilt caught the glint of the sun's rays through the trees.

Now the tracks swerved suddenly to the west, and they were on moist ground and clearly outlined. There was the same pattern of the deeper imprint of the left paw and the lighter one of the crippled right. Even though the wound must be healed by now, John Cooper reasoned, the animal's gait would still be affected. And it was sure to be dangerous if cornered.

Five miles ahead of him, the shaggy black bear halted and turned its head over its left shoulder, sniffed, and then uttered a coughing growl. It was five years old, and it weighed just over three hundred and fifty pounds. It had been docile enough as a yearling, but then its mother and father had been killed within the space of three months by Indian hunters with lances and bows and arrows. Instinctively, it had fled from the hunters and survived. But the next year, it had been set upon by the Ayuhwa brave Mistantoma and his three dogs, and one of the dogs had leaped at it and bitten off part of its left ear. In its unreasoning pain, it had charged the young Sioux warrior and felled him with its paw. It had sniffed at the sprawled, lifeless body, and the dogs had drawn off, yelping and baying in their own cringing fear. Then it had turned and lumbered off to find a cave and to hide there until this strange new pain had left it.

Later, in the summer, it had cautiously ventured forth and, not yet certain of its surroundings, approached the Ayuhwa village. It had come upon a squaw picking berries, an older woman—Degala's mother—and when she had seen it, she had shrieked and flung the basket at it and begun to run. The bear had recognized the scent of her garments as being very much like that of the brave it had slain, and it had raced after her, caught and crushed her with its paws.

After that, several of the braves from Kandaka's village had hunted it down, and one of them had wounded it in the side with an arrow—a wound that inflicted an even greater pain and rekindled the orphaned bear's recollection of those who had dealt it pain before. And two years ago, having found a new cave in which to hibernate during the protracted winter, it had emerged in the spring and been seen by Kandaka's friend, Latiwaka. Two other braves had accompanied the young Ayuhwa warrior, and after launching their first arrows, which missed the bear, they had turned and fled like cowards, leaving Latiwaka to face the bear alone. Bravely, he had drawn an arrow from his quiver, notched it to the bowstring, drawn it back with all the strength of his young muscles, and sped it at the black bear. Even as Latiwaka had drawn another arrow from his quiver and prepared to speed it, the bear had loped toward him with that awkward yet terrifying gait, sprung upon him, and clawed him to death.

It was warier than ever now and angry, for last spring it had endured a new pain, the result of which had been to cripple it and slow its pace in foraging for food and journeying to places of safety.

It stopped again, sniffing the air suspiciously, uttering a low growl, and then fretfully turned back upon its track. Somewhere at the back of its brutish brain there was the dim memory of pursuers. It halted near a stream, and to the west of that stream was a little hill with a small cave near its top, half-hidden by leaves and broken branches from an earlier storm. It made for the cave now, and it waited within, growling softly, pawing the ground with the sharp, murderous claws of its left front paw, lifting its right and whining as it saw and remembered what had been done to it so long ago.

At noontime, John Cooper rested the mustang while he ate some dried buffalo meat which he shared with Lije. The tracks of the bear were fresher and more distinct now, and again he took his rifle out of his sling, inspected it to make certain that it was in good working order, and then mounted the mustang and followed the tracks, more slowly this time.

A stillness seemed to have come over the forest. He could hear the thudding of his own heartbeats as he rode, his eyes unwaveringly fixed on the terrain ahead. Inwardly, he was grateful to Kandaka for having taught him the nuances of tracking, of observing the way twigs were bent or leaves or grass crushed. Looking back now, he knew that he had made many mistakes in his trek from Shawneetown and that he had been fortunate to survive them. He knew, also, that today he dared not make a single error, for it could well prove fatal. And there was always the chance that the bear might double back on its tracks and wait to ambush him. His first shot would have to be deadly. If he met the bear at close range, and only wounded it, there would be no time to reload.

Suddenly he stiffened in the saddle and halted the mustang with a single jerk of the reins, then swiftly dismounted and tethered his horse to a cedar tree. About five hundred feet away there was a cave, its opening half-concealed by branches, twigs, and leaves. The hair seemed to prickle at the back of his neck, warning him that at last he had come upon the elusive killer bear.

He squatted down, slowly easing the rifle out of its sling, leveling it at the mouth of the cave. Lije stood motionless beside him, head held high, tail extended and stiff, his keen brown eyes expectant. For a long moment, John Cooper debated whether to try to flush the bear out of its hiding place and then decided against it. Finally, he left his place behind the cedar tree and moved in a cautious crouch over to his left for nearly fifty feet, hiding behind the huge stump of an oak tree. He glanced at Lije and put a finger to his lips, then put his hand over the wolfhound's muzzle. Lije obediently flattened himself beside his young master, but his eyes were fixed unwaveringly on the mouth of the cave, as if he, too, comprehended what John Cooper sought.

There was a gust of wind from the northwest, and John

Cooper smiled to himself. The bear would not have his scent from that. He would wait and hope that, somehow, Latiwaka's killer would decide that all was safe and emerge to go on its way.

The sun began to descend, and the shadows licked at the foliage and trees with long stealthy fingers as John Cooper crouched behind the stump, gripping the rifle tightly. Then, at last, a dark shape emerged from the mouth of the cave and turned north. Swiftly he rose from behind the stump, leveled the rifle, tightened his trigger finger, and felt the Lancaster's butt thrust bruisingly against his shoulder. The bear uttered a snarling roar of pain and lurched, then turned, opening its savage jaws, and with its right paw brushed at the bloody wound at its shoulder. John Cooper's heart sank; he had only wounded it, not even disabled it. And now the bear had seen him and had begun to lumber toward him.

For an instant, panic seized John Cooper. "Go back, out of the way, Lije," he shouted, sweeping his right hand in the direction from which he had come. Then, frantically looking around him, he saw a young oak tree, about eighteen feet high, sturdy enough to bear his weight. Thrusting the rifle back into its sling, he reached high to grasp its trunk and began to climb.

The black bear was snarling now as it came toward the tree, and Lije barked at, but warily backed away from its charge. It reached the tree and stood on its hind legs, peering up after the boy. Then it snarled again, and began to climb.

John Cooper shinnied up as quickly as he could, seeking secure footing on the topmost branch. Reaching it, he turned round to look down at the bear, his right foot testing the branch to determine whether it would bear his weight. Then, hugging the trunk with his knees, he reached for the rifle and frantically began to reload it.

Below him, the bear was climbing slowly, snarling as it came. Lije leaped at it and nipped its lower right leg near the heel. For a moment, the bear turned and made a swipe at the wolfhound with its right paw, again baring its sharp teeth, its eyes flaming with pain and rage. The distraction gave John Cooper the time he needed. Feverishly, he poured in an extra charge of powder and tamped it down with the ramrod. At last it was reloaded. He maintained perilous balance by the fierce grip of his knees around the thickly barked trunk.

The bear continued to climb. It was only a foot or two

below him now, its sharp, ugly, yellow teeth bared as it emitted a series of ferocious growls. John Cooper could see where its left ear had been torn away by the dogs, and swiftly he put the butt of the Lancaster to his shoulder, tilted down the barrel until it was only a few inches away from the bear's other ear, and then pulled the trigger.

There was a hideous yowl, and then he heard a heavy thud and looked down. The black bear had fallen to the ground, sprawled on its side, motionless. Sweat poured from John Cooper's body, and there was a throbbing in his head. His heart was thudding so violently he thought he would faint and fall from the tree. As it was, in the reaction which seized him, his fingers trembled, lost hold of the Lancaster, and he saw it fall near the bear. Lije circled the fallen brute, barking and snarling.

"Get away from it, Lije, get away, I said!" he shouted as he clung with both arms to the trunk of the oak tree. There was a gust of wind and he felt himself swaying. Suddenly he was nauseated and held on all the more tightly lest he fall.

At last the spasm passed. Slowly, wanly, and weakly, he began to climb down. The rifle lay about ten feet away from the bear, and he retrieved it swiftly and moved off to one side behind another tree. "Get away, I told you, Lije! What if he's playing possum?" he shouted. Opening the pouch tied to his belt, he reloaded the rifle. As he did so, he prayed aloud, "God, don't let him wake up and charge me or Lije until I've got 'Long Girl' primed and ready! Let him be dead, please, God!" When he had finished and backed away to a safer distance, he looked up at the sky and panted, "Thanks, God, thanks a lot! If I didn't get him this time, I'd never get another chance like this and he'd like as not go on killing folks!"

His fingers were still trembling, and he forced himself to steady the rifle as he aimed it at the bear's chest. Narrowing his eyes, he squeezed the trigger slowly, but the impact of the ball did not cause even a tremor. Then he knew that the bear was truly dead.

He sank down on his knees, bowing his head, the butt of the rifle thrust against the ground and its barrel gripped in his right hand as he rubbed his forehead with the other, murmuring a prayer of thanksgiving now that the danger was past. Then, recovering at last, he straightened and moved toward the dead bear. Putting the rifle back in the sling, he took the knife from the sheath around his neck and cut off the torn ear. The people in the village must have undeniable proof that at last the evil bear was dead.

John Cooper rode into the Ayuhwa village at nightfall, bone-weary, drained, and yet comforted by the knowledge of what he had done. He did not consider it a feat of valor or special courage. His only thought had been to rid the village of the lurking, lethal menace of the bear and, more than that, to lift the unjust curse from Degala. He had accepted Kandaka's explanation of the inflexible law of the tribe, and, because he was white and still in a sense an intruder among the Ayuhwas, he would not have set himself up against the law of these people who had given him shelter and friendship. But when he had seen Degala burdened by her armload of wood and observed with what contemptuous scorn Latiwaka's parents had tyrannized her, he had been moved to a pity which gnawed at his conscience and would not let him rest.

He rode the mustang up to the corral, dismounted, removed the reins, and turned it back with the other horses. Then, with Lije at his heels, he strode to Mikanota's lodge. At the doorway, the chief's new wife, a comely woman in her mid-thirties, inclined her head to him and smiled, then went inside to tell her husband that the young *wasichu* awaited him.

Mikanota emerged, and John Cooper drew from the pocket of his buckskin jacket the knife on the point of which was transfixed the tattered ear of the killer bear. "I have slain the bear that has brought death to the mother of Degala and to your braves, O Mikanota," he declared. "Here is the ear which I have brought to show you that I speak with a straight tongue. Kandaka described the evil one to me, and when I killed him with 'Long Girl' this afternoon, I saw also that part of his paw had been shot away by one of my bullets. Let it be known in the villages of the Ayuhwa that the bear is no longer to be feared."

Mikanota's face glowed with joy as he embraced John Cooper. "You have brought news that is welcome, *wasichu*. The mother and father of Latiwaka will say prayers of gratitude to the Great Spirit when they hear what you have done."

"I am glad that is so, O Mikanota. Now I would sleep."

"Sleep well then, brave young *wasichu*. But a word more.

Now that you have proved you are the mightiest of our hunters, think well of what I have already told you, that it is wise to take a squaw. I say this because you are to me almost like a son. The older daughter of our beloved shaman, Letalto, is such a squaw. And Petimaka looks with favor upon you—when he has learned what you have done this day, he will grant you the right to cast the arrow before her."

"Your words do me great honor, Mikanota, but as I have said before, it is not yet time for me to take a squaw. And I do not know that she would want me as her mate. I have not yet seen enough summers to think of this. By your leave, I go back to my lodge."

"Go in peace and may the Great Spirit watch over you, brave young *wasichu*."

John Cooper had flung himself down on his blanket and fallen asleep at once, dreamlessly, out of the deep, over-whelming fatigue which had seized him. The next day, when he walked through the village to the corral to take out the mustang and go hunting with Kandaka, he saw the old women and young girls standing at the entrances of their lodges, watching him. "Though he is a white-eyes, a *wasichu*, I would be proud to share his blanket!" and "How strong and brave he is, to have slain the evil bear without aid from any of the warriors!" he heard them murmur.

Kandaka, beside him, chuckled softly. "Already half the girls in this village would be eager to come to your lodge, John Cooper. And it is not only Yumiquya, who already—I speak with a straight tongue on this, John Cooper—would wish you to cast the arrow at her feet. There, to the left of you, is Oniqua, whose father was once the war chief of the Missouris. She has seen three more summers than Yumiquya, and many of our young warriors have cast the arrow before her. But she has broken it or flung it over her shoulder. I think she would not do that if you sought her out."

John Cooper fidgeted, furious with himself to discover that he was blushing. Frantically, he searched his recollections of the past. His mother had never told him about the differences between the sexes, about the mysteries of mating between man and maid. And all that his father had ever said to him was, "An honest man, John Cooper, doesn't dally with young girls. He keeps himself for the one whom he'll marry one day and have children by." Annoyed and confused by Kandaka's insinuations, he changed the subject. During their day of peaceful foraging, he put the topic from his mind.

That night, after hunting, he fell into dreamless sleep. There was a full moon, and the night was still, save for the distant squealing of a prairie dog. In an elm tree, standing in proud isolation behind the lodge of Mikanota, a screech owl perched, its yellow eyes surveying the placid night, sometimes ruffling its feathers and hunching its beaked head as it watched for a straying mouse.

There was the sound of soft footsteps, and Lije rose and moved to the opening of his young master's lodge, quizzically peering into the darkness. He uttered a low growl, flattening his tail as he saw a shadowy form approaching. But a soft, husky voice intoned his name. And a soft hand, turned upward, offered the wolfhound a piece of buffalo meat. He took it gingerly, still suspicious, and as he bolted it down, the soft hand stroked his head and once again murmured his name. But when the shadowy form moved closer to the opening of the lodge, Lije again stiffened and uttered a menacing growl.

John Cooper woke suddenly. He was instantly alert. "Hush, Lije! Who's there? What is it?" he called. He propped himself up on an elbow, and with the other hand reached for the knife in the sheath he wore about his neck.

"It is Degala, *wasichu*. Tell your great dog I come as a friend, I mean you no harm," the soft, husky voice murmured.

"It's all right, Lije. Let her by, Lije," he soothed. The wolfhound trotted back into the lodge, then lay down beside his master, wagging his tail.

John Cooper sat up, suddenly self-conscious as well as mystified. "I—I'd better make some light so I can see. Degala—you—you must have come all the way from the other village, it's a long way." He spoke in the Sioux tongue, and his tone of voice was uneasy.

"Yes, *wasichu*. I came because I must." In the darkness, she knelt before him. She set something down beside her which he could not see. "But I do not think your dog trusts me. Can you not—will you not send him from your lodge so that—so that I may do what must be done?" she quavered.

Groping in the darkness behind him, he found the tinder box and struck the flint. He had contrived a crude candle, using a lump of buffalo tallow with a reed as wick, and he held the kindled punk to the wick until it was lighted. A tiny flame illumined the small lodge, and he gasped to see Degala kneeling before him, a clay ewer beside her.

"I—I'll take Lije out, he won't bother you. Now that he knows you're not an enemy, he'll be all right." Then, straightening, he muttered, "Come on, Lije, be good now. Come on outside and you stay there and keep watch, you hear me?" The wolfhound, docile to his master's guidance, obediently rose and moved outside the lodge. Then, frowning and shaking his head, still perplexed, John Cooper turned slowly and went back into the lodge.

Seating himself on the blanket and facing her, he stammered, "Now, what is it, Degala? Can I do anything for you?"

She raised her face to his and now, for the first time, there was an exquisite smile on her soft, full lips and in her black eyes. "You have done much for me already, *wasichu*. You have lifted the curse from me. Maniwoka and Tisingua, the father and mother of my dead husband, Latiwaka, told me how you had killed the evil one."

"But—but, Degala, you didn't have to come all this long way—I wanted to kill the bear so that they wouldn't treat you like a slave any more."

"This I know, *wasichu*." Her eyes held his a long moment, and her smile deepened, a smile of infinite tenderness and joy. "I know also how generous you have been in sending the meat of the great shaggy ones to the father and mother of Latiwaka. You are as kind as he was to me. And now, because of what you have done, I may purify myself and I may again be the squaw of a warrior of the tribe, not an outcast. You have given me back my life. It is little I can do to thank you, but it is my wish and my desire."

Helplessly, unable to speak, he watched her as she turned to the ewer beside her, dipped her hands into it, and began to wash away the smudge of ashes on her forehead, and then to scoop up more water and rub the ashes off the buckskin jacket and skirt. When there was no mark of the ashes upon them, she began to remove her garments.

"Degala ..." he could hardly speak. His voice shook and his heart began to pound wildly.

"There is no need for you to speak, *wasichu*. Mighty hunter, you are braver than the chief of the Ayuhwa himself, do not be frightened of me now," she murmured almost teasingly. With a sinuous, feline movement, she cast the buckskin jacket from her and drew away the skirt. She stood naked before him. The golden-coppery tone of her skin, the surge of her round, full, widely spaced breasts, the slimness of her waist, and above all, the long searching look she gave him as she knelt down now before him and extended her supple arms, made him tremble. His sinewy body began to shudder with the awakening for the first time of his strong, young manhood.

She bent her head to the tiny flame and blew it out, and then moved beside him on the blanket, entwining him in her smooth arms. Awkwardly, he put out his hand to touch her shoulder, and in the darkness brushed instead the resilient, satiny curve of a round breast. "Oh, G–God—" his voice was choked, unsteady.

But she, older, knowing, and exquisitely sympathetic, whispered only, "Hush, it will be as it should be between us. Give me your strength as I give you my gratitude for my life which you have returned to me so bravely."

He let her draw him down upon the blanket, not knowing what or how to act toward her, knowing only that this enormous and mystic ritual had cast a spell upon him which he had no power to break. As he felt her soft hands remove his jacket and leggings, tears stung his eyes. And he groaned along with an ecstatic anguish as her soft fingers caressed his wiry nakedness.

Her soft breath was like an incantation upon him. And the warmth and the satiny sleekness of her body, lithe and yet gently cajoling, wrought upon his own male innocence a kind of blessed, natural guidance. With whispered words, with soft hands, she drew him upon her. His head was cradled against the swelling globes of her full breasts, and as his hands clutched her, the terrible brooding loneliness which had lurked within him like a mocking spectre seemed at last to vanish. He wept then, understanding this in the unison of their bodies, of their very beings.

"Oh yes, *wasichu,* give me your strength, make my life strong, so that when at last I become the squaw of a warrior, I will give him strong, brave sons like you!" Her fingers dug into his lean, muscular back and her legs entwined with his.

He had never dreamed that a woman's body could be so wonderfully needed, so gloriously attuned to the urgency and the thrust of his own sinews, to the singing of the blood in his veins. In the darkness of the lodge, the glory of eager flesh that knew neither guilt nor shame was endless, indelible, transfiguring.

Just before dawn, Degala moved away from the sleeping youth, swiftly donned jacket and skirt, then turned and knelt to stroke his tousled hair. Her lips were wreathed in a smile, and her cheeks were wet with tears. Then she moved out of the lodge, stopping only to pat Lije's head and to whisper, "Guard him well, he is beloved of the tribe, he is brave and good, and he will be so all of his days!"

The pale circle of the moon had hidden behind a cloud, and the screech owl opened its beak and hooted softly to herald the oncoming dawn.

TWENTY-EIGHT

In the days that followed the killing of the bear, John Cooper embarrassedly found himself acclaimed as a hero by the Ayuhwa village. When he and the wolfhound walked through the center of the village to meet Kandaka for the start of a hunt or simply for a game of hoop-and-pole or shooting arrows at a distant target, little children would run up to him and touch him, their eyes shining with awe. And the old women would greet him and make his cheeks flush with their extravagant praises and their often ribald urging for him to take a young maiden and procreate sons who would be mighty hunters like their father. More than ever, young Yumiquya regarded him fondly, giggling and turning away when he observed her, and even grave Letalto considered him with an admiring look. He had seen how many of the ambitious young braves, not yet wed, would strut and swagger as they moved through the village, openly seeking the tribute of the maidens; but by contrast he tried to efface himself and not to be aware of the manifold adulation which his feat had brought about.

At the beginning of the last week of April of this year of 1809, Kandaka wakened him early to tell him excitedly that a large herd of buffalo had been seen ten miles away from the village in which Degala lived. And at the day's end, when John Cooper had killed twenty-two buffalo with his father's rifle, Kandaka rode up alongside him and declared, "My father bids me tell you that he would speak with you tonight in his lodge. You have brought our village good luck and good hunting, John Cooper, and he has asked our shaman to make you our blood brother and then to urge you to take a maiden to your lodge so that you are truly one of us."

John Cooper reined in his mustang, his lean, sun-bronzed features clouded with indecision. He chose his words carefully so as not to offend Kandaka. "It is a great honor to be a blood brother. I would willingly be yours, Kandaka. But you know what I have said before when you have bidden me take a squaw. Besides, there is no one in the village whom I desire or who would wish to take me as her mate."

"Is it because you are a *wasichu* that you do not find our maidens pleasing to look upon, John Cooper?"

"No, not that at all. There are surely many who are good to look upon, Kandaka. But you, who are the son of the chief and who have seen more summers than I, should it not be you who first takes a squaw to his lodge?"

Kandaka's face remained impassive. "The time will be when my father bids me. But now he thinks of you first because of the honor and good fortune you have brought us, and he is eager to keep you here with us. But I have said enough. Tonight my father will make known to you his wish."

The old men and the unfledged warriors, as well as the squaws, hitched many travois to the horses to carry back the bounty of the hunt, for over a hundred and fifty buffalo had been slain. It was late at night when they came to the major village of the Ayuhwa, after unloading some of the meat at Degala's village. The feast had begun already, and John Cooper sat beside Mikanota and watched the warriors don their buffalo masks and dance in exultant triumph over the success of the hunt. Petimaka lifted his hands to the moonlit sky and intoned a prayer of thanks to the Great Spirit. Then Mikanota rose and held up both hands to silence his people. He spoke solemnly, and a hushed silence fell upon his listeners as he told of the will of the Great Spirit in guiding the destinies of the Ayuhwa. "He who gives us breath and food decreed that a young *wasichu* should come among us and become one of us. Through His will, our villages are at peace with other tribes, and there is much corn in the storehouse and much meat for the moons ahead. We honor the stranger who came to our village. He sits at my right hand tonight. And it is my wish that he dwell among us, that he become a blood brother of the Ayuhwa, and take unto himself a chosen mate who is beloved of our village. This will be the bond between us, of blood, of sharing, and of the joining together of this mighty young *wasichu* hunter and a beloved woman."

John Cooper, seated tailor-fashion, looked up uneasily at these words. He saw Petimaka, who was seated opposite him, nod and smile.

"I speak of the older daughter of our wise shaman, the maiden Letalto," Mikanota continued. "She of all our maidens is beloved, for her father is the wisest among us and gives us counsel and tells us the will of the Great Spirit. And Petimaka has heard my words and agrees to this, once the *wasichu* mingles his blood with that of the Ayuhwa."

John Cooper turned to look at Kandaka, and his eyes widened when he saw that his young friend's face had suddenly grown bleak. He turned to look at the slim, grave, lovely Letalto, who stood in the doorway of her father's lodge, arms crossed over her bosom, head bowed in docile acceptance of the decree of her chief and of her father. Then, with a flash of sudden insight, John Cooper understood why Kandaka had not yet taken a squaw to his lodge. It was Letalto whom he yearned for. And he remembered how Kandaka had said that the son of a chief must do his father's bidding.

As Mikanota turned to him now, John Cooper rose, searching for words that would not offend, that would show the deep gratitude he felt for the kindness of these simple people. Suddenly, he knew what he must do, the only thing that would show that he truly spoke with a straight tongue.

As they waited for him to speak, silent once more and expectant, he turned to look again at Kandaka, who lifted his head and stared at him, forcing a pleasant smile to his face. He felt a kinship with the young brave and, at the same time, sorrow that he must end that friendship while yet retaining it. "You have been good to me, you have taken me in as one of you," he slowly began. "I have learned that your ways and the ways of my own people are not so different, and that we can live together in peace. It is a good thing to have learned, with my life still before me, so that I shall remember it always, wherever I go."

At this Mikanota's eyes fixed upon him questioningly, and Kandaka looked up again, with a startled expression.

He paused a moment, desperately seeking the right words with which to express his gratitude but reject the honor of a mate, without insulting either the chief and Letalto's father, or shaming the girl herself. He held out his hands with the palms upward in a sign of peace as he resumed, "But I know also that there is this difference between my people and yours. When we take a squaw—a wife as we say in our *wasichu* tongue—it is out of love between both the man and the mate. I respect and honor Letalto, the daughter of the great shaman, Petimaka, and yet my heart tells me that she does not have love for me, and I would not be worthy of her. Yet with all my heart I wish to offer myself in the ceremony of blood brotherhood, and with Kandaka, who has been my friend and whose life has been tied to mine since the day when I found him caught in the beaver trap during the winter of the great snow."

There was a murmur of voices about him, though he could not make out the words. But when he looked at Kandaka, he saw that his friend was smiling at him and that his eyes were warm once again. And thus he continued, "I have said that my people choose a maiden because there is love between her and the man. It is a good thing which keeps them together all their lives. I say, and I mean in no way to offend any of you, for you know that I speak with a straight tongue in all things, that the son of your great chief, Kandaka, who is my truest friend, should be the one to take Letalto into his lodge. I have read in his eyes as in his words that he cares greatly for her. Mikanota, mighty chief of the Ayuhwa, let your son and Letalto share the lodge together because they are meant for each other. And I cannot take her as my squaw, because it is in my heart to leave your village and to go westward."

Now there was a chorus of "No, stay with us, mighty white-eyes hunter!" from the circle where he stood. And when he turned to glance at Letalto, she had turned to one side and her eyes were wet with tears. He knew that he had said what had to be said and said it without hurting any of these who had been his good friends. His voice grew stronger as he concluded. "I shall leave here, as the Great Spirit has told me that I must, but I shall remember all of you. That is why I beg you, O Mikanota, to let my blood mingle with your son's, so that it will be with me always. I shall remember, many long summers from now, the honor of friendship with Kandaka and with all those who are of your tribe."

Mikanota put his hands on John Cooper's shoulders and stared deeply into the lean, young face. Then he nodded slowly. "It shall be as you wish, *wasichu*. Nor shall we forget you when it is time for the buffalo hunt and the planting of the corn. You have learned our tongue well, but we have learned that your heart is good and that wherever you go, others like ourselves will say this of you."

He made a gesture, and Kandaka rose. Petimaka approached them, drawing a ceremonial knife with a bone handle. John Cooper stood beside Kandaka and they extended their wrists to the shaman, who nicked them. Then the shaman pressed their wrists together, bound them for a moment with a thong of white doeskin, and lifting his eyes to the starry night, said, "Let the blood of Kandaka and the *wasichu* mingle, let both of them, through the long summers and winters which await them until their days are done, be brothers out of one mind and heart and blood. Let them remember always how they shared the hunt and the games and the ways of our people, and may these memories go forth to their children and their children's children, so that it will always be said that Kandaka of the Ayuhwa and John Cooper of the *wasichus* lived together in peace, friendship, and brotherhood."

He untied the thong and, as John Cooper put his arms around Kandaka and hugged him, the young brave whispered, "You are younger than I, but you have read what was in my heart as if you were Petimaka himself. I will never forget what you have done this night, John Cooper, my friend, my brother."

John Cooper had packed his belongings in the sack, and Kandaka had made him a present of the mustang which he had ridden during the buffalo hunts. Mikanota had ordered that the squaws fill another sack with provisions, with plenty of dried buffalo meat and corn to sustain the young *wasichu* on his journey west. It was early afternoon in the first week of May when he mounted his mustang, whistling to Lije to follow him, after having said his farewells to the villagers. But as he turned the mustang westward and beyond Mikanota's lodge, a young woman in buckskin stood waiting in his path. It was Degala, standing erect, her head held high, holding up a beaded wampum belt in her slim hands.

"When the news was told in our other village that the young *wasichu* meant to leave us," she said in her soft, husky voice, "my clumsy fingers hastened to complete this gift. Forgive them if it is not well enough made to tell of your courage and kindness, for the time grew short and I have not much wisdom of such things."

He dismounted and approached her, his face reddening at the soft, almost plaintive look in her dark eyes. "You made this for me, Degala?"

"Yes, *wasichu*. The mother and father of Latiwaka instructed me, and they showed me how to sew the colored beads to picture how you killed the evil bear, and drew the curse from me, and made me whole again. I pray to the Great Spirit that, wherever you go, even those who are not friends will read the pictures on this belt and know that you are strong and good and kind."

John Cooper could not speak, and he felt his eyes sting with tears as, very simply, very gently, she clasped the belt around his waist and fastened it, then stepped back and crossed her arms over her bosom. She bowed her head as she murmured, "Thanks to you, a warrior as brave as Latiwaka has cast the arrow before me, and I have said that I will share his lodge. So my life begins again. May yours be long and rich, and may the squaw you choose for your lodge be grateful to the Great Spirit for such a worthy mate."

Awkwardly, he put out a hand to touch her cheek, then hastily drew it back. Finally he said, in an unsteady voice, "I shall always wear it, Degala. I shall never forget you. I, too, pray the Great Spirit will give you long life and happiness with your man. And now I must go."

He could not trust himself to say anything more as he mounted the mustang, whistled to Lije, and then, a wave of regret welling up inside him, rode on toward the west, toward the unknown. He turned once to look back, and saw Degala, still standing there and looking after him. He raised his hand in farewell and saw her wave back. Then, with a long sigh, he quickened the mustang's gait and regarded the valley and the forests ahead which he must cross on his new journey.

TWENTY-NINE

On the evening of the day on which John Cooper Baines left the Ayuhwa village, Don Diego de Escobar arranged a banquet in his new *hacienda* for the purpose of honoring his good friend and neighbor, Don Sancho de Pladero and his family.

For Don Diego, this first event in his own home marked a time not only for celebration, but also for taking stock on what had been accomplished since his departure from Madrid.

Miguel's choice of workers had been thoroughly admirable. Fat, good-natured Margarita Ortiz had proved to be a magnificent cook. She could turn a simple mutton stew into a sumptuous banquet, and, no matter how many unexpected demands were made upon her, she refused to become flustered. Gertrudes Delgado, the soft-spoken, industrious, nineteen-year-old wife of the sheepherder Luis, was both docile and tactful in serving as impetuous Catarina's personal maid. Twenty-year-old Dolores Costilla, the tall, good-natured and relatively well-educated wife of Salvador—whose talents as a blacksmith had induced Miguel Sandarbal to put him to work in that capacity—delighted Doña Inez with her thoughtful service. Educated in the convent school in Chihuahua, Dolores could read and write and express herself fluently. And, because Doña Inez warmed to her at once and treated her graciously, Dolores would have done anything in the world for her.

At Don Diego's suggestion, Miguel had ridden to Chihuahua to attend the great January trading fair, with orders to purchase tables, chairs, beds, and other furnishings to make the new *hacienda* thoroughly comfortable for the de Escobar family. Miguel had bargained shrewdly and saved his master a considerable sum. He had arranged for the shipment of purchased articles by *carretas*. Doña Inez was gratified to be given the opportunity by Don Diego to arrange the new furniture. For her, setting his new house in order and making it comfortable for him in his new life, symbolized the very role she longed to play in the future.

Miguel himself had supervised the first shearing, in the second week of April, and enthusiastically reported to his master that the men had acquitted themselves with skill and conscientiousness. From the herd of sheep, nearly a thousand pounds of wool had been collected, baled, packed, and dispatched by mule train under the escort of soldiers from Santa Fe who would continue their journey on to Mexico City to receive orders from the new viceroy. Teofilo Rosas was sent along with the wool to sell it profitably in Chihuahua and returned with the sum of several hundred silver *pesos*. It was an auspicious start for Don Diego de Escobar's new life in Nuevo Mexico, and it did much to hearten him.

As a former gardener, Miguel had proved invaluable in choosing some of the *peones* and their wives to grow gardens near the *hacienda* which would provide vegetables, herbs, and fruits for the de Escobars' table, as well as for their own subsistence. One of his first acts had been to seek a constant source of fresh water, and he had located a spring some five hundred yards from the house. A well had been dug and a wall built around it. Its flow was such that even in periods of drought, there would be no lack of water.

At the banquet table the night of Don Diego's celebration Tomás de Pladero was seated next to Catarina. Already, at fifteen, she evidenced the radiant beauty that would make her a stunning young woman. Taller and certainly more poised than when she had left the port of Cádiz with her father, brother, and aunt, she was even more conscious of her maturing adolescence.

It was evident that Tomás de Pladero was aware of Catarina's beauty, which was emphasized by the new frock that Doña Inez had purchased in Mexico City at Don Diego's request, and kept as a surprise gift for her fifteenth birthday. He conversed with her during the dinner, but his shyness did not impress Catarina—she thought of him not as a cavalier whose attention should be esteemed, but rather as a young man whom she could easily wind around her little finger.

Though now nineteen, Tomás had been given no freedom in the courting of girls. According to his mother's supercilious opinion, there were few families in Taos whose daughters could be considered eligible for a match with her son. Moreover, being far less athletic than Carlos and more inclined to the study of books, the appreciation of paintings, and the handcrafts of the pueblo Indians, Tomás's high-flown verbal attempts at gallantry very nearly made Catarina titter.

Don Diego sat at the head of the table with Don Sancho at his left. Observing the conversation between his son and his host's daughter, the latter leaned over to whisper, "It seems my son is smitten by your beautiful daughter—and no wonder! Perhaps one day there may be an even firmer bond between our two families. I for one, and my wife for another, would surely welcome this. Of course, it is much too early, and I trust you will forgive an old man's presumption, Don Diego."

But Don Diego de Escobar had already come to the private conclusion that the best way to solve Catarina's flights of sulkiness and loneliness would be to marry her to an eligible suitor. Surely the son of the *alcalde* of Taos would qualify as the most logical candidate. Because of his growing friendship for Don Sancho, he favored his guest with a sincere smile as he whispered back, "I assure you, Don Sancho, it would be a match of which I could approve. But, as you say, let us give the young people time."

When at last the festive evening came to a late end, and Carlos and Catarina had bidden their elders and aunt goodnight, Don Diego turned to Doña Inez. "My felicitations for a most successful evening, Doña Inez. Everything was superbly planned—and you are to be thanked for having supervised the household."

"*Gracias*, Don Diego. It was my pleasure. And it is good for Catarina and Carlos to have some social life."

"Yes, I quite agree. Did you notice how Tomás de Pladero stared at Catarina? Don Sancho said to me that perhaps one day there might be an alliance between our families. Well, my daughter could do worse."

Doña Inez was about to speak, but thought better of it and contented herself with a noncommittal, "I am sure that is true."

"One day, not too far in the future, we must think of finding a proper girl for my son, Doña Inez," Don Diego went on. Then, frowning, "Now that we have our fine new *hacienda* and these excellent servants, it would not be a bad idea to invite the other important *hacendados* and their families so that Carlos could have an opportunity to meet a well brought up, dutiful girl who will make him the right kind of wife. As I think of it now, he seems mainly interested in riding his stallion and befriending all the *trabajadores*."

"They all like him a great deal, Don Diego," Doña Inez observed.

"That is true. But I am not certain it is wise for him to show such a preference—after all, they are only *peóns*. He must not forget that he is the son of a nobleman."

"I do not think he will, Don Diego." Doña Inez could no longer suppress her own convictions. "But from what I have seen of Taos, it seems to me that this is a country where social classes mean very little, where survival is much more important. I think that Carlos's ability to make friends among what you call his inferiors will be extremely valuable to him when he comes to manhood. It will teach him justice and humanity and honesty." Then, aware that she had, perhaps, said too much, she lowered her eyes and added gently, "Forgive me, my dear brother-in-law. I have no right to interfere. And I am happy that you thought the banquet went well. I bid you goodnight, Don Diego."

He bowed to her as she left the room, then went over to the sideboard, took the cut-glass decanter, and poured himself a glass of Canary wine. He sighed, took a sip of it, and reflected aloud, "Trust a woman to always have the last word on everything, no matter what!"

It was early June, and two weeks before, John Cooper and Lije had crossed the wide Missouri at one of its shallower bends as they continued to travel westward. The Great Plains were verdant now under the blue sky and warm sun, and the wide-flung panorama of lush grass and leafy trees, of valleys, green hills, and running streams, stretched out as far as the eye could see. Game was abundant, from the white-tailed deer and the wild turkey to pheasants and chickens, as well as mule deer, antelope, and bustling flocks of sharp-tailed grouse. He and Lije ate well, and the wiry little mustang found rich and constant grazing whenever they stopped to make camp.

On his journey, John Cooper had seen isolated parties of white traders and one evening, just before crossing the Missouri, had been welcomed by a group of six trappers in whose packs were nearly a hundred cured beaver skins. They were heading to the northwest to trade with the Teton Sioux, they had told him, and by winter they would be back in Winnipeg. They were Frenchmen, but their leader, Jacques Pondierre, spoke enough English to make himself understood to the towheaded youth. They had trading goods of beads, knives, powder, and trinkets for the squaws, and they would bring back buffalo robes and hides from their dealings with the Sioux.

From the tales which stocky, bearded Jacques Pondierre told, John Cooper sensed the magnitude of this vast country. They had left Winnipeg the previous winter and, very much like himself and Lije, had lived off the land. They had encountered hardship and danger—two of their original party had been killed in an ambush by hostile Indians. Learning that John Cooper was homeless, Jacques Pondierre invited the youth to join them, but he politely declined and, the next morning, after having secured powder and lead from them, bade the trappers farewell and good luck.

On the evening of the nineteenth day of June, John Cooper and Lije came to a high, grassy knoll overlooking the Middle Loup River, northwest of Grand Island. He had shot a wild turkey early that afternoon, and the wolfhound stood expectantly beside him as he roasted the bird over a small fire.

"I swear, Lije, you and I are getting fat from all this game." He chuckled as, drawing the knife out of its sheath, he cut off a slice of the breast and tossed it to Lije, who bolted it down in a single gulp and wagged his tail for more. "If you keep that up, you'll be so fat and sassy you won't be much good to me on a hunt. Oh, all right, here's some more. You know we share and share alike."

Just as he was finishing his meal, he stiffened and crouched low, reaching for the rifle which he kept primed and loaded at all times, even when hunting for the day was over. He had heard a rustling in the bushes to his left, and he put out his other hand to touch Lije's muzzle, warning the wolfhound to silence.

Then to his right he heard a sharp crack and knew that someone had stepped on a twig. He cradled the rifle butt against his shoulder and called out in the Ayuhwa tongue, "I hear you! But I come in peace, not in war upon you!"

Then suddenly, surrounding him on every side, from behind the trees and out of the waist-high grass, there appeared a group of Indians. Their hair was cropped close to their skulls, and some of them had pierced their left ears and wore strings of colored beads in them, dangling like earrings. Their cheeks were painted with diagonal bars of red pigment, and their foreheads with a broad, red band in the center.

John Cooper sprang to his feet, aiming his gun at the one who appeared to be the leader. "My dog can kill as can I with this stick which speaks with thunder and shoots fire!" he exclaimed in the Ayuhwa tongue.

The leader, who faced him and carried a spear which he held with the point upward, grunted and pointed to the wampum belt, then turned to speak to the brave nearest him in a tongue John Cooper could not understand. In halting Sioux, he said in a deep voice, "I say to Mikaskwa that you are not enemy, but great hunter. The belt says you have killed an evil bear."

"I have said that I have come in peace. Are you Sioux?"

The leader shook his head. "Skidi Pawnee, white-eyes," he again replied in the Ayuhwa tongue. "We speak Caddoan. The Ayuhwa are not our enemies, but there are other Sioux who are."

"I have hunted with the Ayuhwa and now I go west." John Cooper accompanied his words with the sign language which Kandaka had taught him, and again, when he had finished, extended his hands palms upward, having lowered the rifle to the ground. Lije stood guard, the hair on the back of his neck bristling as he bared his teeth with a soft growl.

"Your dog does not fear us," the leader said, eyeing Lije.

"He has already killed a thief who tried to rob me of the bearskin from which I made the coat you see tied to my horse," John Cooper replied.

The leader grunted, glancing at Lije again with grudging

respect. "I am Tarskowa, war chief of the Skidi Pawnee. There are tribes who attack us, though we live in peace. We mean you no harm. Come with us. Our village is not far from here."

John Cooper pondered a moment and then agreed. They seemed friendly enough. The land was good and rich, and there was plenty of game. He and Lije could hunt to their hearts' content, at least through the summer. And if he found life onerous with the Pawnee, he could always move on. Extinguishing his fire, and indicating in sign language that he wished to make a gift of the remainder of the wild turkey to the war chief, he packed his belongings and mounted his mustang, Lije obediently trotting along beside him.

An hour later, he entered the village of the Skidi Pawnee, a series of large, circular, dome-shaped houses with turf roofs, supported by log frameworks. The houses ranged from thirty to forty feet in diameter, and were ten to fourteen feet tall. The floors were made of earth, and in the center of each was a large fireplace, with a hole in the roof to permit the smoke to escape. Between the houses stood high platforms made of poles, upon which food could be stored and dried and skins aired, out of reach of the hungry thieving dogs which barked and bristled at the sight of Lije. The village was not far from the river, and there were many patches of corn, beans, and squash in the lowlands near it. Yet, from the sight of the buffalo skins which many of this war party wore, John Cooper divined that their main food was buffalo meat.

They led him to the largest house at the far end of the village, dismounted, and signaled to him to do the same. Tarskowa approached the house, cupped his hands to his mouth, and called out in Caddoan, "Great chief Peltalaro, we bring a white-eyes hunter to you!"

From the entrance of the lodge there emerged a strong-featured, tall Pawnee in his mid-forties, dressed in a buffalo robe decorated with picturegraphs of multi-colored beads. He was thin-lipped, with a hawk nose and a high forehead, and his brows were plucked. His stern face was tinted on both cheeks by red and black-pigmented bands, and both his ears were pierced to hold short strings of red and black beads.

"He is our chief. He, too, speaks some Ayuhwa, white-eyes," the war chief muttered to John Cooper. Then, raising his voice, he spoke respectfully, inclining his head toward Peltalaro, explaining how he and his men had come upon

John Cooper and brought him back after seeing the wampum belt which told of his prowess as a killer of bears.

Peltalaro nodded, held up his hand, and then, staring coldly at John Cooper, declared in Ayuhwa, "Tarskowa says you are friend. But you have lived with the Ayuhwa, and they are of the Sioux who are our old enemies. You must be purified of their ways and learn ours if you are to live among us."

John Cooper glanced at the painted, suspicious faces clustered around him, and then nodded. He held out his hands with the palms upward to signify that he came in peace, and he said in Ayuhwa, "I have hunted with them, I have shared their ways, but I am not your enemy. If that is what you wish, I will agree to it. I speak with a straight tongue."

Peltalaro grunted noncommittally. Then he pointed to Lije and said, "Never have I seen a dog so large as this. There is much meat on him, and you shall eat of him yourself at the ceremonial feast after you have passed the tests of purification."

John Cooper tried not to show his alarm at this grisly statement. He remembered his father telling him that many Indian tribes looked upon dog as a rare delicacy. Then, summoning his wits, he replied, using the most solemn of Ayuhwa words and phrases, "If this were an ordinary dog, I would gladly sacrifice him for the feast of purification to prove I come in peace and would live among you. But this dog has within him the ghost of a great warrior from far across the seas. Yes, from where my own father was born, in a land where there are evil spirits, demons, and devils. If you kill him, these demons and evil spirits will come to dwell in your village and cast a spell which not even all your magic can turn aside."

Peltalaro grunted again, turned to a white-haired elder beside him, who was one of the village priests, and spoke in a low voice, glancing again at Lije and pointing to the wolf-hound. John Cooper watched anxiously, and saw the old man nod and whisper back to Peltalaro who in turn nodded and then declared in Ayuhwa, "We have no wish to bring the evil spirits in our midst, since we worship Morning Star and the Mother Corn. Say unto your dog and his ghost, then, that we will not harm him so long as he sets no demons free upon our village."

"I hear you, O Peltalaro, and I will speak to the ghost of

my dog and tell him what you have said. While he sees that I come to do no harm among you, he will not loose the demons."

"It is good. Tonight you will sleep inside my lodge on the ground. When the sun is ready to set tomorrow, you will submit to the tests of purification. Once that is done, we will tell you of our ways and teach you our tongue."

"It shall be as you wish, O Peltalaro," John Cooper responded, and once again made the sign of peace. Then he untied his sack and took the bearskin coat from the mustang, which one of the younger braves led away into a corral at the other end of the village. Peltalaro gestured for the youth to enter the lodge, and John Cooper turned to Lije and stroked the wolfhound's head, then told him, "Stay, Lije. Stay here and be a good boy. It'll be all right. They're friends."

A murmur of wonder was heard from the braves as they watched the wolfhound obediently trot over to the side of the lodge and lie down, resting his head on his front paws. John Cooper breathed a sigh of relief and closed his eyes, blessing the sixth sense which had let the wolfhound obey a verbal command and thus, as perhaps nothing else would have done, convinced the superstitious Skidi Pawnee that the dog indeed was the embodiment of a powerful spirit. Then he followed the chief into the lodge. Peltalaro turned to him and said quietly, "If Morning Star smiles upon you, I will welcome you as a dweller in my lodge. See now how we live."

There were many tiny rooms around the circular wall inside, and three women were kneeling around a fire in the very center of the house. There was room between the fire and the tiny rooms for the storage of wood and food, and one of the squaws took branches and cast them on the fire to replenish it, while another stirred an iron pot from which came a savory odor, the meat of buffalo cooked with corn and beans. As Peltalaro entered, the third squaw rose, crossed her arms over her bosom, and inclined her head in respect. "That is Siritanka, my first squaw and the mother of my first-born, white-eyes," Peltalaro gravely informed him. "My other squaws, those you see at the fire, live with me as do my other three sons. Also, my old mother, and my cousin and his family. And there——" his face grew grave as he turned to point to a tiny cubicle at the opposite side of the entrance, over which a buffalo robe served as curtain, "is the sacred bundle of Morning Star. As chief of the village, it is in my keeping so long as I am leader of the Skidi Pawnee. But this you will learn once you have been purified. Now I will take you to the place where you may cast your blanket and sleep well, for you will need your strength when the sun sets tomorrow."

THIRTY

When John Cooper wakened the next morning, food was brought to him by one of Peltalaro's wives, and, as he seated himself to eat from the clay bowl with his fingers, he made the sign of thanks. She turned away without a word, thus giving him to understand that until he had endured the tests of purification which her husband had decreed, he was still an intruder with whom there could be no real communication.

After he had eaten, John Cooper went outside to find that a warm, sunny day awaited him, as well as an overjoyed Lije, who reared up on his hind legs, placed his front paws on his young master's shoulders, and promptly licked his face to show how much he had missed him during the night. As the youth stared around at the other houses in the long, rectangular shape of this Pawnee village, he noticed with some surprise that one of the braves was leading his mustang directly into the house and, a few moments later, emerged without it. He shook his head and wryly told himself that there was much he would have to learn about these Indians, whose language was totally unintelligible to him. He noticed, also, that the Pawnee had round faces and were large of stature, much more so than the Ayuhwa; and they decorated themselves far more with mystic symbols, smeared in paint on their cheeks, chests, backs, and arms, as well as the inevitable beaded ear pendants. Since these pendants were of different lengths and of different colors, he was certain that they were meant to designate the status of the warrior, perhaps his skill in battle or at the hunt.

From the lodge at the right of the chief's, Tarskowa now emerged and, seeing John Cooper, grunted a greeting and approached him. He carried his lance, around the wooden handle of which were entwined rings made of painted duck feathers. Looking up at the warm blue sky, Tarskowa lifted the lance in his right hand as high as he could and drew a circle in the air before lowering it so that its haft touched the ground. Then he approached John Cooper and, in the harsh, deep voice which made his limited knowledge of Ayuhwa even more difficult to understand, declared, "Your ghost-dog is a warrior like you, white-eyes. Last night, while you slept, three of our dogs challenged him, and he bit two so badly that they were killed and will be served at the feast tomorrow night." Then, with a grim smile, "At which you will join us, young white-eyes, unless you fail the tests of Peltalaro."

"I will do my best to be worthy of these tests, Tarskowa."

"That is to be seen. When you hunted with the Ayuhwa, did the ghost-dog hunt with you?"

"Many times." John Cooper reached down to stroke Lije's great head. "By himself—and I saw it several times—he ran into the woods and brought back a rabbit in his jaws. And when I killed a quail or a duck with the long stick that thunders and spits fire, he would bring it back to the village with me."

"I think you speak with a straight tongue, white-eyes. Though I tell you now, one of the tests will be that you must go into the woods and, without knife or lance, without your long stick or this ghost-dog, bring back game for our cooking fire."

"That will be the easiest test of all," John Cooper straightened his shoulders and purposely bragged. That was one thing Pa had always drummed into him, from as early as he could remember: never let an Indian know you're afraid of him or back down from a dare; Indians respect bravery as much as they do honesty. And, from all Kandaka had taught him about setting intricate traps, he was pretty sure that he wasn't really boasting when he told Tarskowa that.

Since there was little for him to do until sundown, he spent most of the day walking through the village with Lije, noting with concealed amusement that the mongrels gave the wolf-hound a wide berth. As for Lije, he did not even bother to recognize their existence, but walked along, head erect, tail stiffly thrust behind him, glancing up now and again at his young master and, as if to show that he shared in John Cooper's private joke, occasionally opened his mouth and let his pink tongue loll out.

About an hour before sundown, he returned and stood before Peltalaro's lodge to show his readiness to submit himself. Since he wasn't exactly sure where the tests would take place, he decided to tie Lije up so that he wouldn't try to attack or bite anybody in case he saw them being mean to his master.

Just as he had finished, Peltalaro came out of the house, and at the same moment, from the house which stood at the left of the chief's, John Cooper saw an old man emerge. His face was completely covered with red paint, and he was swathed in a buffalo robe, his leggings decorated with human scalps and eagle feathers. There were soft down feathers in his white hair, and a single eagle feather stood upright in his scalplock. In his left hand he carried a dry ear of corn and in his right a little pipe filled with tobacco.

"He is Kiskawe, priest of Morning Star," Peltalaro told John Cooper. "It is he who orders the tests of purification to say whether you shall be one of us or be sent away from our village forever. The time approaches. Strip yourself to breechclout and moccasins."

John Cooper grimaced as he obeyed. Kandaka had given him several pairs of moccasins, and they had been most comfortable on his journey to the Loup River. Somewhat self-consciously, he stripped naked except for the breech-clout, flexed his muscles, drew a deep breath or two, and waited.

As the sun began to set, John Cooper saw Pawnee braves emerge from their houses. With another grimace, he observed that all of them carried switches and cudgels, and then he guessed what the first test would be: he was to run the gauntlet.

Kiskawe advanced and lifted the pipe above his head, then touched his left shoulder with the ear of corn and spoke in a shrill voice. Peltalaro translated for John Cooper. "If you are true warrior for Morning Star, Mother Corn will give you strength. If you are brave, you will smoke the pipe of the priest of Morning Star. Now run!"

At first glance, he counted at least two hundred braves in that double line, each pair spaced well apart so that they would have ample opportunity to rain their blows upon the victim. The muscles of his thighs and back tightened as if in anticipation of the stinging, bruising blows those switches and cudgels could inflict. The first two braves in the long, double line were young men, the one at his left holding a stout cudgel of hickory wood, with a cruel knot at the end. He grinned evilly, lifted the cudgel to menace John Cooper, and then gestured with it to urge the youth toward him.

John Cooper took another deep breath, squatted down, and flexed his fingers. There was sandy dirt around him, and he stealthily dug his fingers into the ground and filled his fists with the dirt. Then, while pretending still to ready himself, he suddenly darted forward toward the youth with the cudgel, flinging the dirt into the Pawnee's eyes and at the same moment tripping him to the ground and wresting away the cudgel. As he did so, the switch of the other youth cut across his neck and shoulders, and he whirled, still in a crouching position, and slammed the knotted end of the cudgel against the Pawnee's belly. The latter let out an astonished grunt, dropped the switch, doubled over, and sank down on his knees.

Swiftly, John Cooper seized the discarded switch in his left hand and then flung himself forward, launching blows with both his newly acquired weapons at the braves on either side of him. One of the braves stumbled back and fell full length, stung by a blow to the cheek; another howled as the switch cut round his middle. Now John Cooper raced forward, suddenly halting and turning on the nearest assailant at his left with a vengeful blow of the cudgel which knocked the brave's heavy switch from his hands and sent him sprawling. There were shouts of both approval and anger from the others who awaited their turns, but a voice louder than theirs halted the gauntlet. "Enough!" Peltalaro called. "The white-eyes is no coward and he is cunning. Let the first test be done with now."

John Cooper was about to rush forward, his cudgel up-raised, when he saw the others up ahead in that long line lower their switches and cudgels and move away. He turned, staring at the chief, who beckoned to him with a faint smile on his thin-lipped mouth.

"You have done well, white-eyes. Let us see if purification

by smoke and fire which will burn in the honor of Evening Star will find you as worthy!"

Peltalaro made a sign, and John Cooper felt himself seized by two braves. Lije, who had been growling softly all through the gauntlet, now lunged against his leash, but it held, and he barked angrily.

"Still, boy! It's all right, I'm fine! Now you stay still, you hear me?" he called. Then he nodded, to reaffirm the order, and the wolfhound, with an uneasy whine, slowly lay down, his keen eyes intent on the proceedings.

At Kiskawe's sign, four other braves approached, carrying a long pole between them. The two Pawnee holding John Cooper now bound his wrists and ankles with rawhide thongs. They lifted him in the air beneath the pole while the other four passed the pole through the loops left in the thongs so that he was trundled, face upward to the sky, through the village and finally to a small, earth-covered house which was set back from all the others. The outside of the house was painted with red, black, and yellow pigments. Inside, four old women were preparing a fire of twigs, branches, leaves, and dry corn husks. On each side of the fire, there stood a pole with a Y-shaped top, rising four feet from the ground. The braves lifted the pole to which John Cooper was bound and settled it into the two forks and then left the little house. John Cooper could hear the crackling of the flames, and soon the pungent heavy smoke drifted up to him, making him choke and cough. His limbs ached from the suspension, and the thongs which bound his wrists and ankles had been tied cruelly tight, not enough to cut off the circulation but to add to his discomfort.

Below him, he heard the old women break into a monotonous, eerie chant, in which the incomprehensible word "sharo" was repeated many times. He could feel the heat of the flames, though they did not quite reach him, and his skin grew dry. The pain grew worse and worse.

Now the old women rose and began to jab at him with twigs and sharp stones. He gasped and writhed as the smoke swirled into his nostrils. He clenched his teeth as he felt the sweat on his body oozing in his armpits and as swiftly drying from the intense heat below him. Out of both sudden inspiration and a frantic attempt to distract himself from the intolerable discomfort, he suddenly began to sing. All that came to mind was "Yankee Doodle" and he hoarsely shouted out, "Stuck a feather in his hat and called it macaroni!" with all his remaining strength.

There were pleased murmurs from the old women, and then he heard their footsteps receding as they left the little house. He tried to make sense of his dazed, reeling thoughts —what had made him sing out like that? Maybe it was because way back, he remembered hearing that when Indians were put to the torture stake and wanted to show how brave they were, they sang their death song to defy their torturers. But at least they'd stopped poking him with those twigs and stones, and that was something to be thankful for.

The crackling of the flames seemed to die down, but the smoke redoubled, and he coughed violently, writhing and twisting on the pole, his body aching, his wrists and ankles numb. His head was throbbing violently and when he tried to repeat the words of the song, his voice cracked and dwindled. He tried to gasp for just one tiny breath of fresh air.

Then suddenly he heard voices, and he felt the pole to which he was attached being lifted and carried out of the house. Half-conscious, deathly sick, he coughed and choked, all the while drawing in the blessed, clean, cool air. He had kept his eyes closed tightly throughout his ordeal, and now, cautiously, he blinked them until his vision cleared. He could see the full moon overhead.

Kiskawe stood beside him, touching him with the ear of corn on the forehead, putting the pipestem to his parched, cracked lips, saying something he couldn't understand. Then they lowered the pole, and one of the braves cut the thongs that bound him. He slumped, panting and gasping, to the ground. It was over.

Although dazed and weak from his trial of fire and smoke, John Cooper's first thought was of Lije. When two of the Pawnee led him, stumbling and gasping for breath, back to the chief's lodge, he disengaged himself from their supporting hold, sank down on his knees, and made the sign that he wanted a knife to cut the rawhide leash. Peltalaro awaited him in the doorway. "One test remains when the sun rises, young white-eyes. Let your dog who has the ghost of a great warrior enter with you and stay with you this night. But he will not follow you when the sun rises. Let your spirit reach out to his, that you may have skill for your final test."

John Cooper flung himself down on the blanket in the little cubicle, and Lije lay down beside him. Scarcely had he reached out to stroke the wolfhound's head when exhaustion claimed him. He fell asleep at once, to be wakened at daybreak by Peltalaro gripping his shoulder and urging him to present himself for the last ordeal. He staggered to his feet, wincing at the aching of his body.

"This is what you must do if you will stay among us," the Pawnee chief explained. "You will go from this village, without the ghost-dog, without the long tooth which you wear about your neck, and without the long stick that thunders and spits fire. You are to bring back meat for the fire of my house, for this will show truly that you are a mighty hunter. Go now, tell your ghost-dog to remain with us, and go as you were clad for the tests of courage."

And so, in breechclout and moccasins, John Cooper walked out of the village and toward the forest which lay to the north and the west, after first ordering Lije to stay behind, inside the chief's house.

He was well aware of the difficulty of the task. He could hardly make a trap without anything with which to fashion a running slipnoose that would tighten when the quarry set foot within the perimeter of bent-over saplings. He had neither cord nor the hairs from a horse's tail. He didn't even have a knife to whittle the posts of such a trap. As he started into the forest, he listened to the sounds of the birds and the chittering of squirrels, and his keen blue eyes studied the ground, the grass, the bushes, and the trees.

After walking for about half a mile, he came to a little creek. His moccasined foot struck a small, oblong, white stone. He stooped to retrieve it and thoughtfully continued toward the creek. Before he reached it, he saw a heavy, gnarled, oak branch lying in his path, a cudgel not unlike those with which the Pawnee had armed themselves to form the gauntlet. This, too, he picked up, swinging it and testing it for balance, and then smiled wryly.

As he approached the nearer bank of the creek, he sank down on his knees and began to crawl quietly. He had glimpsed a covey of brown-tailed partridges on the opposite bank, busily pecking and scrabbling for grubs and insects. Keeping his head down, he headed for a thicket of waist-high bushes which fringed this nearer bank and would hide him from the partridges.

He waited a few moments, flattened himself, and crawled forward, parting the bushes with his hands until he could see the birds plainly and yet was still concealed. He examined the stone and then the branch, which was a few inches longer than his arm. Laying down the stone at his left, he straightened until only the top of his head appeared above the bushes. Then he drew back the branch, calculating how far and how hard he would have to throw it. It was a distance of about twenty feet, and the creek was shallow. There was no wind to give momentum to the throw; the sun was already very warm and the air was humid.

John Cooper took a deep breath, drew back his arm as far as he could, then stood up and flung the branch with all his might toward the covey. Some of the birds took flight with a whirring of wings, but his aim had been true, and he let out a boyish whoop as he saw three birds felled by the heavy branch. One of them lay dead; the other two, with broken wings, squawked and tried to hobble away. Rushing out of the thicket, he waded into the shallow creek and wrung the necks of the two crippled partridges. There was a patch of coarse and sturdy weeds halfway up the bank, and he tore out a handful and began to fashion a crude carrying-rope, tying one end around the necks of the three partridges and using the other end as a handle to carry them back. He retrieved the cudgel, found a heavier stone, about the size of his fist, at the top of the bank, and trudged onward to the west.

About a quarter of an hour later, he saw a wild jackrabbit nibbling at a leafy plant near a large cedar tree. He laid down his improvised cudgel and the string of partridges and, holding his breath and gripping the round hard stone, drew it back and flung it. Once again he let out a whoop of exultation. The stone had hit the rabbit in the head and killed it. He found more of the weeds, tied one end of the makeshift cord round one of the rabbit's hind legs, then made the other end fast to the gripping end of the string of partridges. He turned back toward the village, using his cudgel as a walking stick.

When he returned, late that afternoon, he was embarrassed as he had been in the Ayuhwa village, to see that some of the young girls and mature squaws were standing near their lodges, pointing at him, laughing, and making comments which he knew had to do with his near-nakedness. Ignoring these ribald greetings, he walked to the chief's lodge. Lije, hearing his master call out the name of Peltalaro, bounded out to greet him, once again standing on his hind legs with his paws on John Cooper's shoulders and licking his face as if they had been separated for many years.

The Pawnee chief grunted his approval when he saw the partridges and the rabbit. "You have shown that you are indeed a hunter and warrior and that you have courage. If it is your wish, stay with us and, with your long stick that thunders and spits fire, join our braves in hunting the great shaggy ones."

"This I will do gladly," John Cooper replied again in Ayuhwa. "But if I am to live among you, I must learn to speak your language. Is there a young warrior of your tribe who can teach me?"

"Yes, there is Narkinawa," Peltalaro answered after a moment's thought. "When he was a child, he was captured by the Dakota, and his father traded horses to their chief so that after many moons he returned to us. In the Dakota village, there was a young maiden of the Ayuhwa who had been captured also, and she became his squaw. His father had to give many more horses to let her return with him to us."

"I would gladly meet him, O Peltalaro, for I wish to learn quickly how to say what is in my heart so that you will understand me."

"That is good, young white-eyes," the Pawnee chief retorted gruffly, with an approving nod. "Narkinawa will teach you also why it is we worship Morning Star and Mother Corn." He looked up at the sky and his face took on a mystical expression. "Only the great Pawnee of the plains are blessed by Morning Star and Mother Corn. You cannot know our ways until you understand this." Then, more matter-of-factly, he added, "You will eat with us this night in my house, young white-eyes."

"You do me great honor." John Cooper inclined his head and crossed his arms over his chest, knowing from Kandaka that this was the sign of utmost respect to a shaman or a tribal leader.

THIRTY-ONE

On October 23, 1809, the wealthy Mexico City royalist, Augustín Iturbide, pledged his finances, his support, and his unwavering loyalty to the cause of Ferdinand VII, thus defying the will of the Corsican conqueror. Through his efforts, the Central Junta of Spain replaced Pedro Garibay with Archbishop Francisco Javier Lizangay y Beaumont as the fifty-seventh viceroy of New Spain.

On this same day, Carlos de Escobar celebrated his eighteenth birthday, and his proud father gave a great feast in honor of the occasion. He invited not only the de Pladeros, but also many of the wealthy landowners of Taos. He confided to Doña Inez that he hoped in this way the groundwork could be laid for a match between his handsome young son and the daughter of some eligible *rico* whose blood was distinguished enough to mingle with that of the de Escobars. Although his sister-in-law privately believed that Carlos was still much too young to contemplate marriage, she rightly reasoned that her forthright nephew would himself veto his father's matchmaking plans.

Doña Inez's belief in her nephew's common sense was more than justified at the latter's birthday fiesta. A month before, Don Diego had been visited by a wealthy landowner,

Don Sebastián de Galvez. "I, like yourself, Don Diego," Don Sebastián declared, "am a true Spaniard. My dear wife and I lived in Barcelona for many years before we came here to Taos to live near her cousin. I, for one, resent taxes levied to support the brother of a man who, not content with proclaiming himself emperor of the French, seeks to rule all of Europe into the bargain and to plunge our country into bloody, impoverishing wars. These taxes, you well know, Don Diego, will go to strengthen Napoleon's armies in the Peninsula, and many good Spaniards have died because of this."

"I share your feelings. And I am not yet sure whether the present viceroy has chosen, as his predecessor did, to save all monies until the day when a true Spanish king will once again sit upon the throne in the Escorial. Yet my duty is plain, as is Don Sancho de Pladero's: as officials appointed by the crown, we must follow the laws to the letter. I know that the governor agrees with us on this and that he himself has expressed in many a letter to the viceroy the folly of sending all these funds on to Joseph Napoleon," Don Diego had replied.

From the friendship which had begun at this first, formal meeting between the two men, Don Sebastián de Galvez had been invited to attend the celebration of Carlos's birthday. He brought with him his wife, Doña Matilda, and his elder daughter, Serafina.

It was evident from the outset that, having already noticed Carlos riding his stallion, Valor, and seeing his good looks and poise, Don Sebastián entertained hopes of an eventual alliance between Serafina and Carlos. Indeed, through the dinner, seated at one side of his host, he sought to impress Don Diego with a recital of his daughter's virtues. She could read poetry with feeling, she was well educated, and expert in the domestic arts as well, and even though she was all of twenty-one, she was the most dutiful of daughters. Such a paragon, he concluded, would make the perfect wife for a young man who was, without doubt, a great credit to his distinguished father.

Doña Inez could not help eavesdropping. If she knew Carlos, she thought, he would find these categorized virtues more of a danger signal than a beckoning light. Serafina de Galvez was tall, with an oval face and a supercilious, disdainful expression which made Doña Inez long to give her a good slap, just to see if she could show any emotion.

After dinner, the evening being unusually warm for October, a fandango was held in the patio. Don Diego suggested that Carlos dance with Serafina, and the youth politely invited the young woman to be his partner. Don Sebastián charmed Doña Inez by asking her to dance with him, and Don Diego escorted Doña Matilda to the patio.

Tomás de Pladero selected Catarina as his dancing partner for the fiesta. During the summer, she had spent many hours riding her beloved mare, Marquita, and her soft olive skin was enhanced by a golden burnished tan from the sun. Almost sixteen, she had already begun to ripen into a voluptuous young beauty. Her high forehead and sculptured cheekbones, her flashing green eyes, and her imperious, though sensuous, mouth were set off by her long, glossy, black hair. Fully conscious that she was desirable and nearing an age when she might well consider taking a *novio*, she wore her hair long out of preference.

Tomás had ridden his own horse with her during the summer on those occasions when his shrewish mother permitted him to leave the *hacienda*. Doña Elena had already discussed with her husband the possibility of the alliance which she knew he favored. "I shall grant that the girl is already a little beauty," she had told him, "and that her father is a nobleman. But there is the matter of a dowry, and I am quite certain that you are much wealthier than Don Diego de Escobar. So I do not know whether he could furnish a dowry worthy of his station if—and it is a very great if, I assure you, my husband— I should consent to a marriage between Tomás and Catarina."

For all the talk of marriage among their elders, however, neither Carlos nor Catarina were concerned with such grandiose plans. Even when they rode together, Catarina regarded Tomás as hardly more than a grownup playmate, not to be taken at all seriously. He was so placid, so pompous and awkwardly gallant, and she was quite sure that he was tied to his mother's apron strings. As for Tomás himself, although he considered Catarina to be one of the loveliest girls he had ever seen, he had already noticed certain traits, such as her petulant tirades and her sulkiness, which kept him from thinking of her as a future bride.

Carlos was not too comfortable with Serafina de Galvez this evening, either. He would much rather have been out riding Valor, or going to the bunk house and exchanging tall tales with the friendly *trabajadores*. Also, Serafina, despite her father's description of her, began by questioning him about his likes and dislikes, and rather clumsily remarked, with an affected little titter, "Señor Carlos, you are such a handsome *caballero* that I am sure you must have many *novias* already."

"No, Señorita Serafina," he replied politely, "I have not had such good fortune as yet."

"Ah?" she answered coyly, fluttering her long eyelashes at him, as she curtsied in one of the measures of the fandango. After a few more steps, Carlos observed that she was not really a good dancer. This suspicion was confirmed when, in the concluding measures, she very nearly tripped over one of his feet and, recovering herself, flung her arms around him, only to draw back, blush, and stammer an effusive and overdone apology.

"Let me get you a glass of punch, Señorita Serafina," he proposed, hurrying off to find it for her. When he returned, he sat with her a few moments, fidgeting and glancing at his father, who was regaling Doña Matilda with stories about his beloved Madrid. His father glanced at him, smiled, then went back to his conversation—there was obviously no hope from that quarter. After a few more minutes, during which Serafina de Galvez flirted with him rather openly, Carlos frowned and put a hand to his head, sighed and declared, "I am not used to such an elaborate birthday party, Señorita Serafina. Will you forgive me if I excuse myself? It has been my great privilege to have met you."

"And mine, dear Carlos," Serafina purred as she opened her fan and fluttered it.

Carlos promptly escaped to the bunk house, to Miguel and the Corrado brothers. When Jorge told him that there had been three new lambs that day, he shrugged and declared, "That is to be expected when rams go to ewes, *hombre*. But I should much rather hear about the fairs you had in Chihuahua."

Later, after the Corrados had resumed a card game which they had been playing for months with honors about even, Carlos whispered to Miguel, "Let us go out in the fresh air, *hombre*. I have no desire to go back to the ball."

"As you like, young master. But after all, it is your birthday and the guests will miss you. And your father will be disappointed," Miguel tactfully pointed out. Nonetheless, with an indulgent shrug, he accompanied Carlos outside and stood beside him as the handsome young heir of Don Diego stared eagerly toward the distant mountains and the fringe of stars which seemed to circle them.

"Ah, sometimes I think I would like to live in those mountains, Miguel. A man could be free and close to heaven there," Carlos said pensively.

"If he were truly free, young master, yes. But you are Don Diego's only son, Carlos, and you cannot dismiss that. Here he is, alone in this strange new world, making the best of a new life that is as different from the Madrid we all knew as the sun from the stars. And all the more reason why he is counting on you to bring honor to his name."

"Yes, of course you are right, Miguel. Just the same, I have no stomach for fancy balls or the ceremonies of the court—even if we had stayed in Madrid, I would have wanted to work on the land, to work with animals the way you do, to feel that what I had was what I had worked to gain by myself. And now Father is trying to marry me off to some highborn girl—that is not at all what I want."

"You are young, Carlos, and I will agree that it is a bit early to think of marriage—though do not tell your father I said so," Miguel chuckled.

Carlos frowned and walked a few steps away, breathing in the cool night air. Then, turning back to Miguel, he replied, "All I am sure of is that I have not met any girl I would think of marrying. But when the time comes, I will want her to be someone I love with all my heart and soul. And I think I will know her when I meet her."

"Amen to that, young master. And now you had best go back to your guests. *Buenas noches* and a happy birthday to you, Carlos."

The next morning, Don Diego took Carlos to task. "Remember, Carlos, you are my only heir. One day you will inherit all of this. Therefore, your conduct must be beyond reproach. And, even though you are only eighteen, it is not too early for you to think of marriage. In this primitive land, all the more reason that we de Escobars should think of perpetuating our noble lineage."

"But, Father," Carlos protested, "I should rather be a monk than marry a girl like that Serafina de Galvez. Besides, I am sure she is not interested in me."

"There you are wrong, Carlos," his father retorted. "At the conclusion of the fiesta in your honor last night—and I take it amiss that you should have pretended to have a headache so that you could go out and hobnob with the *peóns*—Don Sebastián himself told me that it would be his daughter's dearest wish to be joined with you in marriage."

Carlos raised his eyes and was silent, knowing that whatever he said would only irritate his father. All the same, he resolved that he would do his best to be absent from the next fiesta or *baile*, if Serafina de Galvez attended it.

On the day after John Cooper had successfully completed the Pawnee tests of purification, Peltalaro led him to the lodge of Narkinawa. It was one of the smaller, earth-covered houses near the entrance of the village and not far from the house in which John Cooper had endured the ordeal of fire and smoke. He took an immediate liking to this Pawnee brave in his early thirties, whose appearance reminded him of his good friend, Kandaka.

Narkinawa's wife, Sepirqua, a rather plump, shy, young woman about twenty-five years old, invited John Cooper into their house and prepared food for him. He made the sign of thanks, Narkinawa smiled and said to him in Ayuhwa, "Our chief has bidden me teach you the Caddo tongue so that you may know our ways. And I am also to instruct you in the meaning of our gods, especially he who is Morning Star."

"All this I am eager to learn, Narkinawa," John Cooper replied.

The young Pawnee thought for a moment, rubbed his chin, then suggested, "Perhaps the best way is to tell you the Ayuhwa word and then our own. It will be slow, and you must listen well."

"The days are long and I am young," John Cooper retorted.

"That is so. Then, I will tell it all to you in our own tongue and see if you can repeat any of the words and put them into the Ayuhwa. We will do this after the sun rises and again after it is at its zenith in the heavens. For Peltalaro says that he wishes you to go on the hunt for the great shaggy ones and to take with you your long stick which thunders and spits fire."

With this preface, Narkinawa began. "Tirawa is our supreme God, and all of the lesser ones, both of the heavens and of the earth, as well as we ourselves, acknowledge His supremacy. His commands are carried out by lesser gods who are subject to Him. After Tirawa and his squaw, she that is called Vault of the Heavens, next in rank is Tcuperikata—the

Evening Star. She maintains a garden in which grow fields of ripening grain and many buffalo and from which spring all streams of life."

"And who is your Morning Star, Narkinawa?" John Cooper asked.

"He is equal to Tcuperikata. In the dawn of the world he overcame her, and had his way with her. It was thus that she became the mother of the first human being upon earth, a girl child. We offer sacrifice each spring of a maiden to honor Morning Star, the father and procreator of this first human."

"Human sacrifice?" John Cooper echoed, astonished.

Narkinawa nodded gravely. "Yes. For that is how the corn flourishes and the herds of buffalo come to us to give their meat to our tribes. Two full moons before you came to us, a maiden from the Blackfoot was brought to our village and greatly honored. Then her blood was spilled upon the ground in such a tribute."

John Cooper shook his head but remained silent. The enormity of this religious act struck at his nature, yet he knew that it would be both tactless and dangerous to denounce it. So he contented himself by saying, "I would know more of your gods and how they shape your ways."

"And I will tell you, *wasichu*," Narkinawa solemnly replied. "Next in rank to Evening Star and Morning Star are the gods of the four quarters of the world, who stand in the northeast, the southeast, the southwest and the northwest, and thus support the heavens. Evening Star, through her four assistants who are wind, cloud, lightning, and thunder, tells us of the will of Tirawa. Then, after the gods of the four world quarters, come the three gods of the north, of whom North Star, Kaririwari, is foremost. Our chief, Peltalaro, is guided by North Star, and North Star presides over all the councils of the gods in the heavens."

As the lesson went on, John Cooper was astounded at the many lesser gods who ruled the lives of the Skidi Pawnee. There were the Great Black Meteoric Star, patron god of all shamans, and Operikahuririwisisu, who stood at the southern end of the Milky Way and received the spirits of the dead, over whom he presided in the Great Spirit Land. And there was Fool Wolf, who was slighted during the earliest councils of all the gods and because of this introduced death into the world. And most fascinating of all to the wondering youth was the ceremonial system of the sacred bundles, for each

Skidi Pawnee village received a bundle direct from its foster-
ing god. In the Morning Star bundle of ritual sacrifice, for
example, the designated priest would choose a warrior to
impersonate Morning Star, and take from the sacred bundle a
pipe, tobacco, paints, and a buffalo hide wrapper. The warrior would select assistants who would participate in the
capture of the chosen maiden destined for sacrifice. To
Evening Star, the sacrifice would be the heart and tongue of a
buffalo and tobacco. "Only the priests trained in our ceremo-
nials can interpret all the signs, the taboos, and the words and
the dancings of our great gods," Narkinawa concluded.

Through the months which followed, John Cooper spent
many hours in Narkinawa's lodge. His quick, retentive mind
enabled him to learn Caddo rapidly and with reasonable
fluency. All the same, he was always happy to leave the
smoke-filled lodge—his tutor concluded each lesson by obliging John Cooper to smoke the ceremonial pipe of friendship
—and to go hunting with Lije.

Late in November, Peltalaro himself accompanied John
Cooper and the wolfhound and observed with delighted
wonder the accuracy of "Long Girl" and Lije's ability to
retrieve fallen game. Peltalaro was equally impressed by John
Cooper's generous sharing of the game with Lije, which gave
greater credence to the youth's avowal that the wolfhound
possessed the spirit of a great warrior from across the seas.
Earlier that month, John Cooper had ridden with the war
chief, Tarskowa, and the latter's good friend, Mikaskwa, on a
buffalo hunt. John Cooper's success—he killed eighteen buffalo—won him jubilant acceptance as a mighty hunter who
had earned his right to live among the Skidi Pawnee.

Also in November, José Ramirez, Don Sancho de Pladero's
capataz, was entertaining Consuela Viola in his cottage. He
was in rare, good humor. This plump *puta* had turned out to
be an invaluable aide in furthering his lecherous enjoyments.
As a matter of fact, he had already begun to tire of her
overripe charms and her abject docility, for she was thoroughly terrified of him. One evening in October, she had
watched in horror as he had marched a tearful kitchen maid
out to the shed near his cottage and flogged her. "You see,
little one," he chuckled, lolling back in his chair while she
hastened to tug off his boots, "little Francesca wasn't very
smart. She thought herself too good for José Ramirez, *¿comprende?* Oh yes, you may be sure I told her many a time that

if she didn't please Doña Elena, she would find herself at the mercy of my whip. And you saw yourself what she did."

"*Sí*, José," Consuela promptly agreed.

"Well, you can be very useful to me. And indeed, if you want to go on being my favorite and getting more *pulque* and tequila, you'll have to begin to earn it."

"What—what do you mean?" she stammered, looking up at him with frightened eyes.

"It's very simple. Every so often, Doña Elena discharges some of her maids. Francesca is on trial right now, and I would not be surprised if she were kicked out before the Holy Day of our Lord's Nativity. Of course," he bent forward with a leer and chucked her under the chin, "you see her every day, Consuela. You might just tell her that if she makes up her mind to be nice to me, if she visits me, here in my cottage, I will talk to Doña Elena. Oh yes, Doña Elena and Don Sancho, too, they take my advice, be sure of that!"

"I will, José, I promise I will."

"*Bueno*. And when new maids come into the house, Consuela, I want you to sound them out, understand? Tell them that if they value their place in the de Pladero *hacienda*, they had best make up their minds to be obliging."

"I promise I will. You know I always obey you!"

"I will let you know which one I fancy, my little dove," he continued, with a guffaw. "And you know, sometimes if a girl is very stubborn, and doesn't get into trouble and does her work, there are ways of making Doña Elena find fault with her. Now, for example, if there is a new maid who makes up the beds very neatly and dusts the furniture as she should, what is there to prevent you from going into the room and undoing all the good work she has done, *¿comprende?* That way, she will be blamed, and, if she isn't nice to me, she will find herself out in the shed. Do you think, stupid one, you can remember all this? If you do not, I'll give you a taste of the quirt, and I won't need an order from Doña Elena to do it, either."

"Oh no, I will do whatever you want, I swear it!" Consuela babbled.

Catarina de Escobar's sixteenth birthday, on the 26th of February, 1810, was the occasion for a gala fiesta. By this time, Don Diego had made several lasting friends, even among the *ricos*. With the growing news of Joseph Napoleon's tyranny upon the Spanish throne and the constant demands for heavier excise taxes, they had come to understand that Don Diego's fierce loyalty to the rightful occupant of the Spanish throne was an attribute to admire and respect.

Just before the formal banquet began, Don Diego closeted himself with his lovely black-haired daughter and, after much hemming and hawing, came to the point. "Tonight, Catarina, there are two very worthy gentlemen to whom I want you to pay particular attention. You see, my dear, it is customary for girls to be married before boys—after all," this with a flattering smile, "you know that already at sixteen you fancy yourself a woman—and you are surely a beautiful one, albeit still young! It is not wrong for you to begin to think of a man who will make you happy. Your aunt, for whose opinion I have the utmost respect, will surely agree with me on this."

"Well, I shall be nice to them if you say so, Father." Catarina tossed her head and went back to primping in her mirror. When Don Diego had left the room, she walked over to the table on which she had placed the silver cage with her cockatoo and began to tease it with her finger, encouraging it to repeat the endearment of which she never tired, *"Quiero, Ca-ta-ri-na."*

Her new, green gown, a birthday present from Doña Inez, enhanced her dark beauty. Moreover, Catarina, whose narcissism had grown with the passing of time, had discovered that if she smiled in a certain way, a dimple appeared at the left corner of her mouth, near her cheek. And she favored the two men of whom her father had spoken with many displays of that bewitching dimple.

One of these was a fifty-year-old widower, Don Pedro de Saltada, whose wife had died eight years before and who was almost as rich as Don Sancho. Catarina had been seated beside him, and for a time she amused herself teasing him and making eyes at him, seeing from the very start that he was smitten with her. Across the table sat the severe-looking, twenty-eight-year-old Felipe de Cortana, who would have taken monastic vows if his father had not died suddenly and left him in control of one of the larger trading posts between Taos and Santa Fe. It was true that this was a rather plebeian occupation for a nobleman, but his father, a practical man who had little stomach for Spanish politics, had wisely preferred to earn a decent livelihood, rather than being reduced to genteel poverty.

Catarina danced with both of these men. She made poor

Don Pedro de Saltada blush by telling him that she thought
he was a dear old man who reminded her of her beloved
father. Felipe de Cortana bowed stiffly, took her hand and
kissed it; and then, in a rather sententious speech, intimated
that he would wish to call upon her again and then eventually
upon her father, if, of course, she thought that she might
favor his suit for her hand in marriage. To this she replied,
"But I have only met you, Señor de Cortana. It is too soon
for me to feel anything about you, except that I think you are
very polite and not a bad dancer. Thank you very much for
coming to my birthday fiesta."

After the guests had left the *hacienda*, Carlos gave his
sister a beautifully hand-tooled bridle and reins for Marquita,
kissed her on the cheek, and said, "My little sister has become
a very beautiful woman!" Then he bade her good night and
went off to his room.

Don Diego approached her now, with Doña Inez behind
him, smiling indulgently. "Well now, Catarina, what did you
think of those two fine *caballeros*?"

Catarina shrugged and made a face. "The one is almost old
enough to be my grandfather, and, as for Felipe de Cortana,
being his wife would be like being married to a priest!"

"Catarina!" he gasped, shocked by such irreverence.

"But it is true, you know, Don Diego," Doña Inez put in
with a wink at Catarina who, recognizing aid from her aunt,
blew her a kiss as she flounced off to her room. "An old
widower and a stiff-necked young man who indeed would be
happier if he had taken religious vows are not for your
daughter. What she really needs, my esteemed brother-in-law,
is a man who will brook no nonsense from her, who will give
her a sound thrashing when she needs it, yet love her fiercely
and make a woman out of her."

Don Diego stared at her, his mouth agape. In the two years
since they had come to Taos, he had come to depend on
Doña Inez more and more, not only as a companion to whom
he could express his frankest thoughts, hopes, and fears, but
also as a gracious hostess. And he respected her for her
abilities in managing the household, which she ran smoothly
and without friction. Most of all, he was surprised and at
times even a little troubled to find that he was considering
her as an extremely attractive and desirable woman. This was
something he had not before contemplated, and at times he
asked himself why he should have such thoughts.

John Cooper and Lije hunted frequently, and the boy's fine marksmanship and his friendly demeanor toward the Pawnee —enhanced by his ability to converse fluently with them— had made him a great favorite. Indeed, Peltalaro had gone so far as to intimate that he would be pleased if the young white-eyes would one day decide to choose a young maiden as his squaw. And, as further bait to induce John Cooper to adopt permanently the ways and the life of the Skidi Pawnee, Peltalaro hinted of a great honor that could be bestowed upon a white-eyes who exchanged blood with the chief and who took a beloved maiden—he could be made a warrior for Morning Star.

John Cooper had not been quite certain what this great honor entailed, and it remained for his tutor and friend, Narkinawa, to enlighten him. "Why, it means that he will lead the braves who go to raid an enemy village and there select a maiden who is holy for the Great Star."

John Cooper resolved that he would do everything possible to decline such an honor. In April, at the time of the annual sacrifice, Peltalaro had purposely sent him and two other braves on a hunt for antelope, saying that a large herd had been seen to the northwest of the village. So John Cooper had not witnessed the complex and dreadful rites by which Skidi Pawnee propitiated their mighty god.

On September 16, some twenty Pawnee braves rode back into Peltalaro's village. Their leader was Mikaskwa, and riding near him, her hands bound behind her back, was a young Dakota Sioux girl. The braves had smeared their faces with soot to tell all that the raiding party had been successful in finding a sacrifice for Morning Star. As John Cooper stopped, his hand on Lije's head, he watched old Kiskawe come out of his house, go up to the pony, lift down the girl, and take her back into his house.

He stared after the girl. She was not more than sixteen, with sun-bronzed skin, a gracefully rounded figure, and two long, black braids which fell below her shoulders. She was dressed in buckskin jacket, skirt, and moccasins. Her face, with its wistful, yet courageous expression, suddenly reminded him of Degala. There had been the same mournful resignation, the same quiet dignity, not only in the way this captive girl looked, but in her demeanor as, her shoulders straight and head high, she walked into the house of the priest of the Morning Star.

THIRTY-TWO

As the year of 1810 came to an end, the population of the young United States had reached 7,239,881, and President James Madison had been faced by Napoleon's Rambouillet Decree which ordered the seizure and the sale of all American ships in French ports. Napoleon had crushed the Austrian army at Wagram the previous year. Although much of his army had been diverted into the Peninsular War in Spain, he was planning a *Grande Armée* of half a million men to attack Russia, his only remaining rival on the European continent.

In Taos, as in Santa Fe, the side effects of Napoleon's domination of Spain were reflected in changes in trade between New Mexico and Mexico itself. The New Mexicans made, for their own use, a rough species of leather, cigars, pottery, some cotton goods, and blankets; yet these were of such poor quality and so costly that they might easily be displaced by competition from better and cheaper imported goods. From Mexico, dry goods, confectionery, arms and ammunition, iron, steel, gold and silver, and even cheese, were being sent to Santa Fe. The caravans took nearly five months to fetch and carry between Santa Fe and Mexico City, and already the custom had been established of making

El Paso a division port, where caravans from north and south met to exchange goods. Ambitious Lieutenant Zebulon Montgomery Pike, the unwitting tool of Aaron Burr and James Wilkinson, published his journal in 1810, in which he anticipated an American invasion of Mexico in the near future. What that journal did was to whet the appetites of American traders for commerce with New Mexico—but the rigorous, Spanish laws prevented any interchange of commerce; Americans who dared come to Santa Fe or Taos faced incarceration and even execution.

Because of all this, the new world of Don Diego de Escobar was limited and isolated, and yet, of necessity, it was sufficient unto itself. If Taos lacked the museums, palaces, and theaters of brilliant Madrid, it fostered a greater dependence on one's friends and neighbors, and it intensified the worth and measure of personal relationships. So, as the year of 1811 began, Don Diego began to see at last that there could be no turning back for him. Spain itself had changed, and even if the longed-for restoration of Ferdinand VII came about, even if Napoleon were deposed, there could be no going back.

For the first time since they had come to Taos, Doña Inez could discern her brother-in-law's complete acceptance of the reality of his new life. Although both Don Pedro de Saltada and Felipe de Cortana had again approached Don Diego to renew their suit for his daughter's hand in marriage, much to Doña Inez's satisfaction he had courteously but firmly let them know that he did not favor such an alliance. And he had even gone so far as to tell Doña Inez, "I must be sure of my daughter's happiness, Doña Inez. I remember how it was for my beloved Dolores and myself. And, since there are so few really eligible suitors in Taos to whom I could entrust Catarina without the gravest concern, it will do no harm to wait a little longer."

Yet, in almost the same breath, he had added, "All the same, it would not displease me if she and Tomás de Pladero came to an understanding. There is a young man I approve of—modest, educated, gentle of manner, and a son who honors and respects his parents—a quality which, alas, I do not find in many sons of the *ricos* in our little community."

Meanwhile, Doña Inez devoted more time than ever to guiding Catarina through this trying period of adolescence. She recognized in the girl's vivid and sensual beauty that Catarina was rapidly approaching the threshhold of impetuous young womanhood. The wives of Porfirio Locada and Manuel Miraflores had brought with them from Chihuahua hand-made wooden looms, and they were able to card some of the finer quality wool from Don Diego's flock, as well as to spin it and weave it. Catarina had evinced an interest in this craft, greatly to Doña Inez's approval, and herself had learned to dye this wool with indigo, brazilwood, and wild plants. Also, since Doña Inez herself was an accomplished seamstress, she instructed her niece in the embroidering of handsome altar cloths, not only for the chapel of the *hacienda* itself, but for the huts of the *peóns*. She intimated to the girl that, if Catarina were to make presents of these cloths to the wives of Don Diego's workers, it would win her their love as well as deepen the harmonious concord between the *trabajadores* and her father. Catarina, always susceptible to flattery and attention, soon discovered that her aunt's diplomacy garnered her not only praise but also charming little gifts of reciprocity from the women themselves. Joanna Miraflores wove her a beautiful scarf and Juanita Locada gave her a little silver bracelet which had been made by Juanita's old father in Chihuahua.

Miguel's *trabajadores*, without exception, took pleasure in their work and had nothing but praise for Don Diego and Carlos. Miguel became a kind of father confessor to them, visiting their huts to inquire after their children and their wives, hearing their complaints and settling them with a frank honesty which made them feel that he was truly one of them. The men had built their own chapel early last year, and several of them carved the figures of the saints out of cottonwood, ground their own colors from minerals, and with their limited but enthusiastic skill, painted religious pictures and altar decorations for the chapel.

For Carlos de Escobar, now nineteen, life was simple and thoroughly enjoyable. To Don Diego's dismay, his handsome, vigorous son showed not the slightest interest in sheep, though he admitted that they helped provide a living. "But they are really stupid creatures, Father," he had commented one evening when Don Diego had taken him to task on the matter. "An old man and a dog can guard them most of the time, and if you have many of them, then you just need a few more sheepherders—and someone to shear them, of course. I admit I enjoy mutton the way Margarita prepares it. But to spend my whole life looking after sheep, no matter how many *pesos* will come to me for doing it? That is not for me, Father."

More and more frequently, Carlos rode out on Valor and took along the wide-bore musket for hunting. It excited him to explore the slopes of the majestic Sangre de Cristo mountains to the east, and to lengthen his expeditions by camping out, for as long as three and four days at a time. Don Diego had been concerned when his son had first proposed camping out by himself, with only his stallion, provisions, and musket. But Doña Inez, using all of her tact and charm, had convinced him that there was slight danger and that his son was certainly able to fend for himself.

It was the second week of March, and John Cooper had become increasingly concerned with the impending sacrifice to Morning Star. The young Sioux girl—whose name, Damasha, he had learned from Narkinawa—seemingly had been given the freedom of the village. She had been treated with the utmost respect, and the old squaws had been kind to her. She had remained in the house of Kiskawe; often John Cooper had seen the old priest talking earnestly to Damasha and smiling benevolently at her. Nonetheless, he knew that before two weeks had passed, the awesome and intricate ritual of sacrifice to Morning Star would take place and that she would be the sacrificial victim.

Until now, he had been unable to learn the exact nature of this ritual, but he had resolved to find out exactly what was in store for her and, by whatever means he could, to avert it. And so, the previous night, when he had been invited by Peltalaro to share food with him in the chief's house, he had said, "Great chief of the Skidi Pawnee, you once asked me to become one of you. I am not yet ready to take a squaw into my house, but Narkinawa has taught me of your great gods. I would know more, and if I am worthy, perhaps one day Kiskawe will choose me as warrior of Morning Star."

Peltalaro's grave, somber face brightened, and he hugged John Cooper as he exclaimed, "This, above all else, pleases me, young white-eyes! You have brought much meat to our lodge, you have been kind to our people, and they respect and love you. Who is to say that great Morning Star, himself a mighty warrior, could not see in you, white-eyes though you be, the one worthy to do him such great honor? I shall tell Narkinawa to begin instructing you in the ways of sacrifice, that you may have deep within your heart and spirit the veneration of our great god."

The next morning, when John Cooper went to Narkinawa's house, the Pawnee brave greeted him more cordially than usual. "Our chief has told me that you truly wish to become one of us. No white-eyes has ever before become the warrior of Morning Star, but it may be that after I instruct you in the holy ritual of the sacrifice, you will feel His spirit take possession of your own. And, if you are worthy, He will make you his chosen instrument."

"That is my wish, Narkinawa, and you know by now that I always speak with a straight tongue," John Cooper responded. Boyishly, he put his left hand behind his back and crossed median and forefingers. Inwardly, he thought to himself, *I remember how Pa begged God's forgiveness for telling a lie about the whiskey to old Pesquetaba. I'm praying Him right now to forgive what I told Peltalaro and Narkinawa—but I just can't let that poor girl be killed so they can have more corn and rain and buffalo, I just can't!* Putting his right palm over his heart, he stared steadfastly into the young Pawnee's eyes.

"That is so. You are almost Pawnee now, as hunter and friend, and you speak our tongue so all can understand you. Now listen closely, and let these words dwell within you, so that you will know how it is done for the glory of Morning Star and the life of our village," Narkinawa stated solemnly.

John Cooper nodded, seated himself before his tutor, and, crossing his wrists over his chest, inclined his head in the attitude of respect for the mystic Pawnee gods.

"Kiskawe is not only the priest of Morning Star, but also the keeper of the Wolf bundle. That is why Kiskawe keeps Damasha in his house until the time of sacrifice, through the period of the winter buffalo hunt and the moons which follow. She is taken to eat her food in the house of Mikaskwa because it was he who, as warrior of Morning Star, selected and captured her and brought her to us."

John Cooper nodded, keeping his eyes fixed on Narkinawa's face, which had taken on a look of ecstatic fervor.

"This is because," the Pawnee brave continued, "the wolf was the first creature to suffer death. From that time on, all living things must die. The girl Mikaskwa took from the Dakota Sioux was first bathed and incensed in the smoke of burning sweet grass. Then her clothing was taken from the Morning Star bundle. She was rubbed with red ointment made of pigment and buffalo fat, dressed in a calfskin shirt tied round the waist by a rope, an overblouse, a warm buffalo robe, black moccasins, and a soft down feather to wear in her hair. When she takes food, she uses a special wooden bowl and a buffalo horn spoon. These things, too, are taken from the bundle. No one else may use these utensils. And while Mikaskwa and his companions were on the winter hunt, he killed a fat buffalo cow. Its tongue and heart have been dried and will be used in the sacrificial ceremony, these offerings being in the honor of Evening Star."

Again John Cooper nodded.

"The sacrifice will begin five days from the time Morning Star gives the signal. The captive will go from house to house, begging a piece of wood. With these pieces, the scaffold will be made. There will be four poles to the scaffold—the elm for the northeast, the box elder for the southwest, cottonwood for the northwest, and willow for the southeast. The willow stands for death, yet it also means the renewal of life in the spring, which Morning Star grants us when sacrifice is made in His honor. And to the willow pole will be fastened an otter skin with sixty-five scalps taken in war—these mean war, death, and also the renewal of life. Do you not see, John Cooper, that the otter is the first animal to come up from the water after the winter ice and take the first breath of life for the year?"

"I begin to understand," John Cooper murmured. Although outwardly maintaining the attitude of respect for the gods, there grew within him an anguished, sickening presentiment similar to what he had felt when Kandaka had told him of Degala's shame and degradation.

"Beneath the scaffold," Narkinawa continued, "the men will dig a rectangular pit about the size of a buffalo robe, and the bottom will be covered with soft down feathers. This pit stands for the Garden of Evening Star, from which all life originates—Kusaru. Then the girl will be taken to the altar to be dressed as the sacrifice. Her body will be painted, red on the right side, black on the left. The red stands for the day, the time of Morning Star. The black means night, the time of Evening Star. She will wear a skirt and a painted hide robe around her shoulders."

Again John Cooper nodded, not daring to speak.

"When the dawn comes, the captive will be led by the Wolfman, and then Mikaskwa, who will wear the otter collar, the otter belt with sixty-five scalps, and who will carry his sacred pipe. The four priests of the directions of the earth will follow. Then the captive will be tied to the scaffold, and songs will be sung as she climbs each rung to reach it. The southeast buffalo man with the burning stick will come out of hiding to touch her on the arms and loins. Then the northwest buffalo man will emerge with his bow and arrow and shoot her through the heart. The northeast man of the Big Black Meteoric Star will take his flint knife and make a small cut over her heart. With her blood, he will paint streaks on his face. The southwest man will come with his war club, and he will make a gesture at her. Her blood will be allowed to drip upon the dried tongue and the heart of the consecrated buffalo, and the Wolfman will make a fire at the southeast, where the burned offering of the sacred meat will be made by him who is priest of Evening Star. All the men and boys of our village, singing war songs, will riddle the captive's body with their arrows, and then they will leave the sacrifice."

John Cooper trembled with loathing, and it was only by a supreme effort that he forced himself to look humbly at the exultant face of his tutor.

Narkinawa put out his hand to touch John Cooper's shoulder. "Yes, already I see that His spirit begins to touch your own. Now listen, for this which we do after the sacrifice assures us the favor of great Morning Star. It will be full daylight by this time, and four men will be chosen to untie the captive's body and to take it to the east, laying it on the ground face down. They will sing that she will turn to the whole earth and then they will speak of nine things that will, in turn, find her. She will turn into a bunch of grass; the ants will find her, the moths and the fox shall come, as well. So shall the coyote, the wildcat, the magpie, and the crow. Then the buzzards, and then, last of all, the bald-headed eagle who will come to eat her. Then all of those who took part in the sacrifice will go to the ceremonial earth house and there they will feast on sacred buffalo meat. All the people of our village will carry Mother Corn, and even the women will imitate the warriors and pretend that they, too, took part in the honor to Him. So it is and so it will be."

At last John Cooper spoke. "Does the captive know what awaits her, Narkinawa?"

"No. She has been told that she is being honored as a maiden of a tribe that is our enemy. This year, the sacrifice will be great tribute indeed to Morning Star, for the girl, Damasha, is the daughter of the chief of the Dakota Sioux."

"What you have told me fills me with wonder, Narkinawa. Thank you for instructing me, and I will remember it all of my days," John Cooper murmured. His voice shook, but Narkinawa interpreted this as the expected reaction to his mystic revelation. He put his hands on John Cooper's shoulders. "The girl is not to know. You will swear this with a straight tongue and on your pledge to offer yourself one day as warrior to Morning Star."

"I will do this," was John Cooper's answer.

"You must understand that you will not be allowed to see this holy ritual," Narkinawa continued. "After it is done, you will go to the house of Kiskawe and he will pray with you, and the spirit will come to both of you to tell whether you are truly chosen to remain among us."

"Let it be so, I am willing," John Cooper said. He rose and made the sign of friendship to Narkinawa.

As he walked back to his own little house, John Cooper scarcely noticed Lije when the dog trotted up to meet him. He was overwhelmed by the complex and bloodthirsty ritual which his tutor had explained, and his pity for Damasha was overpowering. Somehow, he must try to save her. If he failed, they would both die, and he knew his own death would be hideous indeed for having committed such terrible sacrilege. All the same, he must try.

If it was true that Damasha was the daughter of a chief, the raid in which she had been captured must have been skillful indeed. Otherwise, the Dakota Sioux would surely have attacked the village by now. But how could he, by himself, hope to save her when she was certain to be closely guarded? He could do it only on the night immediately before the sacrifice. She would be kept in the house of Kiskawe that last night. To escape, he would need the fastest horses in the corral. And he would have to travel light.

Then there was Lije—if Lije barked, it might wake the village and mean death to both of them, and the wolfhound too. But, most of all, he must somehow alert Damasha to be ready for whatever plan he could devise.

He had seen her often since her capture, going to Kiskawe's for her meals. She had walked with her head held high and her face impassive. Even before he had known the terrible fate which awaited her, he admired her courage and dignity. When some of the old men and the old women had spoken to her, she had inclined her head and gone on without a word.

His mind sought frantically to devise a plan that might succeed, but he forced himself to act exactly as he had throughout his months in the village—eating his meals with Peltalaro and his family, hunting with Lije, returning to Narkinawa's house to continue his lessons.

A week before the sacrifice, he and Lije were preparing to leave the village to go hunting wild turkey. The night before, at the evening meal with Peltalaro, John Cooper had promised the chief a fat turkey hen. As he was about to load his rifle, Damasha emerged from Mikaskwa's house, with the stolid Pawnee brave beside her. At the same moment, another brave came out of his house, his squaw beside him, and called to Mikaskwa, who turned aside to answer him. In that brief moment, John Cooper caught the Sioux girl's eye and swiftly made the sign, "I am a friend, I will help you." Then to make certain that she comprehended and knowing that she must surely understand the general Sioux term for friend or relative, he whispered quickly, *"Hunka."*

She gave no evidence of having seen his sign or heard his quickly whispered word, and, as Mikaskwa turned back to guide her to the house of old Kiskawe, John Cooper industriously concerned himself with inspecting the loaded rifle. Then he called cheerfully to Mikaskwa, "Wish me good luck, and if my stick which thunders and spits fire fells one more turkey than I seek, the meat will be yours!"

Although he bagged four birds by noontime, John Cooper and Lije did not return to the village until nearly sundown. He knew that Damasha would be taken to Mikaskwa's house for her evening meal. He gave Narkinawa one of the turkeys in a gesture of friendship. Just then, he saw Damasha and Kishawe approaching Mikaskwa's house. Her Pawnee captor came out of the entrance, and John Cooper exclaimed, "See, Mikaskwa, your good wishes have brought me luck! Here is the turkey I promised you." He loosened the rawhide thong that tied the three remaining birds, took one of them, and handed it to the Pawnee. Then, quickly turning to the old priest and inclining his head in homage, he announced, "And the fattest of these birds, O Kiskawe, is for you, as my gift of thanks for the wisdom you have taught me." With this, he lifted one of the two remaining birds and handed it to the old priest. As he did so, he glanced at Damasha and with his lips framed the word *"hunka."* "And now I will take this last to our great chief, Peltalaro," John Cooper exclaimed aloud. He slung the last turkey over his shoulder and, again inclining his head toward the old priest, headed in the direction of Peltalaro's house with Lije following at his heels.

It was the night before the sacrifice. John Cooper had made his preparations. He had told Peltalaro when he had returned, purposely empty-handed, from hunting with Lije, that he had seen a great bear in the forests to the northwest and that he had resolved to kill it. "Such a bear, mighty chief," he glibly explained, "slew one of my best friends, and I made a vow to avenge him in this way. I will hunt the bear until I find it, even if I do not return until another sun has set." Peltalaro had nodded solemnly and replied, "This, too, is how a Pawnee would live. What you have said pleases me. Go then, young white-eyes, and keep your vow."

That permission had been so readily granted that John Cooper knew that Peltalaro did not wish him to witness the sacrificial ceremony. So, packing his rifle, powder and balls in a small sack and slinging it over his shoulder, John Cooper left the village with Lije and headed northwest. He had put two sturdy rawhide thongs into the sack to make a leash for Lije. About a mile away from the village, he lay down to rest for a few hours, the wolfhound beside him. Stroking Lije's head, he murmured, "Now this is one time you've just got to do things the way I tell you to, without any mistake, Lije. I'm going to have to tie you up, and I don't want you barking, understand? I'll be back to get you, and then we're going to take off, just as fast as we can. So let's get some rest right now because there's lots to do before the sun comes up."

John Cooper did not close his eyes for fear he would sleep past dawn. He listened to the sounds of the forest and thought of Degala—it was her memory that had prompted the story about the bear. Besides, he could not sleep: his mind was racing, dwelling on all the obstacles he would have to overcome. What if the girl refused to come with him? What if she cried out and roused the village?

It was three hours before dawn when he sprang to his feet, went to the sack, and took out the rawhide thongs to make a sturdy leash. Lije stood beside him, wagging his tail, staring at him quizzically. "Now you stay here, boy. Don't worry, I'll come back for you. And don't you go barking!"

He left the sack with his rifle and ammunition beside the wolfhound, touched the sheath of the knife at his neck, then ran back toward the village. Lije stood erect, peering after his master, and the youth glanced back and waved. He breathed a sigh of relief to hear no disappointed bark.

As he neared the western end of the village where Peltalaro's house stood, he stared at the corral two hundred yards beyond it. There were about a hundred horses held within a wide circle of shoulder-high poles dug deeply into the ground. Near Peltalaro's house, there was a space of about six feet between the two strongest poles, with three widely spaced horizontal poles resting on pegs to serve as a gate. A boyish grin eased the tension of John Cooper's lean features when he noticed it. Then, crouching low, he crept toward the left, to Kiskawe's house, where Damasha was spending her last night on earth.

His heart sank as he saw a brave, naked but for breechclout and moccasins, his chest and face painted with red and black bars, standing at the entrance with arms folded across his chest. As he halted, momentarily in a quandary, he nearly stumbled over a short, thick piece of firewood. Glancing down, he murmured a prayer of thanks for this providential boon, picked it up, and crept stealthily toward the Pawnee guard. Hiding against the wall of the lodge, he waited until the guard turned toward the east to stare down the long rows of houses. Then he leaped forward, drew back the club, and struck the guard on the head. The man dropped without a sound, and John Cooper tiptoed to the doorway of Kiskawe's house. As his eyes adjusted to the darkness, he saw the two figures of the old priest and the girl, lying on blankets opposite each other in the narrow cubicles which served as rooms. He tiptoed toward Kiskawe, raised the club, and struck the old man a brisk, short blow on the forehead. He didn't want to kill him, and he prayed he had only stunned the guard, as well. Kiskawe moaned softly but did not stir. John Cooper bent to him, listened to his breathing, and then moved stealthily toward the opposite cubicle.

Damasha had been wakened by the noise and sat up. He saw that her hands were bound behind her back. Before she could cry out, he dropped the club and sprang to her, forcing his palm against her mouth as he hissed in the Ayuhwa tongue, "*Hunka*—friend, Damasha! I will take you back to your people. These will sacrifice you at dawn, not wed you. I speak with a straight tongue. Come with me, do not call out, or they will kill us both!"

For a moment she struggled against him, and his heart

sank as he feared she might cry out. But as his words registered, her dark eyes widened, and then she nodded. He repeated, "Don't make a sound, please don't!" Then, drawing his knife, he cut the thongs which bound her wrists, and whispered, "There are horses, many horses, in the corral. I'll turn them loose and get two for us. Will you show me how to take you back to your people?"

She nodded, and then rose. He took her hand and peered out of the doorway of Kiskawe's house. At the other end of the village, a mongrel barked at the moon, but otherwise all was still. "This way!" he whispered, and signaled for her to crouch down as they crept out of the house, toward the corral.

Carefully and quietly, he lifted the horizontal bars which formed the gate. Again he murmured a prayer of thanks. In his anxiety to save Damasha, he had forgotten to bring thongs to use as reins for the two horses he meant to steal. Yet most of the horses in the corral were not only reined but also crudely saddled with blankets or buffalo hide. With a sigh of relief, he seized the reins of a gray mustang and led him out, then gestured to Damasha.

The young girl swung herself onto the horse's back as John Cooper turned to pick a black mustang for himself. The other horses had begun to mill around the gate, whinnying and nickering. "Show me the way back to your people, Damasha," he anxiously urged.

She pointed toward the northwest, and in the moonlight he could see that her face had an excited beauty to it, her eyes sparkling, her lips curved in an eager smile.

John Cooper opened the gate once more and the horses nearest to the corral gate raced out. The others followed, as he and Damasha rode out of the village and back toward the forest. There he dismounted, cut Lije's leash, and swung the sling-sack with his rifle and ammunition over his shoulder. Then he remounted the black mustang. "Come on, boy, fast as you can!" he called to the wolfhound.

Kicking the belly of his mustang with his heels, he urged it on in the direction which Damasha had shown him. Behind him, he could hear the thundering of the mustangs' hooves, and, at the distant edge of the forest, he could see the first pale intimation of the coming dawn.

THIRTY-THREE

Damasha rode ahead of John Cooper, glancing back from time to time to make certain that he was following. The wolfhound loped along, his long strides nearly matching the swift pace of the mustangs which carried his young master and the Sioux girl to safety. She had not yet spoken a word to John Cooper, but indicated to him by signs which trail to take. She rode as well as any brave, erect in the saddle, a proud look on her face, her braids dancing in the wind as they headed northwest.

When they crossed a creek, he noticed that she doubled back twice, turning the mustang this way and that so that anyone pursuing them would have difficulty interpreting their tracks. Understanding intuitively the reason for her actions, he imitated her. A little farther on, she paused, gestured to him to wait, and circled her mustang several times around a clump of towering fir trees. Then she urged the horse due north for a short distance, before veering west.

John Cooper had hoped that all of the horses in the Pawnee corral would race away once he had freed them. That would certainly delay their pursuers. It was true that many of the horses were taken into the houses; yet they had gotten a fairly good head start, and it would take time for the Indians to round up the mustangs. Dawn had already broken, but neither he nor Damasha stopped to rest or to eat.

They were heading into the mighty Sand Hills, which contained the richest virgin grassland in this new country. Thousands of years before, winds had blown over the beds of dead rivers and lifted incalculable amounts of sand, molding it into nineteen thousand square miles of great ridges, mounds, broad hills, and angular peaks. The land sparkled with lakes and ponds, with marshes and wet meadows. As they rode, John Cooper noticed ducks and geese, herons and wild swans. To his left, out of a huge thicket, there suddenly sprang a young, white-tailed deer, pausing in its flight to stare at them with wondering eyes. Overhead, a flock of grouse whirred away. The sun was bright, the sky almost cloudless.

At last the girl halted her mustang and wheeled it around to face him. John Cooper breathed deeply and looked back over his shoulder. There was no sign of any life, save that of the birds and the deer. Lije rejoined them, panting, his tongue lolling. "How many suns is it to your people, Damasha?" John Cooper asked.

She did not speak but held up the five fingers of her left hand, closed them, then held them up again.

"Ten days?" He thought quickly. "Why, that's a good two hundred miles or so. But we have to rest and have some food soon." He gestured down at the wolfhound. "He can't keep up like this, not the way a mustang will."

Damasha shrugged, as if it did not matter to her. His first reaction was annoyance, but it soon passed. He thought of the grisly ritual whose victim she would have been. By now, her body would have been left for carrion. He certainly couldn't fault her for wanting to get far away from the Pawnee, as fast as possible—and he refused to let his mind dwell on what would happen to both of them if they were caught. So he nodded slowly and said in Ayuhwa, "Well, my dog and I will just have to do the best we can. We'll try to keep up with you. Besides, it's best for me to stay back and keep an eye out for any Pawnee that might be coming after us."

Her dark eyes considered him a moment, her face again impassive, and then she turned and once more headed her mustang north. John Cooper followed slowly, glancing now and then at Lije. The huge wolfdog seemed none the worse for this exertion; without hesitation, he loped along with

determined strides beside his master. At first, John Cooper's
mustang had been skittish at the nearness of the dog, but now
it had become used to Lije and the youth who handled it
easily.

In the early afternoon, they stopped at last near a huge
sand dune which partly shaded them from the now intense
sun. John Cooper realized that in his haste to save Damasha,
he had forgotten not only to take provisions, but also had left
his tinder box behind. He berated himself as he dismounted.
Then he walked to a nearby bush and began to break off
twigs which could be rubbed together. There was knee-high
grass just beyond the dune. It was dry, for there had been no
rain for over a week. That would do for kindling. But he
would have to find food. Half a mile west, he saw a little
stream and, taking his rifle out of the sling and making
certain that it was primed and loaded, called to Damasha,
"I'm going to see if I can get us something to eat."

Again she did not deign to answer, but he saw her nod
almost imperceptibly and then turn back to her mustang,
stroking it and speaking softly to it in words he could not
understand. He hoped that when they reached her village, her
people would be able to read his wampum belt and know
that he came as a friend.

As he neared the stream, he saw a small mule deer
drinking from it. Its back was to him, and, because of the
gentle southwesterly winds, his scent had not yet reached it.
Kneeling down, he took aim with his rifle and squeezed the
trigger. The deer dropped in its tracks.

Replacing the rifle in its sling, he lifted the dead animal
and staggered back with it toward the dune.

When he reached Damasha, he saw, to his surprise, that
she was squatting down and busily rubbing together the twigs
he had broken off the bush, with a pile of dry grass before
her. He could see a tiny wisp of smoke, and suddenly the
grass began to kindle. He grinned in admiration. "That's even
better than I could do myself, Damasha," he complimented
her.

But still she gave no reply. She didn't even look at him.
Instead, with an almost contemptuous gesture of her hand,
she indicated that he should get more grass to feed the fire.
He cut strips of meat from the deer with his knife, put them
on the fire, and added more grass to it.

Damasha signaled to him to hasten the meal so that they

might continue their journey and outdistance any pursuers who would have set out on their trail. John Cooper was willing, and they cooked strips of the meat quickly. He let the girl eat first, then had a few strips for himself and gave Lije a good sizable portion. The dog gobbled it down as John Cooper ate.

Returning to the carcass of the mule deer, the youth cut more strips and dropped them into his sling-sack. They would stay fresh until the next day, in case he found no game to hunt. Then, lifting the animal's body, he carried it to the dune, scooped away the sand with his hands, and buried it so that there would be no sign that he and Damasha had stopped here. Stomping out the little fire, he hid the burned grass and twigs in the sand, as well. Then they mounted their horses and rode on.

Late at night they stopped to rest, but again Damasha made signs to him to wake her while it was still dark, and he nodded. All the same, he couldn't understand why she would not speak. He knew that she spoke Ayuhwa. Otherwise, she would not have known what he meant when he told her that he intended to save her and asked her what way to take to return to her tribe. He stretched out, pillowing his head on his arms, staring up at the moonlit sky, while Lije whined softly and nuzzled his cheek, then lay down beside him. He did not intend to fall asleep, but the next thing he knew, Damasha was bending over him and shaking him by the shoulder, her eyes sparkling with anger, as she gestured to him that they should go on.

Once again she doubled back on her tracks, fording a little stream several times so that the hoof prints of her mustang could not be read easily. Despite his pique at her continued silence, John Cooper admired her stamina and her cunning, and he carefully imitated her maneuvers.

They headed due north for a time, and then, abruptly, Damasha turned her mustang westward. Dawn began to break. John Cooper shook his head and whistled softly at the breathtaking panorama beyond them. It was as if nature had capriciously formed grotesque patterns of sand to frame the richest grazing land he had ever seen. Some of the dunes were long, massive ridges, a mile across and as much as ten miles long, while others were straight as a buffalo lance, and those near them curved like a strung bow. There were narrow ridges, too, which rose from forty to ninety feet, and still others that resembled abrupt little peaks and flanked the large dunes.

Damasha turned north once again, impatiently gesturing for him to follow her. He continued to marvel at her endurance and glanced back to make sure that Lije was still managing to keep up. At last, when they reached a clump of cedar and fir trees, the girl dismounted and tethered her mustang to the low-hanging branch of a tree. Then she disappeared. John Cooper was about to call after her, when he blushed and kicked the ground with his moccasined foot at his own obtuseness. Then he retrieved one of the strips of meat from the sling-sack and set to work making a fire with twigs and grass. They ate quickly as they had the night before and then went on. As he turned to look back, he saw only the huge panorama of the Sand Hills, vast and empty. Thus far, at least, they had managed to elude their pursuers.

On the morning of the tenth day, Damasha uttered a joyous cry and raised her right arm high in the air. Two days before, they had crossed the Niobrara and then ridden a few miles eastward, until they could see the tributary of the Missouri only a few miles to their right. They were near Miniconju. The land here was thickly wooded, with much high grass, and the air seemed slightly cooler. When Damasha turned to glance back at him, John Cooper could see that her face was aglow. Suddenly, she cupped her right hand to her mouth and emitted three times the loud cawing of a crow.

From a distance within the forest came back an answering call, and then another and another. Glancing up, John Cooper saw that they had come into a pine forest. Then, as he looked back at Lije, he uttered a cry of alarm. Five painted braves were running toward him. Lije suddenly began to bark angrily and prepared to spring. One of the braves, his hair shaved high on each side, leaving only a bristly roach which ran back from his brow to a braided scalplock, lifted a war club by its rawhide grip and brought it down hard against the wolfhound's skull.

"Damn you, I'll kill you if you've killed Lije!" John Cooper shouted furiously. He reached toward his sling-sack for the Lancaster, but two other braves sprang at him from the other side and pulled him off the mustang. He tried to get his hands free to pull out his knife, but the braves held him firmly, and in a few minutes his hands and feet were bound with rawhide thongs to a long pole which was carried by two braves at each end. Twisting and kicking, he called out, "Damasha, why am I treated like an enemy? They've just about killed Lije! Tell them to let me go!"

One of the braves who walked beside him bent and cuffed him across the mouth, mashing his lower lip against his teeth and drawing blood. Infuriated by this ignominious treatment and abuse, he again called out for Damasha to order the braves to release him, and was again cuffed for his pains. When he winced and turned his face away, he could see that several other braves were tying Lije's paws with thongs to a shorter pole and were carrying the unconscious wolfhound back just behind him. He turned his head again and lifted it and could see Damasha riding slowly ahead of the warriors.

The village of the Dakota Sioux was just beyond the western end of the forest. It was comprised of a large circle of tepees which resembled cones, tilted so that the open top was a vent, not a hole that would let in rain. Most of these were covered with buffalo skins, and their size and the number of skins testified to the hunting skill—and consequent wealth—of the owner. A few of the smaller ones were covered only with birchbark, denoting that the owner had little success at the hunt.

The braves who bore the pole to which John Cooper was tethered carried him into the center of the village and laid the pole on the ground in front of a thick, round, six-foot stake. Two of them cut his bonds, dragged him to his feet, and forced him against the stake. Then they drew his wrists behind it and tethered them again, while two others bound his ankles. Damasha sat astride her mustang, staring at him. He turned to stare at her in return and exclaimed, "Is this the thanks I get for saving your life, Damasha?"

The same brave who had walked beside him on the way to the village once more cuffed him across the mouth. Insolently, in the Ayuhwa tongue, he informed the youth, "Damasha is daughter of Weshmatigo, who is our chief. By tribal law, she speaks only to her father, not even to us—and surely not to a white-eyes like you!"

John Cooper turned to look for Lije and saw that the wolfhound had been laid on the ground, still bound to the pole, some distance away. As he watched, Lije regained consciousness, and finding himself uncomfortably bound, began to bark angrily.

The young and old squaws had gathered around the stake. Suddenly, they began to pelt John Cooper with buffalo chips and pebbles, mocking him and seeking to terrify him by calling out, "How brave will this white-eyes be when he feels the fire and the torture knives?"

Damasha had ridden toward the largest tepee in the village. As she dismounted, a tall, stately, gray-haired man came to the doorway. He had high cheekbones and a beaked nose and wore a headdress of white eagle feathers, decorated by a pair of buffalo horns to proclaim him not only chief, but also the tribe's finest warrior. He held a lance decorated with a buffalo tail and painted eagle feathers. As Damasha knelt before him, crossing her arms over her bosom and inclining her head, his dark eyes brightened and he uttered a joyous cry. Thrusting the point of the lance into the ground, he bent to lift her to her feet and to embrace her while a hush fell over the assembled Sioux. Then she began to speak in a low, animated voice, gesturing back toward the torture stake to which John Cooper had been tied. Meanwhile, the brave who had cuffed John Cooper began to taunt him, again speaking in the Ayuhwa tongue. "Your dog will be eaten at our feast of rejoicing that the daughter of Weshmatigo has been returned to us by the gods, and then we shall see how brave you are, young white-eyes!" He drew back his hand to strike him once more, but at that moment Weshmatigo called out, "Hold your hand, Sanimito! You are the war chief of our village, but this *wasichu* is not an enemy. It was he who saved my daughter from the cruel sacrifice of the Pawnee!"

"I obey you, O Weshmatigo," the abashed Sanimito replied, and immediately drew his hunting knife and cut John Cooper's bonds. Then, warily, he approached the pole to which Lije was bound, taking care not to get too close to the wolfhound's great jaws, and set the dog free.

John Cooper rubbed his chafed wrists to restore the circulation, moved to the wolfhound, and, squatting down, stroked him gently. "Are you all right, Lije? That was a nasty clout you got—it's a wonder it didn't kill you—" Then, straightening and turning to glare at Sanimito, he exclaimed in Ayuhwa, "If you had killed my dog, you wouldn't have lived to brag about it, war chief or no war chief!"

"Bring him to me, Sanimito," Weshmatigo commanded. But when the war chief approached John Cooper and made as if to take him by the arm, the angry youth struck Sanimito's hand away and strode toward the chief of the

Dokata Sioux. Lije accompanied his young master after growling menacingly at the war chief.

Weshmatigo smiled, and his eyes were gentle as they studied John Cooper's indignant, flushed face. Then he spoke in his own tongue, making signs to convey the meaning in case his hearer did not totally comprehend. The Dakota dialect differed somewhat from the Ayuhwa, even though it had some words in common, and it was a pleasing language with many soft consonants. John Cooper recognized many words and phrases, and again he was grateful to Kandaka for having taught him the tribal signs which clarified unfamiliar words. "My daughter has told me what you have done. You are a brave warrior, for if the Pawnee had caught you, you would have prayed for death for many suns before they granted your prayer. And now I see your wampum belt. It is plain that you have great courage and a heart that is good. I wish you to know that I am grateful for what you have done."

"Well," John Cooper replied wryly, "I didn't expect to be pulled off my horse, tied to a pole and then to a torture stake, and to have my dog clubbed."

"For this I am sorry. It is because the brother of our war chief was killed last year by a young *wasichu* who spoke with a forked tongue and said that he had come to trade. When the brother of Sanimito came with buffalo skins to the place of meeting, the *wasichu* killed him with a stick that thunders and spits fire. Sanimito saw you ride with my daughter, and he saw the stick and he remembered how his brother had died. That is why it happened."

"I guess I understand that, all right. I came here as a friend."

"And you are more than that. I had begun to mourn my daughter. The Pawnee came with their warriors in the night, and they hid in the forest until they saw my daughter go out at dawn to bring water from the stream. Then they seized her and rode away before my warriors could waken and overtake them. At first I did not know what tribe it was, but by the end of that black day, one of our warriors found a quiver of arrows that had been dropped by one of those who had taken my daughter from me. From this we knew and feared the worst."

"I didn't want to see anyone die like that. I lived with the Pawnee and I hunted with them."

"If you wish, you shall live and hunt with us and be our

friend." Weshmatigo smiled and nodded. "And to show you that I do not speak with a forked tongue, I ask you to let my blood flow with yours to show that we, the Dakota Sioux, know how to thank a brave young warrior who would give his life to save her who is dearest of all to me."

"I—I'd be glad to." John Cooper's rancor had vanished and, when Damasha suddenly glanced at him and her lips curved for a fleeting moment in an exquisite smile, he was suddenly embarrassed. The honor which Weshmatigo offered to him was the highest that could be paid, since it was offered by the chief himself.

"Good! Sanimito, you will take your knife and let our bloods mix as it is done when two warriors exchange the vow of brotherhood and friendship," Weshmatigo ordered.

Sanimito, obviously discomfited by having been taken to task by his chief in the presence of the villagers, approached, with a sullen look on his face. He avoided John Cooper's gaze. The gray-haired chief held out his left wrist, and gestured to John Cooper to imitate him. They stood side by side, and Sanimito deftly nicked each wrist with the sharp point of his hunting knife, then pressed their wrists together and wound a rawhide thong around them until the bleeding stopped.

"It is good," Weshmatigo solemnly intoned. "You, Sanimito, will give your knife to my *wasichu* blood brother, as a sign that you are at peace with him and that you accept him as one of our tribe, as friend and hunter. Let there be peace between you. You see for yourself he could not have been the *wasichu* who slew your brother."

"That is so, O Weshmatigo," Sanimito grudgingly agreed. He tendered the bone-handled knife, handle first, to John Cooper, who took it and smiled, then deftly cut the thong which bound his wrist to the chief's. By cutting the thong himself, he thus announced to the Sioux that he entered eagerly and of his own free will into the mystic covenant which the ritual implied.

"This is good, yes, very good," Weshmatigo repeated. "For the name of our tribe, Da-ko-ta, means friends. We are at peace, the land is rich, there are many buffalo, and the Great Spirit smiles upon us. This we know because He willed it that you, young *wasichu*, should save Damasha and bring her back to me. You will have a tepee of your own, and I shall give you one of my best horses. And tonight we shall have a great feast in your honor, my *wasichu* blood brother."

"But my dog is not to be eaten at the feast, mighty chief of the Dakota Sioux." John Cooper grinned boyishly. "He is as mighty a hunter as I, and he is my friend, too. In him is the spirit of a mighty warrior from across the distant waters."

"I have never before seen so large and so strong a dog. But you need not fear that we shall cook him at the feast," Weshmatigo replied. John Cooper saw that the corners of his mouth twitched as if he were suppressing a smile. "My daughter has told me also how he came with you from the Pawnee village and watched over you at night when you made camp. But we have talked enough for now. Rest, brave young *wasichu* warrior. Go to the tepee of Sanimito, and food will be brought to you. Your tepee will be ready soon, but now, because we are blood brothers, there is no tepee in my village that will not offer you shelter, food, and friendship. You are one of us."

THIRTY-FOUR

John Cooper slept that night in the tepee of Sanimito and his young squaw, while Lije remained outside. Sensing that the war chief felt humiliated by Weshmatigo's reprimand, John Cooper had declared, "Do not be angry with me, Sanimito. I bear you no ill will. If my own brother had been killed by an evil *wasichu*, I would have had hate for him in my heart as you did. But now it is done. I wish to live as a friend to the Dakota and to you. I respect you, because you would not be war chief unless you had been very brave and done mighty deeds."

This speech had its desired effect, and Sanimito's stony face brightened as he gripped John Cooper by the shoulders and nodded. "We will be friends. You have been braver than I, for all my coups. You saved Weshmatigo's daughter from the Pawnee sacrifice. If you will forget what I did to you and your hunting dog, I will stand beside you and be your friend."

By the end of the next day, John Cooper could not suppress a smile of amusement at the extreme contrast between the rude welcome he had received from Sanimito and the honor he was now being paid by the people of the village. A new tepee had been built near the entrance of the village, and it had been covered with buffalo skins. Inside, to his delight, he found a warm buffalo robe which had been painted with rayed sun figures. It even had a picturegraph of him killing the bear, which a tribal elder had painted after seeing the wampum belt.

It was an easy life, easier indeed than it had been with the Pawnee, since Weshmatigo did not at first urge him to adopt the religion of the Dakota nor to take a squaw. The chieftain and Sanimito, about a week after John Cooper's arrival in their village, accompanied the youth on a hunt with Lije, both wishing to see his skill with "Long Girl." Fortune favored John Cooper that day. He shot two large-antlered bucks, two wild turkeys, and, just before returning to the village, aimed a quick shot at a soaring grouse and felled it. Weshmatigo and Sanimito were loud in their approval and praised Lije's ability as a retriever.

Knowing what stock Indians placed upon gifts and gestures of generosity, John Cooper insisted that the game he had killed should be divided between Weshmatigo and Sanimito. But the Dakota chief, although thanking his young blood brother, replied, "Now that you are one of us, wasichu, you must be welcomed by our great shaman, Esintashay. It is he who leads us in the Sun Dance when the leaves begin to turn brown and when we hunt the sacred buffalo. He must cast the sacred bones for you and foretell your future with us. Since your long stick that thunders and spits fire has brought down five meat-giving things, and you have said that you wished to share them with my war chief and myself, give the grouse to the shaman."

"Of course, if you wish it, wise chief of the Dakota," John Cooper replied.

Two braves had been sent back on horses, with a travois, to retrieve the game which had fallen to "Long Girl." Weshmatigo stopped before the tepee which stood at the left of his own and intoned, "Great shaman of our tribe, you who rule at our council fire and tell us the ways of the Great Spirit, come forth and see this brave wasichu who has brought the joy of life to my tepee instead of the sorrows of death."

A tall, solidly built man emerged, wearing a buffalo mask with the great horns intact, clad in a buffalo robe decorated with mystic designs of the stars, moon, sun, and a herd of buffalo. A buffalo tail was tied to his single long braid of nearly white hair. The artisan who had made the buffalo head mask had left slits for the eyes, the nose, and the mouth. John

Cooper shivered at the eerie appearance of this Dakota medicine man.

Behind Esintashay stood a young man in his mid-twenties, naked but for breechclout and moccasins, his body and arms smeared with paint, a single eagle's feather in his scalplock. In a low voice, Weshmatigo murmured to John Cooper, "That is Ikinitse, son of the shaman. If Sanimito were not our war chief, surely Ikinitse would deserve such rank, for he is one of the bravest of all the Dakota."

John Cooper nodded, then held out the grouse and gestured to the shaman that he wished to offer it as a gift. Esintashay in his turn made the Sioux sign of thanks, took the grouse, and handed it to his son. Ikinitse glowered at John Cooper, turned, and went back into the tepee. Weshmatigo spoke again to the shaman. "After the evening meal, great shaman of the Dakota, I would ask you to read the sacred bones. This young *wasichu* brought Damasha back from the Pawnee village, and he has exchanged his blood with mine and is our friend."

The shaman's thin lips moved through the slit of the buffalo head mask. In a grave, deep voice he replied, "The sacred bones shall foretell whether he is worthy to have your blood in his veins, mighty Weshmatigo. Let him come before my tepee when the moon is highest in the sky so that its light will drive away the darkness."

At midnight, John Cooper, as bidden by the Dakota chief, presented himself outside Esintashay's tepee. The old man emerged, carrying a buffalo-hide pouch. He gestured to the youth to seat himself on the ground and then, lifting his masked face to the moon, chanted softly, "Wakan-tanka, Great Spirit, you have taught us your will through a four-legged one, so that your people may walk the sacred path. Moon, you tell of long life, and your helper is the owl. Earth, you are chief of all trees and mother of four-legged animals, and your helpers are the rats and the mice and the snakes. Now all of you know the thoughts I am thinking, and I cast the bones of the great mysteries for this *wasichu* who stands before me."

He squatted down and untied the rawhide cord on the pouch. Opening it, he shook it three times to each direction of the earth, then cast the bones onto the ground before John Cooper. There were the bones of a buffalo, a deer, an owl, a prairie dog, and a water rat. John Cooper stared at the shaman, whose mask made this solemn ritual seem strangely momentous and terrifying.

For a long moment, the shaman did not speak. Then at last he said, in halting Ayuhwa, "Your wampum belt which I read tells of your deeds, *wasichu*. The bones tell this, also. You slew a great four-legged one who had brought a curse upon a squaw, and the curse was lifted. The bones say also that you brought the daughter of our chief back from the scaffold of death to the tepee of life. And they say more. Their meaning is strange to me, but it will come to pass even as I say it, for it is the will of Wakan-tanka, the Great Spirit who ordains all things."

John Cooper stared at the bones and then back at the fearsome mask of the shaman. The night was still, save for the faint sound of a wind from the southeast which moved through the pine forest. It was a strange, almost singing sound. Then there was silence again as the shaman spoke. "You have begun life again, *wasichu*, because those who were closest to you are no more."

John Cooper stared wonderingly at Esintashay. For an instant, a flicker of anguish passed over his lean, sun-bronzed face. He gave no outward sign of what those words had stirred in him but waited for the shaman to speak again.

"You will bring death to one who is loved by all. I cannot see how this will be, but it is there—the owl's bone turns away from the moon and toward you, the sign of death and not life. You will save a life that is like your own, and in the saving you will take a squaw. She will turn from you, though she desires you, but she will be yours. You will know many dangers. The shadow of death will hover over you many times, but your life will be long." Esintashay paused and looked up again at the moon. There was a long silence before he spoke again. "I have never before seen what is foretold for any *wasichu*. It troubles me. There is much I do not understand, but your heart is good, you speak with a straight tongue, and the evil and the death which surround you are not of your own will. There is no more to tell you, *wasichu*."

"I thank the great shaman of the Dakota for what he has told me. I seek to be his friend, as to all in the village." John Cooper made the Sioux sign of friendship with his palms turned upward and then crossed his arms and inclined his head in veneration of the shaman.

Weshmatigo had given John Cooper a sturdy pinto pony, whose speed and stamina were the equal of the Pawnee mustang's which the youth had ridden to safety. By way of showing that he bore no grudge against Sanimito, John Cooper offered the mustang as a gift to the war chief. For his part, Sanimito seemed anxious to make amends for his harshness at their first meeting and volunteered to instruct John Cooper in the Dakota tongue. John Cooper learned easily, since it had many words and phrases in common with the Ayuhwa dialect.

Sanimito was an excellent hunter, and he evinced a great interest in seeing the *wasichu* use "Long Girl." Accordingly, John Cooper often invited him to accompany him and Lije on their daily hunting forays. When Sanimito saw John Cooper kill a buck at a distance of two hundred yards, his admiration and envy were so obvious that John Cooper offered to let him try the rifle. He showed Sanimito how to prime and load it, how to hold it and allow for the recoil, and how to peer along the sight. A few hours later, the war chief aimed at a wild turkey near a clump of bushes and killed it. John Cooper praised him extravagantly, and this further strengthened the bond of friendship between them.

By the beginning of July, John Cooper had acquired a passable fluency in the Dakota language, much to Weshmatigo's satisfaction. The chief intepreted this as a sign that the young *wasichu* truly intended to become one of them. One evening in early July, when he had invited John Cooper to take the evening meal with him in his tepee, he hinted that some day John Cooper could please him mightily by taking one of the Dakota maidens as his squaw, thus solidifying the bond of blood brotherhood between them.

Damasha's mother had died six years before, delivering a stillborn child, and Weshmatigo had taken Tshimaka, a comely young woman in her late twenties, as his squaw. She and Damasha served the meal, and, although Damasha still did not speak to John Cooper—which he now could understand as being the tribal law—she glanced at him repeatedly. When Weshmatigo remarked that it would give him great joy to have the young *wasichu* marry into the tribe, Damasha's dark eyes fixed intently upon John Cooper's face. His own eyes widened at this unexpected sign of interest, and she quickly turned away and busied herself by serving her father's meal.

It was a peaceful, almost idyllic life for John Cooper and Lije. The summer was warm and lazy, without much rain, and John Cooper made many friends in the village. Only Ikinitse, the shaman's son, seemed to be hostile toward him. On those few occasions when John Cooper had spoken pleasantly to him, Ikinitse had glowered and replied curtly, in a way that did not encourage the pursuit of even the most casual acquaintance. Even when John Cooper brought game to his father's tepee, Ikinitse only grudgingly expressed his thanks.

One day in late July, John Cooper and Lije set out alone to hunt for deer. Astride his pinto, with Lije loping along, John Cooper rode south through the pine forest. As he reached the edge of the forest, Lije stiffened and uttered a short bark, then wagged his tail. Then he stiffened again, his keen, brown eyes narrowing and his body quivering with excitement, and turned westward, ignoring his young master. John Cooper stopped his pinto and turned to look in that direction. He caught a glimpse of a gray timber wolf, standing on a little grassy knoll near the last of the trees which fringed the edge of the forest. Then he heard Lije whine softly, and saw the dog bound forward. "Come back, Lije, you fool, don't tangle with a wolf!" he called. But already the timber wolf had vanished. With another low whine, Lije turned back, looking up at his master almost plaintively.

"What's got into you, boy? Don't tell me you wanted to palaver with that wolf—he could have torn you to pieces. Or she could have—hey, wait a minute now, Lije, don't tell me you want to go sparking a wolf—if that doesn't beat all!" John Cooper shook his head.

After they left the forest, John Cooper and Lije turned westward. A week before, the youth had come upon a herd of wild deer drinking from a little stream, about two miles from the forest. When he reached the stream, he dismounted to look for tracks but saw no fresh ones. Lije dipped his muzzle into the cool water and gulped his fill. John Cooper stroked the wolfhound's flanks, chuckling at the recollection of Lije's interest in the timber wolf. Then he looked up quickly, automatically reaching for the rifle slung over his left shoulder. The sound of hoofbeats, approaching him from the west, reached his ears. To his surprise, he saw Damasha, clad in buckskin and riding a white pony, her hair bound in a single, thick braid through which a white eagle's feather was thrust.

She reined in her pony when she reached him and sat looking down at him, her dark eyes intent and fond. Then, hastily glancing about, she said in a low voice, "I have wished all these many moons to thank you for my life, *wasichu*. You understand now why I could not answer your questions from that very first day in the Pawnee village."

"I understand, Damasha."

"I may speak only to my father. Only the shaman, the war chief, and the tribal elders may speak to me. But I may not sit in their council—that is our law."

"Then you shouldn't be seen talking to me now, Damasha. But you don't owe me any thanks. I couldn't let them kill you. I couldn't let anyone be sacrificed."

"How unkind you must have thought me when Sanimito tied you like a deer and your dog with you! But I had no choice."

"That's all forgotten now, Damasha. And I'm grateful to your father for letting me stay here and hunt with Lije. It's a good life."

Again she turned in her saddle to make certain that no one was near. "You are brave and strong, and your heart is good, *wasichu*. The other night, in my father's tepee, he said how it would please him if you took a squaw. That was when I knew how I felt toward you. It is more than thanks for having saved me from the Pawnee, *wasichu*. My father says that it is time that I be wed, and he thinks of the shaman's son, Ikinitse. But there is no feeling in me for the shaman's son, not such as that which I have for you."

John Cooper's face turned crimson and he swallowed hard. "I—I'm very honored that you say this to me, Damasha," he at last stammered. "But I told you, you don't owe me any thanks for doing what I did. And what you say you feel is because I saved you, that's really it."

She shook her head, her face grave, her dark eyes fixed on his face. "You cannot know what I have in my heart, *wasichu*. You are braver than the son of the shaman, you are kind—I see this in the way you are with this great dog of the warrior spirit. You would be kinder to me than the son of the shaman. He takes his pleasure from the scalps of enemies, from the coups of the hunt. And more than this, he hopes one day to be chief. It is his thought that, by taking the daughter of Weshmatigo as his squaw, and since Tshimaka has not given my father even a girl-child in all this time, he will dwell as leader in the great tepee of Weshmatigo."

John Cooper squirmed uncomfortably, patting Lije's head, trying to avoid her steadfast gaze. Finally he managed, "But can't you tell your father you don't love Ikinitse?"

"No. All the Dakota of our village obey my father's will—as chief, this is his right. I am bound to it, also. Yet I think that he would not refuse you if you asked him for me, *wasichu*. First, it is true, you must prove that you are worthy. After the great Sun Dance when the leaves turn brown and when the braves go to hunt the buffalo, you with your long stick that thunders and spits fire will surely kill more than any brave among us. That will be a great coup and you will have shown yourself worthy."

John Cooper sought words that would not offend Damasha. "I do not know what to say to you, Damasha. The words you have spoken gladden me, but I am not worthy of them. And we have known each other such a little time. Perhaps it is too early for us even to think of such things."

For an instant, a soft smile curved her lips. "That is true, *wasichu*. Yet a maiden knows better than a man what is in her heart. When we rode from the Pawnee, when I was alone in the great hills with you, you could have forced me to your will, but you did not. You were gentle and kind, and you thought of my safety above all else. If Ikinitse had been in your place, he would have taken me as his squaw."

Once again John Cooper's face flamed. "That would have been as evil as leaving you to the Pawnee, Damasha."

"Yet all the same, Ikinitse would have taken me." Again she smiled softly. "I know. You have no dreams of being chief like Ikinitse. You think because you are a stranger, a white-eyes, that one such as I cannot desire you as her man. Well then," she jerked almost angrily at the reins of her pony, "if you will not speak to Weshmatigo, it is I who one day will tell him what is in my heart—before he orders me to become the squaw of the shaman's son." Wheeling her pinto, she galloped back toward the village.

"Damn it all," John Cooper exclaimed to himself in exasperation, shaking his head, "here's a fine kettle of fish I'm being stirred into! I think I'd rather tackle that timber wolf than run up against Ikinitse or get Weshmatigo down on me! Come on Lije, let's go find ourselves that buck!"

THIRTY-FIVE

During the hot days of July and August, John Cooper absented himself from the village to go hunting as often as he could. Sometimes he was accompanied by Sanimito, who could always be induced to ride along with the youth by the promise of being allowed to use "Long Girl."

One afternoon toward the beginning of August, when John Cooper and the wolfhound had gone out alone in quest of a flock of wild turkeys, the youth glimpsed Damasha's white pony through the trees in the forest and turned his pinto eastward, hoping to outdistance her. For the next hour he rode aimlessly, until he saw a covey of quail near the bank of a small creek. Dismounting, he drew his rifle from the sling, knelt down and aimed it, and squeezed the trigger. Just as he did so, there was the whir of an arrow, and he saw one of the quail fall, transfixed with the arrow in its breast, at the same moment that his shot felled another of the birds.

As he turned, Damasha raced up to him on her pony, brandishing her bow. "Well, *wasichu,* have I not shown that I would make a good squaw? If you were ill, I could fetch meat for our tepee!"

"That was a fine shot, Damasha," he replied, feeling his cheeks burn. "But if any of the braves see us together, they're sure to tell your father, and he'll think the worst of us."

"No, *wasichu*." This time her smile was teasing and merry. "You see, I have already told my father what is in my heart."

"Damasha, no!"

"But I have. Only last night, he said to me that the shaman had spoken to him, for Ikinitse. I told my father that Ikinitse did not have my heart, but that I loved a newcomer to our village, one who is a great hunter and who is kind and good and who had Weshmatigo's own blood in his veins."

"Oh, Lord!" John Cooper groaned aloud in English. "And what did he say to that?"

"It is as I told you before. To win the daughter of a chief, a warrior must count many coups. I told him that after the Sun Dance, you would bring more buffalo to our village than any Dakota has ever done. He said that if the Great Spirit had chosen you as he who would bring life to our village with the meat of the hunt, he would then decide who has the worthier claim."

Then, before he could speak, she wheeled her pony and rode off toward the village, turning back in the saddle to shake her bow at him and send him another provocative smile.

One afternoon, just before the end of August, John Cooper returned to the village with a brace of partridge, Lije trotting at his heels and proudly carrying one of the birds between his jaws. Damasha emerged from her father's tepee just as he approached it.

"These are for Weshmatigo," he stammered, his face reddening as he handed her the thong to which the partridges were tied. "I'll keep the one my dog is carrying."

"My father is with the shaman and the elders in the council tepee," Damasha whispered. "When he returns, I will tell him of your gift. I will say to him, 'Is not the young *wasichu* a greater hunter than Ikinitse, would he not have much meat for his squaw each day of the year?'"

"I'd rather you didn't tell him that, Damasha. If Ikinitse had my gun, he'd be a better hunter than I am, that's for certain. Look out—you'd better go back into the tepee, Ikinitse is coming out of his," John Cooper whispered back as he pretended to be engrossed in taking the partridge from Lije's jaws.

Damasha swiftly disappeared, and John Cooper patted Lije and said in a loud voice, "Let's go back and get our supper ready. You've earned a good half share of this one, Lije."

He pretended not to see Ikinitse, whose sullen face was glowering with anger. But the shaman's son strode up to him and, putting his hand on John Cooper's shoulder, exclaimed in an angry voice, "My father has already asked Weshmatigo for Damasha as my squaw. You, white-eyes, have no right to her. But I am fair, I will fight with you, and whoever wins shall have her."

John Cooper bit his lips, then tried to calm the angry young Sioux. "There is no need for us to fight, Ikinitse, and I would not have you angry at me. I ask only to live in peace among you."

"Do not think I have not seen you with Damasha. Just now, before her father's tepee, I saw her speak with you—she has broken our law by doing that, *wasichu*. I know that you have saved her life from the Pawnee. Because of that, you may believe she should be your squaw. And I, because my father is shaman, second in importance only to our chief, I believe that I am he who should be chosen to take Damasha into my tepee. Yet, because I wish her to know that I am stronger and braver than you and worthier of her than you, I offer to fight you with the lance, the knife, or the bow and arrow, as you choose. Then he who lives will take Damasha."

"No, Ikinitse, I will not fight you. It is not my wish to take Damasha from you."

"You say this because you are a coward. I say, *wasichu*, that you do not deserve to have the blood of mighty Weshmatigo in your veins. So be it! When I tell my father that you will not fight me, and when Weshmatigo sees that you are not so brave as you pretend to be, he will know who deserves to be the mate of Damasha." Ikinitse spat on the ground at John Cooper's feet and strode back to his tepee.

It was September now, and cool north winds heralded the autumn and the snows of winter. John Cooper continued to hunt with Lije and at times was joined by Sanimito. At the end of the first week of September, while the youth was tracking a large buck, Lije suddenly stiffened, whined softly, and then, to John Cooper's astonishment, raced away from him and disappeared in the forest.

In vain John Cooper called him back; by sundown, the wolfhound had not returned. The youth had gone on, found the buck, and killed it. He made a small travois and hauled the buck back behind his pinto to the village. He presented the buck to Weshmatigo, who promised to divide it with him.

Tshimaka would cure the meat and bring it to his tepee. The chief proposed that the two of them feast on fresh venison that night, but John Cooper politely declined. He was concerned by Lije's disappearance and wanted to look for him.

After a quick supper, John Cooper hurried back to the forest, carrying his rifle as protection against timber wolves. Weshmatigo had told him that sometimes packs of starving timber wolves attacked the edges of Dakota villages. From time to time, he called out Lije's name, but there was no sign of the wolfhound. It was well after midnight when, aching with the sense of irreparable loss and fear for the safety of his beloved companion, he walked disconsolately slowly back to the village.

He slept badly, wakened at dawn, and hurried out of his tepee, hoping that the wolfhound would be there, wagging his tail, nuzzling at him. But there was no sign of Lije anywhere. Later, when he asked Sanimito, the war chief could give him no encouraging news.

During the week that followed, John Cooper was utterly miserable. Twice, as he rode his pinto into the forest and beyond in his anxious search, he caught sight of Damasha's white pony. Each time, he shook his head and waved his hand in the sign that he wanted no company.

It was the late afternoon of September 11, 1811. Once again, as he had done every morning that week, John Cooper gulped down his meager breakfast and saddled his pinto, then set out through the forest.

He rode miles beyond it, to the east, then back to the west, but there was still no sign. Weary, sick at heart, he turned the pinto back toward the village and then, nearing the edge of the forest at sundown, his heart leaped. Rising in his saddle, he shouted hoarsely, "Lije—oh, Lije boy—oh thank God it's you, Lije!"

There, standing near one of the tallest pines, the wolfhound nuzzled the flank of a gray timber wolf, then uttered a joyous bark and wagged his tail. The timber wolf turned its head, saw John Cooper astride the pinto, and loped into the forest, soon lost in the growing shadows. Lije turned to look after her, with a plaintive whine, then barked again and bounded toward his young master. Dismounting, John Cooper, his eyes blinded by tears, held out his arms to the wolfhound, who stood on his hind legs, his paws on the youth's shoulders, and frantically licked his face.

"Oh Lije, Lije, you don't know how glad I am to see you—I thought you'd run off and tangled with a bear like that one you helped me kill—oh, Lije!" John Cooper sobbed unashamedly as he hugged the wolfhound. Lije barked, wagging his tail. Then suddenly he dropped to all fours, pawed at his master's leg, and whined, turning his head in the direction in which the timber wolf had gone. John Cooper understood. "So that's why you left me high and dry, is it, Lije? That wolf—that was the same one you ran into that time we were out hunting deer, wasn't it?" The wolfhound, as if he could understand his master's words, barked eagerly, then whined softly, turning again to look for his mate. . . .

During the next week, as if eager to make up for his absence, Lije often woke John Cooper in the morning. Nuzzling his face, barking eagerly, he would wait until his master rose from his blanket, then bound outside the tepee and wait, his keen eyes alert and eager, until the youth came out to share his breakfast with him.

Because he understood what had taken place, John Cooper arranged to circle back toward the forest by the end of the day. Indeed, Lije would head that way of his own accord when he knew that the hunt was over. The first time this occurred, John Cooper reined in his pinto and waited to see what would happen. Lije ran into the forest a short way, uttering his plaintive wail. Warily, from behind one of the trees, the timber wolf approached. She sniffed the air, and, as Lije ran up and nuzzled her, she turned and nipped his flank, then ran back into the woods with Lije racing after her. John Cooper watched, entranced by this incredible courtship. They seemed to gambol like young cubs, pawing at each other, nipping playfully, until at last Lije broke away and bounded back toward his master.

John Cooper rode slowly through the forest. As he neared the village, he turned to look back. The timber wolf stood, gazing after Lije almost forlornly. The dog halted, turned back, and gave a low whine. Then, as if his old loyalty outweighed his impulse, he trotted beside John Cooper's pinto, back to the village.

On several other afternoons, even after John Cooper and Lije had returned from their hunting, the youth could see the timber wolf at the edge of the last row of pines, looking after the wolfhound and, at last, turning and disappearing into the shadows which crept swiftly over the woods.

On the last day of September, a jovial, fat, bearded Canadian rode into Weshmatigo's village with his Indian squaw and three pack horses laden with trade goods. The Dakota chief bade him a hearty welcome, for his coming was fortuitously in advance of the great buffalo hunt. Moreover, Henri Jobin had married a Dakota girl from this very village three years before, and the women of the village eagerly surrounded her, plying her with questions on her life with the *wasichu* bearded one. Jobin had brought beads, colored cloth, salt and gewgaws for the women, and for the warriors gunpowder and slabs of lead which could be melted down and molded into balls. John Cooper traded some of his finest skins for an ample supply of gunpowder and lead so that he would be well prepared for the hunt. He knew that he must maintain his prowess as a hunter to continue in the esteem of the Dakotas.

In early October, Esintashay solemnly announced the ceremony of the Sun Dance. Two neighboring bands of Dakota Sioux sent their warriors to participate in the ritual. With them rode a handsome squaw in her early thirties, Lesinga, whose husband, the chief of one of these bands, had died from a rattlesnake's bite two weeks before the ceremony was to begin. She had been chosen as *medicine woman* because of her virtue and good deeds. Her relatives had collected bull buffalo tongues in the early summer, dried them, and distributed small pieces to all the squaws of the hunters who came to Weshmatigo's village. Holding the pieces, facing the setting sun, the squaws prayed for the welfare of their men and buried the morsels.

Then came the ritual of the building of the medicine lodge. Its center pole was a tree chopped down by Sanimito, for it was ordained that such a tree could be felled only by a warrior who had killed an enemy. It was lowered into a hole at the direction of Lesinga. It stood erect, and this proclaimed her virtue. Then her role ended, and the men of all the tribes began a round of dances and ceremonies. Those young braves who had made vows to the sun were presented in the medicine lodge to fulfill them. Skewers were thrust into their chests, and rawhide ropes were brought out from the center pole and tied to the skewers. This was a test of courage and skill, since the skewers only inflicted superficial wounds. Then the young braves leaned back and began to dance, facing the center pole until the skewers broke loose, and thus proclaimed their devotion to the sun and to the sacred buffalo.

Weshmatigo had urged John Cooper to present himself in

the medicine lodge as further proof of his willingness to join the great Sioux family. "When that is done, brave young *wasichu*," he had added with a smile, "it will be time for you to think of taking a squaw into your tepee." What he said next filled John Cooper with consternation. "My daughter is spoken for by the shaman, for his son, Ikinitse. Yet she has already told me that she looks with favor upon you. If, during the hunt for the great shaggy ones, you bring honor to our tribe by bringing more meat to our village than the warriors from these two other Dakota camps, then I will choose the fitting mate for my daughter, Damasha."

John Cooper knew that he could not wed Damasha. He did not love her. He had felt only pity and admiration for her, when he had seen the dignity and courage she showed while a captive of the Skidi Pawnee. Also, to ask Weshmatigo for her would mean facing Ikinitse's smoldering hatred and inevitably would provoke a fight to the death between them. Beyond that, however much he respected the mystic rituals of these kindly people, it would be living a lie for him to accept their religion, to take part in the Sun Dance, and declare himself a true brother of the Dakota Sioux.

Summoning all his diplomacy and mustering all he knew of the Dakota tongue, he replied to Weshmatigo. "I have been with your people hardly six moons, mighty chief. I am still not worthy, and I am young in years. The Great Spirit has brought me good fortune as a hunter, but he has not yet breathed into my heart the spirit of the Sioux."

Weshmatigo nodded gravely. These were words he could understand. He answered, "You have learned our ways already. Our thoughts come easily to you. This is a good sign. My daughter, too, may wait yet another summer, and it will give her greater wisdom to be the squaw of a great warrior and hunter such as I believe the Great Spirit will guide you to become. Live with us in peace, and come with us on the hunt. For, in the short time that you have been with us, my young blood brother, you have made many friends. You are welcome here."

So, at least for the time being, John Cooper could forget his growing anxiety over Damasha's unsolicited and obviously increasing fondness for him. He enjoyed the fine exhilaration of the great buffalo hunt. It was as it had been with the Ayuhwa, with his friend Kandaka. Riding beside Sanimito, John Cooper let out a low, boyish whoop when they came to a verdant valley and saw a huge herd of buffalo. There were forty hunters from Weshmatigo's village including himself, and as many from each of the two neighboring tribes. It had been a long procession, with the squaws riding behind them on horses that pulled travois, to await the skill of their men in providing the meat that would sustain them all through the coming winter.

For over six hours, the hunters killed as they circled and pursued the herd, which lumbered this way and that. Finally, as their numbers began to thin from the unerring casts of lances and the flight of iron-tipped arrows, as well as John Cooper's accuracy with the Lancaster, the great, bull buffalo leader turned westward and began to run. The younger bulls followed him obediently. Now the braves became bolder in their hunting, darting in among the thundering animals, heedless of their own safety, guiding their pintos with their knees.

When at last the herd was gone, there were long hours of work for the women, some of the old men, and the unfledged boys, who had followed for the bloody, menial tasks which were the aftermath of every triumphant buffalo hunt. Yet they exulted in the knowledge that, even in this humble way, they shared the excitement of the kill.

This year of 1811 proved to be strange and ominous. There was trouble at sea with Great Britain, with idle ships and goods piling up, and the northeastern merchants became impatient with the government's policy of economic sanctions. The people of the South and West, their eyes on Canada and the Floridas, were eager for war. The governor of Canada encouraged Indian tribes to make war on the whites, since that would inevitably bring war with Great Britain.

The year's disasters had begun in the spring, with flood waters so high on the Ohio and the Mississippi valleys that men would long remember it as the year of great waters. In September, a brilliant comet, always a sign of foreboding, appeared in the heavens and shone through the fall and the winter. And, on November 7, General William Henry Harrison won a resounding victory over Tecumseh's Indian settlement at Tippecanoe on the Wabash.

Tecumseh had gone to Montgomery and talked to William Weatherford, the half-Scottish war chief, predicting that when he returned to Detroit he would stamp his foot upon the ground and shake down every house in the village. All the Indians of his mighty alliance had begun to count the days.

It was December now, and snows blanketed the forest, the plains, and the hills. The wind howled from the north, and the great comet was still visible in the heavens. Esintashay had made medicine to banish the evil spirits, but he remained greatly troubled over the portents. Two weeks before, a weary messenger had ridden into the village and conferred with him and Weshmatigo to tell them of Tecumseh's prophecy. Esintashay had gloomily declared, "Perhaps it is time to hold the Ghost Dance, to drive away the evil spirits, and to prepare for war against our enemies. The great leader, Tecumseh, has said that the earth will tremble; and the days are not far off for the time he has set for that sign. Yet our tribe is at peace, and has been all this year, and there are no *wasichus* who threaten us in our village. Send word that we await the terrible sign, and perhaps then the Great Spirit will make his will known to us."

On December 13, as midnight approached, John Cooper lay drowsing in his tepee. Deep sleep had not yet claimed him, and Lije lay beside him, huddling tight against his young master. Suddenly the flap of the tepee was drawn aside and a shadowy form entered. Lije stiffened, uttering a low growl, and John Cooper sat up. "Who's there?"

"Do not call out," came a soft voice. "It is I, Damasha."

John Cooper sprang to his feet, suddenly wide awake as he whispered hoarsely, "You shouldn't have done this, Damasha! If anyone sees you, it will be very bad for you. And they'll think that I asked you to come here—"

"Everyone is asleep. I made certain before I came. Please, *wasichu*, do not send me away. I have waited these many moons for you to speak to my father, and yet you have not done this. You killed many buffalo with your long stick, more than any other hunter of the three villages. Surely that was a great enough coup to make you worthy in my father's eyes."

"Please, Damasha, please try to understand!" He struggled for words, fearful for her, not wishing to shame or reject her. "You must not love me. I have not yet taken my vow in the medicine lodge to become a true Dakota. Long ago, I made a vow to the Great Spirit that I would not take a squaw until he had sent me a sign. I have not yet had this sign, Damasha."

She moved quickly to him, knelt down and put her arms around his thighs and looked plaintively up at him. "Am I not deserving of a mighty hunter? Am I not fair to look upon?

Am I not the daughter of a chief who humbles herself before a *wasichu*—that which no maiden of our village has ever done before—and offers herself to you? How better may I show what is in my heart?"

"Please, Damasha, you mustn't kneel to me—please don't —get up, now—yes, you're very lovely, you're brave, and you're good, but I told you of my vow. Please go back to your father's tepee before someone sees or hears you—they would say bad things about you if they knew what you'd done, Damasha." He lifted her to her feet, and, with a little sob, she put her arms around his shoulders and pressed herself against him. "No, this isn't right. I'm not worthy of you. Please go back now, Damasha," he said unsteadily, distressed by her poignant yearning, and trembling in response to the pressure of her supple young body.

Forlornly, she dropped her arms to her sides and moved away. "I cannot help what is in my heart," she murmured at last. "But I will pray to the Great Spirit to send you a sign and that it will be soon." Then, turning, she stood and crept out of the tepee, moving to the back of the others in the great circle on her way to her father's lodge.

As she entered Weshmatigo's tepee, Ikinitse stepped out of his father's, his face twisted with anger, and stood, staring after her. Then, folding his arms across his chest, he turned to the last small tepee near the entrance of the village. His face tightening in anger, he said under his breath, "I will kill the white dog with my bare hands for this!"

John Cooper resolved to go to Weshmatigo and tell him that he had made a vow not to take a squaw until the Great Spirit had sent him a sign. It would lend authenticity to what he had told Damasha the night before. Even so, if Damasha continued to profess her love for him, he foresaw that the only solution would be to pull up stakes and move on. He had been happy here, the hunting had been good, the people kind. Yet, sooner or later, he knew that Ikinitse would force the issue, and then it would be impossible to remain in the village.

He was, however, unable to carry through with his resolution. Sanimito casually informed him, as he and Lije came out of his tepee and prepared to go hunting, that the chief had gone to one of the neighboring Dakota villages to confer with Masaminga, the chief. He would not return until the following week. All that day, John Cooper hunted half-heartedly. The wolfhound searched in vain for his timber wolf mate, whom he hadn't seen in some time.

At sundown, he and Lije returned. After he had settled his pinto in the corral, he cooked the one rabbit he had shot and divided it with Lije. His thoughts were gloomy. Not only did winter curtail his hunting forays, but there was now the imminent prospect of having to resume his wandering in search of a place where he could be free and begin a new, satisfying life.

He sat for a long time, pondering, hugging his knees, while Lije nuzzled his face and uttered his low soft whine. "I know, boy. You miss her. But I don't know where she's gone, either. Look at me—somebody wants me, only I don't want her. We're both in a fix, Lije. I don't know how it's going to come out. But I've got to go to Weshmatigo when he gets back next week and tell him the state of things. Then maybe he'll want me to leave—maybe that's the best thing to do, anyhow. Well, no use fretting. Might as well get a good night's sleep."

It was well after midnight, however, before he could fall asleep. He was immediately plunged into a crazy dream. He was riding his pinto and Lije was bounding along beside him. They were being pursued. Then he was at the top of a great canyon, looking down into it and seeing a rider thrown from his horse, and hearing the snarl of a mountain lion—the snarl of a mountain lion—

It had been a growl from Lije. He suddenly felt a hand at his throat. Still in the torpor of this strange yet vividly real dream, John Cooper reached for the hand and gripped it. Then he heard a guttural voice, throbbing with hatred, "Dog of a *wasichu*, you shall not have her! I will kill you first!"

The voice was accompanied by a strong, musky odor. John Cooper recognized both. Now, fully awake, he forced away the hand that reached for his throat. Ikinitse, with a shout of ferocious hate, reached for the sheath of the knife around John Cooper's neck. John Cooper shifted to one side, at the same time gripping Ikinitse's left wrist with his own left hand. It took all of his strength to move it away from the sheath.

Nonetheless, Ikinitse had managed to draw the dagger halfway out of the sheath. Gasping for breath and silently praying for yet more strength, John Cooper twisted his rival's left wrist and dug his fingernails into Ikinitse's flesh. With a gasp of pain, the shaman's son let go of the dagger and, clenching his fist, struck furiously at John Cooper's face, bruising his cheek. Throughout the struggle, John Cooper maintained his vise-like hold on Ikinitse's left wrist, barely keeping his attacker's wiry fingers from his panting throat. He tried to rise, but could not; Ikinitse's full weight was upon him, and he could see the glitter of hate and determination in the dark eyes that stared down into his.

Lije had sprung to his feet and growled again, but John Cooper gasped, "No, Lije! Down, down, stay down!" as once again Ikinitse reached for the knife's sheath. Lije stood, his hair bristling, his teeth bared, obeying his master and yet wanting with every elemental impulse to spring upon the assailant.

John Cooper felt his rival's fingers close on the hilt of the dagger. With all his strength, he smashed his left fist against the side of Ikinitse's neck. Ikinitse grunted in pain and shifted his body to one side; at the same moment, John Cooper rammed his right knee against his rival's groin. Ikinitse rolled off John Cooper with a stifled cry, but swiftly regained his strength and, crazed with anger, crouched low and hurled himself at the youth, both hands seeking John Cooper's throat.

But John Cooper had anticipated just such a maneuver. He rolled over and over to the right and up against the wall of the tepee; springing to his feet, he flung himself onto Ikinitse's back and this time his fingers sought Ikinitse's throat.

Ikinitse was an experienced fighter with superb muscular strength: his strong lean fingers gripped John Cooper's and he broke free, rolled over, then sprang to his feet once more. John Cooper faced him warily. By now, the youth's eyes had grown accustomed to the darkness. "Now, *wasichu*, son of a mangy coyote bitch, you die!" Ikinitse panted. His right hand dropped to the hunting knife sheathed at his belt; then, without warning, he stopped, caught up John Cooper's blanket with his left hand and flung it at the youth's head, charging forward with upraised knife as he did so. Lije, wanting desperately to spring, fixed his gleaming eyes on his young master and awaited the word to aid him.

"No, Lije, stay!" John Cooper panted. Anticipating Ikinitse's maneuver, he had cautiously backed away and, as the blanket hurtled towards his face, he struck it down to the ground with his left arm. Swiftly he drew his knife just in time to parry Ikinitse's savage thrust toward his heart. There was a metallic clash as the weapons crossed and John Cooper, using all his strength, forced Ikinitse's right hand upward above his head. With a guttural, obscene oath, Ikinitse backhanded John Cooper across the mouth with his left hand. The youth staggered back, blood oozing from his upper lip. In retaliation, before Ikinitse could press home his advantage, John Cooper kicked him in the belly.

With a hoarse grunt of pain, Ikinitse stumbled backward. John Cooper, his chest heaving violently as he fought for breath, crouched and began to circle his wily adversary. He held the knife low and angling upwards in his right hand, ready to strike.

Ikinitse circled John Cooper, feinting now and then in the hope of distracting him. His eyes narrow, all his senses keen because of the danger he faced, John Cooper moved with Ikinitse, his left fist clenched, his knife making a tiny lunge from time to time to keep the Dakota's concentration fixed on the long sharp blade.

Now, as he followed Ikinitse's slow, purposeful circling, John Cooper's left foot brushed the edge of the blanket. Suddenly he cried out, "Look there, the chief comes!" in the Dakota tongue. Ikinitse, startled by the unexpected ruse, glanced for an instant back over his left shoulder at the entrance to the tepee. In that instant, John Cooper stooped, retrieved the blanket and, rushing forward with it, threw it at Ikinitse. Realizing he had been tricked, the Indian bellowed with rage and slashed out blindly at John Cooper. As he did so, John Cooper sprang at him from his left and drove his knife into Ikinitse's side. The young warrior staggered back, dropping his knife as he tried to claw John Cooper's throat. John Cooper had already withdrawn his knife from the warrior's body and now thrust it into the heart.

Ikinitse's fiercely blazing eyes dimmed, he sank down on one knee, then slumped forward onto his side and lay still. John Cooper stepped back, the bloodied dagger clutched in his right hand. He stared down at the lifeless body of Ikinitse. He was reeling with exhaustion; every muscle ached.

He stumbled toward Lije, who was still growling, his tail stiff and his teeth ferociously bared, and patted the wolfhound with his left palm. "It—it's all right. It's over now. Be still, Lije. Don't make a sound." *My God*, John Cooper thought, gazing in horror at the corpse, *he made me do it—I didn't want this fight—he could have had Damasha—or she could have told her father she wanted somebody else. But now I can't stay here any more. He's the shaman's son, and they'll all hate me because I killed him, even if it was in a fair fight. If he'd stabbed me with his knife when I was sleeping there, instead of trying to do me in with my own knife, things would have been different.* "Come on, Lije," he spoke aloud, "we've got to leave right now. You stay here and keep still while I get the horse."

He pressed his palm down on Lije's head, and the wolfhound obediently stretched out, glancing at Ikinitse's body and again baring his teeth, but this time without a growl. John Cooper peered cautiously out of the tepee, but there was no one in sight. Donning his buffalo robe, he hurried to the corral, got the pinto, and rode back to his tepee. He collected the sling-sack with the rifle, ammunition and ball and drew over his other shoulder another sling-sack in which he could keep any game he killed on the trail. Then he motioned to Lije and rushed outside, mounted the pinto, and rode out of the village. As they neared the forest, Lije suddenly began to bark, turned back, and whined.

"What is it, boy? Why are you so excited all of a sudden? Maybe you've seen your wolf, is that it?"

Lije barked again and leaped up, then sprang forward and ran into the forest. John Cooper quickened the pace of the sturdy little pinto and followed.

He would head southwest. Months ago, Sanimito had told him that there were great warriors to the southwest, men who lived in the mountains and were free and who admired bravery and honesty. They were called the Apache. He thought to himself that he could understand such people and, too, the winters would not be quite so hard in that area. Yes, he would head south as quickly as he could, for once Ikinitse's body was discovered, they were certain to come after him.

He rode through the forest. Lije ran far ahead. There was no evidence of the timber wolf, but evidently Lije had found her scent. He rode at a gallop now, and Lije, as if imbued by greater vigor than he knew he had, outdistanced him stride for stride. They passed the stream from which the villagers got water and headed due south. Then, suddenly, Lije began to whine. He halted in his tracks and looked back after his master, then bounded ahead, wagging his tail, quivering with excitement.

There was a little coulee, framed by three lone pine trees, filled with snow. John Cooper could see the tracks of the timber wolf leading to it. Lije had already loped toward the coulee. Then the wolfhound stopped and began to bay mournfully, turning back and waiting for his master to come to him.

John Cooper dismounted and strode toward the coulee. The timberwolf lay on her side, dead. There were four puppies beside her, trying to nurse. He saw at once that three of them were near death. But the fourth, yellow-eyed, furry, growled and bared its tiny teeth.

Lije moved toward the timber wolf, lowered his head and prodded hers, then uttered again his mournful, baying cry.

"It's no use, fella. She's dead, and those other puppies are just about the same way. Two of them aren't moving any more—this one's all that's left from her litter. And it's yours, isn't it? All right. I'll take it with me. I'll put it in this extra sling I brought along." He stooped down, carefully lifting the wolf puppy, and gently eased it into the sling. Then, adjusting it over his right shoulder, he mounted the pinto and gestured to Lije.

Beyond him stretched the snow-covered plains and the trees and the hills. Dawn was beginning to break. It was December 15, 1811.

THIRTY-SIX

As Christmas, 1811, approached, citizens of Taos—remote though they were from the other parts of the country—nonetheless had heard the news of nature's terrifying portents. They prayed in their chapels and reverently crossed themselves in thanksgiving that they had been spared such terrors. The spring floods had wreaked havoc, and hordes of squirrels insanely marched from north to south, perishing by the tens of thousands as they swam the Ohio in their rabid frenzy. In addition, there had been the comet, and also an eclipse—the latter they had not seen, the former they had. And war between the United States and Great Britain seemed inevitable. The two countries already had broken off commercial relations. What the people of Taos could not know was that Secretary of State James Monroe intended to cause diversionary troubles for Spain, so that the Spanish settlers of Nuevo Mexico, and Mexico herself, would be too occupied with the problems of their mother country to take sides in any war between Britain and the United States.

Thanks to the vigorous military measures employed by the new viceroy, Francisco Xavier de Venegas, there existed a serene, if monopolistic, relationship between New Spain and Nuevo Mexico. For both Don Diego de Escobar and Don

Sancho de Pladero, it had been an uneventful year. Their circle of friends had grown, and they had worked together closely in the court of magistrates. The pueblo Indians were more cooperative than ever—thanks mainly to several of Don Diego's humane decisions in their behalf.

Carlos, now twenty, continued to distress his father by going off on longer and longer journeys with his horse Valor. Having explored the magnificent terrain of the Sangre de Cristo range, he was eager to journey to the Jicarilla Mountains, some ninety miles west of Taos. Don Diego had given Carlos a fine breech-loading rifle for his twentieth birthday, and the handsome young man spent many hours at target practice during November and December. He had learned, from one of the peóns with whom he was friendly, that there was excellent hunting in the Jicarilla Mountains. Also, although there were fierce *Indios* there, they had not been known to harm the *gringos,* but only the Mexicans, whose villages they occasionally raided. Besides, according to the peón, these Apache lived at the top of the mountains and would not bother a lone hunter who sought only game.

There had been no more suitors for Catarina's hand, but, more and more, Don Diego was leaning toward Tomás de Pladero. Her father gave dinners and parties frequently at his comfortable *hacienda* and tended to limit the guests to a handful of the friendliest landowners, with the de Pladeros principal among them. Tomás was now twenty-one and had grown a neat little beard, but he was still stocky, a physical trait which indicated to Catarina that he would be corpulent and stodgy when he grew older. Moreover, although he treated her with the utmost respect, his conversation was inclined to be flowery and sentimental. She found him badly wanting when she considered him as a possible husband and even less appealing—if she were inclined to be so daring—as a lover or *novio.*

What she did not know and what Tomás had no intention of revealing even to his own parents, was that he considered her little more than a younger sister, a personable and colorful playmate who would go riding with him occasionally.

But there was a new and even more powerful reason for Tomás's disinclination to see in Catarina de Escobar his future wife. The month before, his domineering mother, Doña Elena, had engaged a new maid at the gentle but persuasive recommendation of a kindly old priest, Padre Juan

Moraga. He spent much of his time teaching the pueblo Indians and was also—though it was not known in Taos—the leader of the Penitentes, a cult of mystics who imitated the scourging and crucifixion of Christ as self-punishment for their transgressions. They also acted as vigilantes, punishing those who had oppressed and brutalized the helpless.

The maid Doña Elena engaged was Conchita Seragos, a seventeen-year-old girl with black hair and a ripe figure. She had an exquisite, heart-shaped face, and her hair tumbled over her shoulders. Conchita had been orphaned two months earlier. Her parents had been poor members of Padre Juan Moraga's church, and the girl had begged him to help her find employment.

Doña Elena de Pladero, as usual, was in need of a maid. She had discharged one for thieving only the week before, after having ordered the girl flogged by José Ramírez. He had mitigated it somewhat, intimating to the unhappy culprit that if she agreed to submit to his desires, he would see if he could find her a situation elsewhere in the town.

José Ramírez was not only cruel, but an adroit thief as well. His predilection for filling his purse at his master's expense had grown when he learned that Don Diego paid his *peóns* more than Don Sancho paid his. From that day forth, he had contrived to augment his own wages. It was really quite easy. Don Sancho had such a large flock that an occasional ewe or lamb was not missed. Often, late at night, Ramírez would bind the legs of one of the flock, tie a rawhide thong around its mouth to keep it from bleating, and put it into a cart which he then pulled into town behind his horse. Money would be exchanged, and no one would be the wiser.

Doña Elena worshiped in Padre Moraga's church, as did her husband and son. So, after a quick glance at Conchita and a few curt questions, she pronounced herself satisfied with the new maid. By the next afternoon José Ramírez had learned of the newcomer and seen her and summoned Consuela Viola to his cottage late that evening. "At last you're going to do me a real service, *querida!*" José grinned as he watched Consuela disrobe. "Doña Elena has just brought a charming little maid into the *hacienda*."

"You—you mean Conchita Seragos, José?" Consuela faltered.

"The very same." He burst into a brutal roar of laughter. "Look at me now. Smile lovingly. That's the girl. Do you know, you're getting as fat as an old sow, and I'm losing interest in you. It's up to you, therefore, to do me this favor if you expect me to speak up for you when the mistress wants you thrashed or discharged. Do you understand?"

Consuela forced a pitiful, tremulous smile to her lips. "I'll do whatever you want, you know that by now, José!"

"Very good. See that you do, then." Consuela had come forward and knelt beside him, and he cupped her chin, leaning forward to stare into her tear-filled eyes. "Now you remember what I told you before, do you not? Undo her work, get her off to a bad start. One of these days, and it won't be too long knowing Doña Elena as I do, the mistress will call me in to give this sweet little slut a sound thrashing. You do this for me, and maybe I'll give you a few silver *pesos* and that little bracelet you've been begging for. Well?"

She nodded mutely and stared up at him, knowing that the anticipation of his planned conquest of Conchita Seragos would mean only a more vicious ordeal for her now.

Only three days after she had begun her service in the de Pladero household, Conchita Seragos was called to task by a tight-lipped Doña Elena on the charge that she had not made two of the beds in the guest rooms. In vain, her cheeks scarlet and her eyes misting with tears, the shy young girl tried to stammer out a denial, insisting that she had truly done all the tasks that had been explained to her. This had only infuriated Doña Elena. "Do you dare to say, then, that I am a liar, you impertinent little baggage? You do very badly your first week here, my girl! Take care, maids who displease me are taken out to the shed for a whipping."

Conchita gasped, then covered her face with her hands and began to sob. Just then Tomás, who had been coming down the hall to ask if his mother was going to have breakfast with him, saw the door open and entered the room. At once he was stricken by the poignant loveliness of the young maid.

"A moment, Tomás, if you please," his mother admonished him. Then she turned back to Conchita. "Well, now, you have had your warning. I promise you that the next time you shirk your duties or dare to be impertinent to me, you will feel the lash. You may go now."

Unable to speak, Conchita hurried out of the room. Tomás inclined his head in respect to his mother and inquired, "I came to see if you will have breakfast with me, Mother."

"I was just coming. These stupid maids—they are either Mexican or Indian, and they have no intelligence at all. All they know is the whip," Doña Elena complained.

"Come now, Mother, she is young, she is new, and she is certainly trying to do her best."

"What do you know about such things? After breakfast, I want you to ride out to the fields and tell José Ramirez to make sure that all the sheep are sheltered from the snow. Your father and I are counting on a good shearing next spring. Now then, you can go on ahead; I shall be there in a few moments."

"Yes, Mother." Tomás bowed and left the room. He went down the hall quickly and saw Conchita standing near the kitchen, leaning against the wall, her forehead pressed against the crook of her arm.

"Please, Señorita," he stammered, "do not cry."

"Oh, I—I am not a señorita, I am only the maid, Señor Tomás!" Conchita turned to look at him, her eyes widening and a lovely flush suffusing her cheeks.

"You know my name?" Now it was his turn to blush. Then, fearful that his mother might come upon them, he glanced nervously around and down the corridor.

"Oh, yes, your mother told me your name, Señor Tomás."

"I—I see. But please do not cry. My mother is strict, but I know you will please her. At least—well—I am happy that you are working here. What—what is your name?"

"It—it is Conchita Seragos, Señor Tomás. Oh, I must go about my work now. I do not want trouble. It was very good of you to speak to me. *Gracias*, Señor Tomás." She gave him a swift, grateful look, then hurried off. Tomás stood looking after her for a moment, then sighed and went into the elegant dining room.

By nightfall on December 15, John Cooper and Lije had traveled nearly twenty miles south of the Dakota village. The valiant pinto had been surefooted in the snow. Now, even more than when he had returned Damasha safely from the Pawnee village, John Cooper used all his ingenuity to make his tracks difficult for the expected Sioux pursuers to follow. From time to time he changed directions, sometimes heading southeast, then again west, until finally, after passing through a thick forest, he pointed the pinto south.

After the first few miles, he had paused long enough to chew some pemmican, then feed these masticated bits to the tiny wolf cub. They would furnish both nutrition and moisture, since there was no milk. The week-old cub nipped his fingers, and growled, a sign that it might be able to survive the loss of its mother. John Cooper wondered how long the she-wolf had been dead. When he fed the wolf cub, Lije looked up and whined, wagging his tail.

At nightfall, John Cooper made camp on the gentle slope of a tree-covered bluff. There was a small cave, but no tracks of any animal leading to or from it. The night was still, and there was no wind. John Cooper tethered the pony to one of the trees, then crawled inside the cave with Lije. Again he fed the wolf cub and gave Lije several handfuls of pemmican, contenting himself with a single mouthful. He would sleep only a few hours, and then go on. Surely by now they had discovered the body of Ikinitse and would be after him.

In the Ayuhwa village, young Kandaka stood looking at the comet in the sky. It seemed to him that he felt a tremor of the earth, and he was suddenly afraid. One of the couriers of the mighty Tecumseh had come to their village a few weeks before to tell them of the Shawnee's prophecy. Surely this strange light in the heavens and this trembling of the earth could mean only that the prophecy was being fulfilled, that there would be war between the Indians and the *wasichus*. He wondered if that would make his friend, John Cooper, an enemy. He wondered, too, what had become of the strong young hunter and his great dog. Degala was happy now, married to a brave who was also his friend, as Latiwaka had been. As he felt the tremor again, he looked up at the sky and murmured a prayer that John Cooper would be safe from harm. At sunset this night, the sun had been a dull and fiery red, the color of blood.

The prophecy had indeed come true. On this same night, the first of more than eighteen hundred earthquake shocks (which lasted until mid-March of the next year) took place, with their epicenter being in New Madrid, Missouri. Houses of brick, stone, and log were torn to pieces. Those of frame were thrown upon their sides. There was the cracking of falling trees, the roaring of the river, a dense cloud of vapor, and pools of boiling sulphur shot up into the air. The Mississippi River was turned back in its course for three days, and the steamboat *New Orleans* lay high and dry in a protected cove until the water finally returned. In the yard of one man, bears, panthers, wolves, and foxes, side by side with a number of wild deer, had gathered. They showed no signs of enmity, nor did they seem to fear man. And to this was added the screaming of geese and ducks and other wildfowl that blanketed in vast canopies large stretches of the Mississippi River. Many of them came to settle around the fires of those who had left their dwellings, seeking the company of known enemies rather than face the terror of the unknown. These quakes would be felt as far as New England, Detroit, and Quebec, and far up the Missouri River, even in New Orleans.

A white captive living with the Osage tribe later was to write that the Indians were filled with great terror. The trees and the wigwams shook, and the thick ice which covered the Arkansas River broke into huge, jagged pieces. The Osage felt that the Great Spirit, angry with the human race, was about to destroy the world. To propitiate the Great Spirit, the Delaware and the Shawnee executed many victims in their frenzied zeal to achieve purification.

Esintashay stood before his tepee that same night, mourning his dead son. He no longer wore the buffalo head mask, but stood, his head shaved bald except for a scalplock, showing all the age of his late fifties. His face was solemn, with heavy eyelids, imperious hawk-like nose, and a thin, cruel mouth. He wore a buffalo robe, covered with picturegraphs of the black and red symbols of death and war. Around his neck was a string of bones of the prairie dog, the owl, and the hawk. His arms were bare, and they were tattooed with symbols of animals which proclaimed his magical powers.

Before him stood Weshmatigo, Sanimito, and the tribal elders. "You of the Dakota, I come to you now not only as your shaman, but as an outraged father who has found his son slain by one we took into our midst, one whom we made our blood brother." He stared accusingly at Weshmatigo, who lowered his eyes. "When I read the bones for this *wasichu*, I read that he was ordained to take the life of one dear to all of us—I did not know then that the sacred bones announced the treacherous slaying of my only son, Ikinitse. This *wasichu* has betrayed the trust of our village. Now I see what I could not see then—that the prophecy of our great leader, Tecumseh, is coming to pass. I have seen the strange lights in the sky, I have seen the bloody sun. Soon there will be couriers and the signals of smoke from the neighboring tribes to tell us of even more disasters—this I now know and feel within my spirit."

There was a low, restless murmur from his audience as he looked up at the dark, thick-clouded sky and murmured a prayer. Then, in a voice which shook with anger and emotion, he declared, "And when we have had the news of what these evil signs foretell, we shall learn that it was this traitorous *wasichu* who aroused the ire of the spirit gods. They will make the earth shake with their fury because of the treachery and evil he has brought upon us. He who professed to live with us in peace and to bring meat to our campfires, he in whose veins the blood of our chief, Weshmatigo, still runs, took the life of my son because he coveted the maiden to whom Ikinitse would have been pledged. I decree that this evil *wasichu* and his devil dog must be brought back and sacrificed to propitiate our gods. You, O Weshmatigo, chief of our tribe, must send a war party after him."

"It shall be done, Esintashay," Weshmatigo said in a dull, lifeless voice. "My daughter has sworn to me by the spirit of her mother that this white blood brother of mine did not kill your son because of her. She has even told me that she did not prefer your son, but as a father I understand what was in her heart. The *wasichu* had saved her from the Pawnee, and she believed that she had found favor with him. And yet, because of what he has done to Ikinitse, I shall send six strong and well-armed scouts to bring him and the spirit-dog back before you."

THIRTY-SEVEN

John Cooper realized that he had forgotten all about his nineteenth birthday. His anxiety over Damasha's embarrassing interest in him, with all the dangers it implied, had driven the thought completely out of his mind. Yes, he was all of nineteen now, just about a man. He was sure he wouldn't grow any more—so far as he could tell, he'd put on another inch during the time he'd been living with the Indians—first the Pawnee, and then the Dakota. His hair was shaggy, and he had the beginnings of a beard. Until now, he'd used his sharp knife to hack away at the stubble on his chin. And, especially in the summer, he'd cut his thick hair with it also. Well, this wasn't any time for a birthday celebration, he thought to himself, not with a pack of bloodthirsty Dakota probably on his trail. He had awakened before the first light of dawn, chewed a mouthful of pemmican, given a little more to the wolf cub in the sling-sack and some to Lije, then mounted his pinto and ridden south.

He didn't know exactly how far he had to go before he found the Apache. All he knew was that, heading in this direction, he was certain to pass through some of the country where the Skidi Pawnee were. And he was sure that they hadn't forgotten his escape with Damasha. He chuckled grimly as he kicked the belly of his pinto to quicken its pace. He wanted to cover as much distance as possible before the next big snow or blizzard. It was cold, but he knew he wouldn't be thinking about such minor discomfort if either the Dakota or the Skidi Pawnee caught him. He wouldn't get a quick death from either of them, he was sure of that. But, if he had to weigh one danger against the other, he'd rather take his chances with the Dakota trackers than with the Pawnee. After all, he'd committed the worst crime against the latter, robbing them of the sacrifice to their most important god. So he wanted to get out of Pawnee country just as fast as he could.

Sanimito begged Weshmatigo to let him lead the scouting party to bring back the traitorous *wasichu* and the spirit-dog. The chief readily agreed and urged his war chief to select five others whose endurance and skill as hunters and warriors would equal his own. Sanimito chose well: Migowa, Ekinata, Onagatsu, Wikonemay, and Panokatay. Both Panokatay and Migowa owned old trade muskets, wide-bore, single-shot guns which took longer to load than the young *wasichu's* fire stick. But they were both excellent marksmen and between them, they had killed two more buffalo than the *wasichu* with his weapon. As for Sanimito, he armed himself with a hatchet, with heavy wooden handle and sharp iron head. Two summers ago, when he had come upon a raiding party of Pinuki warriors, he had killed three of them with it. He carried also a feathered lance, and a bow with a quiver of arrows was slung over his shoulder. The others in his party had lances and bows and arrows. And they rode the swiftest horses in the Dakota corral. Even though this young white devil had a head start of a full sun and a moon, Sanimito and his five companions would overtake him. They would not kill him. That would be too easy. Sanimito would tie him to his horse's tail and drag him all the way back to the village and to the tepee of Esintashay. And, during the trip back, Sanimito promised himself, he would taunt the *wasichu* with the many slow tortures the shaman would use to make him beg a thousand times for the gift of death before it was granted to him.

They wore leggings, buckskin jackets, and buffalo robes against the bitter cold. Before they left the village, they presented themselves to the shaman and asked for his blessing and swore an oath not to return without the evildoer, the murderer of the shaman's son. Sanimito was first to see the tracks of John Cooper's pinto and the paw prints of the great spirit-dog. He shook his lance in the air and uttered a cry as he spurred his horse in pursuit through the forest.

In a week, John Cooper had traveled about a hundred and fifty miles. He had paused for only a few hours of sleep each evening, journeying by night as much as he could, letting the sturdy little pinto take what water it could find. When he could not find a creek or stream that was still running, he gathered handfuls of snow, squeezed it, and melted it down in a battered little clay bowl he had found by chance in an abandoned, tattered wigwam some miles back. The pinto lapped the water eagerly, and then he melted more snow and tilted the bowl to the muzzle of the growling little wolf cub.

He still had half his supply of pemmican, and when he entered the Sand Hills, he managed to kill two jackrabbits.

He crossed the North Platte River five days later, and, remembering how Damasha had covered her mustang's tracks, he doubled back several times to make those of his own pinto more difficult to follow. Lije obediently followed his maneuvers.

A week later, he came upon the beginning of the South Platte River. Now he was moving into mountainous country, such as he had never before seen. As he continued south, he could see the snowcapped peaks of the Rockies. He was slowed down somewhat by having to blaze his own trail.

One bitterly cold evening, he shot but only wounded a mountain goat. When he approached it, intending to dispatch it quickly, he found that it was a female and that its udders were full of milk. Tethering its front legs with a thong from his sack, he milked it into the battered bowl and thus could feed the wolf cub, which greedily downed it. Then, swiftly, he ended the goat's suffering with a merciful thrust of his knife and began to carve chunks of it for food. He made a fire in an abandoned cave on the slope of a mountain that night, and he and Lije gorged themselves with goat meat. Even the wolf cub savored the raw tidbits; and, as usual, nipped John Cooper's fingers.

"Tonight we'll try to get a little more sleep, Lije," he told the wolfhound. "It'll be tough going from here on, with all these mountains. The only good thing about it is that our trail will be harder for the Dakota to follow, if they're still chasing us. Let's hope by now they've given up."

Lije moved over cautiously to the sling-sack in which the little wolf cub lay, and whined softly. The wolf cub growled and bared its teeth, its eyes bright and intent.

"It's about time we gave your cub a name, don't you think, Lije?" John Cooper chuckled as he reached out and scratched the wolf cub behind the ear with his forefinger. "I don't much know what sort of breed they call it, seeing as how you're an Irish wolfhound and its mother was a wolf. Let's see now. I remember back when I had my lessons with Ma—" He stopped speaking and glanced up at the low ceiling of the cave. It was now a dull ache, not the overwhelming, torturing agony of soul and heart and mind it had been so long ago. All the same, his eyes were misty as he resumed. "Ma taught me a few words of Spanish. Wolf—Lobo—that's it, Lije! That's what we'll call your cub—Lobo!" Again he scratched the wolf cub behind the ear and again drew his hand away to avoid being bitten, the wolf cub growling at his temerity. "See, Lije? He says it's fine with him. After all, that's what he is. Well now, let's get some sleep, and we'll start real early in the morning."

The village of Descontarti, chief of the Jicarilla Apache, was high in the mountains and could be reached only through tortuous canyons and gullies. One mid-January morning, Descontarti, whose Apache name meant "He Who Defends Us," stood in front of his wickiup, a hut made of brushwood and covered with woven fiber mats. It was the largest in the village, and on the mats were painted in pigments the symbols of the Apache leader's many victorious raids against the Mexicans. He was in his early forties, short of stature, but wiry and powerful, his black hair drawn into two sheaves which fell at each side of his head. He wore a red headband through which an eagle's feather was thrust. His skin was brownish and wrinkled, not only from the stress of leadership of his tribe, but from the ravages of weather which, in this rugged country, ran the gamut from dry dusty heat to raging blizzards. His eyes were widely spaced and keen, his nose straight and somewhat bony, and his mouth was firm. His was the face of a man of intense courage and dignity, from whom youth had not yet fled.

As he stood with his arms folded, staring toward the east

and watching the slow progression of the bleak sun, he turned suddenly to the door of his wickiup from which a slim, lovely girl emerged. Her softly rounded face had a gentle, almost ethereal beauty to it. She wore light-colored deerskin, with long strands dangling from the sleeves and the skirt. Small, silver, cone-shaped amulets which resembled little bells decorated the ends of the strands. About her neck was a heavy turquoise necklace, and her arms were covered with silver bracelets set with turquoise and other precious stones. Her blue-black hair was plaited into a single braid which dropped to the middle of her back, and because she was both a virgin and the daughter of a chief, a white eagle's feather was thrust through that braid at the back of her head. She was seventeen, and her name was Weesayo, which means Light of the Mountains.

"My father is troubled?" she asked in a sweet, clear voice.

"All men are troubled by what they do not understand or cannot see, Weesayo," Descontarti gravely answered. "Many days ago, runners came to the village to tell me of strange things. They said the gods were angry, and they said that a great warrior who dwells far to the east where the sun rises foretold that the earth would shake and the trees be uprooted and the waters of the land change their course."

"What do these signs tell, my father?"

"I do not know. I cannot tell if the signs say death or life. Last night I did not come to my wickiup until it was nearly dawn. I walked in the mountains and I sought a sign. You know, my daughter, it is our custom when our warriors die never again to speak their names. Yet, last night I called upon the names of Tarzay and Teesonsay. They were my lieutenants who fought with me against the Mexicans, and they died with much bravery in battle. And yet, when I sought to summon their spirits, they did not come. It is only because of what the runners have said to me that I called upon the dead. And this is why I am troubled."

"What will you do, my father?"

Descontarti scowled. "I will wait for ten more suns," he finally replied. "Then I will send my scouts to the north to ask if other tribes have learned yet what the runners meant."

"In a month, Catarina will be eighteen," Don Diego de Escobar mused aloud as he sipped his wine and eyed Doña Inez across the table. They were just finishing their noonday meal, and Catarina had excused herself and gone to her room, while Carlos had taken his Belgian rifle and sought out Miguel Sandarbal.

"That is true, Don Diego," Doña Inez replied. "And I can guess what you are thinking."

The *intendente* of Taos shrugged and made a wry face. "You seem to have acquired a genius for that, my esteemed sister-in-law. Well, yes, I shall admit it. It is high time we both thought about arranging a marriage for that impulsive girl. She surely considers herself a mature woman, and you well know that back in Madrid a girl was not only betrothed by then, but in many instances wed."

"That is very true, Don Diego. But this is not Madrid, and in my opinion, the right man has not yet appeared for Catarina."

"Why do you keep saying this, Doña Inez?" he exclaimed, tugging at his beard, a sure sign that he was irritated. "We came to Taos nearly four years ago, if you will recall. And in all that time, there has been only one logical choice—Tomás de Pladero."

"Yes, it is true that there really have not been any impressive suitors. But, you see, I do not consider Tomás de Pladero one, either."

"The devil take me if I can understand a woman's logic!" he expostulated. "Can you tell me what troubles you about Tomás, Doña Inez? You know that I owe Don Sancho de Pladero a great deal. It was he who took us in when we first came here. He gave us the use of his house until ours could be built. And, through these years, we have worked together on legal and judicial matters, as well as on finances—all matters that concern the prosperity and the welfare of the people of Taos. We have much in common. And his son is an estimable young man."

"Everything that you say is true. I do not argue with your reasons, Don Diego," Doña Inez patiently responded. "Yet none of them take into account the most important reason for a marriage—love."

Don Diego reddened and set down his glass of wine with a clatter. "In my father's time, a marriage was arranged between families. And love came later. Marriage was founded on respect, on tradition, on the stability and the breeding of the families who bore these children."

"That was in the Spain we once knew, my dear brother-in-law," Doña Inez replied with a smile that only seemed to exasperate him more. "I had hoped that you had begun to forget Madrid, just as I have. A Frenchman still sits upon the throne. It is not only distance which separates us from the gracious, mannered way of life we once took for granted. Consider yourself, Don Diego. In the years we have spent here, you have grown prosperous. You are respected and have made friends. Your workers are loyal to you and they love you. Your son—well, if I had had a son, I could not wish him to be any more honest and admirable than Carlos. But you see, Don Diego, in this new life, you have been forced to adapt yourself. And that is true of Catarina, too. Only, because she is still young and impressionable, the true solution for her will be a strong man who can put up with her caprices and shape her into the woman she will some day become. That is the only kind of man she will ever really love."

Don Diego downed the rest of his wine. "You must admit that such a paragon of strength and mastery over women has not yet made his appearance in our humble town."

Doña Inez laughed softly. "That is also true, Don Diego. Maybe, because I am a spinster, I cling to romantic notions. But I think he will appear one day, and she will recognize him when he does."

"And if he never comes? And if, perhaps, Tomás de Pladero thinks—or his parents do, more likely—to arrange a marriage with some other girl, what then?"

"I only say, my dear brother-in-law, that Tomás de Pladero is not the right one for Catarina."

"But why? What makes you so certain? I have seen to it that they are together often. Indeed, in the past year, he has been the only young man who has spent very much time with my daughter," Don Diego persisted.

"That is because you look at him as a prospective son-in-law, if I may be bold enough to say so, Don Diego. You do not see him as a woman does, and you certainly do not see him through Catarina's eyes."

"And will you then, out of your wisdom, please enlighten me as to how *you* see him or how my daughter sees him?" He sighed heavily, as if to say, "Who can reason with a woman?"

"I shall be very glad to do so. And I hope you will consider my words carefully, Don Diego. I have watched them both

from the very first. Tomás de Pladero was naturally struck by
Catarina's loveliness—but that is not love. For the past two
years, I have seen that she looks upon Tomás as a big
brother, a playmate, one whom she is certain she can wind
around her little finger. She teases him, and she finds his
courtly and sometimes pompous conversation very amusing.
That is not the way a girl in love treats her husband-to-be, I
can assure you. For his part, Tomás de Pladero is too much
under his mother's thumb. And it would be very bad for
Catarina to have a husband who would dance to her tune."

This time, Don Diego thought for a while, stroking his
beard, before replying. "I admit that he could show more
spirit. However, Don Sancho is far richer than I am, and
Tomás is perhaps burdened by the responsibility of knowing
that he is Don Sancho's only heir."

"Well, to use your own words, may I remind you that the
de Pladeros would expect a handsome dowry, even if you
were able to arrange a marriage between Catarina and their
son. But it is time for us to put aside thoughts of dowries and
hidebound family ties. The man who really loves Catarina
will not give a fig for the dowry she will bring him. He will
want her for herself." Doña Inez rose, as did Don Diego.
"And now, if you will excuse me," Doña Inez said, "I think I
shall have my siesta."

Thus far, Consuela Viola had not yet been able to create a
situation that would turn Conchita Seragos to the brutal
capataz's lecherous profit. But on the same day that Don
Diego and Doña Inez were discussing Catarina's marital future, the plump maid had at last put Conchita into Doña
Elena's bad graces.

Two of the household maids had been absent that morning
because of illness, and Conchita had their work to do, in
addition to her own. Consuela, biding her time, crept stealthily into Doña Elena's bedchamber and swiftly undid the neatly
made bed, tipped over a chair, and then, with a piece of
charcoal, smudged the elegant mirror over Doña Elena's
dressing table.

When Doña Elena returned from the kitchen, where she
had been giving orders for the evening meal, she stamped her
foot and called out in a harsh voice, "Conchita, come here at
once!"

The timid, black-haired girl heard her mistress's furious

order and ran down the hallway, her dark eyes already widening with fear.

"So this is the way you do your work, is it?" Doña Elena scolded. "Look at that bed—and, not content with that, you clumsy girl, you have tipped over this fine chair. Oh, and my mirror—whatever possessed you to mark it?"

"But I did not, I swear it, Doña Elena!" Conchita began to sob. She stared in confusion at the disarray of the room she had so painstakingly tidied.

"Do not lie to me, you flighty baggage! I have been too kind to you, that is what. Just because you are an orphan does not give you any right to neglect your work or write upon my mirror as if you were a child scribbling on a slate in school! I know exactly what you deserve and what you will get, Conchita—a good whipping! Go to José Ramirez, do you understand me, and tell him that I want him to give you fifteen lashes. Perhaps that will make you more careful in the future."

"Oh please, no, Doña Elena!" Conchita sobbed, clasping her hands in prayer.

"You heard me, Conchita! Or do you wish me to send Consuela to get José and have him come for you? In that case, I shall order you twenty-five hard strokes of the whip!"

"Oh have pity, please, I swear I did not do this, I swear it!" Conchita, her head bowed and shoulders slumped, covered her tearstained face with her hands.

"And do not think to move me with your crocodile tears! Be off with you now, I mean what I say!"

Conchita slowly lifted her tear-ravaged face, but she saw only cold anger in Doña Elena's. With a choking sob, she turned and left the room. As she walked slowly toward the kitchen, she was trembling. It was bad enough to have to feel the whip, but to think that José Ramirez, that coarse, cruel man, would be the one to administer it—

Blinded by her tears, she did not see Tomás de Pladero, who was just coming out of his room, and she collided with him. "Oh, S–Señor Tomás—forgive me—I—I did not see you—oh please, I did not mean to—"

"But what is all of this? Why such tears, Conchita?" he demanded, putting a hand on her shoulder to steady her.

"It—I—Doña Elena says I am to be wh–whipped—I am to tell—oh, Señor Tomás, I swear I never did what she said I did—"

"Of course not. Wait, now. You stay here and I shall speak with my mother." He seemed to straighten, and his usually placid and pleasant features took on a determined look.

"Mother, may I have a word with you?"

"Yes, what is it, Tomás? Can you not see that I am in a vile humor? And no wonder, just look at this bedroom! That stupid little Conchita did not even make my bed, and she knocked over a chair when she was trying to write on my mirror—my fine, expensive mirror brought all the way from Mexico City by *carreta!*" Doña Elena stormed.

"Come now, Mother," he wheedled, "I do not like to see you scowl like that. You are beautiful when you smile—"

"Oh, stop it, Tomás! It does not change matters, you know." Nonetheless, Doña Elena could not suppress the faint twitchings at the corners of her lips, the ghost of a smile that this filial flattery had prompted.

"After all, Mother, I am certain that Conchita would not be so foolish. Two of the maids are sick, and she has had a lot of extra work to do. Besides, she still feels as if she is on trial here. Would it make sense for her to go out of her way to displease you? Please, do not let Ramirez whip her. She is a shy, gentle girl, and you can see she has some breeding and education. I am sure it was not her fault."

"Tomás de Pladero, until now you have never shown an interest in any girl at all. Not even Catarina de Escobar. Can it be that you are stooping to favor a lowly servant girl?"

"Of course not, Mother!" Tomás tried to feign indignation, for his mother's question had come dangerously close to the mark. "It is just that I do not like to think of a young girl being thrashed by that brute Ramirez. I am sure there are other ways to punish a girl if she neglects her work—and, from what I have seen of Conchita, she is trying to please everyone in the house. Besides, I do not think she did all this."

"Then I wonder who did? Well, let it pass this once. But just this once. Very well, tell Conchita she need not report to José this time. But if she offends me once more, remind her that she will be certain to repent it under the lash."

"I shall. She—she was going to the kitchen, and I was coming out of my room and I saw her crying—" he said lamely.

"I worry about you, my son," Doña Elena said with a sniff.

"You are a young fool. When your father and I are gone, how do you expect to run this ranch if you let some stupid little servant girl forget her duties and try to charm you? Oh, well, I shall say this much for you: you have stood up to me like a man—I cannot remember when that has happened before. Perhaps this little incident has done some good. Do not stand there mooning, Tomás! Run and tell your precious Conchita she has escaped punishment— for now!"

THIRTY-EIGHT

Sanimito and his companions relentlessly pursued John Cooper and Lije. Despite his head start of a full day, they followed his tracks with a fanatical determination, inspired by the shaman's curse. The powerful war chief had his own strong motive for capturing the fleeing youth. He had not forgotten how he had been made to lose face by Weshmatigo when he had brought the *wasichu* before the Dakota chief, only to be chidingly ordered to free him and to honor him as Damasha's savior. And then, admiring the white-eyes' skill and courage as a hunter, he had painstakingly instructed John Cooper in the Dakota tongue. They had ridden together on the hunt, they had become friends—and the white-eyes dared to betray his trust by slaying one of his own people. Now he longed to watch the slow tortures which Esintashay would contrive for the *wasichu*'s deserved punishment.

He expected that John Cooper would double back on his tracks and do all he could to confound the pursuers. When he came upon the repeated fording of a little creek or a river, he sent two of his braves in opposite directions to look for tracks of the pinto and of the spirit-dog, and they found them. The snow and the bitter cold had, of course, slowed their pursuit, but Sanimito knew that their quarry would be equally hindered.

Not only had he and his braves chosen the strongest, swiftest horses from the Dakota corral, but they contented themselves with little sleep and food.

The *wasichu's* tracks were fresher now, more distinct. He must believe that his pursuers had given up the hunt and turned back to their village since he no longer sought to trick them by covering or altering his tracks. Sanimito smiled to himself. The tracks told him that it would be perhaps only another day of hard riding before he and his braves fulfilled the vow they had taken before the sorrowing Esintashay!

Late on the morning of January 25, 1812, John Cooper reined in his weary pinto and stared up at the jagged, towering range of the Jicarilla Mountains. He had come over six hundred miles in forty-two days, and his body ached for sleep. Lije, now nine years old, had shown incredible endurance, keeping up with his young master throughout this grueling flight. John Cooper sighed deeply. Beneath the snow-capped, foreboding mountains, in the clear cold air of a cloudless day, he suddenly felt a mystic exaltation. Here, in such mountains, a man could be free to hunt and explore. Perhaps the Apache, of whom Sanimito had spoken with such undisguised admiration, would find in him a kindred spirit and let him share their ways.

John Cooper stroked the little pinto's neck and looked up again at the mountains. He was not sure the valiant animal had strength enough left to ascend the winding trail which loomed ahead of him, a narrow canyon flanked by great boulders and snow-covered trees. In his sling-sack, little Lobo growled, and Lije looked up and uttered his soft, plaintive whine.

"Never mind, Lije, Lobo's just fine. We've come through it all now. We can sleep for a spell and then go find the Apache. I can see, though, that I'm going to have to train Lobo to get along with you once he grows up. He's a fierce little devil, isn't he? But he's your get, and you watch and see, we're all going to be good friends." He chuckled softly, reached to pat the wolf cub through the sling, then turned back to look whence he had come, as he had done so often these past six weeks. Suddenly he stiffened, his eyes widening with disbelief. There were tiny, dark figures on the snow-covered valley below, riding toward him. They were about three miles away, and in the clear air he could see that they were galloping their horses. "I can't believe it," he whispered under his breath, "they've come all this way, followed my tracks no matter what I did—well, there's no help for it. I guess we'll try to get up this mountain and stand them off, that's about all we can do." He drew on the reins and patted the pinto's neck, urging it on. The little horse's sides were heaving, and it ambled slowly forward up the gradually steepening incline that led to the mouth of the canyon. The animal was clearly exhausted and winded, and though it obediently tried to climb, it suddenly staggered back, bowed its head, and stood still. A rasping plaint rattled through its frame.

"Poor little fellow, you can't go on any more. You've brought me this far, a lot more than I ever expected," John Cooper said. Gently dismounting, he stroked the pinto's neck, shook his head, and sighed. Then, adjusting the heavy sack, that held his rifle and ammunition, on his left shoulder, and making sure that Lobo's sling was securely fastened over the other, he began to run up the incline with Lije at his heels. As he turned to look back, he saw the little pinto topple onto his side, kick feebly, and then lie still. "I'm sorry I did that to you," he breathed, and then headed toward the winding canyon.

The cold air was like a knife in his lungs, and his legs ached from the exertion. But there was no time to think of such pain now. He needed a vantage point where he could hide and from which he could see his pursuers. He hadn't been able to count them, but they were coming fast. When they found the pinto, they would know he was hiding up here. His rifle was loaded, but at the best he'd need just under a minute to reload.

The canyon wound like an uncoiling serpent, ever ascending, and John Cooper was panting. There was no time now to look back; frantically he sought some perch along the rocky ledge just above him where he could lie in wait. The odds were against him, except for that one slim hope. And, on foot, there would be no way to escape them. Even if the Apache should be nearby, he certainly couldn't count on them to come to his aid.

It seemed to him that he had climbed almost a mile. His feet began to stumble and the ache in his chest almost blinded him with pain. Then, at last, the canyon broadened, and he saw that he had reached the summit of the smallest peak. At the top was a wide stretch of ground, covered with snow, with a huge boulder twice his height. Beyond it, to the west, was another broader and flatter peak, with a chasm between of not more than ten feet. The canyon ended here, turning into the base of the peak itself, and he would have to climb at least ten feet to the top. But he could see that there were footholds in the rocks, and, on this nearest side of the slope, it was not at all precipitous. He glanced at Lije, wondering whether the wolfhound could climb with him, and decided that it was possible. He took a last deep breath and began to climb, setting each foot down cautiously, securing himself, and moving steadily upward. It was easier than he had thought. Lije barked once, moved back, and then scrabbling with his front paws and digging with his hind paws, the wolfhound suddenly bounded to the broad horizontal plain of the peak itself. "That's the way, boy! Now we'll try to stand them off, you and I!" he exulted as he drew himself over the top and lay for a moment, breathing hard.

From where he lay, he could stare down at the winding canyon he had left behind him. Now he could see that there were six riders, in buffalo robes, and two of them brandished muskets. They had found his dead pinto, and he could hear the thudding of their horses' hooves as they resumed their pursuit.

South of him, and far higher than he was, four Apache scouts stood watching. They had already marked his ascent and murmured among themselves as they saw the great wolfhound stand beside this strange young white-eyes. They were armed with lances and bows and arrows, and sheathed knives were fixed to their rawhide belts. One of them pointed, and the others watched as they saw the six horsemen come up the canyon.

What John Cooper had not seen was that, although the peak behind him was separated by this narrow chasm, it was joined to the mountain on the top of which he now prepared to fight for his life. Also, some two hundred yards back down the canyon, there was a gradually ascending slope which formed the northern side of the second peak.

His eyes were glued to the end of the canyon, his heart was pounding furiously as he leveled his rifle, cuddling the butt against his shoulder, squinting along the sight. He glanced at Lije, whispered, "Still, boy, not a sound now!" and waited.

Sanimito, leading the braves, saw the end of the canyon and held up his hand, signaling for them to dismount. He had seen what John Cooper had not seen, that flanking slope which connected the two peaks. Quickly he whispered to Wikonemay and Onagatsu, and they nodded and ran back, crouching low, toward the connecting slope. Sanimito gestured to Ekinata to go forward to the very end of the canyon, cautioning him to draw the *wasichu*'s fire but not to sacrifice himself. Ekinata nodded, notched an arrow to his bow, and crept forward. John Cooper watched as, hugging the side of the canyon, the young brave came forward. Holding his breath, he squeezed the trigger, and Ekinata dropped with a bullet in his skull.

Panokatay looked up, cried out a warning as he saw John Cooper's face over the edge of the peak, and, quickly aiming his musket, fired. The ball ricocheted off a jagged rock two feet below. Meanwhile, John Cooper, rolling over onto his side and keeping out of range, swiftly reloaded the Lancaster. Sanimito had drawn his bow and sent an arrow whistling over the top of the peak, a foot over John Cooper's prostrate body.

Onagatsu and Wikonemay began to climb the gradual slope toward the adjoining peak, and Migowa, after conferring in a low voice with Sanimito, ran swiftly to the slope directly below John Cooper and began to climb. Just as he reached the top, the youth finished reloading. When he spied Migowa's head rise before him, he triggered a snap shot. The tall heavyset brave fell backward, tumbling down the slope until his body thudded against the floor of the canyon, the musket clattering beside him.

Sanimito rushed to the musket and seized it. He drew back, leveled it at the top of the peak, and waited, his face grim, his eyes narrowed and burning with hate. Again John Cooper reloaded while Lije barked his excitement. The tiny wolf cub echoed his bark with a spiteful growl.

Very carefully, lying flat, John Cooper pushed the barrel of the Lancaster ahead of him and over the top of the peak. Instantly, Sanimito fired, the ball speeding harmlessly into the air above John Cooper's head. Now crawling forward, the youth aimed his rifle at the war chief and pulled the trigger. Sanimito whirled, a hand clapped to his throat from which bright blood spurted, then pitched forward and lay motionless, Migowa's musket dropping from his lifeless hand.

A howl of rage from Panokatay rang in the still air, and the squat, older brave rushed forward to the slope beneath John Cooper and began to climb. There was no time to reload, John Cooper realized. Gazing frantically around, he saw nothing that he could use as a club and, with the frantic inspiration of necessity, reversed the Lancaster to use the metal plaque on the butt as a counter weapon. In that same moment, he saw the top of Panokatay's head rise, and then, with a sudden savage burst of energy, the Sioux brave scrambled over the top of the peak, his musket held at his hip with one hand. Instantly, John Cooper struck at the musket's barrel, diverting it from him just as the trigger was squeezed. The loud explosion was deafening. With his left hand, he drew his knife from its sheath and plunged it into Panokatay's heart, then wrenched it out as the brave tottered, his eyes still bright with savage hate. Before the brave's lifeless body could topple down to the floor of the canyon, John Cooper seized him by the arm and pulled him forward to collapse at Lije's feet. He saw the bow and the quiver of arrows strapped to Panokatay's back and, discarding his rifle, seized them.

There was a yowl of pain, and at the same moment an arrow whizzed past John Cooper's head. Turning, he saw opposite him, separated only by the narrow chasm, Onagatsu and Wikonemay. Both had launched their arrows, and Onagatsu's had wounded Lije's rear left paw. When John Cooper lived with the Ayuhwa Sioux, Kandaka had taught him to use a bow and arrow. He rapidly fitted an arrow to the bowstring, drew it, and launched it. Onagatsu emitted a high wailing cry, clutching at his chest, then fell backward and lay still. But Wikonemay, setting himself on one knee to the ground, had already notched his arrow and sped it. It struck Lije in the side, and the wolfhound yowled again. Then, gathering himself, the dog leaped across the chasm, scrambled with his front paws for a hold, dragged himself over the top of the peak, and launched himself at Wikonemay's throat. The Sioux flung up his arms, dropping his bow with a howl of terror that turned into a gurgling shriek as Lije's fierce jaws closed on his jugular. Suddenly, the great wolfhound relaxed his hold, having toppled his victim to the ground. He uttered a mournful howl and rolled over onto his side, his tongue lolling out of his mouth.

"Lije—oh, my God in heaven—Lije—oh, God, oh, God, poor Lije—you saved me and it killed you, Lije—oh my God—" John Cooper cried aloud in his despair. He flung down the bow, moved back to gain purchase, and then ran forward. With all his waning might, he leaped across the chasm, stumbling and coming down on all fours over Lije's body.

Tears poured down his face as he cradled the wolfhound's great head in his trembling hands. "No, Lije, don't die—please—oh, God, you're all that I've got left—Lije, don't die!" But through his tear-blinded eyes he saw the arrow, deeply imbedded in the wolfhound's side. The brown eyes stared past him, sightless.

On the southern peak beyond, the four Apache scouts had disappeared. He knelt there, how long he did not know or care, continuing to cradle Lije's head in his arms, weeping unashamedly. The sky was blue and the air was cold and still. There was a silence of death in the mountains.

At last he rose, haggard, irresolute, his eyes swollen with tears, still staring down at the wolfhound—once so vibrant and eloquent in all his movements, and in his playful and fervent attempts to communicate with the only two-legged creature he had really ever loved. He had come all these hundreds of miles, through the greatest of hazards, adapting himself each time to new life in the villages of the Ayuhwa, the Skidi Pawnee, the Dakota Sioux. And toward the end, he had bred with one of the most savage creatures of the wilderness, known briefly the unison of mating—and now only the tiny, still inimical wolf cub survived him. Lobo, whose life had been spared in the midst of death, now remained the only link between John Cooper Baines and the life, the belonging, he had once known and so readily taken for granted.

The youth turned and slowly walked to the far edge of this western summit. He looked down. He saw that the slope was far easier than the one he had taken in his desperate fight for survival. He could not leave Lije here; he would not. But there was Lobo across the narrow chasm, now yowling for attention, summoning him back out of the agonizing abyss into which his irreparable loss had plunged him. He straightened, took a deep breath, then called, "I'm coming, Lobo, I haven't forgotten you. I can't now, not ever." Then, as desolation once more seized him, he lifted his eyes to the impassive sky and shouted hoarsely, "Oh, my God, my God, I've lost Lije. He saved my life, and now I can never thank him for it. Help me, God, he's gone now!"

Again, his body shook with sobs, and he had to rub his knuckles against his eyes to clear them of the hot new tears.

He wept—though perhaps he did not realize it—not only for the great-hearted wolfhound, but also for his family.

Once again he heard the shrill yowl of the wolf cub, and he clenched his fists and burst into sobbing laughter. Lobo's immediate needs had drawn him out of self-pitying anguish that had seemed too great to bear. "All right, I'm coming!" he shouted, and, stepping back, ran forward to leap across the chasm. Then, picking up his rifle, he thrust it back into the sling-sack, adjusted it over his left shoulder, and bent to lift Lobo's sling and drape it over his right. He waited a moment to be sure of his footing and his strength and at last leaped to where Lije lay.

Squatting down, he thrust his hands under Lije's motionless body and eased it toward the edge of the peak; then he seated himself firmly, laying Lije across his lap and holding him tightly and, with a silent prayer, let himself slide down the easier slope that led to the end of the canyon. The snow-covered rocks bruised him harshly, but they also checked the impetus of his descent; and he managed to rise, staggering under Lije's weight, and slowly turned toward the narrow canyon which led south.

He walked slowly, for the weight of the wolfhound was almost more than his waning strength could bear. As he walked, the murderous feathered arrow which had ended Lije's life rose like a deadly symbol before his eyes. Then, without warning, without sound, shadows fell over Lije's body and the feathered arrow. When he looked up, there were four horsemen waiting, watching him. The leader, oldest of the four, gestured with his lance for John Cooper to follow.

Half-understanding, still confused by all that had taken place—the eerie silence of the mountains and the impassive silence of these wiry brown-skinned men making this moment seem unreal—he nodded. The leader wheeled his piebald mustang to the south, the others followed, and John Cooper walked slowly behind them, carrying his heavy burden.

In about a hundred yards, the canyon broadened, and suddenly he saw a wide, deep hollow in the wall of the slope which here ascended far more steeply than the one he had slid down. Strangely, there was but little snow, and many jagged rocks the size of a deer's head studded the slope.

He turned to it, laid Lije's body on the floor of the canyon, and began to tug out the rocks with his mittened hands until at last he had scooped out a hollow large enough. Then, lifting the wolfhound into the hollow, he studied Lije's motionless body for a moment. The scouts had halted and were looking back with patient curiosity.

He unfastened the wampum belt at his waist. He looked at it for a long moment. This part of his life was over, and Lije had earned the belt for his heroic courage. Almost reverently, he wound it round Lije's neck and began to cover the great shaggy body with rocks until it was hidden from sight. When it was done, he turned, tears running down his cheeks, nodded to the leader, and, sometimes stumbling on the pebbly uneven path of the canyon, followed wherever they would lead him.

THIRTY-NINE

Pastanari, the ten-year-old son of Descontarti by his second wife, Nadikotay, had been brooding for some time over the injustice of his mother's scolding. It was one thing to chide him in the wickiup, but to make him lose face within the hearing of others, especially Medoncasa, who was the son of the war chief, Managonway, and two years older than himself, was a crushing humiliation that no true Apache could endure without rebellion. Pastanari was tall for his age, wiry as his father, with large intelligent eyes. And, because he was the son of the chief of the Jicarilla Apache, it was all the more shameful to him to know that he could not yet take part in the puberty rites and that he had been scolded like a baby.

It was all because he had wanted to ride off with the four scouts his father had sent north to meet runners from other tribes and to learn whether Tecumseh's prophecy had come true. When he had asked his father, Descontarti had shrugged and stalked away, and then he had asked his mother, and she had said with a smile that did not take away the hurt of it, "You are not yet old enough to be a scout, Pastanari. If your father will not let you ride, I cannot, either. But if you wish to be helpful, see if you can find more wood for the fire for

313

the evening meal." Medoncasa, who had overheard all this, had laughed mockingly, and Pastanari had dug his nails into his palms to keep from answering back. Such a reply would be the way of a child, and this he was not.

And so, this morning, when he saw the four scouts ride down the canyon, he bided his time and waited until his father climbed to a high cliff which faced east. There, Pastanari knew, he would pray to the Great Black Mountain Spirit. His father would not think of him during that prayer, and no brave might approach the chief when he thus prayed on the cliff.

His mother was busy making a wicker basket, and his father's first wife, Namantay, Weesayo's mother, would be helping her. He scowled with determination as he crept, dressed in a buckskin jacket, leggings, and his knee-high moccasins, to the corral. No one was watching the horses, and it was easy to slip into the corral and seize the reins of Lanza, the great white stallion that his father had stolen during one of his raids two years ago. "Lanza" was the Spanish word for lance, and Descontarti had so named the stallion because he sped like one at full gallop.

Pastanari's scowl lightened as he thought of the great deeds of his father. He was proud of them. And he would be a true Apache warrior before much longer. If he were to ride Lanza and overtake the scouts and go with them to seek the runners who would be coming from the north with the news of the prophecy, then no one could say he was only a baby. And he could boast to the son of the war chief who, because he was nearing his apprenticeship, thought himself better.

Lanza nickered as he saw the boy approach. The horse was already saddled with a blanket and a rawhide cinch around it and wore a rawhide bridle. He stamped his front right hoof, pawing at the snow-covered ground. The smell of the little two-legged creature told him that his master's scent was there, but he did not understand what this little one meant to do. It was cold, and the air was crisp. He had not raced down the canyon in many a day—perhaps this was the time.

Since no Apache would use the lazy man's contrivance of stirrups, Pastanari stared at Lanza for a moment, perplexed as to how to mount him. Then, taking a deep breath, he leaped and clung with both hands to the horse's mane, dragging himself up until, at last, he was astride. Then, seizing the reins, he kicked his heels as hard as he could against Lanza's belly. The white stallion, whinnying indignantly, bolted out of the corral. Pastanari had not thought to close the gate, nor did he worry that the other horses might follow him down the canyon. He was intent upon catching up with the scouts. Lanza left the stronghold at a gallop, sure-footed and strong, knowing the way without any guidance from the reins. Pastanari was completely occupied with holding on and not being thrown—the speed and the great strength of the stallion were much more than he had dreamed they could be.

As Lanza raced toward the opening of the canyon which was the entrance to the village, there were shouts of alarm as several of the braves saw what was happening. Two of them ran to the gate of the corral, and another dragged back by the reins one of the mustangs that was trying to follow Lanza. They conferred a moment, shaking their heads, for they could not tell Descontarti, from whose presence they would be forbidden until he returned from the cliff of prayer.

The canyon wound tortuously round and round, ever descending, now narrowing, now broad, its western side sometimes completely walled in by great rocky boulders, sometimes bare so that a glance told Pastanari—to his growing apprehension—that a single slip could mean a fall of thousands of feet to the valley below.

Lanza tossed his head and snorted, his long legs stretching out as he galloped at full speed, exulting in his freedom. The boy crouched over the stallion's neck, holding the reins as tightly as he could, his little knees gripping the sides with all his strength until his entire body ached. At times he closed his eyes when the bareness of the left side of the canyon became too frightening. He had already begun to regret his foolhardy impulse.

The four scouts rode up the canyon toward the stronghold at an ambling pace. They did not once look behind—they knew that John Cooper was following them. He trudged on, head bent, shoulders hunched forward, bracing himself against the climb. Every muscle in his body ached, and his heart was pounding. The altitude of the mountains, combined with the desperate struggle for survival and the shattering tragedy of Lije's death, had exhausted him. He was lagging about a hundred yards behind the four riders, who went slowly on without the least concern for him.

Now the canyon turned to the left and broadened. Lanza, with no restraint from his terrified little rider, had reached his full gallop. Pastanari had forgotten all about his resolve to prove himself a true Apache warrior; he clung desperately to Lanza's neck and whimpered, his eyes tightly shut so as not to see the abrupt drop from the canyon.

At the next bend in the canyon, Lanza raced toward the four Apache scouts. With shouts of alarm, they dragged their mustangs' heads off to one side to make room for the galloping white stallion, whose pace was momentarily slackened. John Cooper heard the shouts and saw the stallion bearing down upon him. At that moment, Pastanari uttered a wailing cry of stark terror. John Cooper tensed, reached out his arms while calculating the stallion's speed and distance from him, and as Lanza went by, plucked Pastanari from his back. The shock and momentum made John Cooper stagger and fall, and he sprawled on his back with the boy safely cradled against his chest, dangerously near the unwalled rim of the canyon. In his fall, the sling-sack with Lobo had been flung toward the right so that he had not crushed the wolf cub.

The Apache scouts rode back quickly, their faces no longer impassive. They were grinning with relief. Two of them dismounted, one hurrying to lift Pastanari into his arms and chiding him good-naturedly, the other helping John Cooper to his feet. Then the latter gestured to the youth to mount his horse behind him and startled John Cooper by saying in the Sioux tongue, "We take you to our chief, Descontarti. We watched as you slew the men from the north, and we saw also the great wolf that killed the Sioux who had given him his death stroke."

"You speak the tongue of the Dakota?" John Cooper asked in that language. "But how can that be, since you dwell so far south of the tribe?"

For a long moment there was silence, and the scout—a short, wiry man in his early forties, his face stony and weatherbeaten—at last replied, "Many summers ago, when I was as young as you, *wasichu,* and my friends and I rode north to find the great shaggy ones, because they had vanished from our land, a young squaw rode up to us. She was fleeing from a Dakota village because her man had beaten her very badly. She had borne him a son, but it had died, and her man had said that she was accursed and thus the child died. Because she could not bear her grief, she killed him, and she was an outcast from the Dakota. I took her into my wickiup, and we were happy together for many moons. She gave me a son, and she died in the doing of it. I do not speak her name, one does not of the dead, but I speak her tongue until my own is silent forever. Know this, then, *wasichu*. I am Kinotatay, and my son, Pirontikay, is much like you. He is young and brave. That is enough talk now. We go to Descontarti."

By the time the four scouts rode into the stronghold, the leader of the Jicarilla Apache had come back from the cliff of prayer and stood outside his wickiup, awaiting them. The scout who had ridden back with Pastanari got down from his mustang and led the little boy toward his father. Descontarti's solemn, wrinkled face brightened, and he held out his arms. Forgetting about his ambition to be a brave warrior, Pastanari rushed to his father and locked his arms around the chief's middle. Descontarti bent and murmured to him, and the boy looked up with shining eyes, then hurried back into the wickiup to see his mother.

Kinotatay dismounted, as did John Cooper, and the Apache scout moved toward the chief, crossed his arms over his chest, inclined his head in token of respect, and began to speak swiftly. Almost reeling with exhaustion and grief, John Cooper listened dully. He could make out some words that sounded like Spanish, but nothing more. He saw Kinotatay turn and gesture toward him. Then the scout turned back to Descontarti and continued his rapid narrative.

The Apache leader nodded and then replied to the scout, who turned to John Cooper and said, "I have told him how you fought the Sioux who came after you and how your great wolf killed the one who gave him his death stroke. Also I told him how you did honor to the wolf. He knows that you saved the life of his son, Pastanari, and he owes you a debt. He asks how it is that you come to our stronghold from so great a distance to the north."

"Tell him that I lived with the Dakota and that I hunted with their braves, my wolf-dog and I," John Cooper responded in the Dakota tongue. "I had come there because I saved the daughter of their chief from the sacrifice of the Pawnee. But the son of their shaman believed that I meant to take the girl as my squaw, though I did not. Out of hate for me, he sought to take my life, and in the struggle I had to take his. That was why they sent their braves after me. I ask only to be free, to live and to hunt. I was told by a great warrior of the Dakota that the Apache speak with straight tongues and hold courage and freedom as dear as life itself."

Now out of the wickiup the slim, lovely daughter of Descontarti came, holding Pastanari by the hand. She smiled at John Cooper and touched the head of her little half-brother, then nodded to him again, as if to thank him. John Cooper held out his hands, palms upward, in the universal sign of peace.

Descontarti spoke again to Kinotatay, who turned to John Cooper and translated once more. "Our chief welcomes you. You shall hunt for game and sit at our campfires. But he says that he sees in the sling you have on your back the cub of the wolf. At our feasts, we eat dogs and the cubs of wolves, for when we do, we partake of their strength and courage."

"Tell your chief," John Cooper replied, again in the Dakota tongue, "that Lobo is the whelp of my great hunting dog that you saw kill the warrior of the Sioux. Tell him, also, that my hunting dog had in him the spirit of one of the greatest of all warriors from across the great waters, and that this whelp, Lobo, is the bearer of that spirit. I do not think the mighty Apache chief would seek to destroy the spirit of so valorous an ancestor."

He saw Kinotatay's thin lips ease in an approving smile, as the scout once again translated his words. As soon as Descontarti had replied, Kinotatay turned to John Cooper and said, "He says that your Lobo shall be treated as you are, then. Perhaps one day he, too, will be as mighty a warrior as his sire. Now I am to take you to a wickiup which will be made ready for you, and there you will rest. This night you will feast with our chief and our braves and learn our ways. Because I speak the Dakota tongue which you do, *wasichu*, I have been told that I am to teach you the words of the Apache."

FORTY

To mark Catarina de Escobar's eighteenth birthday, her father held a great *baile* at the *hacienda* on the evening of February 26, 1812. Doña Inez presided as hostess, gracious and lovely in a brown silk gown. Although she would be forty-two on the twentieth of March, she looked a full ten years younger on this gala evening. She glowed with serenity and a quiet happiness as she mingled with the guests and saw to their comforts. Of course, the de Pladeros were in attendance, as well as a dozen landowners and their families who had become steadfast friends of Don Diego.

As soon as her master and mistress had left their *hacienda* to attend the *baile*, Consuela Viola left the house and gone to José Ramirez's cottage. Earlier that day, he had indicated to her with a coarse, abrupt gesture that she was to visit him as soon as she had the opportunity. She came in fear and trembling, knowing that by now he had tired of her and that her sole usefulness to him was as a go-between with the young maids of the household.

Without being bidden, as soon as she had crept into the cottage and closed the door behind her, she stripped naked save for her *huaraches* and humbly knelt down before him.

He sprawled in a chair, wearing only his boots and *calzónes*, a half-empty bottle of tequila on the table beside him and a just-filled glass in his hand.

"That is the way I like to see you," he sniggered, eyeing her as she crouched at his feet. "But you no longer excite me, Consuela. You are much too fat, and I know exactly how you behave in bed. I have saved your hide many times this last year, and you can count yourself lucky that I remember favors, or you would have many stripes on that fat bottom of yours."

"You know I have always done what you wanted me to, José," the young woman sniffled, shivering in fearful anticipation.

"To a point, yes. I know that you did your best to get Conchita into Doña Elena's bad graces, and I know also that it was that puling milksop of a son of hers who rescued Conchita from the whipping I had in store for her. In my opinion, that young fool has got his *cojones* stirred up over that shy little slut, so I will have to forget about her for now. But there is a new girl I have seen—you know who she is, that tall, slim Yolanda Perez. The one who gives herself such haughty airs and thinks herself better than she is—did you not tell me her father died and her ailing mother sent her to the priest to help her find work?"

"*Sí*, José. It was Padre Moraga who spoke to the mistress about her. She works in the kitchen."

"Of course, just a scullery maid, but the way she looks at a man, you would think she was a duchess," José Ramirez sneered, then downed half the contents of his glass and belched. "So now, Consuela, if you expect me to keep on protecting you from the whipping you truly deserve, you will make sure that this fine duchess of a scullery maid is sent out to me with a note from Doña Elena."

Consuela nodded, biting her lips and staring down at her hands.

"I will leave to your imagination, Consuela, how you will manage it. Just do not fail. I do not think Doña Elena's weakling of a son would dare to concern himself over another pretty servant. And remember, I know how servants gossip in a household. If it ever comes back to me that you have said anything about our little friendship—"

"Oh, José, I would never do that, I swear it!"

"Come now, I want to show you something." Reaching down, he twisted the fingers of his left hand into her thick, disheveled black hair and drew her roughly onto her feet. Then, slapping her plump, bare bottom with the other hand, he forced her to accompany him to the little closet at the back of his cottage. He lit a candle and opened the door, then pointed. "Do you see that little bowl there on the shelf, Consuela? Go ahead, go on in and look at it!"

With one hand rubbing the flaming red mark his blow had left on her olive-sheened skin, Consuela obeyed. The shallow clay bowl was filled nearly to the brim with grayish, powdery flakes. José Ramirez stood beside her, holding the candle high so that she could see the bowl, and he chuckled evilly. "Can you guess what that is, Consuela?"

She shook her head.

"Well, little one, it is *leche de culebra de casacabel*—rattlesnake milk."

"*¡Dios!*" the young woman gasped, instantly drawing back from the bowl.

"Don't be afraid," he purred, as he gripped her neck with his hand and forced her to stare down into the bowl once again. "It is harmless the way it is. You could even swallow it with a little tequila. But," his voice took on a soft, sinister tone, "if I were to take a little splinter of wood and cut the eye of a needle into the end, and then lick it and hold it against these dusty flakes, and then if I were to prick you here, like this—" He released her neck and dug the nail of his forefinger against it. Consuela shrieked and tried to twist herself away from him, trembling violently.

"You begin to see the possibilities," he laughed as he watched her run toward the low bed, fling herself upon it, and burst into frantic sobs. "Well now, just remember that I know how to use this. An old sheepherder in Durango taught me a long time ago."

"I will not say a word about what is between us, José!" she moaned. "Please, close that door, I do not want to think—"

"Of course not," he murmured as he came toward her. "That is why you will be a very good girl and get Yolanda into trouble. If you are very nice, I may even let you come here and watch how I make love to her. You would like that, I think. Well, since you are so obliging, I will just pretend you are Yolanda now. And as for you, Consuela, show a little more life than you have the last few months. Otherwise, I will let Doña Elena know what a lazy, good-for-nothing servant you really are. Then you will see how often you are out in the whipping shed—"

"Oh, no, I will do anything, I will be good to you, please, do not send me away!"

He laughed brutally as he gripped her by the shoulders and rolled her over onto her back, then pressed his heavy manhood toward her tear-stained face.

It seemed to John Cooper that all of the years he had spent with the Ayuhwa, the Skidi Pawnee, and the Dakota Sioux had been a kind of preparation for his new life in the mountains. There was a freedom here which his past experiences had only intimated.

Perhaps it was because of the rugged isolation of the terrain that the freedom and adventure seemed all the more precious.

In this village of wickiups, with a population of some four hundred men, women, and children, there was a distinctive culture, defined by arduous work and exacting laws, where honesty, courage, and straightforwardness were the very ingredients for survival. He discovered that the family structure of these proud and indomitable people was based on tribal customs that permitted the more successful hunters and warriors to take as many wives as they could support; yet chastity and virtue were highly prized, and flagrant adultery was severely punished. This polygamy was dictated out of harsh necessity. If a warrior or hunter died, his wife and children would have little chance of survival unless another brave stepped forward to take them into his wickiup.

The boys of the tribe served a long apprenticeship before they could join the elite fraternity of warriors. Every day they would practice with bow and arrow, and often they were sent on sorties into the rugged mountains to teach them survival in the wilderness. By the age of seventeen they would be ready to join the council of warriors.

John Cooper found, also, a great pride of craftmanship among these indomitable people. Their very name, Jicarilla, was taken from a Spanish word which referred to the exquisitely wrought, waterproof coil baskets which they used in trading with the friendly Pueblo Indians of Taos. They were skilled in the making of pottery and of glass beads which were used to embroider and decorate their buckskin garments, particularly those of the women. They raised almost no food of their own, but gathered wild vegetables and hunted buffalo, as well as the mountain goats and the large wild rabbits and antelopes of the mountains. Kinotatay's vigorous son, Pirontikay, showed John Cooper a curved rabbit stick, whittled from the branch of a durable mountain tree, which could be deftly flung to bring down a fleeing rabbit or antelope.

Knowing that he would soon need to replenish his supply of powder and lead, John Cooper accompanied both Kinotatay and Pirontikay to the great summer fair of Taos. Here peaceful Indians and Spaniards and Mexicans alike journeyed to barter for goods, even at times to buy or sell slave-captives. Utes, Comanches, Apaches, even Sioux and many of the Mexican Indian tribes flocked to this festive gathering. John Cooper proved himself to be as shrewd a trader as he was a hunter by bartering antelope and deer skins, as well as two mountain lion skins, for an ample supply of gunpowder and lead.

Although he was glad of such occasions to see and talk to other white men, a warm friendship grew up between Kinotatay and John Cooper, based on mutual respect and admiration. Kinotatay diligently taught the young *wasichu* the language of his people, which was part Athapascan and part Spanish—the latter, of course, because of frequent intermarriages between the Apaches and the Mexican women they had brought back on their raids across the Rio Grande. The Spanish came easily to the young mountain man, and he acquired a passable knowledge of the Athapascan. He learned also, as with the other Indian tribes, there were universal signs that conveyed many words.

Meanwhile, little Lobo began to thrive, and John Cooper spent hours each day training the wolf cub to follow him, to obey simple orders, rewarding Lije's whelp with a piece of meat and stroking the wolf cub's head with a word of praise. By constant repetition, Lobo came to understand what pleased his young master. Now, when he nipped John Cooper's hand, it was done in play, and often the youth and the growing cub would play rough-and-tumble games, to Lobo's great delight.

Here in the mountains of northeastern New Mexico, John Cooper remained isolated from what was taking place in the rest of the world. By April of this year of 1812, the Territory of Orleans had entered the Union as Louisiana, a slave state. A ninety-day embargo had been placed on all vessels in United States harbors. And on June 19, President James Madison declared war against Great Britain. Two years would pass before the signing of the treaty of Ghent with

Great Britain, bringing an end to hostilities. And, on September 14, Napoleon led his *Grande Armée* into Moscow; it seemed that nothing could halt the Corsican usurper from becoming master of all Europe.

During the summer, John Cooper hunted with the braves, among them Kinotatay and his son. After one such hunt, during which John Cooper brought down sixteen buffalo with his Lancaster, there was much praise and rejoicing upon the hunting party's return to the stronghold.

At the celebration which followed, Descontarti honored the youth by making him his blood brother in the elaborate and time-honored ritual of the Apache. The right arms of Descontarti and John Cooper were cut, the blood allowed to fall into two intricately marked silver goblets, then the incisions were commingled for a few minutes. After this, each drank from the goblet that held the blood of the other. After the ceremony, the Jicarilla chief declared, "You, who walk with the wolf you have tamed, are as swift as the mountain hawk—this you showed when you saved the life of my son. You shall be known in our village as *El Halcón*—the Hawk."

FORTY-ONE

In the Jicarilla Mountains there was snow, and the dull sky and the hazy sun indicated that there would soon be much more. A northeastern wind had begun to blow, hurrying the scattered clouds along the pallid sky.

José Ramirez did not mind the danger of an approaching blizzard. His workers had already herded the flock into the shelter along the slope of the Sangre de Cristo range, and for the past several weeks he had been enjoying the favors of tall, formerly insolent, Yolanda Perez. Consuela Viola had done her work well.

For Carlos de Escobar, now twenty-one, the threatening weather of this early December day was no deterrent to his resolve to go on a long hunting expedition by himself. He had explored the Sangre de Cristo range until he told himself that he knew it as well as the palm of his hand, and he had bagged many a wild goat and antelope there. The Jicarilla Mountains, about ninety miles from Taos, were an untried challenge for him and Valor. Besides, there was an even better reason for him to absent himself from the *hacienda* all of this week and perhaps next as well: only yesterday, his father had informed him that Don Sebastián de Galvez, his wife, Doña Matilda, and his daughters, Serafina and Isabella, had been invited to spend the weekend. His father had added, with a twinkle in his eye, "Serafina has still not married, *mi hijo,* although she has had many opportunities. I think you can guess the reason, Carlos. Yes, her father was telling me that although she is three years older than you, you are the most impressive man she has met."

So Carlos left the *hacienda* before his father and his aunt had breakfasted, went to the stable, and saddled Valor. He had already wheedled some provisions from fat Tía Margarita, the cook, swearing her to secrecy.

"A long trip this time of year is not a good idea," Miguel Sandarbal warned him. "From all the signs I see, there will be a blizzard."

Carlos laughed the warning off, clapping Miguel on the back. "Valor and I shall manage quite nicely. After all, this is not the first time I have gone hunting in the snow. Just the same, *amigo,*" his voice grew serious, "I should appreciate your not telling my father. If he asks, just say that I went on a little hunting trip."

"May the saints protect you, then, Carlos." Miguel crossed himself. "I have no worries about you and Valor—you are a superb horseman and an excellent shot. All the same, if you are going where I think you are, you might run into hostile *Indios.*"

"I do not think so, Miguel. From what some of the workers have been telling me, the Jicarilla Apache are friendly with the pueblo *Indios* here in Taos, and if they see I am out hunting, they will not consider me an enemy. But I shall be careful, never fear. *¡Adios!*" Then, spurring Valor, he headed northwest.

On the fourth morning after Carlos had set forth toward the Jicarilla Mountains, there were snow flurries. John Cooper ate his breakfast of dried corn and some of the meat of a mountain goat he had killed two days before. He left his wickiup, followed by the wolf cub, who was now a year old. Lobo weighed nearly a hundred pounds and had become almost as attached to his young master as his sire had been. For, realizing the inherent savagery of this offspring of a wild timber wolf and his own faithful Irish wolfhound, John Cooper had spent many hours each day with Lobo, teaching him not to bite or snap at the people in the stronghold. Early in this training, whenever Lobo had bared his teeth and growled as a curious little child or an unfledged youth approached, John Cooper had rapped him on the nose and exclaimed, "No, Lobo, *amigo!*" And when the wolf cub began to obey such commands, John Cooper always rewarded him with a tidbit.

Already Lobo had proved himself to be a relentless and swift hunter. Once, in full view of Descontarti and Kinotatay, he saw a wild jackrabbit hopping along a ledge on one of the rocky slopes which framed this isolated village. He growled, and John Cooper patted his head and exclaimed, "Hunt, Lobo, kill!" Lobo raced up to the ledge and overtook the jackrabbit, and his powerful jaws snapped the rabbit's neck instantly. Then he trotted back with it to John Cooper, awaiting his master's praise.

This morning, as John Cooper was scratching Lobo's ears, Lipanaka, one of the scouts who had led him to the stronghold after his battle with the Sioux pursuers, approached and saluted him with the sign of greeting. Lobo lifted his head, his yellow eyes narrowing, and bared his teeth but this time did not growl. John Cooper had taken the wolf cub's ear between thumb and forefinger, ready to pinch it as a rebuke if Lobo showed open hostility to the scout. He released it and patted Lobo's head. "And to you good morning also, Lipanaka," he said cordially.

"There is a white-eyes in our mountains, *Halcón.*" Lipanaka, like all the villagers, addressed John Cooper by the name Descontarti had given him. "He comes on horseback with a long stick like yours. I do not think he is an enemy."

"Perhaps he is a hunter," John Cooper said. "It is long since we have seen white-eyes in our mountains, Lipanaka."

"That is so, *Halcón.* Perhaps our chief should be told."

John Cooper shook his head. "No, Lipanaka. I will go to meet this white-eyes. And Lobo will go with me. If you hear the sound of my long stick, then it will be time to send scouts. But if he is an enemy and he is alone, his long stick cannot bring death more quickly than mine, nor will he by himself endanger the stronghold. If I must go after him on foot, I will turn my horse loose."

Descontarti had given John Cooper a strong brown mustang. The youth mounted it, while Lobo, ears pinned back and eyes narrowed, watched him intently. Then, as John Cooper headed down the winding trail, Lobo bounded ahead with an eager growl. John Cooper shook his head as he remembered how Lije had eagerly taken the lead at the start of a hunt. More and more, each day, he could discern some of Lije's traits in this powerful, savage whelp.

Carlos had spied an antelope pausing to graze at a grassy knoll high above the canyon, and he had quickened Valor's pace, ascending the winding trail of the narrow canyon toward that steep incline. Higher up, snow covered the trees and even the rocks—but where the antelope was grazing, there were stretches of luxuriant grass and a profusion of scrub trees which still seemed verdant.

It had taken him four days to reach the mountains, camping at night, making a fire with his tinder box, and rationing his provisions. Just before he had guided his horse into the mouth of the canyon far below, he had seen a jackrabbit and killed it with a well-aimed shot. He had put it into a leather sling he wore over his left shoulder, for his provisions were nearly gone and the rabbit would make a tasty supper tonight. The cold wind began to tug at him, and he saw the first flurries of snow. But the prospect of killing the antelope excited him, and he urged Valor on.

After killing the rabbit, he had reloaded the rifle, an instinctive act. He was sure that if the canyon led close enough to that knoll, he would have a chance at a good shot unless, of course, the antelope heard his approach and took flight. Assuredly, this was far better sport than having to dance with Serafina de Galvez. He shivered at the thought that she still pursued him, three years since the time he had abandoned her after bringing that glass of punch.

At the next turn, the canyon broadened, completely enclosed by rocky walls high above his head. The snow had begun to come down hard—there was every indication of a blizzard. Well, if he had to hole up for the night, he might at least have an antelope to show for his labors. "*¡Adelante, Valor!*" he called eagerly, and the great gray stallion, tossing his head, snorting, responded at once. Carlos grinned. This was the life, alone and free to do as he wished, not back tending docile stupid sheep.

He rounded another turn of the canyon. The antelope was still grazing about four hundred feet above him, its head turned away. Carefully, he lifted his rifle out of the improvised sling he wore over his right shoulder, and halted Valor. Then, suddenly, there was a coughing roar, and the stallion snorted, reared up on its hind legs, and pawed the air. Carlos uttered a cry of alarm as he felt himself flung from the horse and catapulted to the ground, his rifle hurled a dozen feet away. "Valor, Valor, what is the matter with you?" he called, wincing as he tried to rise. His left leg ached painfully, and as he turned his head, he froze in sudden terror. At his left, about ten feet above him on a rocky ledge, was a mountain lion—lashing its tail, its great jaws open, its cruel yellow eyes staring at him. The stallion had taken flight and was racing up the canyon, disappearing at another turn. Gritting his teeth against the pain, Carlos tried to crawl to the rifle, but there was another frightening roar from the tawny beast above him. It was crouched, ready to spring.

"*Señor Dios*, if it be Your will—" he murmured a prayer and crossed himself.

All the world seemed to stand still as he stared up, helpless, at the crouching beast. Then, suddenly, there was the sound of a shot, and the mountain lion, in the act of springing down, jerked convulsively and fell heavily on its side a few feet away from him, its yellow eyes glazed in death.

"*Gracias, gracias, Señor Dios*—but who—" he panted. He turned his head to the right, then uttered a startled gasp.

On a ledge above him, clad in buckskin, with a gray wolf beside him, stood a young man whose blond hair fell to his shoulders.

"You saved my life, Señor!" Carlos called in Spanish. He tried to rise, but a wave of pain shot through his leg and he sank back, grimacing.

"Are you hurt?" his savior called back down to him.

"My leg—it may be that it is broken."

"I'll come down," the young man called. He turned, and Carlos saw the wolf follow him as he walked back down the canyon for about a hundred yards to a gentle slope. Then he slid easily down, the wolf nimbly racing ahead.

The wolf fixed Carlos with narrowed, yellow eyes and uttered a low growl. "No, Lobo, *amigo!*" the young man reprimanded and tapped his nose with a forefinger. Lobo warily retreated a step or two but continued to watch Carlos with an unswerving gaze.

The wind had redoubled in intensity, and the snow had begun to obscure the landscape. "I'll see if your leg is broken," the blond young man offered, then squatted down and gently began to finger Carlos's left leg from the knee down to the ankle. "I feel no broken bone. But I can tell that it hurts a good deal."

"My horse—Valor—he ran away—" Carlos gasped, as he tried again to rise, then sank back on his knees.

"Don't worry. He has gone up the canyon, and the scouts will find him and take him back to the village. It's a long way from here. But there is a blizzard coming. We'd better find a cave—I saw one not far from where the mountain lion waited to leap down on you. Come, put your arm around my shoulder, try to hobble on your good leg."

"I am very grateful, Señor. Are you Spanish, then?"

"No, Señor. My name is John Cooper Baines. I learned Spanish from the Apache with whom I live and hunt."

"*¡Dios!*" Carlos slowly rose with John Cooper's help, standing on his right leg, lifting the other foot in the air. "You live with the *Indios*? You, a *gringo*?"

"I'll tell you once we have found the cave. The snow's getting very bad now, and it may last a long time. Don't worry about food. I have corn and jerky, and Lobo will hunt rabbits and bring them back for us."

"I have a rabbit in my sling," Carlos glanced at his left shoulder. "And my rifle—"

"I have it safely, Señor—"

"Carlos de Escobar, and alive, thanks to you. Your rifle is surely better than mine. That was a most difficult shot, especially as the mountain lion was just about to leap down."

"It was my father's Lancaster. It's saved my life more than once. I'm happy it saved yours. Now save your strength, we must get to that cave a little further up the canyon."

"*Sí, amigo.*" Gritting his teeth, Carlos began to hop as best he could on his good leg, wincing as even the slightest movement redoubled the pain in his injured left leg.

About two hundred feet up the canyon, the wall suddenly dipped, and there was a low wide ledge which ran beneath it, some five feet off the floor of the canyon. Looking up, Carlos could see a narrow cave. "Yes, that's the one I meant. The mountain lion probably lived in it. I don't think he had a mate. Even if he did, our two rifles will be more than enough, and Lobo will give us plenty of warning," John Cooper said.

Tossing the rifle and the sling onto the ledge, John Cooper gripped the edge and pulled himself up, then lay on his belly and reached down to grasp Carlos's hands and slowly drag him up. "There! It wasn't too bad—did I hurt your leg?"

"No, no, I am fine. You are right, there is certainly going to be a blizzard!" Carlos exclaimed.

Lobo had tenaciously climbed to the ledge and now stood at the mouth of the cave, still eyeing Carlos. John Cooper took Carlos's rifle and peered into the dark opening. "Nothing to worry us here. It's low, but it's long enough for both of us, and for Lobo, too. Here, I'll help you in. Then I'll see what I can do for your leg."

"I speak some English, John Cooper. My mother taught it to me," Carlos said. "I understand most of what you say in Spanish, but I can see that it is different the way the *Indios* speak it."

"From the looks of that snow, Carlos, we'll have quite a bit of time to talk to each other," John Cooper chuckled as he took hold of Carlos's hands and gently led him inside the cave. Then, having found the cave full of dry leaves and bits of brushwood which the wind had blown in, he made a small fire, borrowing Carlos's tinder box to start it. Lobo stood at the mouth of the cave, turning now and then to stare at the stranger.

"If you're hungry, Carlos, perhaps I could cook some of your rabbit," John Cooper suggested.

"As a matter of fact, I am. And the provisions I brought from Taos are almost gone."

"Good! I'm hungry too, and Lobo is always hungry." With this, John Cooper reached for a hunting knife strapped to his belt and began to skin the rabbit. Carlos had propped himself up with his back against the wall, gingerly testing his injured leg. "That is a fine knife you have in the sheath around your neck, John Cooper," he remarked.

"Yes. I took it from a man who tried to rob me of a bearskin and leave my dog and me to die in the winter."

"You say that you live and hunt with the Apache. How long has it been? And where did you come from?" Carlos could not contain his curiosity.

"I've been in the stronghold for a year. But for the last five years, I've lived with other Indian tribes—the Ayuhwa Sioux, the Skidi Pawnee, and the Dakota Sioux."

"You prefer, then, to live with *los Indios* rather than with your own people?" Carlos stared at his new friend.

John Cooper Baines's face was impassive as, putting several pieces of the skinned rabbit onto the fire, he answered, "I lived on the bank of the Ohio River with my family, Carlos. One afternoon, drunken Shawnee killed them. I had nothing left except my wolfhound."

"I understand." Carlos was silent a moment, then shook his

head. "And so all this time you have lived with those Indians, hunted and trapped and learned their ways and their language? How I envy you!"

"Why?"

"Because," Carlos shrugged, "I live in a fine *hacienda* near Taos, and my father owns a large flock of sheep and he is *intendente* there. We came from Madrid—why, it must have been about the time you left your home. But I, I do not care for sheep or balls or dinners where I have to stand on ceremony. That is why I came to these mountains to hunt. I have often gone into the other mountains, the Sangre de Cristo, with my horse Valor."

"Here, I think this piece is cooked enough." John Cooper speared a piece of the rabbit from the fire and handed the hilt of his hunting knife to Carlos, who began to gnaw at it ravenously. Seeing that Lobo had come into the cave and lain down at his young master's feet, Carlos asked warily, "This Lobo of yours seems to be all wolf. You said you had a wolfhound, did you not?"

"An Irish wolfhound. He mated with a timber wolf near the village of the Dakota Sioux. She had a litter of four cubs, but only Lobo survived, and I took him with me. He's far more savage than poor Lije, but I've been training him to accept those who are my friends. He won't hurt you."

"I am not afraid of him. I just would not want to get him angry at me, by moving or doing something that might make him think I was your enemy—the good God knows I owe you my life, John Cooper."

"We are both about the same age, I should think."

"Yes, I am twenty-one."

"And I'll be twenty in a few days. Besides, it's not a matter of how many years one has, but how much one learns in the living of them."

"That is a profound truth. And you have learned a great deal to have managed with all those Indians through the years," Carlos declared with obvious admiration. "Yes, I am envious of you. I wish I could lead such an outdoor life, carefree, dependent on my own skill as a hunter for the food I eat. To come and go as I choose, without having to answer to anyone for the consequences of it."

"Sometimes, Carlos, there are consequences even in that freedom. I found that out with the Skidi Pawnee and with the Dakota Sioux."

"I should like to hear about your experiences. At least,"

Carlos looked out of the mouth of the cave and saw the furious blizzard rising, obscuring all but the palest light, "I think you are right when you say that we shall have to wait here for some time. I only hope Valor is safe."

"Before I left the village, I told the scouts that if they heard the sound of my rifle, they were to come, and that I might turn my horse loose. By now they have found both horses and taken them back to the corral. I know what you are thinking. You have a stallion, but the Apache have no mares."

Carlos tilted back his head and laughed joyously. Already he felt a spiritual kinship with this young man dressed in buckskin, who spoke so simply of what must have been harrowing experiences and, he could already sense, a terrible personal tragedy.

"First, I want to look at your leg. Maybe I can tie a splint to it to ease the pain a little," John Cooper offered.

"As you wish, *amigo*." Carlos closed his eyes and leaned back, clenching his fists in anticipation of the pain. John Cooper foraged at the back of the cave and found a stick nearly three feet long. Breaking off a small piece, he took a thong from the sling-sack, placed the stick against Carlos's left leg from ankle to knee, and tightly wound and tied the strap around it. "Is that better?"

"Yes, a little," Carlos gasped, beads of perspiration standing out on his forehead.

"It's a bad sprain, I'm sure that's all it is. When the storm's over, I'll climb up and get a horse, then come back for you and take you to our stronghold. They have herbs there, and they can heal your leg quickly," John Cooper declared.

Then, seeing that the young Spaniard was exhausted, he added gently, "Why don't you try to sleep now, Carlos? Lobo and I will stand watch."

The blizzard raged for three days and nights, and only on the morning of the fourth day, when John Cooper came out of the cave, did he see clear sky ahead of him. The canyon's floor and walls were deep with wind-blown snow. The two young men had lived on the rest of the rabbit which Carlos had shot and on another which Lobo had hunted down in the snow and brought back on the morning of the third day. During that time, they had become close friends; John Cooper had discovered that Carlos's enthusiasm for outdoor life, and for freedom and independence, was very much like his own. And Carlos had been a rapt listener as John Cooper had explained the ways of life he had known with the four vastly different Indian tribes with whom he had stayed. In turn, Carlos described the courtly and gracious life that had once been his in Madrid and his excitement over the proposed journey to a strange but vital new world. He spoke of the challenge of adapting to it and his current boredom with the monotony of running a sheep ranch and remaining in an isolated community that heard so little from the outside world.

The young Spaniard's leg had mended; it had, indeed, been only a bad sprain, and the improvised splint and rest had greatly eased the pain, though it was still extremely sensitive. Carlos was able to limp about, and his first thought was one of rueful concern for his family. "I should like nothing better than to go to your stronghold and meet the Apache with whom you live, John Cooper. But I am afraid that my family will be greatly worried over my long absence. I told Miguel—there is a man you must meet, John Cooper—that I should be back when I was back and not to worry about me. I only hope that my father did not take it into his head to send out a search party for me."

"I'm going to fire a shot now. It will tell the scouts that I'm here. When they come, I'll have them bring your stallion, Valor."

"Will you not come home with me to Taos, John Cooper? As a matter of fact," Carlos gave a self-conscious little laugh, "your presence may do much to keep me from getting a tongue-lashing from my esteemed father. I know he will be furious with me for not having left word where I was going. Besides, there is a girl I want you to meet."

"A girl?" John Cooper warily echoed.

"Yes. My sister, Catarina. Come now, *amigo,* do not look at me like that. I know you want your freedom and think you are too young—you told me all about Degala and Damasha. But my sister has spirit and great beauty, and in Taos there are absolutely no young men capable of understanding her nature. They are all sons of *ricos,* like that Tomás de Pladero I told you about. She looks on him as if he were a schoolboy, and what she really needs is a strong man—because I know that Catarina has a great capacity for love if only the right man would find her."

"If you wish, I'll ride back home with you, Carlos. Besides,

I want to be sure that you're all right, with that bad leg. But I warn you, I'm not going because of your sister."

"Agreed." Carlos laughed joyously. "Then tell yourself it is because you are my friend that you want to save me from being dressed down by my worthy father in front of all the workers. Besides, he is a wonderful man, really, and I know he will want to thank you for saving my life."

"I'm glad I was able to. But you mustn't make me out to be important just because of that—I happened to be there when the mountain lion was, that's all."

"Well, by whatever good fortune you were there, I thank the good *Señor Dios*, and I shall thank Him all my life. And now that I have met you, John Cooper, I feel at last I have a real friend, someone who will understand my thoughts. In a way, in spite of our differences in background, you and I have much in common."

"I feel that too, Carlos. Wait—I hear the sound of horses—I'll go outside—it may be the scouts from the village!" John Cooper stooped and left the cave, Lobo beside him.

Kinotatay and his son rode down the canyon, leading behind them John Cooper's mustang and the superb gray stallion. John Cooper lifted his rifle to them in salute and, cupping his hand to his mouth, called out, *"¡Aquí, amigos!"*

"We were worried for you, *Halcón*," Kinotatay exclaimed as he reined in his mustang and looked up at the ledge on which John Cooper stood with Lobo, who peered down and bared his teeth, his yellow eyes alert. "We heard the sound of your long stick four days ago, but the great wind blew the snow and we could not look for you, for it blinded the eyes of men and horses. Then these two horses returned to the stronghold. But when the snow had stopped, we came in search of you."

"I am grateful, Kinotatay, and to you, Pirontikay. It was as I thought—the white-eyes, who is my *amigo*, is a hunter and means us no harm. It may be that I will bring him to the stronghold. But now, since he has been so long away from his family, I will ride with him back to Taos. He hurt his leg—the shot you heard was when I killed a mountain lion that was on a ledge about to spring down upon him. He had been thrown from his horse."

"It is a magnificent horse. It could easily be a bridal gift for the parents of a young maiden in our stronghold," Kinotatay commented with a sly grin. "Also, because we did not know whether you had food during the great snow, my son and I brought dried buffalo meat and some corn."

"That, too, will be welcome on our journey back to Taos. I thank my Apache brothers," John Cooper replied with a smile. Then, turning back to the cave, he called to Carlos to come out. The young Spaniard uttered a cry of joy when he saw Valor, who whinnied and raised his front hooves in the air in his own delight at seeing his master.

"I'll slide down the slope, and then help you," John Cooper proposed. "Do you think you can ride now?"

"Yes, I am sure I can. My leg is a little sore and stiff, but once I am on Valor, he will take me home quickly," Carlos responded.

John Cooper helped Carlos mount Valor, took the sack of provisions which the two Apache had brought, and saluted them. "Say to your chief that I will return after I have seen my *amigo* safely home." Then, putting his fingers to his lips, he uttered a shrill whistle, and Lobo bounded down the gradually declining slope, shaking the snow from his shaggy fur. He uttered a soft growl as he came up to rub his muzzle against his young master's leg.

FORTY-TWO

"You young scoundrel, leaving me and your aunt and your sister to think you dead in the mountains all this time!" Don Diego de Escobar scolded. But his misty eyes belied his anger as he gripped his handsome young son by the shoulders and then pressed him against his bosom, blinking his eyes rapidly to clear them of the tears. "Our cook tried to pretend that you would only be gone for a few days, but I managed to get the truth from her. And Miguel himself was worried! Whatever possessed you to go so far—and then the blizzard! I spent many a sleepless night, I can assure you, Carlos!"

"I am truly sorry, Father," Carlos replied contritely. "But here is the man you should really thank—he is the one who saved my life. Valor threw me when he heard the roar of a mountain lion, and if it had not been for John Cooper and his rifle, I should never have come back."

Don Diego turned to the young man in buckskin. "If what Carlos says is true, Señor, I owe you a debt for the rest of my life."

"It was only by luck that I happened to be in the canyon when your son came riding and the mountain lion was on the ledge, Don Diego," John Cooper modestly replied.

"*¡Caramba!* You speak Spanish very well for a *gringo!*" Don Diego exclaimed.

"I learned it living with the Apache. But your son speaks better English than I do Spanish."

"It is most gracious of you to say so. But please, come in, come in, *mi casa* is yours!" Don Diego invited, standing to one side and gesturing for John Cooper to enter.

It had taken Carlos and John Cooper nearly five days to make the journey back from the mountains. The snow was deep and the footing treacherous for their horses, and Carlos's injury kept him from riding long hours at a stretch.

As they entered the spacious and elegantly furnished living room of the *hacienda,* Doña Inez uttered a joyous cry. "Carlos, my prayers are answered! I thank the good God that He has sent you back to us! It was thoughtless of you not to leave word where you were going or how long you would be away."

"I know, *Tía Inez.*" Her nephew approached and, bowing his head, kissed her hand, making her flush with pleasure. "But, as I told my father, it was my friend, John Cooper, who saved my life and brought me back."

"Then I shall pray to Him to bless you always, Señor." Doña Inez turned to John Cooper, her lovely eyes sparkling through the tears, a luminous smile on her attractive face.

"I'm well repaid already, Doña Inez." John Cooper inclined his head in a sign of respect, which delighted the handsome spinster all the more. She turned just as Catarina entered the living room, "Catarina, *querida,* come meet the man who saved your brother's life!"

Catarina stopped short, her green eyes widening with surprise at the sight of the tall young man with long hair and a straggly beard. There was a flicker of disdain on her exquisite face which she at once quelled; forcing her most dazzling smile to her sensuous lips, she said, "Then you are very welcome to this house, Señor. My brother means much to me."

"I can understand that, Señorita. He is already a dear friend. We had a good deal of time to share our thoughts and our experiences in the cave, during the blizzard."

"How horrible! But what were you doing in the mountains?" Catarina could not help asking.

John Cooper stared at her, thinking her the loveliest creature he had ever seen. With a deprecating shrug, he replied softly, "The fact is, I live there, Señorita."

"Oh! But is it not terribly hard—I mean, the blizzards, and it must be so lonely—"

"I live with the Apache. They have been good to me. We hunt together, and we are friends."

"Oh." Catarina could think of nothing more to say to this and bit her lips, lowering her eyes and flushing as she observed that John Cooper's eyes were fixed on her.

"Well, well," Don Diego boomed, "now that we have had the introductions, please be kind enough, Doña Inez, to tell the cook that we are hungry. It is something like killing the fatted calf for the prodigal son, ¿no es verdad, mi hijo?" He grasped Carlos by the shoulder and gave him an affectionate little shake.

Before sitting down to the festive supper, Carlos had lent John Cooper a fine razor of Damascus steel. One of the maids had heated a jug of water, and John Cooper had flushed self-consciously when Dolores brought the water to him. Her gaze was unabashedly admiring.

At the table, Catarina was seated opposite the young mountain man and watched him intently as the lavish meal was served. Doña Inez, seated at the other end of the table and across from Don Diego at the head, smiled at Catarina's reactions. The handsome young stranger managed knife, fork, and spoon as if he had learned to use them from earliest boyhood. Doña Inez interpreted Catarina's surprised look as an indication that her niece found it incredible that this stranger from the mountains who had lived with the Apache did not disgrace himself at the table.

During their first evening, John Cooper was reticent about his past, but Carlos could not say enough about the courage and skill his new friend had displayed in killing the mountain lion, and then managing to survive the blizzard in a cave. Nor did he forget to startle his family with the story of how Lobo had gone hunting for a rabbit and brought it back to the cave when they were out of food.

Before going into the main house, John Cooper had made a leash for Lobo and tied him up in a little shed, with plenty of food and water. After the meal, he politely excused himself. "I don't want Lobo to think that he's been abandoned. I'm trying to teach him to be friendly to everyone, except, of course, someone who means to do me harm."

"Lobo—what a strange name for a dog," Catarina mused aloud.

"No, Señorita Catarina, it's a very accurate name. You see, Lobo is the whelp of a timber wolf and my Irish wolf-hound."

"A wolf? A savage beast like that—and you have made a pet of it? ¡Dios!" Catarina gasped, lifting her green eyes ceilingward and then clapping a hand over her mouth as she saw her aunt shoot a reproving glance down the table.

Don Diego cleared his throat. "I insist that you stay with us several days, Señor Baines," he eagerly declared.

"If you wish it. It's been a long time since I've sat at a table and eaten supper—and never such a supper as this," John Cooper grinned.

"Of course he will stay, Father," Carlos broke in. "I want him to meet Miguel and the rest of the workers. John Cooper, perhaps you will show them how well you can shoot your Lancaster rifle. It carries farther and it is much more accurate than mine."

"Thank God for that," Don Diego interposed and crossed himself.

Carlos could not wait to introduce his new friend to Miguel and the workers, and almost at dawn, after downing a quick breakfast, he led the young mountain man out to the cottages of the workers. "Valor is safely back in his stable, thanks to you, John Cooper," the young Spaniard declared. "Let me show you the other horses we have. Miguel, this is my good friend, John Cooper Baines. He saved my life. ¡Sí, es verdad! Valor was scared by the roar of a mountain lion and threw me, and if it had not been for John Cooper, you would not have seen me again."

"Then I shall be your friend for life, too, Señor," Miguel Sandarbal answered gravely as he held out his hand to shake John Cooper's. "May I see that rifle of yours—ah, wonderful workmanship."

"A Lancaster, made in the east of our country, Señor Sandarbal."

"I should be honored if you would call me Miguel. Yes, I can see how well made it is. And the metal plate at the butt?"

"When there isn't time to reload, it can be used as a club against an enemy," John Cooper tersely replied.

Miguel nodded. "Comprendo. And your mustang, it is a fine horse."

"The Apache capture mustangs on the plains, break them in, and take them into their corral. They have much endurance and courage."

"That is plain to see. In Spain, at the bullfights, swift, brave horses like these are used by the *picadores*. Now, here in our corral, John Cooper—may I call you that?"

"I would much rather be called that than Señor, as you would rather be called Miguel." John Cooper grinned, and the two nodded to each other, already friends and content with their appraisal of each other.

"That gelding there, the piebald one, what do you think of him?" Miguel asked shrewdly, winking at Carlos.

John Cooper studied the horse. "He's in need of shoeing, and his front left fetlock is just a trifle shorter than the right. I wouldn't use him on a long hunt, that's for certain."

"Your friend knows horses, that is plain to see," Miguel exclaimed. Then, cupping his hands to his mouth, he shouted, "*Amigos*, come meet a good friend, one who has saved our young master's life in the mountains!"

The Mexicans crowded around John Cooper, and he readily answered their questions in passable Spanish, acknowledged their greetings, and inquired of their families—so that within half an hour all of them had accepted him almost as one of them. "Now," Miguel decided, "we shall see how well this rifle shoots. Jorge, give him a difficult target to shoot at."

Jorge Corrado grinned and nodded, went into the stable, and came back with a dried fir cone. Then he strode to the end of the long corral and placed the cone on the top of one of the posts, a distance of about four hundred feet away from where John Cooper stood.

"You first, *amigo*," John Cooper turned to Carlos with an engaging smile.

"Very well, I accept your challenge." The young Spaniard loaded his rifle, aimed it carefully, squinting along the sight, and then squeezed the trigger. The ball brushed the side of the top of the pole, but without touching the fir cone.

There was a cheer from the workers, but it was silenced when John Cooper cradled the butt of the Lancaster against his shoulder, drew a deep breath, squinted carefully, and then touched the trigger without seeming to move. The fir cone leaped into the air and split in two amid loud cheers, and Miguel clapped the young mountain man on the back. "By all the saints in heaven, I have never seen a better shot by anyone—no, not even by you, young master!"

At supper that night, Carlos, brimming with excitement over the way his new friend had won the hearts of the workers and of his dear friend Miguel, insisted that John Cooper tell about his life with the *Indios*. "What do the Apache call you, John Cooper?" he urged.

"*El Halcón*. That is probably because I am swift with my rifle on the hunt."

"What you are, *amigo*, is far too modest. But how do you live with them?"

"In a wickiup, a frame of brushwood which is covered with skins. And I assure you it keeps out the cold, especially if one has blankets and good thick buckskin, as I wear."

"And before that you lived with the Dakota Sioux and the Skidi Pawnee and the Ayuhwa Sioux—five years of your life with *los Indios!*" Carlos exclaimed.

"Yes, that's true. And yet their way of life is as good a way as any other. They respect a man who tells the truth, who is brave, who can hunt and bring meat for the campfire. And they hate liars and thieves. They love their wives and children—yes, in many ways they are not unlike us."

"But, John Cooper, I should have thought you would hate all Indians for what they did to your family."

John Cooper shook his head. "I can't blame all of them for what a few did. To begin with, the Shawnee who killed my family were drunk, and they were after more whiskey. I've been told of white men who went crazy after they drank too much whiskey. No, the Indians I've lived with have treated me fairly by their sights, and to my way of thinking you can't ask more than that of anyone."

Catarina, who had been listening to all this with a supercilious expression on her lovely face, broke in haughtily. "Really, I do not understand that at all! Why, if *los Indios* had killed *mi padre* or dear Carlos, I should want to kill all of them!"

"But suppose a river bushwacker or maybe even one of your neighboring ranchers did that, Señorita; would you then say you'd want to kill all rivermen or ranchers?" John Cooper countered. "If you were to see how the Jicarilla live, you'd learn that there are good men and bad in their village, just as there are in any town or village, no matter what the color of the peoples' skins."

"Oh, it—it is useless to—to talk to a savage!" Catarina exploded, tossing her napkin onto the table. She rose abruptly, icily excused herself to her father and her aunt, and walked out of the dining room.

"I am overwhelmed with shame, Señor Baines." Don Diego scowled after his daughter. "I do not know what has gotten into her."

"Please don't be upset, Don Diego," John Cooper replied. "I can understand why so well bred a young lady, who perhaps has never talked to an Indian or even seen one, would think me a savage for having lived with them."

"Yes, but the fact is, Señor Baines, that when we were on our way from Mexico City here to Taos, we were attacked by *Indios*. So you see, she has seen them, but only as she believes them to be—savage and warlike."

"They are not all like that. But, you see, Don Diego, they have enemies among other Indian tribes, as well as the whites who wish to take their land from them and kill the buffalo which give them their food. And then there are the traders who cheat them with trinkets in return for valuable skins. They've had to survive in wildernesses and in mountains, and so they're simple people. But they're honest."

Don Diego plucked at his beard. "You have given me much to think about this evening, Señor Baines. I have never before met anyone like you. But again, I beg you to forgive my daughter for her inhospitable outburst."

"I've forgotten it already, Don Diego. All of you have been so gracious to me that I have only the warmest feelings toward you," John Cooper replied.

During the first two days of his stay at the de Escobar *hacienda,* John Cooper had gone out to the shed and released Lobo, but had kept the leash around the young wolf's neck. Lobo was not happy, but grudgingly allowed his young master to lead him along on frequent walks. Each time he returned, John Cooper rewarded him by talking to him and stroking his head and giving him a piece of raw meat. But on the third morning, John Cooper declared to Carlos, "It's time that I return to the stronghold. Lobo isn't happy being locked up in a shed, and because I do not know how he will react to your workers or to your family, I won't take the chance of letting him run loose as he's used to doing."

"I understand." Carlos hesitated, then said earnestly, "I

should like to go back with you to your village in the mountains and meet the Apache. What you have told me of them makes me want to learn to know them."

"I would be happy to take you with me, Carlos. But you'd best ask your father."

"Of course. I shall do that before we leave. But Miguel wants to see you again, and besides, I shall have the cook pack a big sack of good food to take with us on our journey." John Cooper chuckled and patted Carlos on the back, nodding in agreement.

Just then, Carlos caught sight of Miguel Sandarbal. "*Hola*, Miguel, a good morning to you."

"And to you, young master, and you, John Cooper."

"I have asked John Cooper to take me with him to the Indian village, Miguel. I shall get permission from my father. So be sure to give Valor a good breakfast for the long journey."

"I shall do that, Carlos. And one for your mustang, too, John Cooper."

As John Cooper approached the shed in which he kept Lobo, the wolf heard his master's voice and growled. To the right, about fifty feet away, was a smaller shed, its door partly open. Esteban Morales, a young Mexican sheepherder, was standing there talking with his lovely young wife, Concepción. They had a two-year-old boy named Bernardo and were radiantly happy in their new life in Taos. Esteban, who had met John Cooper the previous morning, had insisted that his young wife come out to meet him and bring their little son. Concepción, holding the child's hand and looking toward the tall young mountain man, exclaimed to her husband, "How tall and handsome he is, and dressed like an *Indio!*"

"*Sí, querida*, that is because he lives with them. I told you, he saved our young master's life with that long rifle of his. It is good to see our young master have a new friend. I know that he does not care for sheep. Maybe now he will have someone to hunt with."

"It would be better for him to find a wife, Esteban," Concepción giggled. She gave him a sly pinch and in so doing released little Bernardo's hand. The child moved back, and then began to walk slowly toward the little shed.

In the back corner, there was a large scorpion which had been dormant all through the winter. Now the scorpion stirred, just as the little boy ventured inside the shed.

John Cooper came forward with Miguel, who gestured toward Esteban and declared, "You know Esteban Morales already. This is his *mujer linda,* Concepción, and their son Bernardo—*Dios,* what is the *niño* doing?"

Concepción screamed as she turned to stare into the shed. Little Bernardo, in moving into it, had pushed the door farther to one side, and she could see the huge scorpion. The child was now only about three feet away from it.

John Cooper drew his knife from the sheath, balanced the point between right thumb and forefinger, and flung it with all his strength. The point transfixed the hideous arachnid, whose long, narrow, segmented tail had already drawn back to inflict its venomous sting.

Esteban uttered a sobbing cry and rushed into the shed, picked up the little boy, and carried him back out in his arms. Concepción burst into tears and covered her face with her hands. "Señor, Señor," Esteban said hoarsely, "I am your man for life. Call on me whenever you will to pay back this debt I owe you."

"You owe me no debt, Esteban Morales," John Cooper replied. "I did only what you would have done if you had my knife. But there is one thing you could do for me—"

"Anything, Señor, anything in the world!"

"Miguel has told me that you make wooden flutes and play them to the sheep." John Cooper chuckled as he looked at the shed in which Lobo was now growling loudly. "Perhaps you could give me one of your flutes. It might help soothe Lobo's temper."

FORTY-THREE

Reluctantly, Don Diego de Escobar agreed to his son's visit to the Indian village. At first he protested, "But that means you will miss out Christmas together, my son!"

"*Mi padre,* truly, it is the only Christmas present I really want. Besides, John Cooper saved my life—at least I owe him the keeping of the promise I made to go with him," Carlos countered.

Then Carlos told his father how John Cooper had saved the life of Esteban Morales's little son. The Spanish nobleman heaved a sigh. "Very well, *mi hijo,*" he finally said, "I am convinced you will be in good hands. And if the *Indios* of the mountains look upon Señor Baines as a blood·brother and you accompany him, I shall try not to worry too much." Then, with a characteristic tug at his beard, he added with some irritation, "All the same, I suspected your motives in going off hunting by yourself after you were told that Serafina de Galvez would be a guest at our *hacienda.* She inquired after you and professed great interest in your well-being."

"I hope you made my apologies, Father," Carlos replied. "As for myself, I am sure that my well-being will be the greater if Serafina de Galvez expresses her concern about it from a respectable distance. I have not the least affection for her, but I do hope that she finds someone who does."

"Very well, then, *vaya con Dios,* my son." Don Diego sighed as he embraced Carlos and then gripped John Cooper's hand.

During last summer's trading fair in Taos, Carlos had purchased a hunting knife of fine Castilian steel in a sheath affixed to a tooled leather belt, and he had strapped this around his waist. "I should like to make a present of it to the Apache chief in return for his hospitality, John Cooper," he said to the young mountain man as he mounted Valor.

"Such a gift will please him greatly. As I told you, these are simple people, and when one deals fairly with them, they can be staunch friends, even to defending your life if need be. Well," John Cooper looked up at the clear, almost cloudless sky, "we won't have a blizzard to reckon with this time, and by now the mountain trail should be much easier. *¡Vamanos!*"

"It is good to have you back with us again, my blood brother," Descontarti solemnly declared. Then he turned to look at Carlos. "And this is the white-eyes who came to hunt in our mountains and whose life you saved?"

"That is true, Descontarti. And we have become good friends. Like myself, he wishes to be free, to hunt and to ride his horse, and to understand the people of your tribe. I have told him that they believe in truth, honor, and courage."

"Then he is more than welcome." The Apache chief turned to Carlos and said in halting Spanish, "Because *El Halcón* speaks well of you and because we in the stronghold know that he has never spoken with a forked tongue, I welcome you. Tonight we shall have a feast in your honor. And tomorrow, I invite you to join our braves and my young blood brother in tests of skill with the bow and arrow, the knife, and the long stick. When we raided across the border, our warriors sometimes brought back old muskets. They can still be used, but they do not shoot very far. Yet it is good sport for our young men to practice with the weapons of the white-eyes—because there are those who would use them against us even though we are at peace. If the time should ever come when we are attacked in our stronghold, they will stand ready to defend our women and our children."

"I thank the great chief of the Apache for his welcome.

And I wish to give him this gift which will speak my thanks and which I hope, when he uses it, will remind him of my pleasure as a guest of his village."

The Apache chief smiled and took the belt with its attached sheath, lifted the finely honed blade out of it, and held it up toward the sun. "It is a fine gift, and I thank the friend of my young blood brother." Then, turning back to his wickiup, he called, "My daughter Weesayo, will you not come forth and take our guest to the wickiup where he will stay during his visit with us?"

Carlos caught his breath as the slim young Apache girl emerged. Their eyes met, and hers widened at the intense admiration in his gaze. Modestly lowering her gaze but unable to suppress the sudden coloring of her cheeks, she murmured gently, "I bid you welcome here because you are the friend of one who is loved by all of us and whom we trust."

John Cooper glanced at Carlos, then pursed his lips in a silent whistle. He could readily understand his friend's wondering surprise at the first glimpse of Weesayo. Until he had met Catarina, he himself had believed Weesayo to be the loveliest young girl he had ever seen. Her poise and quiet dignity, as well as her youthful femininity, elicited both respect and admiration. When he saw Carlos smile as she came forward to lead him to the wickiup, he at once engaged her father in conversation so that Carlos and Weesayo might have a few moments alone together. Dimly, he now remembered what his mother had said to him—how very long ago it all seemed!—that sometimes people fell in love at first sight, and sometimes that was the deepest, sweetest, and longest-lasting love of all. Because he felt himself more closely drawn to the young Spaniard than even to his Ayuhwa friend Kandaka, he hoped that it would happen to Carlos.

"Is there news of any importance to the village since my absence, my blood brother?" he asked.

Descontarti frowned. Then he led John Cooper into the wickiup. "Again there have been runners from the great chief of the east," he replied gravely. "We have been told that the earth trembles many times because the Great Spirit is troubled by the hatred which the white-eyes have for people like ourselves. Also, it is known that the white-eyes fight against their own people from across the great ocean."

"You mean, the United States is at war with the English?" John Cooper exclaimed.

"So the runners said. And they spoke also of a war party of Mescalero from the south who go to raid the Mexicans across the border. But these, so the runners say, are outcasts from the tribe. Such outcasts may attack the white-eyes and we, the Jicarilla, may well be blamed for what they do."

"But the Mescalero are many miles to the south, Descontarti."

"Yes, it is so. But these outcasts are bold enough to raid where they choose, and they have strong horses and take weapons from those whom they kill. I do not think they will come up the road which leads to our stronghold, and there are not enough of them, even if they did. All the same, I do not like to hear such news."

"Nor I, Descontarti." John Cooper rose to his feet and made the sign of respect for the chief in sign language. "But this is a time for feasting and for good friendship, for I wish my *amigo* to learn, just as I have learned, the kindness and the honesty of the Jicarilla."

Descontarti smiled and nodded. "His manner has already pleased me, *Halcón,* and it was a very fine gift that he thought to bring me. Besides, it is not hard to like a man who is your friend."

"My chief honors me with such kind words. May I always deserve them." Then, remembering the glances Weesayo and Carlos had exchanged, he paused and asked, "Would the chief of the Jicarilla allow a white-eyes to take his daughter as his squaw?"

To his surprise, the weatherbeaten face of the Apache chief crinkled in a knowing smile. "Not any white-eyes, *Halcón.* But it has been in my thoughts that if you, my young blood brother, were to say to me that you sought to live among us and have my daughter share your wickiup, I would gladly give my consent."

The blood surged to John Cooper's face and he lowered his eyes. Suddenly, he saw in his mind's eye the green-eyed, insolent, black-haired Catarina de Escobar. For a moment he could not speak, having realized the feelings for her that he had not before suspected. Finally he said, "Among your people, as among mine, Descontarti, a man and a woman come together in love. This has not happened between Weesayo and myself. Yet it may happen for my friend, who is now your friend, and Weesayo."

Descontarti pondered a moment. Then he replied, "I have already seen that there is much good in him. He does not look down upon us. I say to you that if it should happen between him and my daughter, I would consent if it meant her happiness. Now I must go to see that the feast, the dancing, and the games for our warriors are being prepared as I ordered."

After he had placed his gun and sling in the wickiup to which Weesayo had led him, Carlos emerged to find her standing there with her back turned to him. "*Gracias*, Weesayo," he said softly.

She turned and her large, dark eyes were very wide. There was an exquisite shyness to her face as she said in Spanish, "You know my name?"

"*El Halcón* has told me. And he has said what it means. *Luz de montaña*. It is a name that suits you."

Weesayo blushed as she quickly looked away and pretended to pluck at a loose bead on her jacket. Finally she murmured, "It was the name given to me as a child, Señor."

"Can you say my name?" Carlos pursued boldly. He saw that her hair was drawn tightly against her head and gathered together on the nape of her neck. It was, although he could not know it, the proclamation of her unwed status. The sun touched deep, blue shadows in through the black of her hair. It seemed to him that the sound of her voice was like that of a gentle flute, played in the stillness of the night. Suddenly, foolishly, he ached to hear her say his name.

"My father has told me. It is Señor Carlos," she murmured back.

"I thank you again for bringing me to the wickiup. I think you are very beautiful, Weesayo."

"Oh! You must not say this to me. We do not even know each other."

"But," Carlos found his heart pounding, "it is in my heart that we shall know each other. I would stay here and know the ways of your people, and of you most of all."

She flashed him a sudden look in which there was both maidenly fear and a naive pleasure at such unheard-of-flattery and then hurried away without another word. Carlos stood looking after her. He felt himself trembling. "I did not know that a girl could be so innocent and yet more teasing than my own sister," he thought to himself. "I wonder how it is that John Cooper has not fallen under her spell. But for myself, I have already." Then, delighted with himself at this discovery, he grinned and went back into the wickiup to wait until he was summoned to the feast.

Carlos, on his walks with John Cooper through the village, had seen the women scraping skins, making gourds and baskets, sewing clothing, preparing food. Men were fashioning arrows and new lances, refitting bowstrings, and those who owned old wide-bore muskets were cleaning them. Even the little children were at work, the girls helping their mothers while the boys fashioned toy weapons and dreamed of the day when they would be warriors and go on raids or hunt the buffalo.

Lobo trotted beside John Cooper, with an occasional wary glance at Carlos. There was a sense of peace in Carlos now, and it was not the elevation of the mountains which made him feel such serenity and joy. He said to John Cooper, "I begin to understand why you are happy here, *amigo*. I think I could be also."

John Cooper glanced at him and smiled to himself. It was still too early to tell Carlos that if, as he suspected, the young Spaniard had already fallen in love with Weesayo, Descantarti would not forbid such a union.

At the feast, there were roast antelope and buffalo meat, cold cakes made of mesquite beans, honey from the stalks of the mescal and yucca, and a jelly made from the roots of algerita. There was fruit from the prickly-pear cactus, and there was tiswin, a weak beer which was the favorite drink of the Apache, drawn from skin vats and poured into huge gourds.

In the darkness, the campfires blazed and made long shadows on the ground. The music-makers sat before the fires, chanting, pounding their drums, drawing strange, eerie music from the fiddles and guitars which they had obtained at the trade fairs in Taos. The warriors wore their ceremonial costumes. The women came to form another circle outside the men's circle, and both swayed back and forth to the rhythm of the music. Descontarti appeared, dressed in robes of soft buckskin painted with pictures which showed the elements of the hail, rain, snow, and sun, with lightning blazing in red jagged bolts across his chest. On each of his arms there were leather and silver bands set with silver-colored stones, and bright seeds which glittered in the light of the fire. On his head was a red sash stuck with two eagle feathers, one painted bright red, the other in its natural white.

He was preceded by the chief shaman, Gonordonotay, a small, wiry, gray-haired man with broad nose, thin lips, and high-arching forehead. Gonordonotay wore his holy shirt on which were painted the marks of the buffalo, the mountain lion, the antelope, and the eagle, and in his right hand was a medicine cord of four strands with painted gourds at the end of each. He swung the cord in a great circle over his head as he began the chant of welcome for the return of their young blood brother and to the latter's friend, who came in peace as a hunter.

Carlos, seated next to John Cooper, watched and listened, and when at last, at the very end of the dancing, Weesayo appeared, John Cooper saw that Carlos could not take his eyes from the slim young girl.

The men passed gourds of tiswin among themselves and told stories of Coyote, whose cunning often tricked his enemies and, alas, as often out-tricked himself.

Late at night, when John Cooper and Carlos returned to their wickiups—that assigned to Carlos was located near John Cooper's—the young Spaniard gripped his friend's hand and said, *"Gracias, mi amigo.* You cannot know what it has meant to me to come here today. It is as if I had just begun to live."

"Listen, Carlos," John Cooper said warmly, "I think I know what you have felt. Don't be afraid of it. I tell you this—Descontarti likes you, and he has already said that you are his friend. If it should happen that you and his daughter fall in love, he wouldn't say no to it just because you are white and she is Apache."

"Do you think so? *Amigo,* do not joke with me on such a matter—I cannot believe myself what has happened to me. But when I first saw her, and now tonight—" Carlos did not finish, then shook his head and said, "There are no words for it."

"That is how it happens. I wouldn't joke about such a thing, Carlos. I asked Descontarti what he would say if you and Weesayo should fall in love. And I tell you he would not oppose it."

"But it would mean marriage, there would be no other way for me—"

"That goes without saying. You are an honorable man, *amigo.* There would be no other way, with an Apache maiden. If you only wanted a girl for a night, then you could choose among the widows, or women whose men have walked away from them—those who have knowledge of men. With such, the Apache allow a man who has no squaw to have a woman in his wickiup. But clearly you want Weesayo, and her alone."

"I do not know if she would marry a white man, John Cooper. All I know is that suddenly, after just this one day, I feel that I have wanted her all my life."

"Then win her. Tomorrow, in the games with the warriors, try to exceed them. Show that you are as strong and clever as any of them, and she will see it and she will smile upon you," John Cooper declared. Again he gripped Carlos's hand and then went into his own wickiup.

Well into the next afternoon, the Jicarilla braves competed with the bow and arrow and the lance. One of the games was for a warrior to ride his mustang at full gallop and, with the point of his lance, pick up a small gourd and lift it high above his head without dropping it. Astride Valor, having tested the lance for balance, Carlos missed at the first try. But the second time, he deftly scooped up the gourd and held it aloft amid the cheers of the women and the old men. He was less successful, to be sure, with the bow and arrow, but John Cooper consoled him by saying, "Don't forget, since children they've been instructed in its use and you've begun to handle it only just now. Even I am not the equal of the scout Kinotatay who taught me to speak the Apache tongue. But now, you'll shoot with your rifle against the five who have the old muskets. And I won't use 'Long Girl.' "

"But why?"

John Cooper smiled. "Because I want you to win and I want Weesayo to watch you. We're friends, aren't we?" Carlos's eyes blazed with joy and he gripped John Cooper by the shoulder, then strode off to the target range. It didn't take long to show that the Belgian rifle was far more accurate at a greater distance than any of the muskets, and Descontarti himself praised Carlos's shooting.

At the end of the games, the Jicarilla chief turned to John Cooper. "You are my blood brother and the Señor Carlos is much like that to you," he said. "Well, since he has shown that he is the equal of many of my young warriors, I will make him my blood brother as you are."

Carlos was overjoyed when John Cooper translated the

chief's words. Then he said in Spanish to Descontarti, "I ask *Dios* to bear witness to my promise that I shall never dishonor this bond between us."

"Already you begin to think like one of us, Señor Carlos," Descontarti remarked as he beckoned to Gonordonotay.

Once again the Apache ritual of blood brotherhood was enacted, and John Cooper, now a spectator, was moved by its profound significance. First the chief and Carlos knelt, facing each other, while the shaman drew a circle into which he stepped and placed on the ground before them two small, beaten silver goblets. Next, building a fire of twigs and leaves, he drew his bone-handled knife from its sheath and held the blade in the fire for a moment. Then, raising his face to the sky, and holding Descontarti's and Carlos's right wrists in his hands, he said, "There is all of a man in each drop of blood. A man is made of his blood, which came from his father, and which his father had from his father, which he gives to his son, which his son gives to his son." He released their wrists, waved the knife to the four directions of the earth, then thrust it into the ground and said, "The blood is the man and the earth is his mother." Then he drew the knife out and put the blade in the fire again for a moment.

When the blade had cooled, he cut a small slash in each right arm about eight inches above the wrist and held each arm over one of the goblets and let blood flow into it. He placed their arms together so that the blood commingled and then released them and bid the two men drink. Carlos and Descontarti lifted the goblets and touched them to their lips in the ritualistic symbol, each thus drinking the other's blood.

When the two young men went back to their wickiups, John Cooper said to Carlos, "This is the first time that Descontarti has accepted a man of the Spanish race into the people of the mountains. He has paid you a very great honor. He accepts you as being of his own blood—and thus, if you truly love Weesayo, a union may come to pass. There is one thing more you should know about the Apache, *amigo*. The parents do not choose husbands for their daughters. They, like the white men, believe in love."

Carlos's face was shining with happiness. "It is all I could dream, and yet it is the most exciting life that I have known. These two short days—I still cannot believe it. But I know that my father will be worried about me, and so I must go back. John Cooper, please, come back with me and stay for at least a week. Enjoy the luxury of living like an *hidalgo* instead of this rugged life with your Apache friends."

"Well, maybe one day," John Cooper replied.

"No, tomorrow, for I shall go back then. Besides, *amigo*, I should not be surprised if you wished to see my sister again. For all the airs she gives herself, I think she was very much impressed by you."

John Cooper stared at him. Could it be that Carlos suspected what he himself had only just realized when he saw the young Spaniard and Weesayo together? The thought that he might be able to communicate with Catarina and break through her glacial reserve was a kind of challenge. And again, when he remembered how Weesayo had smiled at Carlos after the latter had won the shooting game, he knew that he would give a good deal to have Catarina smile at him like that.

Abruptly he decided. "Very well, Carlos. I'll admit I enjoyed the meals your cook, Tía Margarita, prepared when I was there. And I very much like your father and Doña Inez, and Miguel and the workers."

"Of course, I know you are coming just so you can stuff yourself with Tía Margarita's special dishes. She is going to make a big *flan* for me when I get back. Oh yes, I am sure that is reason enough," Carlos teased. John Cooper laughed and made a playful swipe at his friend, who went into his wickiup laughing at his own joke. John Cooper went back to his dwelling. He realized, sheepishly, that he knew exactly what Carlos had really meant.

On this same afternoon, Doña Inez had found herself with an unexpected admirer. A week ago, as she and her niece were returning from the village after a call on old Padre Moraga, a tall distinguished-looking gray-haired man driving his own horse and *cabriolet* had drawn on the reins, then doffed his hat and bowed to her. "A good afternoon to you, Doña Inez," he had politely declared. "And to you, Señor," she had smilingly and wonderingly responded.

After the interlocutor had driven on, Doña Inez looked quizzically at Catarina. "Now who in the world could that have been? I confess I have never seen him before."

Catarina giggled. "Oh, I know, Tía Inez! His name is Enrique Portofino, he's a lawyer from Mexico City who has come to Taos to look after his old sister, who, they say, is very ill."

"I see," Doña Inez teasingly countered, "that you have already accustomed yourself to your new home, so much so that you know all the gossip of the town."

"*Sí, es verdad,*" Catarina giggled again. "And he must like you very much to find out your name so he could speak to you in public like this. Why, if we were not driving our own little carriage, I wager he would have offered us a ride back to the *hacienda*—yes, as an excuse to tell you how much he admires you."

"Minx, be still!" Doña Inez gasped, her cheeks flushing hotly as she strove to maintain an air of complete indifference.

"But, Tía Inez, I did not say that to offend you. You are very pretty and it is only natural men should notice you," Catarina propitiated.

Doña Inez sighed inaudibly and closed her eyes. *Only natural,* she thought to herself. *Perhaps so, but not for Don Diego. Sometimes I wonder if he'll ever see me as a woman, comprehend that what I feel for him is more than being the sister of his mourned wife and the duenna of his wonderful children. And the truth is, even if a man were to court me—though heaven alone knows why he should!—I would still say no in the hope that one day Don Diego will, indeed, see me as a woman who can give him love and respect and take joy in the knowledge that I can share his life and ease his burdens.* Aloud, she said, "I thank you for the compliment, my dear niece. It's very flattering. But now we must get home quickly. I have to see that Margarita prepares a special dish for your father. It is something new, of my own recipe."

"Do you know what I think, Tía Inez?" Catarina murmured with a roguish sidelong glance at her aunt. "I think you just might be in love with Father yourself."

"Hush! You must not say such a thing, even in jest, Catarina!" she rebuked her niece. "I am devoted to him, because he was such a wonderful husband to my sister. And I have responsibilities to him, because I offered to look after you and Carlos in our new home. Now you must not embarrass me—promise you will never say such a thing again, *querida.*"

"Very well, I promise, Tía Inez," Catarina solemnly proffered. But when she turned to look at the road ahead of them, her eyes twinkled with a secret amusement. . . .

Just a week later, when Doña Inez had ridden into town

alone to visit one of Padre Moraga's ailing parishioners and
bring her some soup and blankets, she saw the gray-haired
lawyer chatting with the town clerk across the street. Espying
her, he broke off his conversation with the latter and crossed
the street, again doffing his hat. "Forgive my inopportune-
ness, Doña Inez, but I wish to introduce myself formally to
you. It occurs to me that last week, when I spoke to you when
you were riding with your lovely niece, you must have
wondered who I am. My name is Enrique Portofino, I am
abogado and I am thinking of settling in Taos to be with my
sister, a widow, who is very ill and alone."

"It is a pleasure to meet you, Señor Portofino. And you did
not offend me, be assured of that," she smiled at his earnest-
ness.

He hesitated a moment, glanced down the dusty street to
make sure that no one was watching, then spoke quickly, "I
should never wish to offend one so gracious and estimable
and lovely as you, Doña Inez. You see, Señor Arronzo, the
town clerk, had told me who you were when I first saw you
some weeks ago. That you are the sister-in-law of our
illustrious intendant Don Diego de Escobar. And also—"

"Yes, Señor Portofino?" she gently prompted.

He bit his lips, lowered his eyes, then took a deep breath.
"Forgive my bluntness, Doña Inez. You would be right in
thinking me a great fool to speak to you on such short
acquaintance—indeed, ours has hardly begun. Yet—it is this,
Doña Inez. I myself have never married, and now that I have
come to stay in Taos, where I shall pursue my profession, I
feel the loneliness of one who has no one he can care
for—except of course, my sister. Please—do I offend you?"

"Not at all, Señor Portofino. I admire honesty above
pretense. Say what you wish to say," she reassured him.

He twisted the brim of his hat between his lean hands,
hesitant a long moment, then at last blurted out, "Why, it is
just this, Doña Inez—I wish your permission to call upon you
at the *hacienda* of Don Diego de Escobar. I have, I assure
you, only the most honorable intentions—I am not a rich
man, but I could support a wife without her incurring the
least hardships—and—"

Tears filled her eyes as she put out her hand to touch his.
"You do me a great honor, Señor Portofino. I can tell you are
the most honorable of men, and no sensible woman could
possibly be offended by so flattering a declaration. That is

why, out of consideration for your feelings, I must tell you that I could offer you no ultimate hope in—in the regard which you imply."

His face fell. "Forgive me—I had no right to accost you and speak of marriage before we even met, as it were."

Again she touched his hand, her eyes gentle and tender. "You have paid me the highest compliment a good, upright man can pay a woman, and you must not belittle yourself. It is only that—well, there is someone else."

"I—I understand." He took another deep breath, straightening. "I wish you and your intended every happiness."

"Thank you, Señor Portofino. God grant you the same and soon. But be sure we shall always be friends. And let me hear from you. Never fear, there will be the right woman for you one day, one who will recognize your fine qualities and assuage your loneliness."

He took her hand and kissed it as he would that of a queen. Then, bowing low, he said, "Gracias, Doña Inez. I shall never forget your kindness. ¡Vaya con Dios!"

Doña Inez watched him until he disappeared inside the town hall and then uttered a heartfelt sigh. "At least," she said to herself, "I've had someone willing to ask for my hand. It is a sign that my waiting for Don Diego to consider me as a wife is not just an obsession or a penance—because now I can tell myself I have a choice—yes, but it is still Don Diego I want with all my heart!"

FORTY-FOUR

The two young men returned to the *hacienda* on the last day of December, in time for the fiesta of New Year's Eve. Once again, John Cooper leashed Lobo and led him out to the shed, promising the wolf cub that he would come out several times during the day and turn him loose once they had gone beyond the *hacienda* and the shelters in which the sheep were quartered.

There was a great banquet that evening and the de Pladeros were present, but not Tomás, who had come down with a bad cold and remained at home. Don Sancho expressed great interest in meeting John Cooper, for Don Diego had already told the *alcalde* how the young mountain man had rescued his son from certain death. At the table, both Don Sancho and Doña Elena asked John Cooper many questions about his life with the Indians, and the other guests were equally interested. Embarrassed by all this attention, John Cooper responded to their questions without embellishment. Throughout the conversation, Catarina watched and listened attentively; but though she was gracious to him, as she would have been to any guest of the *hacienda*, she showed little more than impersonal interest.

After the banquet, Don Diego invited his guests to enjoy

the fandango in a large chamber off the dining room, which had been cleared for the occasion. The musicians were his own workers, with Esteban Morales playing his little flute and others playing fiddles and guitars while Jorge Corrado strummed on an old mandolin he had brought with him from Mexico City.

Somewhat to Carlos's dismay, the de Galvezes were there with Serafina and Isabella, and this time Carlos was unable to escape dancing with the former. Yet, no sooner had they begun to execute the intricate steps of the dance than Serafina breathed, "I hope you won't be too desolate, dear Carlos, but Papa has just betrothed me to Felipe de Cortana. We are to be married next month." Then, with a coy look and a fluttering of her long eyelashes, she whispered, "You know, I can tell you, since I am to be Felipe's wife, that I had really hoped you would care for me. But I forgive you now, because I have found dear Felipe to be such a fascinating, educated man, so thoughtful and considerate."

"I am desolate indeed, Señorita Serafina," Carlos replied, trying to hide his smile of relief. "Yet I am happy that you have found a man who cares for you, and you care for him."

"Thank you, dear Carlos," she purred, glancing over at her husband-to-be, who stood in a corner chatting with Don Diego. "You must try to hide your broken heart and not hold me too tightly in the fandango. Felipe will be very jealous."

John Cooper was watching Catarina, standing across the room in her beautiful green silk gown and chatting with her aunt. Catarina wore the little gold locket which Doña Inez had given her. She noticed John Cooper staring at her and tossed her head as she turned back to her aunt. "That savage is staring at me, Tía Inez," she whispered. "Of course I would not expect him to know how to dance, living with those dreadful *Indios* all these years."

"Do not be catty, *querida*," her aunt rebuked her with a smile. "I do not weigh a man and find him wanting in the balance because he does not know how to dance. That young man has shown great courage, surviving after what happened to his family and adapting himself to the hardships which were forced upon him. I admit he is not a polished *caballero*, but of all of that species I have observed here in Taos, there is not one I should choose for you."

"Tía Inez!" Catarina gasped, her eyes widening. "Are you daring to suggest that I could possibly be interested in that—that savage? He would not even begin to know how to court a girl. I do not wish to discuss him any more, if you please."

But Doña Inez looked across the room at John Cooper, and there was a little smile on her lips as she did so.

At midnight, everyone toasted the New Year, and soon after the guests began to take their leave. Don Sancho lingered, and when he saw his opportunity, approached Don Diego. "May I have a word with you, *amigo?*" he asked.

"Of course, my old friend. Come with me into my study. We shall have some fine brandy with which to exchange our own good wishes for the year ahead."

Inside the study, Don Sancho came directly to the point. "You know, Don Diego, that for some time it has been my fondest hope that my son, Tomás, and your beautiful daughter, Catarina, might be joined in marriage. It has been my great joy and privilege to work with you in the governing of our little town, and I have no better friend in all this world than you."

"You are far too kind, Don Sancho. To your health, and to that of your lovely wife and your fine son," Don Diego lifted his glass.

Don Sancho bowed and touched his glass to Don Diego's. "And to you and your family, long happy years," he toasted. Then, somewhat hesitantly, he resumed, "What I am about to say is in strict confidence, please understand this. There is the matter of a dowry, and unhappily my wife still clings to the traditions of old Spain. Sometimes, alas, she judges a family by its wealth rather than by its character and noble blood."

"Say what is on your mind, *amigo,*" Don Diego urged.

"It is this, Don Diego. I suspect that my son is enamored—though I hasten to assure you he is a decent, well brought up young man who I am sure would never stray from the paths of virtue—of one of our servants. I am not quite sure which one, but at his age it would be only natural for him to have—shall we say, the temptations of the flesh."

"But of course," Don Diego replied. Then, frowning, he said, "For that matter, Carlos should think of marrying, too. It was St. Paul who said that it was far better to marry than to burn. Well, you were saying?"

"Yes—well now, I know that my son has great fondness for your Catarina. And it would delight me if a betrothal could be arranged."

"I, too, have thought about this idea for some time now," Don Diego responded. "By the end of next month, my daughter will be nineteen, and it is high time she had a proper husband. I respect your son as I do you. Yes," his expression became decisive, "I give my consent. It is true that my dear sister-in-law is of the opinion that Catarina looks upon Tomás rather more as a good friend than as a possible husband. But once the marriage vows have been spoken, Catarina will be an obedient and loving wife, I am certain. Tomás is dependable and a gentleman. Yes, Don Sancho, I shall speak to Catarina soon and acquaint her with my feelings on the matter."

"You have made me very happy, old friend." Don Sancho clasped Don Diego's hands and shook them warmly. "Well, I shall say good night now, and a happy New Year. Doña Elena will be wondering where I am. But I shall not tell her out little secret, not until you have formally advised me that everything is in order."

"I shall do that. *Vaya con Dios, amigo.*"

Two nights later, after Carlos and John Cooper had finished supper and gone off to the former's room to chat, Don Diego cleared his throat and, nervously glancing at his sister-in-law, said, "Catarina, there is a matter of great importance I wish to discuss with you. Will you please accompany me to the study?"

Doña Inez looked at her brother-in-law in surprise, glancing first at him and then at her niece, and quietly interposed, "May I come with you, Don Diego?"

"Well—er—yes, yes, of course," he almost snapped, "since in a sense it concerns you, also."

Catarina gave her aunt a doubtful look, but Doña Inez nodded and smiled to reassure her. A few moments later, Don Diego seated himself at his desk, feeling the need to prepare himself in advance for his daughter's anticipated reaction. "On New Year's Eve, Catarina," he began at once, "Don Sancho de Pladero came to me in all confidence and made to me his proposal on behalf of his son for your hand in marriage."

"I, to marry Tomás de Pladero?" Catarina exclaimed, arching her brows, her green eyes bright with indignation. "Do you honestly mean that, Father? He is a weakling, a milksop, a mother's boy, no matter how old he is. Why, I ride horseback with him and I even dance with him, because it is expected of me, but never would I consider having him as my husband!"

"Now, Catarina, I know very well that you have been used to having your own way, and I only wish that your adored mother could have been spared to bring you up as an obedient daughter so you would understand such things," he said testily.

Catarina stamped her foot. "That is cruel of you, Father. You know how much I miss her, as you do, too. But that has nothing to with Tomás de Pladero. And even if she were alive and told me that it was my duty, I still would not do it, do you understand? No, I do not love Tomás, and I never shall, so please tell his father to look somewhere else for a wife for him!"

"Take care, Catarina, you go too far!" he exclaimed. "In Madrid, a daughter who defies her father's wishes is sent to a convent where she is chastened and shriven for her rebelliousness!"

Doña Inez could be silent no longer. *"Mi hermano,* in this new world, so far from our homeland of Spain, surely now you must know that things are not the same. In Madrid, children were betrothed years in advance. Why is it wrong in this new life of ours to let them marry for love when they are old enough to understand it? If Catarina does not love Tomás, marrying her to him will not bring that about. And I said before, he is not the man for her."

"My dear sister-in-law," he glared at her, "I cannot begin to express my gratitude for the way you have managed the household and the infinite kindness you have shown to my children and to me. Yet on this point I remain firm. As Catarina's father, I still control her and I wish to announce the betrothal."

"You can cry it from all the housetops, Father, but it will not change anything! And I refuse to listen to it any more. I am going to my room!" Catarina burst into tears. She walked to the door of the study, opened it, and slammed it. Doña Inez and Don Diego could hear her unrestrained sobs as she hurried down the hallway.

"Dios, I thought that by now she had matured enough to be sensible," Don Diego grumbled.

"Please, Don Diego, do not think of her as a child any longer. She is already a woman, and she is lonely—yes, just as I am—but she still has not found a man she can truly love. Be patient with her a little longer, I beg of you."

His face hardened as he shook his head. "But it is almost five years since we came to Taos, Doña Inez. I must be concerned about her happiness, and marriage is the only way to insure it."

"Undoubtedly, but not to Tomás. I earnestly wish you to think very seriously before you make any public announcement. I know Catarina perhaps better than you do, Don Diego."

"I shall never understand women," he groaned as he rose from his desk. "Well, perhaps I broke it to her too hastily. Let her take a few weeks to think it over. Perhaps she will come around to it. And a few words from you—"

"I am afraid I must take her part this time, Don Diego. We have spoken of this before, and you know my convictions. Good night, my dear brother-in-law."

FORTY-FIVE

Catarina was not able to sleep that night, fuming as she was at the thought of an alliance with Tomás de Pladero. Just before dawn, she dressed in her riding habit and donned her thick cape against the cold, then went into the kitchen and prepared a cup of hot chocolate. After drinking it, she went out to the stable to saddle Marquita.

Miguel Sandarbal had wakened early, too, this frosty morning. Last night, one of the workers had brought him a piece of gossip that had disturbed him. José Ramirez had been up very late, carrying off a ewe in a *carreta* into Taos. That could only mean that he was stealing sheep from Don Sancho's flock and pocketing the money. A man who would do that could easily take his knife and notch the ears of Don Diego's sheep and then claim them as his own master's.

He left his cottage in time to see Catarina lead Marquita, already saddled, out of the stable and prepare to mount the mare. "Señorita Catarina, it is not even morning yet!" he called to her. "And with all the snow on the ground, it is not a good idea to go riding."

"I shall do what I please!" Catarina retorted as she wheeled Marquita to the south and, kicking her heels into the mare's belly, rode off at a gallop. Miguel Sandarbal scratched his head and swore under his breath. What that *muchacha* needed was a strong man who would take her over his knee and teach her how to behave. Then he grinned to himself. He knew just such a man: Señor John Cooper. To be sure, a fine lady like Catarina de Escobar would never consider a man who had lived with *los Indios* and who had neither noble name nor fortune. All the same—

He scowled, not certain what to do. She must be in a fine rage about something, he concluded. Doubtless this was her way of working it out. Yes, a good hard ride until she was exhausted, and then she would come back and be able to think things over calmly.

But by eight o'clock that morning, when Catarina had not returned, Miguel went to the *hacienda* in search of his master. Before he could find him, John Cooper came out of his room, and Miguel uttered a grateful cry. "Oh, John Cooper, I am glad I have found you! Señorita Catarina saddled her mare and rode off almost three hours ago. She is not back yet and it worries me. She seemed very angry about something—she did not tell me what it was."

"Did you see in what direction she rode, Miguel?"

"*Sí*, John Cooper, to the south."

"That is where—" John Cooper checked himself in time. He remembered what Descontarti had told him of the party of renegade Mescalero who by now had certainly crossed the Mexican border and might well be in the vicinity. "Don't disturb anyone, Miguel," he urged the wiry foreman. "I'll ride after her."

"That is good of you, John Cooper. But you are right, if she is only out for a ride and I told her father and aunt, they would be greatly worried. I hope you find her and bring her back soon, John Cooper!"

"I promise, Miguel. Now go have some breakfast, and I'll get my horse and take Lobo with me. He's been growling ever since I locked him back in the shed last night, and he needs a romp too!"

Taking a buffalo-skin robe and slinging his rifle over his shoulder, John Cooper urged his mustang toward the south. It was easy to follow Catarina's trail—Marquita had left fresh prints of her hooves in the snow and they led directly southward.

There were thirty Mescalero in the renegade band who had broken away from their tribal village in southern New Mexico. They had chosen their own leader, Lachisay, and early in December ridden south across the Rio Grande to attack a little village near Durango. They had stolen a dozen fine horses and a hundred sheep but had managed to bring back only two Mexican women in their early twenties and a middle-aged *rico*. Twenty-two of the renegades had taken the sheep and horses to a deserted stretch of plain about seventy miles south of Santa Fe, but Lachisay and his seven strongest warriors had brought along the three captives. In his pride over having been proclaimed chief, he had determined to travel far north and capture even more women. To prove himself worthy of leadership, he had boasted that he would return with at least a dozen more squaws.

Lachisay, his seven braves, and their three captives had skirted Santa Fe and had come this morning upon a mesa surrounded on all four sides by rocky-ledged walls, the rocks allowing a narrow entry and exit at each end. It was a good place to camp. They had ridden all night long, and the women were hysterical and exhausted. The *rico* was babbling prayers for his life, promising much gold if they would only spare him.

On the mesa there were many large cacti and stunted, gnarled trees. Lachisay ordered that the two women be tethered to trees, and, to amuse himself over the *rico*'s woman-like cries, had the unfortunate man bound to a large prickly-pear cactus. He laughed uproariously as the man arched himself against his bonds, trying to hold his breath so that the sharp needles would not score his flesh. "If you cry out now, *viejo*," he taunted his victim, "what will it be like when we roast you over a slow fire while we shred your greasy skin with our hunting knives?"

When the man sobbed in terror, Lachisay grinned and spat into his face. Then, hugely satisfied with his triumph, he took provisions from his saddlebag and signaled to his braves to eat and rest before they resumed their raid.

Catarina de Escobar wanted only to put as much distance between herself and the *hacienda* as she could. She had never before gone so far south, and the terrain was strange and new to her. As she neared the narrow entrance to the mesa, she did not attempt to turn Marquita's head away from it, but rode toward it out of curiosity. It was Lachisay who saw her first and barked an order. Two of the Mescalero leaped astride their mustangs and raced toward her, uttering strident cries. Catarina screamed and tried to wheel Marquita back to the narrow entrance of the mesa, but the two Mescalero cut her off, one riding around behind her to block the exit, the other dragging her off Marquita and onto his mustang as he galloped back to Lachisay. His companion grasped Marquita's reins and forced the snorting mare to ride back with him.

Lachisay was short and stocky, the hair on the left side of his head cut even with the top of his ear, while the hair on the right fell to his waist and was adorned with feathers and trinkets. His face was streaked with red war paint, and he wore a buffalo robe over his buckskin skirt, leggings, and knee-length moccasins. His dark eyes seemed hollowed out, set over the bridge of a broad, large nose. As Catarina was dragged before him by her captor, he appraised her quickly. "This one I take as my squaw," he announced. Her captor, tall and wiry, began to argue, but Lachisay put his hand to the knife at his belt and snarled, "Am I not your chief? Have I not promised there will be squaws for all of us in our village? Now, tie the girl to one of those trees near the other two women and her fine horse to a mesquite branch. After we have eaten, we will amuse ourselves a little."

Catarina cried out and struggled as her tall captor dragged her by the wrists to one of the stunted trees near the two weeping young Mexican women, forced her hands behind and around the trunk of the tree, and bound them tightly with a rawhide thong. Squatting, he applied another thong around her knees and made it cruelly tight. Then he began to unbutton her cape, but Lachisay barked a command, and he sullenly desisted and went back to finish his meal.

Lighter and far younger than Lije, Lobo had no trouble racing along with the sturdy little mustang. His yellow eyes gleaming, his sharp teeth bared in anticipation of a hunt, he often outdistanced John Cooper, who urged his horse on, knowing how much of a head start Catarina had. The fresh tracks of Marquita led him unerringly along her trail. He came in sight of the mesa, flanked by its rocky walls, and drew on the reins when he saw that Marquita's tracks led toward that narrow entry between the walls. His call halted Lobo, who turned and trotted back, growling softly, quivering with eagerness.

Dismounting, he cautioned Lobo with a gesture to remain where he was and crept ahead to peer into the mesa. He could see in the distance the horses of the eight Mescalero, and he heard Catarina's scream. What he couldn't see was Lachisay who, having finished his meal, approached her and, unbuttoning her cape and shoving it open about her shoulders, began to rip off her jacket, telling her in broken obscene Spanish what he intended to do to her.

John Cooper ran back to his mustang, mounted it, and spurred it toward the northern side of this desolate, walled-in enclosure. He was seeking a way to climb to the top of the wall where he could ambush Catarina's captors; there were too many of them to chance a bold dash into the mesa.

The rocky wall dipped and rose erratically. At first glance, it seemed too preciptous to climb, but as he reached the middle, toward the east, he reined in the horse and dismounted. Here there was a gently rising, hill-like stretch of ground and the wall was only about fifteen feet high. Beckoning to Lobo, he began to climb the hill-like slope, cautiously setting one foot ahead of the other because the deep, drifted snow gave little indication of the footing beneath. He managed at last to reach the top and haul himself up onto the surface of the ledge. Lobo stood, looking up at him, then with a soft growl gathered himself and bounded onto the ledge.

Catarina, her head tilted back, her face contorted in revulsion and fear, tried to twist away from the renegade Mescalero chief's pudgy fingers which now, having ripped away the jacket, had begun to tear at the bodice of her dress. Her breasts heaved wildly, and she shrieked again as he viciously cupped them and squeezed, muttering, "You not want Lachisay, *muchacha?* You be his squaw—he will teach you to want him!"

Stretching himself out on his belly along the flat ledge, John Cooper drew the Lancaster out of its sling, leveled it, held his breath, and peered along the sights. Lachisay was standing far too close to the writhing shrieking young woman; he estimated the distance to them to be about six hundred feet. He saw the renegade Mescalero tear down the bodice of Catarina's dress and step back. At that moment, John Cooper squeezed the trigger. The sound of the shot reverberated in the walled-in mesa, and the other Mescalero stiffened, turned, and uttered startled cries as they saw their leader, shot through the side of the head, pitch lifelessly in front of the tree to which Catarina was bound.

Even as he saw Lachisay fall, John Cooper reloaded swiftly, working with grim precision. His second shot, forty seconds later, killed the Mescalero who had pulled Catarina from her horse. Marquita neighed in terror, rearing up on her hind legs, and, breaking away from her tether, began to gallop toward the distant exit between the rocky walls. Again John Cooper primed and reloaded the rifle with desperate speed. As the other Mescalero who had blocked Catarina's exit ran toward his musket, John Cooper felled him with a ball through his back.

Two of the five other renegades had retrieved their muskets and both fired at him, but at that range their balls did not even reach the rocky wall. The other three mounted their mustangs and, crouching low over their horses' necks, galloped toward the nearest exit. They sought to flank their ambusher and pick him off, exposed as he was on top of the ledge.

Again John Cooper reloaded with a dexterity and speed he had never before equalled. His next shot brought down one of the renegades in the act of mounting his horse to join his fellows. His companion, turning toward the ledge on which John Cooper lay, brandished his fist in blind frustration, then ran to his mustang and rode through the farther exit toward the south, abandoning the battle.

The three remaining Mescalero had seen the low, hill-like ascent to the top of the rocky wall. One of them, gripping his mustang with his knees, leveled his musket and fired at John Cooper. The shot only grazed the young mountain man's shoulder. Having reloaded, he whirled, dropped to one knee and squeezed the trigger. But the ball whistled by his attacker. With threatening shouts, the three renegades dismounted and, crouching low, ran up the slope. Two of them had bows and arrows, and the third hugged the low wall while he swiftly reloaded his musket.

Frantically, John Cooper tried to reload, but the two Mescalero had already strung their bows and were sending arrows toward the top of the ledge, forcing him to lie on his belly to keep out of range. One of the arrows narrowly missed Lobo, who was snarling viciously.

One of the two bowmen began to haul himself up to the ledge, drawing his hunting knife as he did so. As his head appeared over the top, Lobo sprang, slashing at the Mescalero's face with his sharp fangs. The renegade uttered a wailing screech of terror and fell backward and down to the plain. His head was tilted to one side: in the fall, he had broken his neck.

The second bowman waited, just below the ledge, pressing himself against the rocks while he notched an arrow to his bow. Meanwhile, the third Mescalero with the musket, by now having reloaded, knelt down at the base of the hill and trained his weapon on the ledge. He waited for John Cooper to rise.

The bowman below the ledge now dropped his bow and drew a knife. He lunged up to the ledge and dragged himself over. As he did so, Lobo's fangs sank into his neck. His desperate swipe with the knife scored a slight bleeding slash along Lobo's side before he pitched backward and fell, his head smashing against the jagged tip of a rock.

John Cooper had at last finished reloading, and, crawling on his belly, carefully peeped over the rim of the ledge. Instantly, the Mescalero beneath pulled the trigger of his musket, and the ball splattered against a rock just below, fragments scratching John Cooper's face and drawing blood. John Cooper fired, but the reflex of turning his head as the fragments struck him sent the ball whistling harmlessly over the Mescalero's head.

With an exultant cry, the renegade drew his knife and began to ascend to the ledge, gripping his unloaded musket by the barrel with his left hand. As he neared the top he swung the musket at Lobo, striking the wolf's head and felling him onto his side, where he lay dazed but still snarling. John Cooper sprang to his feet and reversed his rifle. Holding it in both hands by the end of the barrel, he swung it down with all his strength. The metal plaque fixed to the heavy butt crashed against the Mescalero's forehead. His musket dropped, and he hurtled backward to lie sprawled beside his two dead companions.

John Cooper made his way down toward the body of the last attacker, gripping the rifle in his left hand as he drew his knife from its sheath around his neck. Mortally injured by his fall and the crushing blow of the rifle butt, the dying Mescalero stared up at him. Again his hand feebly lifted the hunting knife as if to strike. John Cooper thrust his knife into the man's throat, drew it out, and wiped it on the dead renegade's Mexican jacket. Then he straightened, shuddering with fatigue and revulsion, and stood staring down at the three dead Mescalero. Finally, remembering Lobo's plight, he warily made his way up to the ledge.

The wolf soon righted himself, still snarling, his eyes narrowed and bright. "It's all right now, Lobo, we've won. Easy,

Lobo, easy," John Cooper soothed him. He patted the wolf's head and gradually the fierce young predator ceased his snarling.

"He cut you, Lobo—let's see—it's not bad, thank God for that! I'll rub some snow on it, it's just a scratch. All right now, let's go back down and take care of those Mexicans they captured—and Catarina! What in the world made her ride so far? I don't understand her, I just don't."

He straightened, drew a deep breath, and then made his way back down the gentle hill, careful of his footing lest he slip in the snow or trip over a hidden rock. Lobo, fully revived by now, bounded down to the base of the hill and stood growling over the three dead renegades.

John Cooper's mustang was patiently waiting for its master, and he mounted it. The Mescalero's three horses had galloped off, but there were still several in the mesa, John Cooper had observed.

He rode back into the narrow opening, with Lobo at the mustang's heels. As he reached the tree to which Catarina was tethered, she uttered a cry of joy. "Oh, Señor Baines, you saved me, oh, *gracias a Dios*, you saved me—it was so horrible—" and burst into hysterical tears.

He glanced at her, then rode on past her to where the two young Mexican women and the terrified *rico* were tied. Dismounting, he quickly cut their bonds. The *rico*, blubbering with gratitude, sank down on his knees and grabbed John Cooper's hand, kissed it effusively. Embarrassed, John Cooper drew his hand away. "Act like a man now, *hombre*," he ordered, almost rudely. "There are horses here which the Mescalero left. Take them and the women back to safety. You are near Santa Fe if you head south, and there are soldiers who will escort you back across the border."

"*Sí, sí*, Señor, they were going to torture me to death—oh, the blessed God sent you to us, Señor! We owe you our lives!" the man sobbed as he rose to his feet, staggering slightly. The two young women, weeping together in their relief, were in each other's arms, consoling each other, and John Cooper turned to the *rico* again. "Get those horses, *hombre*. I was told that there were many more in the raiding party, and they may be nearby. Get the women on the horses and get yourselves out of here as quickly as you can!" At last the man nodded and began to untie one of the Mescalero mustangs, urging the two young women to emulate him.

John Cooper hurried back to the tree to which Catarina was tied and cut her bonds. Instantly and impulsively, she flung her arms around his neck and burst into tears again. "You saved me, against so many—what a hero you are—oh—" Then, blushing furiously when she recalled that only her camisole covered her ripe, firm breasts, she drew away. "You could have untied me first, you know," she observed haughtily, "but you went to those Mexicans! Do you know what that dreadful *Indio* was going to do with me?"

"You're safe now, Señorita Catarina, that's all that matters. I wanted to get them out of here quickly—I'm sure the Mescalero raiding party captured them across the border and was taking them back to whatever village they were going to settle in. You'll be all right."

"Where is Marquita?" Now she stamped her foot, as if nothing had happened to her. "And you put your arms around me—yes, it is just as I supposed, you are really a savage. You tried to take advantage and make love to me just because they tied me to a tree—it is not to be tolerated, Señor Baines, do you understand? Marquita—you must find her at once! She is a valuable horse, I do not want to lose her! Go after her, I tell you!"

John Cooper's mouth dropped open and his face flamed. He couldn't understand her mercurial changes of mood. He had a sudden impulse to take her over his knee and discipline her as one might a spoiled child. "Well, what are you waiting for? Find Marquita this minute!" she ordered, again stamping her foot.

He clamped his jaws together, for a moment almost ready to yield to that impulse. Then he shrugged. "I'll do that at once, since you wish it, Señorita Catarina."

He walked back to his mustang, mounted it, and then rode to the end of the mesa and out through the narrow gateway which the rock walls formed. Half an hour later, he came upon the mare, whinnying, standing near a low gully. Gently soothing the horse, he took her reins and rode back toward the mesa.

"Here is your mare, Señorita," he said as he released Marquita's reins and dismounted. Catarina, meanwhile, had been attempting to restore her torn garments to order, but it was impossible. John Cooper flushed and, turning away, doffed his buffalo-skin robe. "Put this on, Señorita, it's very cold."

"Gracias," she said curtly as she wriggled into the heavy robe. "A real *caballero* would help a lady mount her horse, Señor Baines!"

John Cooper looked skyward, and he sighed deeply. It was impossible to understand a woman—or, at least, a woman like this one. With a wry grimace, he knelt and cupped his hands so that she might step into them and mount Marquita. "Very well now, I'll ride you back to the *hacienda*," he declared and wheeled his mustang to the other end of the mesa.

When Don Diego and Doña Inez discovered that Catarina had left the *hacienda*, the worried Spanish nobleman went in search of Miguel Sandarbal, who reluctantly informed him of Catarina's impulsive flight. However, when Miguel added that John Cooper had gone off in search of her, Don Diego's anxiety was considerably lessened. All the same, he urged Miguel to come to the *hacienda* to bring him news the moment the young mountain man and his daughter returned.

It was about four o'clock that afternoon when Miguel uttered a joyous cry as he saw John Cooper riding beside Catarina and her mare. Don Diego and Doña Inez came out of the *hacienda*, wearing capes against the penetrating cold air. Don Diego was nearly in tears when John Cooper, dismounting, helped Catarina down from Marquita and led the black-haired young woman toward him. Miguel at once took the two horses back to the stable.

"In God's name, my child, you have given me such a dreadful fright!" Don Diego broke out, his voice trembling with emotion. Then, to John Cooper, "I shall be forever in your debt, Señor Baines, for bringing my daughter back to me."

"She had ridden a long way, but her tracks were clear and I had no difficulty finding her," John Cooper replied.

But Catarina, giving him an indignant glance, flung herself into her father's arms and began to sob distractedly. "Oh, Father, I thought I was going to die—there were some terrible *Indios,* and they captured me and tied me, and they were ready to take me back to their village—and he—he saved me—he and that wolf of his—oh, he was so brave—"

Don Diego looked up with wondering eyes. "Is this true, Señor Baines?"

"Yes," the young mountain man answered reluctantly.

"There was a raiding party of Mescalero—when your son and I were in the mountains with Descontarti, he told me that a band of them from the south had gone across the border, broken away from their tribe, and might head in this direction to take more captives and horses."

"It is a miracle, Señor Baines—I have not words to thank you—I can never repay you enough—"

"There is no need to talk of that, Don Diego. I'm happy that I could bring your daughter back safely. And now, if you and Doña Inez will excuse me, I must see to my horse and to Lobo's wound. One of the Mescalero cut him with a knife—it's not serious, but I want to make sure."

"Of course, of course, Señor Baines—God be praised for a man like you, so resourceful, so courageous—my little Catarina, my poor, sweet girl, come inside the house—you must be frozen to death—why ever did you do such a thing—to ride off like that without telling anyone where you were going? Come along, *querida!*" Her father led Catarina back into the *hacienda*. Doña Inez stood looking at John Cooper, a radiant smile on her lips. And she said softly, for only him to hear, "The more modest a man is about what he does, the braver I know him to be. I will say only, God bless and thank you, Señor John Cooper Baines."

Doña Inez had sent soft-spoken Gertrudes Delgado, Catarina's personal maid, to her niece's room to make certain that Catarina would be tenderly cared for after her harrowing experience. Gertrudes soothed and comforted her young mistress, helped her to change her clothes, and later that evening brought her a supper tray. Catarina had sent back word that she did not feel up to taking her place at the table.

Later that night, before she went to sleep, she stood before her mirror, critically examining herself. When her Mescalero captor pulled her down from Marquita, his powerful grip had left faint bruises on her olive-sheened shoulders. Apart from these, there were no blemishes on her voluptuous young body. She stared at her reflection and then shook her head. It had been a dreadful nightmare. She could still remember what that filthy *Indio* had said to her in his broken Spanish, and she shuddered.

She recalled how, even as he was about to rip off her camisole, there had been the sound of a shot and he had fallen at her feet. She had looked up and seen the buckskin-clad figure of the young mountain man on the rocky ledge beyond her, and Lobo beside him, baring his teeth. Such a wave of hope and gratitude had flooded her at that moment that she had wanted to apologize for how badly she had always treated him and to thank him for coming to rescue her from these dreadful savages.

"Dreadful savages," she repeated the words aloud to her reflection in the mirror. "And yet, he and that wolf of his were savage, too. How they both fought to kill all those filthy *Indios* who were going to carry me off to their village—just he alone and that wolf against all of those horrible *Indios!* He—he was like some primitive god—oh, but it is silly to think of Señor Baines like that—"

She frowned at herself, disconcerted by her jumbled, irrational thoughts. "Yes, he can read and write, and he uses a knife and fork well enough," she mused angrily while she studied herself in the mirror. "But he is still a savage." Color flooded her cheeks and her eyes widened over a new thought that had suddenly leaped, unbidden, into her mind. "But this is ridiculous! How could I ever bring myself to love a savage like him? And yet—and yet—it is true he is more of a man than Tomás de Pladero will ever be. But that does not mean I would take him as my husband. *Madre de Dios,* why should I even think of such a thing? Of course I am not going to marry a—a young savage!"

Turning from the mirror, she blew out the candle and climbed into bed, pulling the sheets up about her neck and making a face.

FORTY-SIX

It was February 13, 1813. John Cooper had returned to the
Apache village some four days after bringing Catarina safely
back from her capture by the Mescalero. Carlos had gone
with him, having entreated his father to allow him to accompany the young mountain man back to the stronghold. He
had not yet told his father the real reason for his wanting to
return so soon after his first visit; but he had told John
Cooper, who had enthusiastically agreed that he should press
his suit with lovely, gentle Weesayo.

Catarina's brother had stayed nearly a week, taking part in
the warriors' games and, somewhat to John Cooper's amusement, had spent many hours with Kinotatay, acquiring a
rudimentary knowledge of the Apache language so that he
could court Weesayo.

Carlos was able to see her several times alone when she
was out gathering wood for the fire or shaping the coil
baskets which the Jicarilla used in trading with the merchants
of Taos. He was shy with her, not wanting her to think him
overbold, but he could not hide his growing love. One
afternoon, when he sought to tell her in Apache that she was
truly named, for the light she cast was so dazzling that it
blinded him, Wessayo turned away and put her hand over her

377

mouth to suppress a soft little laugh. Flustered, Carlos stammered, in Spanish, "But, *querida,* Kinotatay has taught me these words which I now spoke. I meant them as a compliment."

In Spanish, without turning her face to him, Weesayo replied in her sweet, clear voice, "You must not call me *querida,* Señor Carlos. It is true that I have had the purification rites which prepare me for marriage, but I am not yet spoken for by any of the braves. What you said to me was that my light was so hot that it kindled a fire in your heart."

"And that is also true, *mi dulce!*" he blurted.

An exquisite blush suffused her golden skin as she rose hurriedly, taking the basket in her soft, shapely hands and holding it against her bosom. "I must go now. It is not proper for a maiden to be alone and to talk of such things with a man."

"But I speak with a straight tongue and from my heart, Weesayo. I love you. I want to marry you and be with you always and care for you."

"This you surely must not say to me now. You are a white-eyes and I am Apache."

"That is true, Weesayo, but do not forget that your father has made me his blood brother. So in my veins there is Apache blood, too, and that is why I say what I do to you."

She glanced at him, half-fearfully half-shyly, and then, with a hint of a smile, ran back to her father's wickiup.

Carlos once again sought out Kinotatay to teach him more of the Apache words, and he took John Cooper aside and almost desperately asked for his friend's help in furthering his courtship of Descontarti's beautiful daughter. "You must go to Descontarti, Carlos, and tell him what is in your heart," John Cooper replied. "If he consents, you must marry Weesayo in the Apache way. Of course, I am sure she would go back with you to be married in your faith. You could explain that this would bind the marriage."

"I never thought I could love a girl so much," Carlos exclaimed. "She is so young, but there is a mystic, wonderful gentleness to her, a wisdom and a kindness. I do not think of her as just an Apache girl, but as a girl I want to marry and have children with and live with to the end of my days."

"If you say this to Descontarti, and if he approves, you need have no fear then, Carlos. If you want, I'll put in a good word for you. You know I already did, as I told you, and Descontarti didn't say that he would prevent Wessayo from marrying a white-eyes."

"I owe you a lifetime of gratitude, John Cooper," Carlos declared as he shook John Cooper's hand, "first for saving my life, and then for bringing me here to meet Weesayo."

"Tonight there will be a feast, and the shaman will make medicine to bring the buffalo herds to the plains this spring. You and I will talk to Descontarti together about this."

"*¡Gracias, mi amigo, gracias por todo!*" Carlos exclaimed. Then, his face sobering, he asked, "I do not mean to pry, John Cooper, but I think that you and my sister could be as happy together as I long to be with Weesayo."

"Yes, it's true that Catarina is in my thoughts, *amigo*," John Cooper replied slowly. "But she still thinks I'm a savage, a white man dressed in buckskin who lives the Indian way. Yes, I saved her life, and yet I don't expect that to obligate her to care for me."

"Catarina is lonely, John Cooper. In two weeks she will be nineteen, and back in Spain many girls that age are already married and have children. There is no one in Taos she cares for. But I am certain that she really cares for you—it is her way to pretend that she is still back in a life that was filled with presentations at court and balls and parties. That does not exist anymore, not here. I think even Father is beginning to understand it. We have all begun over again, and for me it has been wonderful. It can be that way for my sister, too, if you show her that you really love her."

"Well, it won't be easy doing that." John Cooper gave a nervous little laugh. "But since I'm going to help you with Weesayo, perhaps when you go back this time you can put in a good word for me in return."

It was a joyous feast, and Carlos was rapt with admiration at the skill of the dancers who pantomimed the hunt of the buffalo. Weesayo danced, too, at the head of the women dancers, dressed in white buckskin, her face ethereal and poignant. Carlos could not take his eyes from her, and John Cooper squeezed his arm and nodded sympathetically.

When the dance was over and the gourds of tiswin were being passed around, Kinotatay ran into the dancers' circle and held up his hand. "Our scout, Magagonsay, has come back badly wounded! Two of our braves lifted him from his horse and bore him to the wickiup near that of *El Halcón*."

The Apache chief strode forward, his face grave with

concern. "Wounded? And what of the other braves who went
with him to the border village of Benitez to trade for horses
and to learn whether any of the Mexican *mujeres* would be
proud to come back with them as squaws for our bravest
warriors?"

"They are all dead, Descontarti," Kinotatay solemnly replied. At this news, the women of the stronghold whose
husbands had ridden out in that scouting party uttered loud
wails and began to blacken their faces with ashes from the
dying campfires.

"He still breathes?" Descontarti anxiously demanded.

Kinotatay nodded. "But he has lost much blood, and his
spirit ebbs from his body. Come, I will take you to him."

Descontarti hurried to the wickiup and stepped inside, while
Kinotatay looked at the old woman who was tending the
wounded brave. She shook her head as she applied a poultice
of herbs to his forehead, which was wrinkled with pain and
beaded with sweat. Descontarti could see the bullet hole, its
edges bluish and black, in the left side of his chest just beside
the armpit.

"Magagonsay," he said gently, putting his hand on the
brave's cheek, "it is I, your chief. You have come far to bring
me news. The Spirit of the Sky has given you great strength
to ride so far with your hurt—speak that we may know what
you have learned."

Magagonsay opened his eyes and stared into the face of his
chief. Then his lips formed words, but at first there was no
sound. Slowly, laboriously, as if the sight of Descontarti had
given him strength, his voice returned. "Outside Benitez, we
were ambushed by *bandidos*. My comrades—all died. I played
dead and lay still as the *bandidos* talked. I heard them say
Santomaro is their *jefe*."

Descontarti sent Kinotatay a wondering look. "Santomaro
—that is the name of the *bandido* who was hanged by the old
intendente of Taos."

"Yes—yes, my chief," the wounded Apache gasped as he
tried to lift his head, "that is what I heard them say, O
Descontarti. Seven years ago—the brother died by the order
of the *intendente*—now Santomaro plans to raid the ranchos
of the *ricos* at Taos to have his revenge.... And I heard them
say that he who is now *intendente* shall be first. They will take
gold and horses and the women of the *ricos* for their
revenge."

"How long ago did you take your wound?" Descontarti demanded.

Magagonsay winced as a spasm of pain surged through him and sank back on the rude pallet. His eyes closed, he forced himself to gasp out, "Fifteen times the sun rose and set from when I mounted my horse until I came here. And the *bandidos* said they would raid along the way, to take weapons from the *gringos* so that they would be strong and Santomaro would have his revenge—I do not—" his eyes opened and remained glazed and staring as he died.

Descontarti rose, his face troubled. "He was truly Apache," he said to Kinotatay. "The village of Benitez was always friendly to the Jicarilla. Even today there are four squaws who came willingly with our warriors to live in our stronghold. We did not need to raid that village when we sought women. But now we must tell *El Halcón* and the young Spaniard—for he is the son of the new *intendente* of Taos, and it will be against his *hacienda* that the *bandidos* of Santomaro will ride."

The Apache chief went back to seek out John Cooper and Carlos and tell them what the dying scout had said. "He did not tell me how many there were of the *bandidos*, but I remember well the brother of Santomaro and how he lusted for gold and women until he was caught and put to death by the old *intendente* whom your father replaced," he told Carlos.

"And it was fifteen days ago that your brave was wounded and rode back here with the news?" John Cooper mused. "From the Mexican border, with fast horses, they could easily be in Taos within a week. Carlos, you and I must ride back at once to prepare to defend your *hacienda* against them, and we must also warn your father's neighbors."

"Yes, above all others, Don Sancho de Pladero, who is the *alcalde*—if a man like Santomaro seeks vengeance for his brother, he would wish to avenge himself also on the *alcalde* of the town, for I am sure that Don Sancho sat in judgment upon his brother at the time of the trial," Carlos responded. He glanced at Descontarti, and John Cooper understood. There would be no time now to pursue his courtship of Descontarti's daughter. Consolingly, he put his arm around Carlos's shoulder and murmured, "After it's over, we'll come back, and I'll speak for you if you wish, *amigo*. Now let's ride!"

There were forty of them, wearing sombreros and thick *calzoneras,* fitted trousers with bottoms that flared out when unbuttoned. Jorge Santomaro was forty-one, coarse-featured, with a huge mustache and thick black stubble on his fat jowls. He and his men had been *peóns,* all of them working long hours for pitiful wages in the silver mines of a *rico* in the province of Coahuila. That had been ten years ago. When their tyrannical *patrón* had, as an example to all of them, ordered one of the workers flogged to death because he had been caught stealing some of the rich ore from the mine, they had revolted, killed him, ravished his wife and daughter, and then killed them too, so that they could not be witnesses. They had become *bandidos,* preying on obscure little villages, skillfully avoiding the occasional royalist troops sent to pursue them. Of the two brothers, Manuel, five years younger than Jorge, had been the more daring. It had been he who had proposed to raid Santa Fe and even Taos. Jorge had demurred, calling such a venture madness; there were garrisons at both Santa Fe and Taos, and both were well armed and constantly on patrol.

Nonetheless, Manuel had taken fifteen men with him. That had been in March of 1806. Manuel and two of his confederates had been captured, the others shot down on the outskirts of Taos, and the three captives brought to trial before the old, ailing *intendente,* Juan de Morena. They had been hanged in the public square, and their bodies were left for a week as an example to other outlaws.

When the news reached Jorge Santomaro, he had taken a blood oath of vengeance, but the carrying out of that oath had been deterred for some years. First, many of his band had left his service, calling him a coward for not having gone with his brother. Also, a large contingent of royalist troops had patrolled the province of Chihuahua and made several forays near the known bandit camp, forcing Jorge Santomaro to change his headquarters.

Now, however, Jorge's plans were ripe and the time ideal. He had learned that Juan de Morena had gone home to Spain and that there was a new *intendente* in Taos, but that Don Sancho de Pladero, the same *alcalde* who had presided with Morena at his brother's trial and supervised the execution, still prospered in his post. He would capture Don Sancho, take him and his wife and the prettiest of their servant girls back into Mexico, and Don Sancho would watch his wife being ravished before he himself was put to agonizing death.

The *intendente* would be dealt with as if he were Morena himself, and there would be much booty—there was certain to be gold, plenty of horses, and young women. As he planned the campaign, he could see that his men were eager to take part in it. Lately, their pickings had been all too slim.

The *bandidos* gathered near Benitez, a little town near the Rio Grande, and there they had seen the Jicarilla braves riding into the town. They had killed them all, taken their sturdy mustangs, then raided Benitez itself. There had been only two women worth capturing, but the stupid creatures had fought so violently against their captors that, after the men had slaked their brutal lusts, Jorge Santomaro had ordered their throats slit.

By now his men were well enough armed to risk the danger of crossing the border and making that long journey into Taos. All of them had *pistolas,* at least half of them had old, wide-bore muskets, and a few had the newer Belgian rifles. They also had knives—cold steel, in Jorge Santomaro's opinion, had far more power to terrify than did *pistolas* or rifles.

To avoid detection, they traveled at night, averaging no more than twenty miles a night, and had taken a route which avoided the larger towns of Nuevo Mexico. They crossed the Rio Grande at Agua Prieta, turned northeast, following the river up beyond San Marcial and Magdalena, then went northwest, almost to the boundary of Nuevo Mexico.

They crossed the Rio Grande again near Espanola and made camp just before dawn. It was about seventy-five miles to Taos, and they meant to strike at dawn three days hence, then head back with their captives and booty. As Jorge Santomaro shrewdly pointed out, they could replenish their supplies of food and water in the little towns along their path.

Descontarti had dispatched three of his best scouts— Kinotatay and his son, Pirontikay, and Menogoches—to accompany John Cooper and Carlos. "While you bid your workers prepare for the attack by the *bandidos,*" the Apache chief declared, "these men will ride south, southeast, and southwest to find the band and bring back news of them, so that you will be ready."

The five riders, with Lobo eagerly racing at their heels, left the mountain trail and, at Kinotatay's direction, took a shortcut toward Taos which would save them nearly ten miles. Riding day and night, pausing only for brief rests and a little food and water, they came, by the third day, to the grazing range beside the Sangre de Cristo Mountains which bordered Taos from the east.

"Carlos, go at once to the ranch of Don Sancho and tell them to arm their workers and be ready for the *bandidos*," John Cooper urged his friend. "Kinotatay will follow you and go on, southeast, while his son will ride with me to your father's *hacienda* and then due south. Menogoches will go southwest. One of the three is certain to learn where Santomaro's men are camping and how far they are from us."

Carlos nodded, then spurred Valor toward the estate of Don Sancho de Pladero. He dismounted in front of José Ramirez's cottage. The foreman was giving orders to the sheepherders and scowled to see Carlos approaching him. "What do you want with me, Señor?" he demanded.

"To warn you that a large band of *bandidos* is on the way to attack your master, because he was the *alcalde* who had the brother of the leader of the bandits hanged some years ago. Tell your men to bring out all the guns they have and to station themselves near the *hacienda* where they can defend it."

"I give the orders here, Señor de Escobar, not you," José Ramirez sneered. "Who is this *jefe* of *bandidos*, that we should fear him?"

"He is Jorge Santomaro, and his brother was Manuel," Carlos curtly retorted, and smiled grimly to see Ramirez make a face and hastily cross himself. "I see you have heard of him. I am sure he has brought a large force, or he would not be bold enough to come all the way across the border bent on this revenge against your master. Now, this Apache scout, Kinotatay, will head southeast to learn where the bandits are camping. He will come back to you and tell you what he has found. There is no time to lose, *hombre!*"

John Cooper and Kinotatay's son had ridden swiftly to the *hacienda* of Don Diego de Escobar, and the young mountain man at once sought out Miguel Sandarbal to inform him of the danger. Without an instant's hesitation, the wiry foreman barked orders to his workers, and an hour later all of them were armed and ready to take positions as Miguel assigned them. Those with rifles would lie atop the flat roof of the *hacienda* itself, to act as snipers if the bandits reached the *hacienda*. Others would hide behind boulders or mesquite thickets near the grazing fields, to pick off the bandits both as they came to attack or as they retreated to regroup. Menogoches, meanwhile, urged his mustang on, riding southwest.

Carlos soon rejoined his young friend and went into the *hacienda* to tell his father, while Lobo sulkily accepted being put on his leash and locked up in the shed for the time being. Quickly, Don Diego acquainted Doña Inez and Catarina with the news of the danger and urged them to remain in their rooms and to lock the doors. Miguel took the precaution of giving Don Diego's daughter and sister-in-law a *pistola* and a musket apiece, quickly refreshing their memories on how to use these weapons as a last resort. "Our workers and I will see to it, never fear, that these *bandidos* never set foot inside the *hacienda*," he pledged grimly.

John Cooper gestured to the capable, loyal foreman and they went outside the *hacienda* to confer. "Miguel, if the bandits make a frontal attack, they're certain to try to break into this connecting passageway. Do you see, the *hacienda* is like two rectangles, and in my opinion, if they are driven back from the front, they may try from the back, toward the kitchen."

"*Es verdad*," Miguel admitted. "What do you propose, *mi compañero?*" In calling John Cooper this, Miguel paid him the highest compliment he could to someone who was not his master.

"Suppose you were to dig a trench just in front of the walled-in passageway, facing the kitchen side of the *hacienda?* We might cover it with branches or clumps of mesquite. Carlos and I, and the three Apache scouts, as well as Lobo, could be concealed in it. Lobo will obey me—he is trained to attack on command. Do you have any more Belgian rifles you can spare?"

"Señor Carlos has a fine gun, and I think there are two more, now that all the workers are armed," Miguel replied after a moment's thought.

"That will do very well. Kinotatay has a musket which he uses very capably. That should give us enough fire power to surprise the *bandidos* if they try to attack from the rear of the *hacienda*," John Cooper grinned.

"I will have some of the men begin to dig this trench at once—it is an excellent idea. All of us, and my master and his family, are fortunate to have such a friend as you." Miguel Sandarbal extended his hand, and John Cooper grasped it as they smiled at each other. "*Por Dios*," Miguel swore, "I feel like a young man again, as I did in the fencing school. You have brought me back to life—and I am not the only one—but we shall talk of that later." He gave John Cooper a meaningful wink which made the young mountain man flush as he well understood the allusion.

About two hours before dawn, Kinotatay rode his lathered mustang into the courtyard of the *hacienda* of Don Sancho de Pladero and hammered on the door until a sleepy servant finally admitted him. Don Sancho was wakened to the news that the bandit forces were only about an hour's ride away to the southeast and would come along the little valley below the Sangre de Cristo range, with his *hacienda* as their first objective. Don Sancho at once sent a servant to José Ramirez and the foreman lost no time in summoning his workers to the defense of their master's estate. Several of them climbed onto the flat roof of the *hacienda* and stationed themselves with their old muskets, while one man, part Navaho, armed himself with his bow and a quiver of arrows.

Jorge Santomaro had sent two of his band ahead to a little village to the southeast of Taos with orders to find either an *Indio* or a *peón* who would know where the *haciendas* of the *alcalde* and the *intendente* were located. They had broken into a *jacale* and dragged out an old man, threatening to kill his ailing wife and his two terrified daughters unless he directed them, and the *peón* had given them exact directions.

When his two men galloped back to the band, Santomaro grinned evilly. "It means that the *hacienda* of this upstanding *alcalde* of Taos is first in our path, *hombres*. *¡Vamanos, adelante!* If we strike at dawn, they will all be asleep, and it will be easy. From there we go to find the *intendente*. Kill the men, spare the *mujeres*—that is, those who are appetizing enough, *comprende? Ahora, ¡muerto a los gringos!*"

They came along the southeast side of Don Sancho de Pladero's *hacienda,* spreading out like the wings of a fan and firing into the huts of the workers and into the *hacienda* itself. There was a stifled cry as one of the bandits dropped with an arrow through his lungs, and then there were the explosive reports of two muskets firing simultaneously. Two more bandits toppled from their saddles. Jorge Santomaro halted, wheeling his horse so abruptly that the mustang squealed and reared high in the air. *"Diablo,* who could have warned them?" he swore; and then, angrily, to his men, "Charge the *hacienda*, break into it!"

José Ramirez, brutal and coarse though he was, was nonetheless a fighter; impressed by the fearful name of Santomaro, he had swiftly instructed his workers after having pretended to ignore Carlos's warning. The workers had hidden in some of the storage sheds, so that the bandits' fire into their huts had no effect. The women and children had been told to lie flat on the floor and not to move until their own men ordered them to do so. Now, as the first wave of riders rode toward the *hacienda*, opening fire at the shuttered windows, the doors of the sheds opened, and the workers returned fire with their muskets and old rifles. Six of the bandits went down, mortally wounded, and two sustained minor wounds. Demoralized by this unexpected counterattack, the survivors wheeled their horses away and galloped off toward the north. Young Tomás de Pladero, who had armed himself with an old Belgian rifle, poked it through one of the shutters and, squeezing the trigger, brought down one of the fleeing bandits.

Jorge Santomaro shouted hoarse, blasphemous oaths at the cowardice of his men; but the others beside him muttered among themselves, and he could read their moods. "Very well, we will let the *alcalde* wait his turn. Let us go north and kill the *intendente* and take his women and horses!" he finally decreed.

Brandishing a sword which he had taken years ago from the body of a royalist officer, he rode ahead of his men toward the *hacienda* of Don Diego de Escobar.

Meanwhile, Don Sancho's workers hurried out of the sheds as soon as they saw the bandits gallop off and swiftly gave the *coup de grace* to the wounded attackers.

As he drew up within a hundred yards of Don Diego's *hacienda*, Jorge Santomaro lifted his sword and ordered, "Do you see that connecting passageway between the two parts of the *hacienda*, *hombres?* Three of you, go find a log or a heavy boulder and smash it in. Then we can get inside the *hacienda* and make short work of those accursed *gringos* who helped to hang my poor brother!"

Three of his men dismounted and found in a shallow gully nearby a gnarled tree trunk which they lifted and carried back to their horses. Two of them balanced their improvised battering ram between them and rode slowly forward, while the third drew his musket out of its sling, ready to support their advance. Jorge Santomaro gestured with his sword to aim his other men toward each rear wing of the *hacienda* and then, drawing a *pistola* from his belt, galloped forward to the attack.

Don Diego's men on top of the hacienda instantly opened fire, killing two of the bandits and wounding a third; they swiftly reloaded, lying flat on their bellies and keeping out of sight as much as they could. Jorge Santomaro's horse reared up on its hind legs, pawing the air with its front hooves and whinnying at the sudden unexpected detonations. *"Por los cojones del diablo,"* the bandit leader raged in his frustration, "who has betrayed us? *Adelante,* Fernando, Pablo, break in the wall quickly, quickly, before we lose more men!"

The two men with the tree trunk and their companion with the musket had skirted the camouflaged trench under which Carlos, John Cooper, Lobo and the three Jicarilla scouts lay waiting. Dismounting, the two men seized the trunk and, drawing back, rammed it against the adobe structure repeatedly, while the man with the musket shouted back to the leader, "It begins to crumble, *mi jefe!*"

"¡Con fuerza!" he shouted back, then gestured to his men to follow him into the enclosure formed by the two rectangles. Once again, from the rooftop of the *hacienda,* the three workers fired with telling effect. Three of the bandits pitched from their saddles, lifeless. Carlos, who had taken several loaded *pistolas* from the storage shed, now turned around, poked one barrel through a chink in the covering of brushwood, and pulled the trigger. The bandit with the musket staggered and fell heavily to the ground, kicked once, and then lay still.

Now, from the rear, Miguel Sandarbal and ten of the workers—armed with muskets, Belgian rifles, and *pistolas,* crouching low as Indians might during an attack—came behind the bandits and opened fire. At the same moment, the three Indians flung the brushwood above their heads to one side and they, Carlos, and John Cooper fired almost simultaneously. Four of the men went down, and Jorge Santomaro uttered a shriek of rage and pain as a ball imbedded itself in his right shoulder. One of the bandits, with the foolhardy desperation of a lost cause, rode up toward the men in the camouflaged trench and aimed his pistol at John Cooper. But, with a savage growl, Lobo sprang from the trench and buried his fangs in the Mexican's throat. The bandit screamed in agony, his hands scrabbling at Lobo's shaggy neck, then he toppled from his horse with the wolf's savage fangs still digging into his throat.

"Back, back, *hombres!* We have been betrayed! May all these *gringos* fry in hell on the devil's pitchfork! I swear to return, and the next time it will be different, I swear it in my dead brother's name!" Jorge Santomaro, almost frothing at the mouth in his frenzy, shouted. Waving his sword, heedless of the blood oozing down his body from his wound, he galloped off to the southeast, followed by only four of a band that had been forty. Fernando and Pablo, trapped all this time between the passageway and the trench, had fallen to Carlos—who, a *pistola* in each hand, had fired with unerring aim.

John Cooper scrambled out of the trench and hurried to Lobo, retrieving the leash and ordering the growling young wolf off its lifeless prey.

Miguel Sandarbal came running to him, his face bright with joy. "We saved the *hacienda!*" he cried.

"Yes, Miguel, because you and your workers fought in loyalty and love for your *patrón* and his family," John Cooper responded. "These men," he gestured toward the sprawled dead, "came only to kill and to plunder out of hate and greed."

FORTY-SEVEN

An hour after the bandit attack against the *hacienda* of Don Diego de Escobar, a worker from Don Sancho's ranch rode over to convey his master's good wishes and his hope that none of the de Escobars or their workers had been hurt. On questioning him, Don Diego learned that the *alcalde*'s men had beaten off the first attack and that only two men had been slightly injured. "Tell your master," Don Diego joyously exclaimed, "that we finished the good work here and killed all those scoundrels off except for a few who, if they are wise, will not try to test our strength again. Tell him also that our losses were only three men slightly wounded and one of the wives whose face was grazed by a bit of wood when a bullet ricocheted into the hut. We are all grateful to el *Señor Dios* for His merciful protection. I go now to pray in the chapel to thank Him for watching over us."

John Cooper followed Don Diego back into the *hacienda* and said in a low voice, "I need to say my prayers, too, Don Diego. And maybe this is the time for me to tell you straight out that I want to marry your daughter, Catarina."

Don Diego stopped and stared, nonplussed, at the tall young mountain man. Then, with a deep sigh, he replied, "Señor Baines, Miguel told me how cleverly you organized the defense and the counterattack. Those were your orders that led Miguel and the workers to attack the main group of the bandits from the rear and thus drive them away for good."

"It was only simple strategy, Don Diego," John Cooper replied.

"Yes, but you were calm and poised enough in the face of danger to think of it and to show Miguel how it could be carried out. Then, the bold and brave act of hiding yourself in the trench where you would be in the greatest danger if the bandits discovered you—Señor Baines, my words alone cannot express the debt I owe you. You saved my son, you saved my daughter, and now you have protected this *hacienda* and my family. I give you my blessing in advance—but I do not think it will do you much good. I am afraid that my daughter is as stubborn as a man, and she will despise you because you were not born an aristocrat."

"Well," John Cooper laughed, "it's true that I don't have blue blood in my veins. The fact is, I even have some Indian blood in me—because I was made a blood brother of the Sioux and the Apache. But I'd still like to take my chances with her, and I'd be true to her and stand by her and protect her. Also, I love her, even if she doesn't seem to have much use for me because I dress in buckskin and live with Indians."

"I shall be as frank with you as you have been with me, Señor Baines." Don Diego put his hand on the young mountain man's shoulder. "I frankly confess to you that I had been planning for some time to marry her to young Tomás de Pladero. His father is from Madrid, as I am, and I suppose it was natural that both of us in our declining years should think of an alliance between our houses. Yet now I can see he could never be the man for her that you are, Señor Baines. So I grant your request, but I also feel it my duty as a loving father to warn you that I am not sure she will agree."

"Then I'll try to make her understand me. I'll have to teach her how to lead the life that the woman of a mountain man must accept. After that, we'll see what she thinks of me."

"You have my blessing, Señor Baines. I shall pray for you in the chapel that Catarina will be wise enough to weigh what you have done for her and for all of us. I realize now that aristocracy means very little in this new country. You see, Señor Baines, Don Sancho and I are getting old, and we think of the past as it once was. But it is young people like you who are facing the realities that we would prefer to ignore." With this, he turned away and walked down the hallway to the little chapel.

Doña Inez had been standing in an archway while Don Diego and John Cooper were talking. She could not help overhearing what they said, and now she beckoned to him. "Señor Baines, a word with you, *por favor.*"

"At your service, Doña Inez."

"No, Señor Baines, not mine," she gave him a warm smile, "but my niece's. I heard what you were saying to Don Diego about wanting to marry Catarina. And I thought I might give you a little advice—since, after all, I have known her much longer than you have."

"I'd certainly be grateful for it, Doña Inez." He smiled ruefully. "I don't seem to be making much headway. She still thinks I'm a savage."

"I know. And yet I think that inwardly she respects and admires you. Somehow, you must break through the barrier she's set up against you. A little persuasion—not the courtly, wordy kind our local *caballeros* use with the girls. But—well, I am just thinking aloud, John Cooper—if somehow you could get her to see exactly what sort of life you lead, it might win her over."

"But how could I do that?" He stared at her, puzzled.

"You will have to figure that out for yourself, I am afraid. But be sure, John Cooper, that I know you to be an honorable young man, worthy of complete trust. And if Catarina is somehow shown how to depend on you and your courage and goodness, I feel sure she will share the vows with you in Holy Church."

He grinned, then impulsively kissed her on the cheek. "Now I'm the one who's in *your* debt, Doña Inez. Frankly, if I hadn't met Catarina and fallen in love with her, I'd very likely be asking Don Diego for your hand in marriage instead."

"*¡Madre de Dios!* Go along with you, you young scoundrel! Why, I am old enough to be your mother!" In spite of her expression of outrage, Doña Inez was unable to suppress a smile of pleasure. "Well," she added as she turned to go back to her room, "I wish you good luck with your persuasion, John Cooper. *¡Vaya con Dios!*"

"And you also, Doña Inez," he respectfully inclined his head. After she had disappeared, he grumbled, "Now how am I to persuade that girl, when she won't even hear me out?" He left the house, scowling. Then he looked back and had a sudden inspiration. "Wait a bit—what was that Doña Inez said about showing Catarina the life I lead? Yes, that was it! Well now, what if I were to take her to the mountains and show her I could care for her, get food and find shelter for her? Maybe even let her see how friendly the Apache are? Yes, that's it—I know what I'll do, I'll take her there right now!"

With a cheerful whistle, he went back to the door and banged the brass knocker. After a moment, Catarina herself opened the door, and her eyebrows scornfully arched as she saw him. "Oh, it is you! Excuse me, I was just going out to the stable to have a ride on Marquita."

"You remember, you got her back, after all," he said gently.

"Yes, yes," she testily answered, "you are right about so many things, Señor Baines. And yes, I am grateful to you for saving me from those horrible *Indios*. But please excuse me now, I would like to ride a while before it gets dark. After this morning and that frightening attack by the *bandidos*, I just must go out into the air and feel free again."

"Perhaps you'd do me the honor of riding with me, Catarina," he politely suggested.

She eyed him a moment, then shrugged. "Oh, very well, if you like."

"I know a lovely place you've probably never ridden to before, Catarina. You'll like it very much."

"All right. I shall have Miguel saddle Marquita for me." She turned to go.

"And I'll get my mustang and Lobo."

Catarina whirled, frowning. "Why do you have to take that wolf? He—he's dangerous!"

"No he's not. I've trained him to know my friends as well as my enemies. Well, are we going riding or are we going to argue?"

"Señor Baines, you—you are impossible! Riding, of course." She flounced off, and John Cooper walked slowly behind her with a knowing smile on his face.

While Miguel saddled Catarina's mare, John Cooper brought out his mustang. His rifle sling and buffalo robe were in the stable, and there was, as he remembered, a package of pemmican in the sling. He went to the shed, where he had locked the wolf cub after the surviving bandits had fled, and let Lobo out.

Mounting his mustang, he waited for Catarina to emerge

from the stable, then pointed to the direction of the Jicarilla Mountains. "There's some wonderful country out there."

"But it is too far, Señor Baines. I told you I want to get back before dark."

"Perhaps you're afraid you won't ride as well as I do?"

She stiffened, her eyes large and angry. "I can ride as well as any man, even if it is side-saddle, Señor Baines. I will show you!"

"Good! Then let's see if you can keep up with me," he grinned.

Giving him a scornful glance, she bent to whisper into her mare's ear, then rode off at a canter. Lobo, running easily beside his master, looked quizzically up at John Cooper. "Easy, Lobo," he cautioned. He watched her ride far ahead and then quickened his mustang's pace to catch up with her.

Exhilarated, her cheeks rosy and her eyes sparkling, Catarina exclaimed, "Is that the best your mustang can do?"

"No, of course not. But we're on the right trail. Soon you'll see the place I had in mind, Catarina. There'll be time enough to race then."

John Cooper had purposely taken the long way toward the mountains, and doubled back now and again around dense clumps and thickets and towering trees till he was sure Catarina could not find her way back. Half an hour later, she turned back and vexedly declared, "This is far enough, and I do not see anything so lovely!"

"We're not far from it, Catarina."

"You had better be right, Señor Baines. Oh—I—I want to rest for a moment." A vivid blush suffused her cheeks.

"Of course, Catarina," he nonchalantly agreed as he halted his mustang. "Over there is a large thicket of mesquite. And Lobo won't bother you, I'll keep him by me."

"Ohh—you—you brute, to dare to mention such a thing— you're no better than those Indians who captured me!" she stormed as she dismounted. Then, as she hesitated, she added, "At least, Señor Baines, have the decency to turn your back!"

"Of course, Catarina. There. When you come back, tell me so we can go on with our ride!"

Holding her long skirts above her slim ankles, Catarina hurried off toward the thicket, glancing back once to make sure he had kept his promise.

Lobo peered after her, then quizzically looked back at his master. "It's all right, Lobo. She's a friend. You'll have to get used to her, and I don't want you to frighten her, you understand?" Lobo seemed to sniff, then lifted his head and peered intently at the trail beyond them.

"You might at least be *caballero* enough to help me back on Marquita," he heard her call out after a few moments.

"It will be my pleasure, Catarina." Dismounting, he came to her and deftly lifted her back onto the mare.

"*Gracias,*" she said grudgingly. "And now, how much farther is it? And do not forget, we must get back before it gets too dark to see. Oh, I ought never to have let you talk me into this."

"Not much farther. Come on. So far, you haven't shown me that you can ride better than I do," he teased.

Flashing him a scornful look, she made Marquita break into a canter, and again he let her go ahead of him for a time. They had reached a little ravine that had once been the bed of a tiny creek at the base of a gently sloping hill. There had not been water there for many years, and a few tall trees formed a protective shelter from the wind. Suddenly she halted her mare, and, pointing toward the west, accusingly cried, "Look, Señor Baines! The sun has begun to set, and now we shall never get back in time. Oh, you have tricked me, you—you savage!"

"Tarnation," he mumbled to himself, "I hope I didn't bite off more than I can chew." Aloud, he told her, "Here's a fine place to camp for the night."

"Camp for the night?" she echoed incredulously. Then, drawing herself up, she burst out: "I suppose this is the way you get all your Indian wives, having them ride with you till they are lost and then threatening them with that savage wolf!"

"You're very wrong, Catarina. I've never had a wife, Indian or any other kind. It's you I want." He turned to stare intently at her.

"Oh yes, you would like me to believe that! And now I suppose—I suppose now that I am lost and alone and helpless, with that wolf growling at me—just look at the way he stares at me with those cruel gleaming yellow eyes!—you're going to—you're going to—"

"I'm going to have some pemmican and then go to sleep. We've a long ride ahead of us, at least two more days before we reach the stronghold," he replied.

"The *stronghold?* What are you saying, Señor Baines?"

"Why, the stronghold of the Jicarilla Apache. After all,

that's where I live. I want you to see just how I do, because maybe then you won't keep saying I'm a savage."

"You mean you are taking me to a c–camp of wild *Indios?*" Catarina hastily crossed herself. *"Madre de Dios,* save me, Holy Virgin, I—I'm afraid—"

"There's nothing to be afraid of, as you'll soon see. Now be a good girl and get down off Marquita. We'll make camp here." Dismounting, he came toward her.

Catarina's first instinct was headlong flight. Then, seeing how dark it had suddenly become, she realized that she could never find her way back by herself. The imagined dangers of this darkness and the unknown trail far outweighed her being alone with him. "I can't help myself, so I suppose I shall have to do what you want," she said in a quavering voice as she slid down into his arms. Before she could remonstrate with him for holding her so securely, he had taken Marquita's reins, led the mare over to a nearby tree to which he tethered it, and tied his mustang to another. Then he began to pick up armfuls of brushwood to construct a kind of windbreak, while Catarina glowered at him.

Darkness had fallen, and she glanced around fearfully, for the presence of Lobo reminded her that there might be other wild animals in this desolate terrain. "I think this will do for the night, Catarina. The trees on the hill will protect us from the wind."

"You mean—you mean you are going to sleep here?"

"Of course. There will be caves along the trail leading up the mountains, but that's still a long ways off. You'll be comfortable enough. I'll give you my buffalo-skin robe."

"And—and I am hungry too—I have not had anything since breakfast—"

"I have some pemmican we'll share," he answered as he completed the windbreak. He brought the pouch of pemmican from the mustang's saddlebag and came back to her. "Put out your hands," he instructed.

Grudgingly, she did so. When she saw the crumbled bits of pemmican, she angrily demanded, "Is this what you consider food?"

"It's dried meat and fat from the buffalo mixed with berries and nuts, Catarina. It's very good and very nourishing. It's all I have when I'm on the trail, that and some water and maybe a little corn."

"I hate you, I wish I had never set eyes on you!" she burst into tears as she seated herself cautiously in the little ravine in front of the windbreak. Looking down at her cupped palms, she made a wry face, then slowly lifted her hands to her mouth and chewed one of the bits of pemmican. "Ugh! I do not like it at all!"

"I'm sorry, you'll just have to go without food, Catarina." As she glared at him, he opened the pouch again, took out a handful, and began to chew at it, then gave Lobo another handful when the wolf began to prod his muzzle against John Cooper's leg.

"And I am thirsty," she complained.

"There's some snow on the ground. Just scoop it up and suck at it. That's what your brother and I did when we were holded up in a cave during a blizzard," he replied.

Catarina clenched her teeth and stared malevolently at him, then flung away the rest of the pemmican. "No, thank you! I see you have brought me out here to starve me to death!"

He ignored her, finishing the handful of pemmican, and put the sack back in the sling. Glancing warily at her, he reflected that during the night she might well try to untie her mare and ride back to the *hacienda*. Quickly, he drew a rawhide thong from the sling-sack and thrust it into the pocket of his buckskin jacket. When he seated himself beside her, Catarina drew away, her eyes fearful and suspicious. "Do not dare to touch me, Señor Baines!" she hissed. "I shall claw your eyes out, I swear I shall!"

"We might as well get some sleep before we continue our journey, Catarina. But since I don't trust you, I'm going to have to tie your hands so that you won't try to go back home alone in the dark."

"Yes, you will tie me, and then you will have your way with me—you horrible savage, you beast, you animal!" she panted.

Sighing in feigned exasperation, John Cooper seized her wrists, drew them behind her back, and swiftly bound them with the thong which he tied as tightly as he could without hurting her. Then, rising, he took off his buffalo robe and draped it over her. "That should keep you warm. Now, good night."

By morning of the fourth day, they could see the Jicarilla Mountains ahead of them, and Catarina no longer spoke to him except when it was imperative that she dismount to ease herself. Two nights before, he had made camp on a grassy knoll surrounded by scrub trees and mesquite, and once again he had bound her hands and covered her with his buffalo robe. This time, she had eaten about half of the pemmican he had poured out into her hands, though making a wry face and expostulating with him over the meagerness and tastelessness of the food he doled out to her.

Also, on this fourth day, she had complained about the hardship of the journey, for he had come at least twenty miles each day, and Catarina resented the dustiness and rumpling of her clothes. Yet she was also piqued by his total indifference to her. She had imagined that, with a bound captive at his mercy, he would coerce her. When he had shown not the slightest sign of attraction, or even attempted so much as a stolen kiss, her vanity was injured.

When they reached the base of the mountain range, John Cooper reined in his mustang. "There we'll camp," he said to Catarina. "Carlos and I spent several days and nights in that cave you can see up ahead. It's quite comfortable."

"Every bone of my body aches," she sobbed. "I need a bath, I am hungry and thirsty, and I despise you for what you have done to me, Señor Baines!"

"I can't prevent your feeling the way you do, Catarina, but I'm afraid you'll just have to put up with it. I'll help you down."

She glared at him as she slid down into his arms, then indignantly pulled herself away. "How do you expect me to get up to that cave? I am not a mountain goat like you, you know."

"I'll climb up and hold my hands to you and pull you up, that's how, Catarina. As for my horse, he'll find his way back to the stronghold, and Marquita's sure to follow him because he's a male. That way, the Apache'll know we're coming."

"I do not want to!"

"In that case," he shrugged, "I can ride on by myself to where I'll be welcome. Since you continue to feel this way, you can simply find your way back alone."

"You would not! Oh, *Dios*, you would not leave me here all alone in these mountains, with the savages and the wild beasts? Oh please—all right, I shall go into the cave—it seems I have no choice." She gave him a withering look and turned her back on him.

Taking his sling and robe from the back of the mustang, John Cooper slapped it on the rump and bade it go back home. Then he gestured to Marquita, who, with an eager

whinny, raced after it. Catarina turned to watch, her eyes
widening with despair, as she saw her horse disappear around
the bend of the canyon. John Cooper deftly climbed onto the
ledge, lay flat on his belly, and stretched his hands down
toward her. Reluctantly she took hold of them, and he drew
her up.

"And you want me to stay in that—that cave with you?
You are truly a monster, Señor Baines!"

"Well, at least you'll have one advantage. I won't have to
tie your hands this time because there isn't any horse for you
to take and ride back home," he countered.

"Oh, you—you are impossible!" She rose, looking down
the trail whence they had come. "I do not see any soldiers—
but I hope they are coming after you, Señor Baines. I hope
they make you pay for all the misery·and suffering you have
caused me!"

"I don't imagine they will, if they're not here by now,
Catarina. You'll have to make the best of it, I think."

"And what are we going to do for food?" She turned to
him, hands on her hips. "You made me eat that awful
pemmican, and it is all gone now."

"Never mind. Lobo will find something for us. Now you'd
best get inside the cave and keep warm."

With a look of high disdain, she stooped and crawled into
the cave, gasping at the ignominiousness of her situation. She,
the daughter of a nobleman, forced to crawl on all fours into
a cave with a barbarian, a man in buckskin who had kid-
napped her and bound her hands and starved her!

"Since you're so exhausted, you'd do well to take a nap. It's
still morning, and we won't really need any food until
evening," he remarked calmly. Then, as she stared incredulously at him, he stretched out on his back, put his head in his
arms, closed his eyes, and was soon fast asleep. With another
gasp of angry indignation, Catarina sulkily followed his
example.

He woke at noon to find her in deep sleep, smiled to
himself, and went outside the cave where Lobo was lying.
The wolf sprang to his feet, looking up at his master. "See if
you can find us a rabbit, Lobo. Go fetch, kill—go!" he
exhorted, sweeping his arm in a wide gesture. Lobo uttered a
low growl, then turned and scrambled along the rocky ledge.
John Cooper watched him and then went back into the cave
and stretched out again. He glanced at the sleeping young
woman beside him and smiled.

When she woke, it was nearly twilight. "Ohh! I—I dreamed I was back in my nice, comfortable bed—I am hungry, I am thirsty!" she exclaimed.

"Lobo should be back soon. He's probably on the trail of a jackrabbit, but this time of year they're not quite so plentiful as in the summer and fall. If you're thirsty, there's some snow outside the cave. You can scoop it up and eat it. It's clean and it'll give you all the moisture you need."

"Oh, it is vile of you to treat me this way!"

"But I treat myself the same way. That's how I drink when it's wintertime and there isn't any spring or stream around, Catarina," he patiently explained.

She sat up, her arms around her knees, staring at the wall of the cave so as not to see his face. At that moment, Lobo sprang into the cave with a rabbit between this jaws.

"Good boy, good Lobo!" John Cooper praised him and took the rabbit. "Well, Catarina, here's our supper. Now suppose you build a fire while I fix the rabbit for cooking."

"Are you completely mad, Señor Baines? I do not know how to make a fire." She burst into tears, covering her face with her hands, her shoulders heaving with her sobs.

"All right, all right," he said, "I'll make a fire. If you watch, I think you're intelligent enough to learn how to do it from then on. I'll expect you to, Catarina."

She dropped her hands and gave him a furious, hateful look. He groped for some twigs, began to rub them together over a handful of dry leaves, and soon heat ignited the leaves and a small fire was going. Catarina watched, absorbed despite herself.

"You're sure you don't want to prepare the rabbit yourself?" he said as he teasingly held it out to her.

Catarina shrank back with an indignant gasp. "I do not know how—besides, it sickens me just to think of it."

"Well, I suppose you can't help being useless. I'd be useless, too, if I'd been brought up in a fine house like your father's, with lots of servants to wait on me," he grinned. Catarina covered her eyes with her hands as he proceeded to skin the jackrabbit, but from time to time he observed with great amusement that she was stealthily watching him.

After having skinned it, he cut the meat and skewered it on green branches stuck in the ground at an angle over the fire.

Again she had turned her back to him and was stonily regarding the wall. But the smell of the cooked rabbit began to waft toward her, her nostrils dilated, and she sighed with a despondence which drew another soft chuckle from the young mountain man.

When the meat was cooked, he began to cut it in smaller pieces, and Lobo, who had been watching all this while, rose and came to him to demand his share. "There you are, boy, you've earned the tastiest part," he praised the wolf as he gave him a piece of meat. Lobo bolted it down, his yellow eyes blazing in the darkness of the cave.

After giving Lobo another piece, he cut one for himself and began to eat with relish. Catarina flashed him a glance, then turned back to the wall, but the sound of his eating finally drew an outburst from her. "Did you drag me away from my father's house and bring me here to starve me to death, you contemptible wretch?"

"You haven't earned your food," he shrugged, "but here, this should be enough nourishment until morning." With this, he tossed her a piece of the haunch. Catarina glared at him, then picked it up, put it to her lips, and tasted it tentatively. It was surprisingly good, and she began to eat quickly and with relish. She eyed him pathetically as if to intimate she would like more. When he observed this, he smiled and shook his head. "Oh, so you like rabbit after all? There's no understanding women. Very well, here's another piece."

Catarina had turned sideways and was surreptitiously licking her lips. Pretending not to notice, John Cooper stabbed another morsel of meat with his hunting knife and held the hilt out to her.

"Let it cool a bit," he warned.

"Do you think I am a stupid child?" she flashed at him.

"You certainly behave like one."

"How long do you intend to keep me here?" she finally asked in a low, shaking voice, after she had finished eating.

"I really hadn't thought about it, Catarina. Maybe as long as it takes to make you fall in love with me."

"We would both be dead before that happened!" she hissed, but all the same she blushed as she again turned to stare at the wall.

"Suit yourself," he yawned. "I think I'll take a little nap. Then I'll go outside and see what's stirring."

He stretched out, putting his head in his arms, while Catarina gazed at him incredulously. His eyes were closed, his breathing was regular, and after about five minutes

Catarina stealthily sidled up to him, then reached out for the knife in its sheath around his neck. Hardly had her fingers touched the hilt when he sat up and thrust her back. "I wouldn't advise trying that again, Catarina," he warned.

"I wanted to kill you—and I shall!" she cried out as she flung herself at him, her left arm around his neck, her right hand groping for the dagger.

In total exasperation he gripped both her wrists, drew her to face him, and shook her soundly by the shoulders. "You're behaving like a spoiled child, I declare, Catarina. I thought you were a real woman, with all that education and a fine house to live in and advantages I never had. Now, what's the sense of trying to kill me, when all's said and done? You'd never find your way back alone, for one thing. For another, I'm not sure what the Apache would do with you, either. Now, you can act like the girl I'm really in love with— because, consarn it, in spite of all your trying to put me down, I can't help loving you, Catarina, and that's the gospel truth."

He let go her wrists and stared at her. Catarina's green eyes were hugely dilated and luminously misty. With a sob, she suddenly flung her arms around him and, to his astonishment, kissed him passionately on the mouth.

"Ca—Catarina!" he gasped, turning red with emotion. "I—I didn't mean to treat you so rough, honest I didn't! It was only—well, I didn't think I'd ever get you to see that I really care for you, that I'd like to spend all the rest of my life with you—"

Now, in her own turn, she was flushing furiously as she averted her face and said shyly, "I—I think I—I hated you because something inside me told me you weren't like those prancing dandies, those conceited *caballeros* of Taos. And— and I know I've been cruel to you."

"Not now, when you kissed me, darling Catarina," he whispered.

"I—I must make it up to you for all that," she whispered, and her arms locked tightly around him as her mouth fused to his.

When his lips responded to hers, her kisses became more fiery, more ardent. For the passion that swept her being had been held in check through these years in which no real man had ever claimed her.

It was he who at last disengaged her arms from him and in an unsteady voice, murmured, "Catarina, my darling one—

but I want us to be married. And your father would want that too."

"*Sí, querido.*" Self-consciously, she drew back. "And Doña Inez would think I am a sinful girl to let a strange man hold and kiss me like that before we are betrothed."

"Surely Doña Inez wouldn't think you that, my dear one. But we'll wait, we'll be sure of each other."

With a flash of her former tempestuousness, Catarina asked, "How could I know you cared for me, *querido?* Why, when I was tied to the tree and that *Indio* had torn my dress, you did not even look at me—"

"I'll look at you once we're married, you can depend on that," he chuckled; and she blushed vividly as, this time, she gave him a gentle little kiss. Then she murmured, "Do you know, *mi corazón*, I do not even know your full name—I thought I hated you, and so I forgot it and drove it from me—tell me, I shall never forget it again, *querido.*"

"It is John Cooper Baines," he whispered, kissing her eyelids and the tip of her dainty nose.

As their lips met, she whispered, "Cooper? That is a word I do not know, *mi corazón.*"

"It is the name of a man who makes barrels to hold wine or water or whiskey, Catarina."

She laughed softly, cupping his unshaven face with her soft hands. "Then I shall call you Coop."

"As you will, *querida*," he whispered back, "but you will never coop me up for long in your nest. In love, as in my life, I must be free."

"Let me share that freedom with you. I promise I shall learn the way you live, to understand it and share it with you —oh, I do love you, there could be no other man for me— you must know that now," she pleaded, trembling.

"I do. You will be my mate, my wife. I'll take you to the stronghold, and you'll see what good people they are."

"But your horse—you sent it away—"

He laughed softly as he stroked her hair and kissed her forehead. "That is a sign agreed upon between the chief and myself, Catarina. When my horse returns, they will know that I am in the mountains. This I did with your brother in this very cave."

"They will not come too soon?" she murmured, her face flaming at her own daring.

"Not until tomorrow, my dearest, my sweet Catarina," he told her. "We'll sleep now and dream of our wedding."

"Oh yes, *querido!*" she breathed. "Now I am no longer afraid. Oh, if only I were not a good girl brought up so strictly by my mother and Doña Inez—I almost wish I were one of the maids so we'd not have to wait so long, dear Coop!"

The next morning, Lobo awakened them with a growled warning at the sound of horses' hooves. When John Cooper and Catarina, hand in hand, emerged from the cave, they saw Kinotatay and his son leading John Cooper's mustang between them. This time, Catarina rode behind her chosen mate, clinging to him, resting her chin on his shoulder, her eyes dreamy with the remembrance of their kisses, the anticipation of the union in the little church of Padre Moraga.

They rode into the stronghold, where Descontarti, Weesayo, and Pastanari welcomed them. The Apache chief, seeing the serenely happy look on both their faces, chuckled and said, *"El Halcón* has taken *la Paloma* as his mate. I do not need a shaman to tell me this. We welcome, then, you, my young blood brother, and you, Señorita, for now you have come upon a happy time in our stronghold."

"How is this, Descontarti?" John Cooper asked.

"Because it is the fourth day of the ceremony of marriage among our people, *Halcón*. Our custom is that for three nights the man and the woman shall sit side by side, forbidden to speak to each other. Tonight our shaman will join them. You will watch it. You, Señorita," he turned to address Catarina with a benevolent smile, "will understand how it is with us and how, even though we are warriors whose enemies tremble before us, we know how to respect and admire the love that binds two people together."

That night, seated before the fire, their hands clasped, John Cooper and Catarina watched Gonordonotay, dressed and painted for the final ceremony of marriage, leave his wickiup and come toward the circle in which a young Apache couple stood. Raising a long wand in his right hand, he moved it in a majestic arc and then beckoned to the young man and the lovely Apache girl. Both knelt before the shaman. Laying the wand before them, he took the man's right hand and the young woman's left, and with his knife made a small incision under the first joint of the index finger of both hands, pressed the two cut places together, and quickly bound the fingers with a twisted thong. Then he chanted, "There is no rain for you, for one is shelter to the other. There is no sun for you, for one is shelter to the other. There is no night for you, for one is light to the other. For you the snow has ended always, for one is protection for the other Thus it will be from now on, from now on, and there will never be loneliness, now, forever, there will never be loneliness."

Then he sprinkled the pollen of flowers on both their bowed heads and, picking up the wand and making a circle over their heads, he intoned, "There are two bodies before me in the circle of our marriage rites, but now there is only one blood in both of them, and they are the same person."

Then he turned and went back into his wickiup. Descontarti rose and, extending both hands with palms upward, said to the young couple, "Go." They moved out of the circle, their faces radiant, and they were lost in the shadows beyond the campfires. At the edge of the camp, there were two white mustangs, and they mounted them and rode away.

"Where do they go, *querido?*" Catarina breathed, spellbound by what she had seen and heard.

"They will go to their secret place, Catarina," he explained. "The bride went long before to build their wickiup, to decorate it, to bring blankets and food. They will stay there ten days, and then they must leave it. By custom, they will never again return to it. Because, you see, there can never be such happiness, such perfection again, and that is why they must not go back, for it would be to tempt the gods into bringing them sorrow."

"How beautiful it is!" she whispered.

"Yes. But when we leave the stronghold, Catarina, I will marry you before the priest. Your father and your aunt would not want it otherwise—if you will have me?"

She turned to him with a soft little laugh and put her arms around his neck. "If you do not yet know that I shall have you, Coop," she murmured, "then please take me back now to the place where you live when you stay here, and I shall prove it to you. You see how shameless you have made me, *querido* savage?"

FORTY-EIGHT ·

On March 11th, 1813, old Padre Juan Moraga presided in the chapel of Don Diego's *hacienda*, as the tall mountain man held hands with his white-gowned bride. Don Diego and Doña Inez stood behind the young couple, Catarina's father having given away the bride and Doña Inez acting as the maid of honor. There were a dozen other guests, including Don Sancho an Doña Elena de Pladero and their son, Tomás.

The *hacienda* was gaily decorated, and, after the ceremony had been completed at mid-afternoon, Don Diego made an eloquent speech in which he seemed at last to recognize the vast difference between Old and New Spain.

Doña Inez watched him, her eyes glowing with approval. Her lips slightly parted, she dabbed at her eyes with a lace handkerchief as she saw John Cooper take Catarina in his arms and tenderly kiss her. Now at last, for her, the cycle had been completed. After all these years, the man who had cherished her beloved sister, and whom she had respected and admired long before he had chosen Dolores to be his wife, had made his peace with the past. It was what she had hoped for—and yet much life lay ahead for both her and Don Diego.

He, too, was watching his son-in-law turn to Catarina and

whisper to her as he kissed her. He saw her cling to her husband, her eyes shining with the promise of constancy, devotion, and passion. When he cleared his throat and turned away for a moment, Doña Inez sympathetically understood how this reminded him of the ceremony in the great church near the Escorial where he had stood beside her sister and pledged his eternal constancy and devotion.

Doña Inez turned to watch Tomás de Pladero, and she smiled knowingly as she saw that his pleasant young face was eased and that there was a new jauntiness to his bearing. Catarina's marriage had lifted from his shoulders the unwanted burden of being her elected suitor. For the first time, he was left to decide the pathway of his own life. She saw Doña Elena sniff and wipe at her eyes as she turned aside to whisper to her husband. She pitied them both with a compassion that was mellowed by her own, finally serene, coming to terms with herself.

She had been patient, she had hidden her loneliness until it had become almost benign and no longer cruelly tormenting. She was contented to know that her niece would be the wife of a young man whose great strength and honesty would surely, for all time to come, rid Catarina of her selfish foibles, her vanity, her sense of insecurity, and awaken in her all the happy and enlightened instincts of the woman she should be.

After the wedding ceremony, the bridal couple and the guests enjoyed a collation, the spectacular feature of which was Tía Margarita's three-tiered wedding cake. Once again, Doña Inez watched smiling, as John Cooper took the silver knife and cut a slice, then divided it equally and handed the little silver plate first to his radiant young wife. He whispered to her again in a way that made her blush and stare at him with eyes that saw no one else.

Then there was a long traditional siesta until the formal wedding dinner, at which Tía Margarita surpassed herself. The smiling maids carried in huge platters of roast mutton, antelope, and venison, casseroles of stewed rabbit and chicken with spicy herbs, and filled the silver goblets with Spanish and French wines and rare brandies.

Then came the *baile*. A week before the marriage, Doña Inez had explained to John Cooper that he would be expected, as the bridegroom, to lead Catarina out as the first to dance the fandango. He explained that he had never danced before, and Doña Inez herself undertook to teach him the basic steps so that he could acquit himself in the proper tradition of a Spanish wedding. As she danced with Don Diego now, she watched him carefully lead Catarina; she nodded a smile of encouragement when he caught her eye, to let him know that he had been an apt pupil.

The gay music went on well past midnight, but before then, Catarina and John Cooper had made their apologies and slipped away. By the light of a candle, the tall mountain man stared with some embarrassment at the elegant dresser with its broad mirror, the hand-carved chairs, and the spacious, canopied bed. He tried not to look at the bed and flushed to think of the ecstacies he and Catarina would know this night and in their life to come. He suddenly wished he could spend a lifetime alone with her, high in the mountains where he had first won her love.

But now he was within four walls, and for him a new life was beginning. After Padre Moraga had united them, his father-in-law had come to him and clasped him by the hand, his voice shaking with emotion as he declared, "Now I can call you *mi hijo*. I can see that Catarina loves you and will be happy with you. I gave her to you with a joyous heart. But I ask, because of your strength and your youth and the wisdom that you have had in coming to us a stranger out of the wilderness, that you become a true son to me. Let Catarina enjoy the advantages of a proper home and you in turn begin to acquaint yourself with the affairs of a husband who has married a young woman of property and means."

John Cooper had pondered a moment and then carefully replied, not wishing to affront the man who was Catarina's father, "Don Diego, I will be faithful to her all my days. And I will honestly try to live the life that will be easier for her. I can't be sure it's what I want for myself, but because I love her, I'll do everything I can to make her happy."

"I could not ask more of you, *mi hijo*," Don Diego had said, then blew his nose and pretended that the smoke from all the *cigarrillos* was affecting his vision.

John Cooper caught his breath as his young bride came out of her dressing room in her white silk, lace-trimmed night shift, her hair unbound and falling to her waist in a lustrous cascade. He felt himself trembling, and he turned to the candle and blew it out. Then he went to her and took her in his arms. She trembled too as her arms linked around him and her lips sought and found his in the mystic darkness of sweet union.

Discovering each other anew and finding each other steadfastly ardent and adoring, neither John Cooper nor Catarina heard in the distance the mournful baying of Lobo, locked in the shed and bitterly resentful over it. Perhaps he, too, yearned for a mate who would solace this imposed loneliness that struck at his savage freedom.

Tomás de Pladero had come to a decision, but it was to be José Ramirez who would precipitate it from thought to action. On the afternoon of the day following Catarina's wedding, the amiable young Spaniard left his room and went in search of Conchita Seragos. Since the day he had interceded with his mother to spare her a flogging, he had thought of her constantly. To be sure, because of his mother's strictness, he had not dared to profess his growing interest in her. That would only have endangered her situation in the household and led either to her dismissal or an already deferred whipping.

Nonetheless, whenever he saw her performing her duties, her eyes downcast, attentive to her tasks, he sent her an intent glance or a quick little smile and a nod of his head. For her part, Conchita, innocent though she was, understood that he was infatuated with her. Indeed, many a night in her little room she had knelt to pray to the Holy Virgin to protect her not only from José Ramirez but also from any clandestine involvement with Tomás. Yet, sensing his more than compassionate concern, she had often found herself dreaming of what it would be like to have so kind and gentle a *caballero* as her *novio*.

She had gone out this afternoon to draw a bucket of water from the nearby well. As she turned to go back to the kitchen, the oily voice of José halted her and made her bite her lips and tremble with a sudden fear. "*Hola, muchachita,* do not run away. The *patrón* and Doña Elena have ridden off to visit old Don Pedro de Saltada. I hear he is very ill and that his housekeepers sent for the priest."

"M—may God preserve him." Conchita hastily crossed herself. "Please, Señor Ramirez, I must bring this bucket to the *cocinera.*"

"But there is no hurry, as I just told you. Come now, *linda,* you know you have been avoiding me. Now do not be afraid. It is true that I am ordered to whip the naughty girls who displease Doña Elena, but you have been good as gold from all I hear. No, *querida,* it is time you had a *novio.* What you really need is a man who can protect you and look after you because he is looked on with great favor by the master and mistress. That is myself, *linda*. You please me greatly, as I have known from the first day you came into service. Now, why do you not visit my little cottage this evening? I will have a bottle of tequila, we can talk and get acquainted."

"Oh no, Señor Ramirez, I—I could not! Please, I am not for you—and besides—" In her ingenuousness, Conchita tried to propitiate José with what she knew of his proclivities, having been informed in sometimes salacious detail by the gossiping *cocinera*. "You—you have many girls, like Francesca and Consuela—yes, and Yolanda, too. Surely you do not need me with so many sweethearts, Señor Ramirez."

"*Por Dios y los santos!*" he swore, laughing, "I think I know who has been talking out of turn. That fat Magdelena, who stirs her tongue as much as she does her ladle in the kitchen." He put his arm around her waist and with his other hand took the bucket out of her trembling hand. "But those girls cannot hold a candle to you, *querida*. You are much prettier, much younger, and so very sweet and shy. I am just the man for you. Just give me a nice little *beso, un beso poquito*, and you will see how much you like it."

Conchita uttered a cry and tried to twist out of his embrace, but José Ramirez flung the bucket to one side and, with a lustful snarl, seized her by the shoulders and crushed his sensual mouth on hers. Her cry of revulsion was stifled as she desperately tried to disengage herself, striking him with her little fists.

"Well, you are a tigress, not a shy little dove, you really are! *¡Bueno!* But wait until you are in my bed tonight, *linda*, you can claw and scratch all you please, that is just what I want. The others, like fat Consuela, they have no life in them and are not nearly so pretty—try to scratch me, would you, you little hellcat?" In her frantic terror, she had raked his cheek with her fingernails and then, horrified at her own temerity, drawn back.

At this moment, Tomás de Pladero came out of the kitchen and stood staring incredulously at Ramirez and the young maid. At first his heart sank at the thought that so sweet and modest a girl could lend herself to the lecherous overtures of Ramirez, but when he heard her cry out and saw the scratch on his face, he called out angrily, "Now that is enough, Ramirez! Get back to your work!"

José Ramirez blinked, startled by the unexpected interruption, and then stared insolently at the young Spaniard. A crafty smile made his coarse-featured face still more sinister. "But, Señor Tomás, there is surely no need for you to interfere. *Madre de Dios,* there is a misunderstanding, you see. Why, little Conchita and I—well, you know how it is, Señor Tomás, I am sure you're a man of the world—she wants to be my *novia,* you see. Only, just so I won't think she is too easy, she pretends to fight me."

"Oh Señor Tomás," Conchita sobbed, clasping her hands and holding them out before her, "tell him it is not true—never in the world would I do such a thing—I pray each day to the Holy Virgin to teach me my place—"

"Never mind, Conchita," Tomás said in a low, trembling voice. "He is a filthy liar. And you, Ramirez, I told you once before, get back to your work or I shall have you dismissed. That should have been done a long time ago. I can guess how you have brutalized many of these poor girls in the past, though my mother won't listen to a word against you when I have tried to tell her. But I swear you shall not touch Conchita!"

"No? And who, my fine young master, will stop me? Your father would not have any other foreman. I have made him rich with the way I have handled his sheep, and he is the first to admit it. If I tell him that you are not man enough to order Conchita to your bed, but tried to get me to share her with you because it is really me she wants—"

"Oh I swear that is not true, Señor Tomás!" Again Conchita sobbed wildly, tears running down her cheeks.

"Then I shall dismiss you myself, Ramirez. Leave this ranch at once. I shall get your pay for you."

"I do not take orders from you! Go ride your horse and see how the sheep are doing. Conchita and I will patch up our little difference once you have gone," José Ramirez boasted. "Now let us be sensible, Señor Tomás. I saw her first, so she is mine. But I tell you what, after I've broken her in, I will let you have her now and again. Why, it would do you no harm to come to my cottage and watch how a real *hombre* gentles a little dove like this one."

The young Spaniard's face turned red with both fury and embarrassment for the unfortunate young girl. He strode forward and struck José Ramirez on the side of his jaw. Ramirez, taken by surprise by this unexpected attack, staggered back with his mouth agape. Then, slowly rubbing his jaw, he grinned wolfishly. "So it is a fight you want, Señor

Tomás? Fine. But I promise you, when I am finished with you, Conchita will not find you very pretty to look at." Then, with a bull-like bellow, he launched himself on the young Spaniard.

Tomás defended himself manfully, but his heavier opponent knocked him down and bloodied his upper lip. Conchita uttered a groan of anguish, her hands at her mouth, her eyes huge with terror.

"Come on, Señor, you are not *macho* enough to take my place with the willing little hens," Ramirez taunted. His fists doubled, his eyes glistening with sadistic joy, he approached the fallen young man. "Did you really think you could dismiss José Ramirez and drive him away after he has made your worthy father *muy rico?*"

Ingeniously, Tomás de Pladero kicked out with his right foot and caught the foreman in the shin. José Ramirez uttered a yell of pain and stumbled back, and the young Spaniard flung himself at the foreman. His fists thudded home against Ramirez's jowls and plump belly.

Conchita watched with astonishment to see Tomás defend himself so resolutely against the brutal foreman. But Ramirez, recovering quickly, again knocked Tomás down with a vicious blow to his midriff, and the young Spaniard crouched on the ground, gasping and panting for breath. To further his advantage and terminate the fight more quickly, the foreman now advanced toward his fallen adversary and kicked out with his right foot. Tomás agilely gripped it with his hands before it could find its target and, righting himself, yanked hard and upward. With a yell of dismay, Ramirez fell backward, his head striking the ground, his coarse face twisted with pain and hate.

"I said you were dismissed, and I meant it, Ramirez," Tomás de Pladero panted. "Get up. You will never again touch any of the servant girls, do you understand?"

"Hijo de puta," the foreman gasped as he stumbled to his feet, "I will kill you!" He hurled himself forward like a bull at a matador. But Tomás ducked and, with all his strength, sent his fist hard into the foreman's belly. Ramirez, the wind knocked out of him, uttered a gurgling cry, stumbled back and fell. He rolled over onto his side, clutching at his belly and drawing up his knees as he moaned in agony.

"Now it is your turn to get up, Ramirez! Who is the coward now? All you are fit for is taking a whip to innocent girls and forcing them to your dirtiness! Take your belongings and leave! You can get your wages from Señor Marcante at his shop!"

Wincing, José Ramirez got to his feet. In a last and desperate attack, he aimed a kick at his young adversary's groin. But once again Tomás, anticipating just such a move, caught the foreman's leg with both hands, wrenched it violently, and flung the foreman to the ground. *"Madre de diablo*—you have broken my leg—all right—all right, I'll go, I'll go! Take your little *puta*, then—I did not know you wanted her so badly."

After a few moments, José Ramirez tentatively tested his leg and found that it was only sprained, not broken. He dragged himself to his feet and, with a last glaring look at Conchita's young champion, hobbled back to his cottage, muttering blasphemously under his breath.

"Oh Señor Tomás, oh *gracias, gracias*—I was so afraid for you—he is so cruel, so strong—" Conchita sobbed.

"Do not cry, *querida*. Here, I shall fill your bucket again. Please do not cry. But you see, it is true. Yes, Conchita, I do want you—but I want you to be my wife."

"No—you cannot mean that—I am a poor orphan, Señor Tomás, only a *criada*—"

"No longer," his voice was firm and crisp. "When my mother comes back, I shall tell her that I have found the girl I love. And if she does not like it—well—well—" he drew a deep breath, "then I shall move into town and we shall have a *jacal* all to ourselves, *querida.*"

She flung herself at him, her arms locking around him, and she rained kisses on him, sobbing in her joy and gratitude. Tomás blushed like a schoolboy, nervously glancing around to make certain that no one was in sight. Then gently he disengaged himself and whispered, "You do not know how I have longed to have you do that, Conchita dearest. Please— let me fill the bucket and take it back to the kitchen. Then we shall make our plans."

"What are you telling me, Tomás?" Don Sancho stared at his son, his mouth agape. "You dismissed Ramirez?"

"Yes, *mi padre*. He was molesting Conchita, and I would not have it. I—we—we fought and I told him to leave and he did. I am going to take his pay to the shop in Taos."

"I cannot be hearing you right, my son." Don Sancho slowly shook his head, while Doña Elena caught her breath and crossed herself. "If it were the summer, I should say that the sun has touched your brain. Do you mean to say that you forced Ramirez to leave by fighting him?"

"Yes. And now there is something else I want to tell both you and mother. I want to marry Conchita Seragos."

"I—I think I am going to faint, Don Sancho," Doña Elena gasped.

"No, Mother," Tomás fiercely interrupted. "All these years I have done everything you wanted me to. Well, I know what you thought of me. I guess I deserved it. But I am my own master now, and I know my own mind. You tried to get me married to Catarina de Escobar—well, she is married now, and I never really wanted her in the beginning. It is Conchita I want and it is Conchita I am going to marry, whether you like it or not!"

Don Sancho and Doña Elena looked at each other, and it was Doña Elena who was first to speak. "Who would have thought Tomás would show such passion? I cannot believe I am hearing such words from his lips—he has always been so dutiful and obedient—"

"I shall always be obedient, Mother, but I am old enough to decide on my own happiness."

"My dear wife," Don Sancho at last put in, "perhaps we had best let him have his own way. As he has just pointed out, Catarina is married to someone else and there is no other eligible girl."

"But, my beloved Sancho, do you realize what you are saying?" Doña Elena gasped. "This Conchita is only a servant, an orphan, there is no dowry—"

But Don Sancho had seen the determined look on his son's bruised and bloodied face, and he was secretly admiring him. "Once Tomás marries Conchita, my dear," he told his wife, "she will have the de Pladero name, and it is as a fine a name as any in Taos. Please have the goodness not to forget it. Besides, she is a sweet, modest, industrious girl, and one could not ask for a more devout Catholic—Padre Moraga has often told me how she comes to his little church to pray and to thank him for having brought her into our household. I, for one, approve."

"Father!" Tomás de Pladero joyously exclaimed as he went forward to clasp his father's hand. Greatly moved, Don Sancho coughed, then flung his arms around Tomás and embraced him.

Doña Elena, realizing her defeat, made the best of it with a sigh and an indulgent smile. "Very well then, my dear son.

Both your father and I live only for your happiness. We shall arrange this marriage, and I, too, shall give my consent."

Muttering to himself, José Ramirez reached for the half-empty bottle of tequila and swigged almost all of it down before he flung it against the wall of his cottage. "I will show them! That young puppy, making a fool of me in front of that stupid little bitch! Well, he is welcome to her. I will find employment somewhere else, and it does not have to be in this backward village, either. A good foreman is worth his weight in gold—there will be others who will appreciate me."

It was well after midnight, and he was very nearly drunk. Consuela had timidly knocked at the door of his cottage a few hours ago and been profanely told to get back to the *hacienda* if she did not want to be flayed alive. José Ramirez had already packed his belongings, but now a sudden idea occurred to him. He turned to the closet, opened the door and, lighting a candle, stared at the bowl which contained the grayish, powdery flakes. A diabolical smile twisted his lips and he nodded to himself. "I will give them something to remember. Don Sancho is counting on the lambs, and it is almost shearing time. Only there will not be so many lambs this season. And that other *rico* who gives himself such airs, and that fancy son of his, that Carlos de Escobar—they have had it easy since they brought their flock to Taos. It is high time they learned that you cannot always have things your own way. Sheep can die, and who will say what kills them?"

He chuckled to himself, went back to the table, and, taking a piece of brushwood, began to whittle at it with his knife.

FORTY-NINE

Teofilo Rosas was out of breath, and his face was contorted with anger and fear as he hammered on the door of Miguel Sandarbal's cottage the morning after Tomás de Pladero's fight with José Ramirez. Dawn was just breaking, and the wiry foreman was tugging on his shirt as he opened the door and exclaimed, "*¿Que pasa, hombre?* From the way you were hammering on my door, I thought it was the Day of Judgment."

"The sheep, Señor Sandarbal, the sheep!" the plump little Mexican gasped out. Twisting his sombrero in his hands, he dolefully shook his head. "Juan Ortiz, who as you know is getting ready for the shearing next month, could not sleep last night. So he was up about two hours ago and wandered into the grazing fields—*¡mi Dios!*"

"Calm yourself and take a deep breath, *hombre*." Miguel clapped him on the back. "What happened to the sheep?"

"It is dreadful, Señor Sandarbal! He came to waken me as soon as he had seen it."

"You are like an old woman who tells the story of her first and only flirtation, drawing it out to infinity, *hombre!*"

Teofilo Rosas forced a faint smile to his sweating face, but he sobered quickly. "Señor Sandarbal, Juan Ortiz woke me to tell me that he had found at least ten of our best rams dead. But that is not all. As you know, the sheep of Don Sancho graze with ours, and there has never been any trouble because Don Sancho's have their left ears notched. Well then, I could not believe what Juan told me—there are at least thirty lambs dead in Don Sancho's flock. This Juan himself verified when he saw how their ears were notched."

"The devil! Who could have done such a monstrous thing? And to kill lambs especially—they are what every rancher looks to for his next year's earnings. But how did they die?"

"Juan Ortiz says he is sure it was poison. Their faces were blackened and swollen, and their eyes were bulging as if they had seen the devil himself."

"The devil himself," Miguel Sandarbal slowly repeated. "I have an idea who that might be—Don Sancho's foreman, the one who was carting that ewe late at night into Taos to sell it and keep the money for himself. And yet, Teofilo, why would a foreman kill his own master's sheep as well as those of a neighbor?"

"I do not know, Señor Sandarbal." Teofilo Rosas glumly shook his head.

"Mount your horse, Teofilo, and ride over to the de Pladeros's and see if their foreman is still there. If he is, play innocent—just tell him that some of our sheep are dead, and we were wondering whether he had any losses. If he did, try to get him to tell you what he thinks killed them. Get back to me as quickly as you can. I shall have to tell Don Diego, but I shall wait until he has had breakfast. Meanwhile, tell Juan Ortiz to put all the sheepherders on watch and let them guard the sheep through the night in shifts—at least we can prevent any further losses."

"At once, Señor Sandarbal!"

But when Teofilo Rosas returned a little over an hour later, it was with the news that José Ramirez had been discharged the day before, had taken his possessions and left the ranch, and that no one had seen him since.

Carlos had come to breakfast early for the express purpose of conversing with Don Diego. After courteously greeting his father and Doña Inez (Catarina and John Cooper were not expected; they had asked for a tray in their room) he came right to the point. "Father, I have something to say and I hope you will not take it badly."

"After all that has happened in this household the past several months, Carlos, I think I may say that I am prepared for surprises," Don Diego chuckled. At this, his sister-in-law sent him a quick glance and smiled to herself. "What do you have to tell me, my son?"

"You know I have spoken to you about Weesayo, the daughter of the Apache chief, whom I met when John Cooper took me to the stronghold."

"Indeed I do. If I am to believe you, she is a paragon of beauty and virtue."

"She is all of that and more, Father. So much so, indeed, that I intend to marry her."

Don Diego nearly dropped his spoon into the bowl of porridge which Tía Margarita had just set before him. "Are you serious, Carlos?"

"I have never been more so, Father."

"But she is an Apache."

"That is very true, Father. But that is not the point at all. I should love her if she were from the Sandwich Islands or the Straits of Magellan. She is kind, good, gentle, and thoughtful. Her people love her, and she is called the beloved woman—which is the highest tribute the Apache can pay to their womanfolk. And I think she cares for me."

"I do not know what to say, Carlos."

"I assure you, Father, that if she will have me, we shall be married according to the ways of her people first. But then we shall come back here so that we can be married in the chapel by Padre Moraga."

Don Diego's face brightened, and he stared reflectively for a long moment at his handsome son. Then he sighed and nodded. "You are the last of my line, *mi hijo*. And yet, these years here in Taos have taught me more than I realized. I have begun to believe that Spain is no longer a great power and that she will play no part at all in this strange, constantly changing new world in which we find ourselves."

"I did not mean to bring back sad memories for you, Father. I know how much you miss Madrid—"

"No, Carlos, it is not that now. I feel I shall never see Madrid and my king again. The die is cast, and for better or for worse my life is here. Since you are my son, my only son, my last days must certainly be devoted to seeing to your happiness. If you truly feel that you want to marry this girl, then do as your heart bids you. I promise you I shall welcome her as a daughter, and I shall be kind to her, and I shall love her because you love her."

Doña Inez stealthily reached for her handkerchief and dabbed at her eyes, then sent Carlos a warm, affectionate glance.

"In that case, Father, I shall ride to the stronghold today and ask her father, the Apache chief, Descontarti, for her hand in marriage."

"Now that is proper. Perhaps in some ways their customs are not so strange after all," Don Diego mused aloud. Then, with mock-paternal sternness, he added, "But you are letting your breakfast get cold, Carlos. If you are going to ride all the way to those mountains to court your wife-to-be, you need your strength."

Carlos had joyously taken leave of his father and aunt, dressed warmly for his journey, then gone to the kitchen to wheedle the good-natured cook into putting up a sack of provisions for him. "This time, Tía Margarita," he teased her, "you will have another bride to cook for and to send trays to—I am going to bring one back."

"Oh, that is wonderful news, young master! And whoever the girl is, she will be very lucky with a wonderful *caballero* like you."

"Go on, Tía Margarita, you say that to all the *caballeros* of Taos," he laughed, then whirled her round and round to leave her breathless, and kissed her resoundingly.

He went out to the stable to saddle Valor. As he was packing his rifle in its sling and fixing the sack of provisions to the pummel of his saddle, he saw the foreman hurrying out of his cottage with a worried look on his face. "Miguel, why such a long face?" he called.

"Oh, it is you, Señor Carlos! I have bad news for your father. Some rogue has poisoned many of our finest rams, as well as many of the lambs belonging to Don Sancho's flock. I think I know who it is, because Teofilo Rosas rode in to tell me that José Ramirez was discharged yesterday and has not been seen since. But where are you going?"

"Off to the mountains to bring back a wife, Miguel," Carlos laughed, too happy to be very much concerned over the sheep. "And that reminds me—John Cooper tells me it is customary to give the father of the bride-to-be some horses by way of purchase price. Can you spare any, *por favor?* I shall give you the money to buy replacements in Chihuahua when I get back."

"Of course, Señor Carlos. There are three you could take, and they are in excellent condition."

"Well, she is worth more than three horses, but I remember also that John Cooper said the gift should not be too extravagant because then it would be in bad taste. If one gave a rich present to the parents, it would be said that they could not refuse. And you see, Miguel, horses are the most valuable possession the Apache has."

"Well," Miguel teased him with a straight face, "if these three are not enough, I daresay you could always throw in Valor."

"Valor?" For a moment Carlos's face fell. *"Por Dios,* for Weesayo, yes, I would give up even Valor. I shall take them then. Is there anything I can do about those sheep, Miguel?"

"No, no, young master. That is my work. We shall find out soon enough if that thieving Ramirez was the one. And we shall know what to do. You see, some of the workers have joined the Penitentes. They will punish the transgressor in their own way. It is cruel, but it is also justice. But now, I am keeping you from your happiness—and I wish you *salud, amor, dinero, y tiempo por gustarlas."*

"That is a wonderful wish, Miguel."

Tethering the three horses together and holding the lead in his left hand, Carlos mounted Valor and, his face radiant with expectation, set out for the Jicarilla Mountains.

On the morning of the fifth day of his journey, he rode Valor into the stronghold and dismounted in front of Descontarti's wickiup. The Apache chief emerged and at once smiled broadly as he came forward to welcome the young Spaniard. "You are welcome, my blood brother. Kinotatay has told me how bravely you and *El Halcón* defended yourselves against the *bandidos* of Santomaro."

"And he should have told you also, chief of the Apache, that he fought like a true warrior beside us. I am proud to have your blood in my veins. And I would ask more of you," Carlos responded.

"Between brothers, one does not have to hide one's feelings behind words. Say what is in your heart."

"You see the three horses I bring to your wickiup, Descontarti. I ask if you will take them as my pledge to be husband of your daughter, Weesayo."

Descontarti's smile broadened. "What you ask is not unexpected. I had seen it already in my daughter's eyes. Yet, while you were gone from the stronghold, the warrior Nesantayah spoke for himself and offered ten horses."

Carlos gasped, his face falling with disappointment. Then he took his rifle out of its sling and handed it, butt foremost, to the Apache chief. "I add this also to show you that I love her as much as life itself. And if it is not enough, you have seen my stallion Valor, which brought me to your stronghold. Him, too, I give you in the purchase price."

Descontarti pretended to frown. "It is true that four horses and a rifle—and especially your stallion—make a very fine gift. Still, one cannot gainsay ten horses, and Nesantayah has counted many coups and is esteemed among us."

Carlos bit his lips and stared down at the ground disconsolately. Then Descontarti said softly, "It is a good joke. Your horses are much better, and then, too, Nesantayah did not offer me the gift of a rifle."

Carlos uttered a cry of joy and at that moment Weesayo came out of the wickiup. The young Spaniard walked toward her, saluting her with the sign of palms upturned in friendship, then took her hand and kissed it as he would that of a princess. "I have just asked your father if he will give his consent to me as your husband," he said gravely.

An exquisite blush suffused her golden skin, and she lowered her eyes. He felt her hand tremble in his.

"Does it please you, my daughter?" Descontarti gently asked. Weesayo did not speak, but she raised her eyes to his and nodded slowly and then turned and went back into the wickiup.

Carlos was beside himself with joy, and he could hardly speak. Descontarti put his hand on his shoulder. "You will keep Valor, for you and Weesayo will ride back to your people after the marriage has been performed. El Halcón has told you of our way. You will sit together but not speak for three nights, and on the fourth the shaman will make you one person. And now, my son, go to your wickiup and remain with us until Weesayo prepares your secret dwelling."

On the fourth night, after the shaman had mixed their blood, Carlos lifted Weesayo in his arms and set her astride Valor and then mounted. He felt her soft arms cling to his waist, and he was trembling with an ecstasy such as he had not dreamed possible. The beauty and simplicity of the symbolic ceremony had touched him deeply. Nor did he feel it to be the slightest sacrilege against the beliefs in which he had been reared as a child. There was a pure candor to the Apache ritual that expressed perfectly to him the wonderful sanctity of marriage.

He and Weesayo rode for almost an hour until they came to the far end of the southern canyon and then, at her whispered instruction, he turned Valor's head up the sloping trail ahead and rode a little while longer. At last they came to a flat platform jutting out over the canyon. On the rock platform was a newly made wickiup, with silver bells tied to the sides of the door. The night air was gentle and strangely warm, and when it stirred, there was a tinkle of bells that matched the music singing in his heart. He dismounted and lifted her down, and hand in hand they walked toward their bridal dwelling. Inside, it was filled with desert flowers. Weesayo turned to him and put her hand to the side of the door. "The bells had already begun to sing in my heart when the shaman made us one, *mi esposo*."

"And in mine, beloved."

"You speak our tongue well, *mi esposo*," she whispered.

"You speak mine more beautifully than I have ever heard any woman speak it, light of the mountains, light of my life." His voice trembled with his longing for her.

"But you must see if I am a good wife, Car-los"—his heart almost stopped beating in the joy of hearing the delicious hesitation with which she accented his name in her sweet, clear voice. "Come, see. Here are containers with mescal cakes, sacks of ripe acorns, cakes baked with juniper berries, roasted pinyon nuts, dried mustard seed, roasted yucca fruit, and many other things. And I have brought also spoons made of yucca leaves and containers made from the hard inside of the saguaro that will hold water."

She led him into the wickiup. "My beloved one, my sweetheart, my wife," he said hoarsely, as he took her hand and kissed it again.

"You are content with me, Car-los?"

"Do not ask such a question. Content is not the word. There are no words to tell you. We shall make our own language, you and I, Weesayo. And when we must leave here—"

"Yes, *mi esposo*, after ten days, it is so written."

"I know, beloved. And when the time is up, you will ride back with me to Taos where my father and my aunt will meet you and they will know why it is that I rode here to choose you out of all the women in the entire world to live with and to be my sweetheart and my wife."

"Do you truly wish this?"

"Yes, beloved. I would ask only one thing of you—because my father came from far across the seas and my mother died just when he had to do so, he looks to me as his only son to carry on his name. He is used to his customs. Will you not marry me again in our ceremony? It is as loving and as honest as yours—though it is not more beautiful. In this way, Weesayo, we shall be married twice."

"Oh yes, if that is what you wish, I wish it also with all my heart. But sometimes," this almost wistfully, "you will come back with me to the stronghold, that I may see my father and my mother—and you know you must not look at my mother now that we are one."

"This I have learned, also, and you will teach me many more things. Of course I shall bring you back here. We shall come back often, and when we have children, we shall show them the happy people of the mountains that they may honor and respect and love them as I do, Weesayo."

With a soft little cry of delight, she put her arms around him, cradling her head against his chest, and he breathed in the night air and the sweetness of the scent with which she had adorned herself. Outside, the silver bells tinkled in what was for him a celestial music.

Early on the afternoon of April 21, 1813, another wedding took place at the de Escobar *hacienda*. This, too, was held in the chapel, and old Padre Moraga stood before Carlos and Weesayo to hear them repeat the vows that formally united them in the faith of the lovely Apache girl's husband. John Cooper stood in back of Carlos as his best man and handed him the ring. He smiled warmly as Carlos, his lips forming the silent words of *"gracias, amigo,"* reverently put the ring on Weesayo's slim finger and then kissed her hand.

Catarina was there as a bridesmaid, her eyes misty with happiness, but she stared more at her own young husband than at her brother and his Apache bride.

Behind them stood Don Diego and Doña Inez. Don Diego was greatly moved by the beauty and gentleness of the young Apache girl. During the week before the ceremony, he had been enchanted by her exquisite beauty and still more by the conversations he had with her. Well before Padre Moraga had pronounced them man and wife, Don Diego had accepted Weesayo as a daughter-in-law, and he had approved his son's choice of a bride.

As Padre Moraga made the sign of the cross above the young couple's heads, Don Diego turned to Doña Inez and saw her dabbing at her eyes with her handkerchief. When she had finished, he took her left hand and murmured gently, "By rights, there should be another wedding in this chapel soon. Let it be between us, Inez."

She turned to regard him with a startled gasp, then put her handkerchief to her mouth and looked around to see if anyone had overheard him.

"Yes, Inez. Make my happiness complete. Do you not see we shall be alone now? Carlos and Catarina are starting their new lives and they will not need us any more. But I know now how much I need you, how much I have always needed you without really understanding it. It took all this time, fool that I was, to forget what I had left behind me in Spain and to see how greatly you had enriched my life. Will you have me, Inez? There is so much of Dolores in you—and yet there is much more all your own that I see now as if for the first time."

She could not speak, but she moved closer to him and squeezed his hand and nodded as the tears began to flow unchecked. Together they watched Carlos and Weesayo turn toward them, their faces radiant, their hands clasped.

FIFTY

For over a month there had been no news of José Ramirez. Tomás de Pladero, greatly to his father's pleasure, had himself replaced the brutal foreman. He and Conchita had been married by Padre Moraga exactly one week before the cermony in which the daughter of Descontarti had accepted the faith of her young husband. And, basking in Conchita's adoring and grateful love, coming to discern how his mother's attitude toward him had subtly altered to one of respect and even grudging admiration, he was finding his double role of husband and foreman vastly rewarding. The workers, who had never really liked José Ramirez, warmed to his natural friendliness and easygoing way. Yet they soon discovered that this mild-mannered young man knew almost as much about sheep as they did. Moreover, with a diplomatic shrewdness that Doña Elena herself would have applauded, Tomás had the disarming habit of asking the workers for their opinions and seriously weighing them, which increased their self-respect and forged a greater bond of camaraderie.

As for Don Sancho, overjoyed at the way the tensions of his household had begun to ease, he faithfully promised Doña Elena that he would take her on a second honeymoon to Mexico City and meet the popular and powerful new viceroy.

With the disappearance of José Ramirez, the maids of the de Pladero household found life eminently more bearable. Doña Elena herself seemed to be less tyrannical in her dealings with them. Yet Consuela Viola remained cowed and reticent, speaking but seldom to her companions, and, whenever she had occasion to pass by the cottage which José Ramirez had formerly occupied, she furtively crossed herself and murmured a prayer.

There had been gossip throughout the household among the servants that José Ramirez, in his spiteful retaliation for his dismissal, had poisoned his master's and Don Diego's lambs. There was, of course, no proof of this, but the lack of news of the foreman's whereabouts heightened these suspicions.

Only Consuela Viola knew for sure. Just three nights previous, a Navaho boy had come to the kitchen to ask for food. When the impatient *cocinera* had called Consuela to give him a few scraps, he had gestured to Consuela to come outside with him. Glancing nervously back at the *cocinera,* Consuela followed the boy outside and demanded, "What do you want of me?"

"I have a message for you. You know who it is from. You are to go tonight to meet him at the shop of Barnaba Canepa."

Consuela gasped and crossed herself. "But I would not dare. Señor Canepa is a dreadful old man who they say has books on witchcraft and sells strange potions. Besides, are you sure the message is for me?"

"Yes." The Navaho boy bobbed his head and grinned. "He said I was to find the fat one, the one who was his *novia* in the old days. The one who knows what he keeps in his closet. Thank you for the food, I go now."

Again Consuela crossed herself as the wiry boy darted away. She was trembling, and her lips had suddenly gone dry. The reputation of Barnaba Canepa was unsavory indeed, and some of the older servants had whispered that if a girl got into trouble, he could give her herbs which would make it vanish.

She rubbed her sweating face with her apron and went slowly back into the kitchen. She had not noticed that the tall, cadaverous-looking Mexican, Ignazio Peramonte—one of the de Pladero sheepherders—was standing beside a shed near the kitchen door and listening attentively.

At eleven o'clock, when the *hacienda* was still, Consuela slipped out and went to the stable. In his more indulgent moments, José Ramirez had taught her how to ride a horse. She rode through the darkness like one who fears the devil pursuing her, frequently crossing herself and praying aloud to all the saints to guide her and protect her.

She came to the eastern edge of the town. At the edge of the pueblo where the christianized Indians lived, she awkwardly dismounted, falling onto all fours, which she interpreted as an ill omen. She rose to her knees, clasped her hands, and began to pray aloud. In the midst of her prayer, a mocking voice assailed her. "This way, you fat sow. And do not make so much noise. Señor Canepa is tired and wants to go to sleep."

In the darkness, she saw the glowing light of a lantern, and behind it the mocking, leering face of José Ramirez. He had shaved off his mustache and cropped his hair, but those narrowed eyes and that wet full mouth were unmistakable.

"I swear by all the saints—"

"Save your prayers, *puta*. In with you!" He made an abrupt gesture with the lantern, showing her the narrow door to the back entrance of the shop.

She could scarcely move. Her limbs felt as if they would turn to jelly as she stumbled into the obscurity of Barnaba Canepa's shop. The lantern cast a weird glow on shadowy vases and jars, and she saw one that contained a dead toad and another a rattlesnake. She crossed herself, closed her eyes, and stumbled again. José Ramirez gripped her by the fleshy part of her arm and swore, "Stupid bitch, look where you are going! Here we are now. Barnaba, go to bed. I will deal with this *puta*."

Barnaba Canepa was a man in his late sixties, wizened, with sparse white hair, a wispy goatee, and cataract-blurred eyes. "Very well," he cackled, "don't make too much noise. Just make sure she brings back the rest of that venom. You were a fool to have left it there in your hut. I have use for it, and it will earn us much *dinero*."

"*Caramba, amigo,* I thought I had used most of it up poisoning Don Sancho's accursed sheep. In my haste to leave his *hacienda,* I left the bowl behind. But there is no harm done. The stupid peóns who work there, even if they find it, will not know what it is."

"Just be sure she brings it back, José. Let us have a look at her." With this, he gripped his cane and hobbled toward her, while José Ramirez held up the lantern so that the old man could squint at the cowering young woman. "Eh, José, if I were a bit younger, I would stay here and keep the *puta* company. But my old bones ache for sleep. *Buenas noches.*"

Consuela found herself alone with the man she most detested and feared in all the world.

"Well, Consuela, you have missed me, I am sure," he chuckled nastily. "But you still owe me one last service. Remember how I spared you from the many whippings Doña Elena wanted to give you. I was always your friend, was I not, *puta?*"

Automatically, she stammered, *"Si,* José."

"*¡Bueno!* Now then, do you remember what I showed you in that closet of mine, eh?" Shuddering, Consuela could only nod and again cross herself.

"Has anyone discovered it yet?" he demanded, bringing the lantern closer to her face so that it almost blinded her.

"I do not know—I mean—Señor Tomás has taken your place, José. I do not think anyone has gone to the cottage—I am sure they have not—"

"That is better than I had hoped. But then, they are all idiots. Now, listen. You are to ride back there at once and get that bowl, *comprende?* Bring it back to me. Maybe, just maybe, I will give you a few *pesos.* I might even take you with me. There is a chance I shall have a post as foreman in San Luis Potosi. Well, are you going to do what I want?"

She nodded.

"Good. Now get on that horse of yours and ride back and be quick about it. I will wait up for you. Go now. But one thing, Consuela—if you ever breathe a word—"

"I know, I will not betray you, I swear it in my soul! Please do not hurt me!"

He uttered a coarse, cynical laugh. "That is as may be. We will talk about it when you come back with what I want."

He gripped her elbow and forced her to walk outside through the back of the shop, held the lantern until she mounted the horse, and laughed at her clumsiness. Then he called mockingly after her, *"Vaya con Dios*—and come back quickly! If you fail me on this, Consuela, I will know what to do with you."

She thought she would faint on the way back. Her heart was pounding furiously, and a cold sweat drenched her. The night air had turned cool, but she felt as if a raging fever gripped her. At last she reached the *hacienda,* dismounted, and stumbled toward the abandoned cottage.

Hesitantly, she tried the door, opened it, and in the darkness, groped her way toward that terrible closet with its ghastly secret. She found the door of the closet, opened it, and her trembling hand brushed against the bowl. "Holy Virgin, forgive what I do. I must, I am so afraid—I—" she sobbed aloud.

Then a dry, cold voice hurled at her out of the darkness, "Why do you call on Her, Blessed Mother of our Sacred Lord who tasted the scourge and the cross, to do evil?"

"*¡Ayudame, Dios—!*" she cried out almost hysterically as she whirled.

She saw before her a tall, gaunt man, his face hidden in a black cowl, his body almost skeleton-like in the clinging black robe. His feet were clad in thong sandals, and in his right hand he carried a scourge made from three supple yucca branches bound at their ends with rawhide.

"Who—who are you?" she panted, clinging to the closet door to steady herself.

"I am the *sangrador*—the bloodletter of Los Penitentes. My name is Ignazio Peramonte."

"I—I know you, S–señor," she quavered. "You—you are a sheepherder here."

"By day. By night, I am one of those who glorify Our Lord and who dispense justice to the evildoers. What do you seek in that closet, woman?"

"Oh, Señor Peramonte, in the name of heaven, do not make me tell you—I am afraid of him—he sent for me—"

"José Ramirez," the gaunt man dryly interrupted. "We of the Penitentes have watched him for many weeks. We know of his evil deeds, his lusts, his thefts, his treachery. One of the peóns who works for Don Sancho de Pladero is a Penitente like myself. When the sheep were poisoned and José Ramirez vanished, he suspected the *capataz* of this abomination. And when he searched Ramirez's cottage, he found the bowl with rattlesnake venom, the final proof. This monstrous deed demands that he be brought to our tribunal. Again, woman, I ask you to tell me what you sought here—was it not that bowl of venom which Ramirez, in his haste to escape justice, left behind him? Speak!"

Consuela fell upon her knees, wringing her hands, and confessed what she had been told to do. Because the dread name of Los Penitentes was even more terrifying to her than the vengeance of Ramirez, she told Ignazio Peramonte about that night José Ramirez had shown her how the gray, powdery flakes could take life.

"You have done well to confess this, woman. You are without guilt. What you have done adds to his, since he compelled you by force and by cruelty. You will testify against him at our tribunal. Come. Our brothers wait." Then he added, "Take that bowl, and carry it carefully. Wrap it in a cloth—there is certain to be one in this cottage. Be quick, woman. Justice has been delayed, but tonight José Ramirez will learn that our dear Lord does not long condone a sinner."

He held the light while the half-fainting, half-hysterical young woman found a piece of cloth and covered the bowl with it, hugging it against her bosom. Then he led her back to her horse and, putting his left index and middle finger to his lips, emitted a shrill whistle. From behind the cottage came a dozen black-robed, cowled figures. They led four horses among them, and Ignazio Peramonte mounted one and bade three others accompany him with Consuela Viola to the shop of Barnaba Canepa.

Before they reached the rear entrance of the shop, the *sangrador* whispered, "You will lead us to him. You will call out, and you will say that he must come out because you are afraid of the darkness."

"I will do whatever you wish." Consuela crossed herself.

She walked toward the rear of the little shop, obscure in the darkness of the night. Only a crescent moon hung in the sky, the wind rose, and the branches of trees moved. There was a stirring in the air that increased her superstitious terror.

Then, drawing a deep breath, she forced herself to call out, "José, come out, I cannot see—come out, *por favor!*"

The door was flung open and José Ramirez, holding the lantern, strode out and snarled at her, "You stupid bitch, you will wake the entire town with your caterwauling! Well now, did you get what I want?"

"Sí, José. Please—I am so tired—come closer with the lantern, I cannot see in the dark, I will stumble and spill it—"

"Quiet, you whore!" he hissed. "I should have killed you when I had the chance, Consuela. You fat, clumsy sow, you are—ah, what is this—did you bring—you bitch, you Judas bitch—you betrayed me—I will kill you—" As he drew a knife from his belt, two of the black-robed Penitentes rushed at him from out of the darkness and disarmed him, and the two others swiftly bound his wrists behind his back. One of them pressed a gag into his mouth and covered it with a bandana. Then, forcing him toward one of the horses, they lifted him astride it, and one of them mounted behind him, his left hand pressing a knife to the back of Ramirez's neck, while with his right hand he grasped the reins of his horse and turned it back toward the *hacienda* of Don Sancho de Pladero.

But they only stopped there to join the others who waited in the darkness beside the cottage where once José Ramirez had reigned as lecherous tyrant over the household of helpless female servants. The four rode, and the others walked slowly, toward the grazing range at the slope of the Sangre de Cristo Mountains. One of them carried a huge cross made of the branches of an oak tree. He who carried it was Padre Juan Moraga.

They came at last to the gentle slope where the sheep grazed, and Padre Moraga and two of his black-robed aides hammered the cross into the ground. Two others dragged José Ramirez from his horse, tore off his shirt, and then the *sangrador* cut three gashes along each side of his spine with the sharp edge of a flint. José Ramirez writhed and cried out, but the gag muffled his prayers and threats.

They bound him to the cross, and then the *sangrador* took the scourge and began to flog him. Consuela, kneeling, crossed herself and prayed aloud for her own redemption and for pardon in having betrayed another human being.

They left him, fainting, his back bloodied. As dawn rose, he hung there, tied with rawhide thongs, crucified and chastised in the brutal justice of the Penitentes.

It was a bright April morning, and John Cooper had left Catarina sleeping with a serene smile on her soft lips, to take breakfast with his father-in-law, Carlos, and radiant Doña Inez. Their banns would be proclaimed by Padre Moraga a week from today, and they would be married in his little church.

"It is time I let Lobo out for his run," John Cooper explained to Don Diego after he had drunk his chocolate.

"By all means, *mi hijo*," Don Diego chuckled. Then, with a fond glance at Doña Inez, he added, "My two sons, indeed. And their two brides sleep the happy sleep of happy wives, *¿no es verdad?*" Then, quite unlike himself, he added with a playful wink at Doña Inez, "When you and I are married, my dearest Inez, we shall send for a tray and have our breakfast served alone. I find the prospect intensely pleasing."

"Diego—one does not talk of such things," Doña Inez reproved him, but her eyes were dancing and she surreptitiously blew him a kiss.

John Cooper hurried out to the shed and unleashed Lobo, who growled his greeting and rubbed his muzzle against his leg. Saddling his mustang, he rode off toward the now green peaks of the Sangre de Cristo Mountains. Over them was a shroud of soft white clouds, and the sun was bright. As he knew the day would quickly grow hot, he took with him a canteen of water.

Lobo raced ahead, his eyes gleaming, eager for the sport. "We'll go back to the mountains one of these days, Lobo," John Cooper mused. "But you'll have to learn to become a household pet for a while, I'm afraid. And I honestly don't know how good a job I can manage with that. Well, we'll see. Why are you growling?" he spoke aloud. "What do you see over there?" The wolf had bounded ahead, his hair bristling, uttering a low growl.

Spurring the mustang, John Cooper quickened his pace to catch up with Lobo. The wolf was baring his fangs at a cross of oak branches to which a man was bound, his head drooping, his back bloodied.

John Cooper quickly dismounted and ran toward him. Then, as he recognized José Ramirez, he removed the gag and demanded, "What has happened to you, *hombre?*"

With a supreme effort, Ramirez lifted his head, his face pale and contorted in unspeakable agony. "*¡Agua, por piedad, Señor!*" he croaked, and his dry lips trembled convulsively.

"Ramirez—who did this to you?"

"*Los—Los—P–Penitentes*—help me, Señor—they whipped me—nearly to d–death—I have sinned—I wish to confess it— forgive me—only give me water and untie me—" José Ramirez moaned.

Lobo had crouched, showing his teeth again and growling,

but John Cooper silenced him with a peremptory wave of his hand. Quickly he cut Ramirez's bonds and helped the half-conscious man to his feet. "Now then, what do you want to confess?"

"It was I—I who poisoned—the sheep—*Los Penitentes* —they judged me—they had known what I had done—I sent C—Consuela for the poison—I could sell it to Canepa and there are those who would pay much to rid themselves of an unwanted wife or husband, S—Señor—forgive me—"

"It's not for me to forgive you. They have judged you, and you killed the sheep for revenge, didn't you?"

José Ramirez nodded feebly. *"Agua,* I beg of you, Señor," he gasped.

John Cooper reached for his canteen and held it to Ramirez's lips while the former *capataz* drank thirstily. Taking the canteen away, John Cooper said to him, "Now listen. Go back to Mexico, and never come back. Do you understand? Perhaps you have learned a lesson. Maybe you will have another chance at being an honest man."

"God will reward you, Señor." Ramirez took a halting step toward John Cooper, who was already swinging into his saddle.

"I owe you nothing, Ramirez," John Cooper said. "A man who would poison sheep is worse than a renegade Indian. But I'll take my time riding back to the *hacienda,* and you'll have a head start. Use it to get back into Mexico, *comprende?"*

"¡Si, gracias, Señor, *gracias!"* With a groan, the half-naked man stumbled toward the south, casting only one furtive glance back at John Cooper.

He had said nothing to Don Diego or Carlos or Miguel about finding José Ramirez hanging from a cross at the base of the Sangre de Cristo Mountains. But he did not think that the *capataz* would ever come back, and he knew the mystic justice of the Penitentes. They had given an evildoer justice; John Cooper freed him that he might profit from his lesson; and God alone would judge whether that lesson would be learned.

That night, alone with Catarina, he banished all such thoughts—reveling in his complete delight in her. As he held her close to him, he smiled to hear her say, "It is still our honeymoon, *mi amorcito,* and I am so new to it that you must be very tolerant of me."

"You are no longer a child, sweet Catarina, you are my wife and I love you," he said gently as he kissed her throat.

"Will it please you if I go camping with you in the mountains now and then?"

"Very much."

"And I shall, dearest Coop, if you will help my father with the ranch. You know, he looks on you as his own son. And of course Carlos will never be a rancher. So I think it is Father's hope that you will take his place, if only for a while."

He stroked her as he pondered her words. Then, kissing her eyelids, he said, *"Querida,* even a dove can be restless for its freedom. Well, you are my dove and I am your hawk. You shall keep the hawk with you, until it can no longer bear living within four walls and away from the blue sky. Then we'll go to the mountains to be free again—as we were when I took you away to make you my true love."

"Sí, querido," Catarina sighed as she cupped his face in her hands and kissed him passionately. "But perhaps I shall have a child—and I want a child, my dearest Coop. Perhaps that will keep the hawk from flight."

"We shall see, my dearest one." He kissed her eyelids again, and his hand thrilled to the ardent surging of her firm young breasts. "But for now, let us make this night last forever."

A Special Preview of
the stirring opening pages from
Book III of the
Colonization of America series

WAR CHIEF
by Donald Clayton Porter

WAR CHIEF continues the passionate
saga of Renno, the intrepid white
Indian whose blazing story began in
WHITE INDIAN and THE RENEGADE.

Chapter I

The sound of the throbbing drums that originated in the main town of the Seneca, the most powerful of the six Indian nations that made up the Iroquois League, rolled across the fields of corn and squash and beans grown by the women and echoed through the endless forest of evergreen and elm, oak and maple that surrounded the community. Families left their huts, and the unmarried emerged from long-houses to watch the solemn procession of the nation's leaders.

Leading the group was Ghonka, the Great Sachem of all the Iroquois, wearing the beaded buffalo robe and headgear of many hawk and eagle feathers that were the symbols of his exalted rank. Revered as the wisest of the wise and renowned for his exploits in battle, he was lean and muscular, and though in his middle years he was still capable of performing feats that no other fighting man could match.

Directly behind him, with clusters of feathers trailing down his brawny back from his scalp lock, came Sun-ai-yee, the main town's war chief, whose skills and acumen belied his portly appearance. Then marched the chiefs of the lesser Seneca towns, along with the principal medicine men and the elders who were also members of the nation's highest governing body, the potent council of the Seneca.

Bringing up the rear was a young man whose

appearance created a stir in the otherwise impassive crowd. The elderly nodded their approval, the younger warriors looked at him in admiration and awe, and the unmarried women brightened, casting provocative glances at this most eligible of bachelors. Renno, the son of Ghonka and his wife, Ena, was the only Seneca other than the Great Sachem himself ever to have achieved the distinction of being made a war chief prior to his twenty-third summer.

Renno was truly extraordinary. He stood more than six feet tall. He wore a magnificent headgear made from the feathers of the hawks who watched over him on behalf of the supernatural spirits of earth and sky and netherworld. Around his neck was a necklace of bear claws that not only identified him as a member of the Bear Clan but served as a reminder of his extraordinary relationship with the huge brown bear, now deceased, whom he had called Ja-gonh.

But in addition to these marks of distinction, there was something else about Renno that made him truly unique. His bare torso and face, although browned by the sun, revealed that his skin was not as dark as that of other Indians. His eyes were pale, an intense blue, and the hair of his scalp lock, although heavily greased, was the color of sand. The son of Ghonka and Ena, adopted by them soon after his birth when one of the first English settlements in Western Massachusetts Bay had been destroyed in an Indian raid in the late 1600's, was actually white.

Renno hadn't become aware of his heritage until he had grown to manhood and become a warrior. Since that time he had become a vital link between the Iroquois and the northern English colonies of the Atlantic seaboard. He had earned his high rank by fighting with distinction in two campaigns, leading his Seneca at the side of the colonists in an attack on the French at Quebec and in the successful siege of the great French fortress, Louisburg, on Cape Breton Island. He had traveled to far-distant England, where he had won the support of King William III for the joint expeditions of the English colonists and Indians against the supposedly invincible French. Thanks to him the Seneca and three other Iroquois nations—the Mohawk, the Oneida, and the Onondaga—now possessed and had become expert in the use of firearms. Thanks to him, trade between the northern English colonies and their Iroquois allies was flourishing.

He had learned the language of the English and had become familiar with their customs and manners. But he felt truly at home only here, in the land of the Seneca. So at this moment, knowing the reason the council of the Seneca had been called into session, his heart was heavy.

A war chief of the Seneca never revealed his feelings, however, regardless of whether he was sad or happy, so Renno's handsome features remained immobile, his expression wooden. As the procession moved past Ena, Renno paid homage to his mother by inclining his head to the dignified, graying woman in the dress of supple buckskin, and only she knew, when she saw his eyes, that he was unhappy. Beside her stood her younger son, El-i-chi, recently promoted to the rank of senior warrior, and although he and Renno were inseparable, even he could not guess that his brother was steeling himself for the ordeal that lay ahead.

Renno's composure was threatened just once, when he marched past a girl in her teens, and a slightly older boy. Ba-lin-ta, his younger sister, was defying Seneca tradition as usual, her broad grin making it plain to everyone that her pride in Renno was unbounded. He needed his lifetime of rigorous training to prevent himself from returning her smile or, even worse, laughing aloud.

He noted with satisfaction that her companion was appropriately somber, even though his shining eyes indicated that he shared the girl's feelings. Walter Alwin, the son of a recently remarried Fort Springfield widow, was a deaf-mute who somehow had managed to communicate his thoughts to Ba-lin-ta from the time they had first met. Renno was convinced that the manitous, the spirits of the wilderness, were responsible, and at his instigation Walter had been living with the Seneca for many moons. The youth had become remarkably self-reliant in this land where his affliction was not regarded as a handicap, and one day he would take the manhood trials that Seneca youths were required to endure. Walter insisted on becoming a candidate for these tests of strength, courage, and endurance, and if he passed them he would be a full-fledged junior warrior. Renno would sponsor him and felt certain he would succeed.

A fire was already burning in the log council house, the smoke escaping through a hole in the ceiling, and as the members entered they sat in a circle around it. Spring was at hand, so the day was warm, and as there were no windows in the lodge, the heat of the fire was noticeable, but no Seneca would admit he was uncomfortable.

Ghonka filled a clay pipe, lighted it with a coal from the fire and, after puffing on it, passed it to Sun-ai-yee. Not until every member of the group had taken a puff did the Great Sachem speak.

"My brothers," he said in his deep, resounding voice, "I have called you to this place to solve a new problem that confronts the Seneca. May the manitous who watch over us guide us and help us to make the right decision."

The war chiefs, elders, and medicine men folded their arms across their chests, and during the long silence that followed, each in his own way implored the manitous for their help. Every Seneca of high rank had seen visions at one time or another, and because these experiences had been so different, no two prayed in the same way.

Renno thought of the hawks that had led him out of dangerous situations, and then an image of Ja-gonh appeared in his mind. The spirit of the bear who had been his companion since both had been very young had mingled with his own spirit and, he knew, would not allow him to blunder now.

"My brothers," Ghonka said at last, "you who fought against the French at Louisburg and conquered them will remember Austin Ridley. To you who stayed at home I will explain. Austin Ridley is the war chief of the colonists from Virginia. He fought beside us and became the comrade of the Seneca. He is a man of honor and courage."

Sun-ai-yee nodded in sober agreement, as did Renno and the others who had participated in the long, arduous campaign.

"Wilson," Ghonka said, "has sent a message to me, a message of grave importance, which must be weighed carefully by the members of this council."

This time Renno was the first to nod. Brigadier Andrew Wilson, a wealthy western Massachusetts Bay land-owner who had recently succeeded to the command of that colony's militia, had demonstrated repeatedly that he was the staunch ally of all Iroquois.

"The English of Virginia seek only peace with their neighbors," Ghonka said. "But the strongest of their neighbors, the Pimlico nation, are sending their warriors to raid the towns and farms of the colonists. It is the hope of Ridley that the Seneca will send a special messenger to the Pimlico, asking them to exchange the wampum of peace with the people of Virginia."

A grizzled elder was the first to reply, his voice querulous. "The Seneca live far from the land of the Pimlico," he said. "Even the swiftest of our warriors would need to march for almost a moon before he would reach that land. Why should the Seneca interfere in the wars of others?"

"It is because we are the strongest of all nations that the Pimlico might listen to us. Those who make war against our allies need to understand that they also make war against us."

"The land of the Pimlico is too far from the land of the Seneca," the old man said.

Several of the other elders and medicine men nodded to indicate that they agreed with him.

Renno looked at his father, who inclined his head

a fraction of an inch, granting him the right to speak.

"The Virginia colonists," Renno said, "like the colonists of Massachusetts Bay and New York, swear fealty to William, the Great Sachem of the English. It is William who has given firesticks to the Seneca and the other nations of the Iroquois. He has given us knives and tomahawks and other weapons of metal. He has given us blankets that warm us when the weather is cold. He has given us cooking pots of metal and fine tools to cut the wood of the forest so we can make better homes and stronger fences. William is our firm friend. We would lack honor if we refused to come to the aid of his subjects."

"Men with white skins," Sun-ai-yee declared, "have come to the lands of the Indians in such large numbers that we cannot drive them into the Great Sea. Of these, only the English are our friends. The French have become the allies of our ancient foes, the Huron and Ottawa. We cannot desert our friends in their time of need."

"The men of all nations tremble when they see the war paint of the Seneca," Ghonka said. "None seek combat with us. So it is my hope that the Pimlico will agree to make peace with the English of Virginia."

"Who among us will make the long journey and reason with them?" the querulous elder demanded.

The Great Sachem's reply was blunt. "Wilson of Massachusetts Bay has told us they have asked that Renno be sent to them."

Everyone seated around the circle turned to stare at the youngest war chief.

"Is it the wish of Renno that he go to reason with the Pimlico?" the principal medicine man asked quietly.

Renno shook his head, feeling the need for complete candor in this company of his peers and superiors. "I will go if it is the order of the council," he said. "If I did that which pleases me, I would stay home, hunt in our forests, and fish in our lakes and rivers. I have fought in two long wars against the soldiers of the French. I spent many moons in London, the great city of the English. It is true that I have prospered, but now I would like to find the pleasures that I have earned. Even so, I will not shrink away from my duty."

"When any ally cries for help, that cry must be answered," Ghonka said. "But Renno has made so many sacrifices for our people that I have told him I will not command him to make another. If this council wishes to send an emissary to the Pimlico, I would rather choose to take his place."

His son shook his head. "I alone speak the language of the English and know their ways. If it is the wish of the council to send a mission, I will accept."

The Great Sachem called for a vote.

A twig lay on the ground beside each member's place. Those who wanted to send an emissary voted accordingly by throwing a twig into the fire, while those who were opposed to the dispatch of a mission would refrain.

Renno folded his arms across his chest to indicate that he did not intend to participate in the balloting. He had stated his position bluntly, and now he awaited the verdict with Seneca stoicism.

Custom decreed that the Great Sachem vote last, so Sun-ai-yee cast the first ballot. Renno was his friend and protege, the most dependable of his subordinate commanders, but the grizzled war chief unhesitatingly placed duty above personal considerations. His own face masklike, he threw his twig into the fire.

The other war chiefs voted as he did. Only some of the elders and medicine men were so advanced in age that they could afford to show sympathy for the young man who had already done so much for the Seneca nation.

By the time Ghonka's turn came the issue was no longer in any doubt. The vote was more than two to one in favor of sending Renno on the journey that would once again take him far from home for many moons. A lesser man might have been tempted to make a gesture in behalf of the son he loved. But the Great Sachem always thought in terms of high principle and cast his twig into the flames.

Renno bowed his head in submission to the council's will, and the meeting came to an end. Within a short time those who lived in other Seneca towns would be homeward bound, accompanied by their escorts of warriors.

The residents of the community saw the bleak look in Renno's eyes, and no one halted him as he made his way across the fields, where the year's crops soon would be planted. He walked deep into the forest and did not halt until he came to a tiny clearing that only he and El-i-chi knew. It was here that he had held his private meetings with Ja-gonh after the bear had grown too large to continue to dwell with humans.

Studying the sky with unblinking eyes, Renno caught no glimpse of a hawk anywhere, even though he was renowned for vision greater than that of other warriors. So be it, he thought. The manitous were choosing not to reveal whether they approved of his mission and would offer him their protection.

Then he spoke aloud in a clear voice, "Spirit of Ja-gonh, my brother, return from the land of our ancestors and hear my plea. Lend me your strength and your wisdom in the moons that lie ahead. Keep watch over me, and help me to stand again if I should stumble."

He remained in the forest for a long time, and dusk was falling when he finally returned to the town. Although he lived in his own small dwelling, a privilege to which his rank entitled him, he continued to eat most of his meals at the house of his parents, and he arrived just as the others were seating themselves around the cooking fire in front of the hut. Renno inclined his head to his father, then to his mother, and took his place between them.

The family of the Great Sachem ate a special meal that night, which was Ena's quiet way of demonstrating the depth of her feelings for her elder son, who once again was placing the welfare of the nation above his own desires.

Ba-lin-ta had cooked the first course, and even before she removed a bulky mass of baked clay from the coals with two sticks, Renno knew what she had prepared. Her bright grin confirmed his guess, and when she broke the clay by tapping it with a tomahawk he saw a large fish with white flesh that Walter had caught in the lake that afternoon. Everyone in the family knew the baked fish was one of Renno's favorites, and Ba-lin-ta served him a portion as large as that which she gave to her father.

This was a breach of Seneca custom, and although Ghonka ordinarily insisted on the observance of protocol, he conveniently pretended not to notice. Ba-lin-ta well knew she enjoyed a special place in his affections and that he indulged her as he had never indulged his sons.

Ena had cooked the main dish in a large iron pot that Brigadier Andrew Wilson's wife, Mildred, had given her on her one visit to Fort Springfield. Chunks of smoked venison had been stewed with wild onions, dandelion greens, and beans for hours and were served with baked squash and still-steaming cornbread.

Only Ena ate sparingly and enjoyed watching the others relish the meal.

Not until Ghonka was done and wiped his mouth with the back of his hand did he break the silence. "When will you leave for the land of the Virginia colonists, Renno?"

"As soon as I can."

"I suggest you go in two mornings' time," Ghonka replied, settling the question. "Before you visit the Pimlico, go first to the town of Ridley to learn what new developments may have taken place in their war."

Renno nodded, having already made up his mind to confer with Colonel Austin Ridley in the town the settlers called Norfolk.

"You will want to impress the Pimlico with the

might and majesty of the Seneca," the Great Sachem said, "so I have decided to send an escort of two times ten men with you. Choose your own companions, of course. Let two or three be senior warriors."

El-i-chi promptly cleared his throat.

Renno grinned at him. "I choose my brother. The season of growing is farther advanced there than it is here, so perhaps the manitous will guide us to some plump ducks and fat deer."

Walter Alwin, sitting cross-legged like his Indian hosts, strained forward.

Ba-lin-ta instantly interpreted for him. "Wal-ter wants to go with you, too, Renno."

It was easy to understand the boy's eager desire, but Renno regretfully shook his head. "No one less than a junior warrior will march with me," he said. "One never knows what foes one will find in the forest, or what hardships one will encounter."

Ba-lin-ta added a word on her own initiative. "Please, Renno! Wal-ter would be a help, not a burden."

Renno smiled at the boy. "I promise I will take you with me on a mission, Walter, as soon as you have passed your manhood trials and become a junior warrior."

The girl took hold of her good friend's wrist, and by applying a series of pressures known only to the two of them, translated what her brother had said to the deaf boy.

Walter reacted admirably, folding his arms across his chest and concealing his disappointment.

Even Ghonka glanced at him approvingly for an instant.

Renno quickly gave El-i-chi the list of the warriors he wanted to take with him, and the younger brother, acting the familiar role of his brother's deputy, hurried off to tell them their good fortune. Ba-lin-ta and Walter were excused so they could swim in the nearby lake with the children before bedtime, and Renno was alone with his parents.

"Your father and I," Ena said, "wish to discuss with you a matter that long has been on our minds."

The ordinarily inperturbable Ghonka looked uncomfortable.

Renno saw the subtle expression of determination in his mother's doelike eyes and braced himself. Ena, as everyone in the family well knew, was an extraordinary woman. She worked in the fields with other wives and in most matters she subordinated herself to her husband's will, but she had a backbone as hard as metal, and when there was something she deemed important she invariably got precisely what she wanted.

"My son," she said, "few warriors are chosen as war chiefs, and many are men of twice your summers before they reach such a high place."

"That is true," he murmured, and tried not to look apprehensive.

Ghonka began to fidget, which wasn't like him.

"The time has come," Ena said with calm finality, "for you to be married."

"I know of no one I want to marry, my mother." Renno tried without success to match her serenity.

"The mothers of as many young women as I have fingers on my hands have come to me, offering their daughters to you. Some of the fathers are war chiefs. Others are medicine men. You may choose from the highest level of our people."

Renno wanted to protest that he knew virtually every eligible young woman in the entire Seneca nation and wasn't interested in any. But there were times when it was best to retreat into silence, his only defense.

"You have had two women, as far as I know," Ena said. "Perhaps you have taken others, too, but they meant nothing to you and I prefer not to hear about them. I wonder if the thought has ever come to you that both of the women you have loved have pale skins."

It was true, Renno realized. Deborah Jenkins was

now happily married to Fort Springfield's leading clergyman, and Adrienne Wilson, a French Hugenot refugee, had found contentment as the wife of his closest friend in Massachusetts Bay, Jeffrey Wilson. He was delighted for both of them, but he could not ignore his mother's observation that both happened to be white. Now that he thought about it, his casual affairs, in the main, had been with white girls, too.

"It may be," Ena said, "that the destiny the manitous have in store for you is a marriage to a woman with pale skin. If that is so, you are responsible for finding her and making her your wife."

Ghonka cleared his throat. "Renno," he said, "I have tried to explain to your mother that no white woman would be at home in the land of the Seneca."

"That is so," Renno said. "I have never met any woman in the English colonies or in England who would be happy to live in this town. But I am a Seneca, and a Seneca I shall remain, even though I no longer find the ways of the pale-skinned people strange."

Ena had her own logic. "Then you should be married to a woman of the Seneca," she said.

"Renno goes on a mission that is important to all nations of this land," Ghonka said, trying not to show his irritation. "The Seneca cannot afford bad feelings between the English colonists and tribes that do not understand how difficult life will be for us if the French drive out the English and take their places. Yes, and Andrew Wilson has told me the men of Spain are even worse than the French! So do not fill Renno's mind with thoughts of women when he has a mission to establish peace."

"I will be silent," Ena said. "But while Renno is absent from home on his mission, I will study each of the young women whose mothers have come to me with offers. I will determine which of them would be the best wife for Renno. When he returns I will tell him what I have decided."

A flicker in Ghonka's eyes indicated that, although

he knew how his son felt and sympathized with him, this was a matter in which his own ordinarily un-limited authority was meaningless. Renno would have to deal with his mother alone on the issue.

Ena went off to wash the gourds and iron pots in a small stream, and her husband and son were re-lieved. Now they could turn their attention to matters they regarded as significant.

"When you speak with the sachem, war chiefs, and medicine men of the Pimlico," Ghonka said, "do not threaten them unless you find it necessary. But make it plain to them that the English colonists are the firm allies of the Seneca and all five of the other nations of the Iroquois Confederation."

"They may not believe," Renno replied thought-fully, "that we would go to war against a nation that lies so far from our own land. That is the weakness of our position. But I intend to make it clear to them that we traveled just as far when we fought the French at Louisburg."

"It is important for you to remember at all times that the reputation of the Seneca is at stake. No In-dians, not even the Huron or the foolish Erie, would willingly go into battle alone against our warriors."

"I know what you mean, my father. We have given our word that we will stand beside the English colonists, who have treated us fairly, and we shall not fail them. How far may I go in making our po-sition plain to the Pimlico?"

The Great Sachem removed two strips of wampum from his belt, one decorated with white shells and the other studded with black shells. "Take these," he said, "and use them as you see fit."

Renno was stunned by the magnitude of the au-thority he was being granted. If he presented the white shells to the Pimlico it would mean that the Seneca and other Iroquois would remain at peace with them. But if he gave the black wampum to the Pimlico he would openly declare war. He was being granted a degree of responsibility that Ghonka normally reserved for himself. His father was demonstrating complete faith in his judgment, Renno realized, and he vowed to live up to that sacred trust.

Renno's daring mission takes him beyond the Virginias into the untamed, exotic land that would become Florida. This bold warrior is little prepared for the peril in store for him—dangers that more than once threatened his very life.

Read the complete Bantam Book, available October 1st, wherever paperbacks are sold.

WATCH FOR
Book II in the tumultuous new
SAGA OF THE SOUTHWEST series

WINGS
OF
THE HAWK

By Leigh Franklin James

This triumphant novel continues the series
begun with THE HAWK AND THE DOVE.
WINGS OF THE HAWK follows
the lives of John Cooper Baines and Catarina
as they face untold adventures and
new dangers in this untamed land.

It is April, 1814, when Doña Ines and Don Diego de Escobar are married. Catarina soon tells John that she is pregnant. John, thrilled by the news, admits to her his frustration with the quiet life at the ranch. He is anxious for the wide open spaces, and understandingly Catarina gives her consent.

John heads for the mountains, accompanied by Lobo, his now-tamed wolf cub. There, John finds over 300 perfectly preserved dead bodies and—buried with them—many ingots of pure silver. Soon word of his discovery reaches the ears of the Governor's evil aide who plots to steal this treasure from John. Meanwhile, Catarina gives birth to a son named Andrew. But she is soon plunged into peril when renegade Mexicans attack her and kidnap her baby.

WINGS OF THE HAWK

Read the complete Bantam Book, available February 1981, wherever paperbacks are sold.

★ WAGONS WEST ★

COMING IN SEPTEMBER, 1980
Book V in the Wagons West Series

TEXAS!

DANA FULLER ROSS

The time is 1843. The fledgling Republic of Texas
is fighting for its life. Sam Houston, first President
of the Republic appeals to his old friend Andrew
Jackson for help, and "Old Hickory," though
ailing, responds to the challenge with a bold
plan: the recent settlers of Oregon, who know
so well the cost of freedom and the hardships of
building a new home, will help the Texans secure
their liberty.

Immediately a campaign is organized on several
fronts. Americans everywhere, as well as the
Oregonians, rally to help their countrymen in
Texas:

—Rick Miller, brave young captain in the
   Texas Rangers, leads a band of volunteers
   all the way from Oregon to Texas. Their
   mission: to aid Texas in the building of a
   navy.

—Lee Blake, veteran commander of the wagon train in its journey to Oregon, is promoted to brigadier general and placed in command of a new wagon train, this time traveling on barges down the Mississippi and crossing Louisiana to Texas.

—A munitions train carrying stacks of rifles, boxes of Colt revolvers, and cannon, and escorted by a regiment of U.S. cavalry, is dispatched to Texas, a gift from Americans to the people of Texas.

Along the way, romance is sparked, notably by a red-haired spitfire named Melissa Austin, who is so eager to see Texas that she becomes a stowaway on Rick Miller's expedition. There, she breeds trouble between two old friends of the Oregon Trail—Danny Taylor and Chet Harris.

Meanwhile, in Texas, Anthony Roberts, expatriate American with a score to settle with his native land, plots with the British and Mexicans to bring ruin on the Americans. He stops at nothing, including murder.

The stage is thus set for a mighty confrontation: an epic struggle between Americans and Texans under the command of General Zachary Taylor, "Old Rough and Ready," and the crack Mexican troops of the President and Supreme Commander of Mexico, Santa Anna.

TEXAS! continues in the tradition of OREGON!, WYOMING!, and the other books in Dana Fuller Ross's Wagons West Series. It is his biggest book to date!

Read TEXAS!, a Bantam Book available September 1st, wherever paperbacks are sold.

THE LATEST BOOKS
IN THE BANTAM
BESTSELLING TRADITION